the
sinner

SP♠DE
HOTEL

the
sinner

SPADE
HOTEL

USA TODAY BESTSELLING AUTHOR
MARNI MANN

Entangled Publishing, LLC
644 Shrewsbury Commons Ave., STE 181
Shrewsbury, PA 17361
rights@entangledpublishing.com

Amara is an imprint of Entangled Publishing, LLC.

Visit our website at www.entangledpublishing.com.

Edited by Jovana Shirley/Unforeseen Editing
Cover art and design by Hang Le/By Hang Le
Interior design by Britt Marczak

ISBN 978-1-64937-789-0

Manufactured in the United States of America

First Edition June 2024

10 9 8 7 6 5 4 3 2 1

AMARA
an imprint of Entangled Publishing LLC

ALSO BY MARNI MANN

For the women who love a protector—a man strong enough to be her safe haven and fierce enough to let the world know that she's his to protect…and no one else's.

Playlist

"Heaven"—Jelly Roll

"Smoking Section"—Jelly Roll

"I Was Wrong"—Chris Stapleton

"Chainsmoking"—Jacob Banks

"Like You Mean It"—Steven Rodriguez

"Lucky"—Dermot Kennedy

"Parade"—Jacob Banks

"Higher"—Chris Stapleton

"Shake the Frost (Live)"—Tyler Childers

"Faust Road"—Allan Rayman, featuring Adria Kain

"Outlaw State of Mind"—Chris Stapleton

"Talk"—Hozier

"Wolves Cry"—Bryan Martin

"Sin So Sweet"—Warren Zeiders

"Death Row"—Chris Stapleton

Chapter One

Brady

Commercial airlines weren't for people who had billions' worth of assets. But since my younger brother had booked our private jet before I had the chance to reserve it, that was exactly what I'd been stuck with—waiting for my flight to take off to Edinburgh to look at property for a new hotel. It didn't matter that I was stretched out in my own pod or that I'd been greeted with a glass of scotch when I stepped into first class or that a five-course meal was being offered during the seven-hour flight.

I was fucking pissed.

I didn't want to people—my family would say that was because I was a grumpy asshole; I referred to it as being selective. I hadn't wanted a three-hour layover at JFK that I'd just barely recovered from since I couldn't get a direct flight from LAX. I didn't want to deal with the crowd during the chaos of deplaning and claiming baggage and locating my driver when they'd normally be parked directly outside the plane.

Macon had already gotten an earful when I found out he and his girlfriend were taking our jet to Hawaii to visit her family. But the conversation I'd had with him a few days ago over this wasn't enough. He needed a verbal whipping because there was no reason he couldn't be on a commercial flight and I could be the one flying in luxury across the Atlantic.

I pulled out my phone, getting ready to send him a scalding text, when Dominick's name came across the screen. I connected the call and held my cell up to my face. "Tell me something good."

Like myself, Dominick was the oldest Dalton brother—a group of lawyers my family not only did business with regularly, but we were also extremely good friends with them. And since Jenner, Dominick's brother, had married my cousin, Jo, the Daltons were basically family now.

"As opposed to something bad?" He chuckled.

"Listen, not even a down pillow and a foot massage could make me a happy man right now."

"We both know there's only one thing that makes you happy, and you're not getting it on that flight."

Pussy.

There was nothing else that could turn this day around.

But I hadn't seen anyone in this first-class cabin or in the flight crew who was hot enough to even make my dick hard. So far, during this entire trip, there was only one woman who had the power to do that. A flight attendant I'd seen about thirty minutes ago when I was coming out of the airline's lounge to go to my gate. A blonde, far too fucking beautiful for her own good, with a body to die for. And just when I'd gotten a solid look at her, when I got the chance to appreciate her curves in that uniform, she'd disappeared into the sea of passengers.

I breathed in, wishing it were the scent of the blonde's cunt rather than the bullshit recycled air that came through the vents. "You're right. Damn it."

"I hoped to catch you before you took off. I'm finalizing the plans for this weekend, and I wanted to make sure you're still good to go to Kentucky. All the boys are in—Jenner, Ford, Declan, Camden—and I've confirmed with your brothers too. Just waiting on you, buddy."

The Daltons; their soon-to-be brother-in-law, Declan; and my brothers would be going on a trip to the country's best whiskey makers.

I could already taste the bourbon.

"Fuck yeah. Wouldn't miss it."

"Excellent," he replied. "You're in Edinburgh for just a couple of days, right?"

"Long enough to make an offer on a piece of land or purchase an existing hotel that I'm going to gut and make my own."

Now that the Spades had merged with the Coles, our biggest competitor in the hospitality space, and the elders of both companies had retired, the seven of us—my two brothers; my cousin, Jo; the three Coles; and me—were running the business. Together, we'd decided that Edinburgh was the next location to house one of our five-star resorts, and I would be spearheading the project. The six others were an opinionated group, but I'd made it clear when I left LA that this was *my* hotel. They had picked the city; I chose everything else, and I gave zero fucks about what any of them thought, going forward.

"Do I dare guess that you're taking a commercial flight back home?"

"Fuck off, Dominick."

He laughed as I drained my last sip of scotch, setting it a little too hard on the small table beside me. The tumbler wasn't out of my hand for more than a few seconds when a flight attendant, carrying a glass of amber liquid, started making her way over to me.

Not just any flight attendant.

The goddamn blonde I'd seen earlier at the airport. A woman so fucking gorgeous that my cock was throbbing inside my pants.

Man, wasn't that some luck?

Things hadn't gone my way when Macon scored the jet out from under me, but things were changing. Because it certainly wasn't a coincidence that the flight attendant I'd gotten a semi over earlier wasn't just on my flight, but was also assigned to the first-class cabin.

Now that I was much closer to her, unlike when we had been in the airport, I could take my time gazing at every inch of that face and body. Her long hair was curled around her cheeks, like I'd circled the locks around my fist and caused kinks in the strands. Her eyes were the deepest, most piercing blue. Her uniform, consisting of a light-blue button-down and knee-length skirt, left everything up to my imagination, and my imagination was wandering to a far-off, naked land. But what I could see from here was the outline of one perfect, extremely sexy body with tits that were perky and hips that were so enticing that I wanted her legs straddling me.

My stare bounced from her full lips to her nipples, so hard that I could see them poking into her shirt.

Damn it, she was a fucking dime.

She stopped at the entrance of my pod. "Mr. Spade, I thought you could use a refill."

Hearing her say my name made my pre-cum bead at the tip of my dick.

She took my empty glass and replaced it with the one she was holding, her fingers clutched around the girth, like it was my cock. "Oh"—her hand covered her mouth when I turned my face, showing her that I was on the phone—"I'm sorry. I didn't realize you were busy. Excuse me—"

"What's your name?"

She was trained to smile, but what came across her mouth wasn't fake. It also wasn't forced. I could tell we were mutually satisfied with what we were looking at.

This was going to be fun.

"Lily."

Lily.

Oh. I liked that.

And I liked having only inches between us, the nearness giving me hints of her fruity scent.

I lifted the drink in the air, moving it toward my chest. "How about you come back in a few minutes, Lily, and bring me another one of these?"

In addition to her grin, she gave me a fluttering of her lashes before she walked away.

"*Fuuuck,*" I groaned to Dominick. "Things are about to turn around, my man."

"You're telling me you're going to hit that mid-flight?"

I would have hit it in the airport, but she'd taken off before I had the opportunity to speak to her.

This was my second chance.

As Lily made her way toward the galley at the front of the plane, I watched her ass, admiring her cheeks that had just the right amount of padding and thickness. "Brother, I'm going to taste her before dinner is even served."

"I don't doubt that for a second. Have a safe flight, buddy. I'll see you when you get back to LA."

"You will," I said and hung up.

I tucked my phone away and took out my laptop and headphones, prepping for takeoff and the long flight ahead. Had I been on the Spade jet, I would have had access to a queen-size bed and a private restroom, my own flight attendant and food that I'd ordered ahead of time, a series of courses I could eat whenever I desired rather than when it was served. Most of all, I would have had silence and privacy—things I was desperate for right now.

I put on my headphones.

But, shit, that didn't even help because I could still see the people walking by and feel their eyes on me. Their stares strong enough to get me to glance up, this time meeting Lily's stunning eyes.

She'd returned. Wasn't that a pleasant surprise?

If I approved of anyone looking at me, it was her.

I pulled the cups off my ears. "Bringing me a refill?"

"And water, in case you're in the mood for some." She set a small bottle and the new glass next to the full one that was already on the table. "Can I get you anything else?"

"It's like you already know me."

"I try." She smiled.

Fuck, I remembered that grin. I'd seen it in the airport when she was talking to another flight attendant.

It wasn't just lips and teeth.

It was a mood.

A sensation.

And it triggered a pull, starting at the base of my stomach and lifting all the way to my chest.

When I'd seen it the first time, I'd questioned how an expression could make me feel that way, and now, it was doing it again.

"You want to hear something funny, Lily?"

"Always. I love to laugh."

"I saw you in the airport before we boarded the flight. It was just a little more than a glimpse, but you made such an impression that I could recognize you anywhere, in any other location, in or out of your uniform."

"Interesting." She hesitated. "And what was I doing?"

"Nothing. But honestly, you wouldn't have to be doing anything, and you'd still capture my attention. You have the kind of face that's easy to stare at."

She moved an invisible hair off her cheek. "I don't know about that...but thank you." Her hand cupped the side of my cube. "Tell me, did you see me before the baby almost threw up all over me or after?" She laughed. "It was quite a scene, so hopefully, you saw me pre-vomit face."

I chuckled. "Fortunately, I missed the puking."

"I wish I had missed it." She sighed.

"Don't tell me that happens often?"

She moved in a little closer, and when I went to fill my lungs again, I took a deeper whiff of the air, realizing what I'd smelled earlier was pineapple, like a piña colada.

Just when I thought she couldn't get more perfect, she came in smelling like the tropics.

"Baby vomit? It happens enough. But not at the airport—usually, that occurs on the plane. You'd be blown away by some of the things I've seen on flights."

"Share a good one with me."

And just keep talking because, fuck, I can't get enough of you.

She looked toward the galley, as though she was seeing if anyone wanted her, and glanced back at me. "Couples in the restroom together—that's been popular this month."

"The Mile-High Club."

Her cheeks reddened. "And when they break the lock in the process and we have to ground the plane because we can't get them out of the lavatory—yep, good times."

"Amateurs."

She laughed. "Rule one: steer clear of the lock—am I right?"

"If they don't know that, they shouldn't be fucking on a plane." I took in her beautiful lips. "Tell me another."

"*Hmm.*" She rested her chin on the wall that her hand was holding. "Last week, we had a service dog flying with us. An eighty-pound golden retriever. Poor thing was terrified when we hit some heavy turbulence. He left his owner and came bolting to the galley, climbed onto my lap, and sat on top of me until the plane leveled out."

"Lucky dog."

Her smile widened. "I was flattered that he'd picked me to cuddle with. I just love animals."

"I should have brought a dog with me, then."

"You'd let me hold it the whole flight?"

"Lily…" I chuckled, ending my sentence there since it didn't feel like the right time to tell her I'd not only let her hold my imaginary dog, but also me. "Give me one more. The best one you've got. Something I'll never forget."

She was quiet for a moment. "Years ago, I had to break up a fight between two passengers. While I was holding one back, the other threw something at us." Her eyes closed, her head shaking, like the memory traumatized her. "I wish I could say it was her fist, which sounds silly, I know, but I would have rather had that than her dentures."

"Hold up. She threw her teeth at you?"

Her hand flattened against her chest, drawing my attention there. "Sadly, they hit my cheek. Spit and all. The thought still makes me want to die."

I made sure my stare rose to her face when I said, "And here I thought, biting was the only way to use those as a weapon."

"Right? I swear, my passengers teach me something new every day."

Here was my in.

"So, what are you going to learn from me, Lily?"

I liked the way she reacted whenever I said her name, the sound of it causing her lips to tug wider each time.

"I don't know…what do you plan on teaching me?"

Shifting the focus, smart move.

I nodded toward her face. "I bet a lot of your passengers comment on your beautiful smile."

"I've gotten a remark or two in the past, yes." Her brows lifted. "Why? Are you a dentist? Are you going to teach me a trick about flossing that I don't already know?"

I laughed. "I was going to tell you that I wanted you to reserve that smile just for me."

"Make it all yours, huh?"

"That's right."

"That's going to be hard to do, Mr. Spade. This is a seven-hour flight. That's a long time, especially since I'll be passing out multiple courses of food and drinks. Not smiling at anyone while I'm doing it?" She shook her head. "Not sure I can pull that off."

"Let's make a deal, then." I held out my hand. "In exchange, how about I promise not to flirt with any other flight attendants?"

"Boy, you're a charmer."

My fingers waved in the air. "So? Do we have a deal?"

"I'll see what I can do."

Her hand clasped mine, and the second we touched, I felt something. A goddamn buzz that jolted through my arm, up my chest, and straight to my cock.

I was positive she felt it too.

I saw it in her eyes. I felt it in the way she gripped me.

I sensed it when she didn't immediately release my hand.

"I've got to go." Her voice quieted. "Can I get you anything else?" She pulled her fingers back.

I pointed at my glass. "How about another one of these after takeoff?"

The hand that had touched me was dangling at her side, fingers tightening and loosening, just like mine were doing. "Sounds like I'll be seeing you soon."

Chapter Two

LILY

The passenger in 3B wasn't just the handsomest guy I'd ever seen in my life, he was living, breathing sex. The kind of sex that was liquefied, like chocolate fudge, and poured over me like I was one of the sundaes we were serving for dessert. I assumed he was my age—twenty-eight—or a few years older. His hair was the darkest black and styled, his eyes light blue and piercing, his nose a sharp slope. His beard was trimmed and manicured along the edge of his chin, his whiskers a length that would tease rather than scrape. His skin was tan, as though he'd just spent the week in Hawaii. The combination of features made a perfect blend.

A blend that I needed to see again.

Now that we had reached cruising altitude, I got to work on another scotch. This time, one finger's worth rather than two, so he'd be asking for a refill sooner rather than later, giving me another chance to stare into his stunning eyes.

Something I could do for the entire seven-hour flight.

Just stare.

Nothing more.

But, oh, what a gaze-fest it would be.

One full of smiles, which made me laugh to myself. He wanted to make a deal that my smile was reserved just for him, and he wouldn't flirt with any of my colleagues.

That was the first time in my whole career that a deal had been presented during a flight.

A story I could add to my collection.

But one far more fascinating because the harmless flirting made my body throb in a way that I hadn't felt in a long time. It made me feel wanted, something else I hadn't experienced in forever. And for just a fleeting moment, I could focus on something other than the things that constantly ate at me.

"We're going to start preparing the first course," Martha said from behind me.

I put the bottle of scotch away and replied, "I'll help."

"No need," she said. "Just make a sweep and check on everyone. Katy and I will do the food prep."

"Works for me," I told her, and I started walking toward the third row.

I was only a step past the galley when I connected eyes with Mr. Charmer.

He had reclined his seat all the way back, not quite into a bed, but enough that his legs were extended out and his arms were folded behind his head. A position many of the passengers were currently in, yet none of them made it look as sexy as Mr. Spade.

"She's back."

I set the scotch on his side table. "Are you doing all right? Anything else I can get you?"

"I'm extremely disappointed with the service so far." He kept his voice low. "Is there a manager I can speak to?"

His smile made me laugh.

"I'm the manager, Mr. Spade. What can I help you with?"

"There's this flight attendant I'd like to spend more time with, and I'd like to have her relieved of her duties so she can pull up a chair and have a drink with me."

I shifted my stance, my body turning so tingly. "Unfortunately, I can't allow anyone on my staff to do that. Drinking isn't allowed on the job."

"What about conversation?"

My head tilted. "I could possibly arrange that." I looked toward the galley. "Why don't you tell me which flight attendant you're interested in talking to—"

"The one I can't take my eyes off of."

Why did that simple statement sound so intimate?

"That would be you, Lily."

I felt the heat from those words move across my face. "I promise, I'm not that interesting."

"Now, that's where you're wrong." His stare dipped down my body. "Can I be honest with you?"

"Of course."

"No, Lily, can I be *really* honest with you?" He paused. "Because once I say this, you can't unhear it. So, decide now if that's something you want hitting your ears or not."

"You're sure it's not just the scotch talking? If I had as many drinks as I've poured for you, I'd probably end up proposing to that golden retriever who sat on my lap."

He laughed. "I can hold my liquor."

"Okay, I'm intrigued. Tell me all the things, Mr. Spade."

"Brady."

"Let's stick with Mr. Spade." I winked.

"You're sure?"

"I appreciate the warnings, but now, they're only just adding to the buildup, and I'm one of those people who reads the ending before the beginning because I can't handle surprises."

"You're ruthless."

I shrugged. "I like to be prepared."

"Even for this?"

"Maybe." I smirked. "Whatcha got for me?"

"I'm going to give you a fact."

"Please tell me this isn't going to make me math? That's a subject I cannot handle."

He chuckled. "I've seen no less than twenty thousand women in my life—passing them on the street, eating across from them, working with them, flying with them."

"Okay..."

"And not one has ever been as gorgeous as you."

He was silent for a moment, but what was happening inside me was so loud that it was piercing my eardrums.

"Ah, there it is, Lily. My favorite smile."

. . .

"Hey, Lily," I heard as I was just about to pass Mr. Spade's row, holding the bowl of ice cream 6A had just finished.

I turned toward his pod. "Another scotch?"

"I'm good in that department." He nodded toward my hands. "What do you have there?"

I glanced down at the soupy leftovers. "Strawberry ice cream with walnuts."

"Yours?"

I laughed. "No."

"What's funny about that?"

"Obviously, you don't know this about me, but I don't like nuts on anything. Salad, dessert, sweet potato casserole—no to all of that."

"No nuts. Noted."

"Not *no* nuts, just no nuts *on* anything."

"I was beginning to worry you were going to kick me off the

plane for having nuts."

My eyes widened. "Mr. Spade!"

"On my ice cream. Did you think…oh, your mind went there." He rolled a little onto his side. "Sounds like you're flirting with me, Lily."

"Never."

His head nodded. "Never or just not right now?"

I set my arm on the wall of his pod. "Has anyone ever told you that you have this magical skill of getting people to do whatever you want?"

"If I was getting what I wanted, things would look very different than they do right now."

"How so?"

A smile came across his face, one that I recognized because I'd worn a similar one when he told me how gorgeous I was. "We'd be sitting in a restaurant in the Old Town section of Edinburgh, sharing a bottle of wine, and you'd be telling me more stories from your years as a flight attendant."

"Mr. Spade—"

"You don't have to decide now if you'd like to join me after this flight. We still have a few hours to go before we land." He mashed his lips together. "But I want you to think about it."

Chapter Three

BRADY

Unlike all the other women I'd been with, Lily didn't give in easily.

In fact, she hadn't given me an answer at all.

I liked that.

And I liked that every time she walked by my pod, she didn't always connect eyes with me, as if she was trying to make me miss her stare.

The truth was, I did.

I needed this woman.

I needed her taste on my lips.

I needed to lick her until she smiled.

And the only way any of that was going to happen was if I told her exactly what was on my mind.

I waited until the plane landed, after the captain made his announcement, and when the first-class cabin began to depart, I walked over to her as she stood in the front of the galley.

"Mr. Spade, it was a pleasure to smile for you during this flight."

I laughed—I couldn't fucking help it.

"For the record, I held up my end of the deal," I told her. "Zero flirting with anyone but you. How'd you do? Were there lots of other lucky bastards who got to see your smile?"

She shrugged. "I did my best."

"I have another deal for you."

Her arms crossed. "You always win, don't you? You're one of those."

"Yes."

She swung her upper body, but her feet didn't move. "Can you guess the type of woman I am?"

"That's tough." I adjusted my collar. "I'm going to go with one who's my perfect match."

"Clever, but you're wrong. I'm the type who doesn't win or lose. Because I don't play."

She could say anything she wanted.

Words held no weight.

Actions did.

And every expression that had come across her face, along with each second in which she held my gaze, told me Lily wanted me.

"I don't need you to compete," I said. "I just need you to say yes."

"To wine in Old Town?"

Since it was getting louder behind me, I waved her closer. With her ear not far from my lips, her scent filling my nose, the smoothness of her skin in my direct line of sight, I said, "To spending your entire day off with me. I assume you're free until you fly out tomorrow."

She leaned back to look at me. "Your assumption is right, however, I've already made plans. This is my first time here. I've curated a list of the things I want to see. Why would I forgo those plans for you, Mr. Spade?"

"Museums? Castles?" I chuckled. "Come on. I'll be giving you something much more memorable than those."

"Oh?" She rubbed her lips together. "What would that be?"

"An orgasm. Well, multiple, if I'm really being honest."

She filled her lungs quickly and deeply. "My God, you're shameless."

"Something tells me you like that about me." I waited for her to argue and then added, "Do you want more of my honesty?" I paused again, her eyes answering when her voice didn't. "I've been thinking about you this entire flight, dreaming of every way I want to make you come. My tongue, my fingers, my dick—I want to give you all of me."

The color of her cheeks rivaled any previous time she had blushed on this flight.

"You want to go down on a woman you barely know?"

Out of all comments, she'd come back with that one.

Damn it, I really liked her.

"It's not about wanting to, Lily. It's about needing to. A desire so strong that I *have* to taste you. Have you ever experienced anything like that? Something you can't move on from unless you have it?"

She pursed her lips. "But that's it…just a taste?"

I was already dreaming about the flavor that would hit my fucking tongue the second I swiped it against her clit. "A taste that's going to last all day and into the night."

Her hand moved to her face and surrounded her chin, showing nails that were a light pink—a color far too angelic for a woman who gave me naughty vibes.

"And then what?" she asked. "We part ways? Two strangers going in opposite directions to never ever see each other again?"

"Yes."

I didn't do relationships.

I didn't exchange phone numbers.

I didn't ever do a second round.

One and done.

I had my work, my family, and my friends.

And I had a different woman every night of the week.

That was all I wanted.

All I needed.

"But what I can promise is that nothing on that list of plans will even compare to what I want to give you," I said.

She was smiling without showing her beautiful white teeth. "God, you're cocky."

"I'm confident."

"It's the same thing."

"It's vastly different." I handed her a piece of paper, where I'd written the name of the hotel and my room number. "A cocky person would say you're coming to my hotel room, where you're going to be blown the fuck away by the size of my dick. A confident person would show you the way, knowing you'll find out on your own."

She slid the paper into her apron. "How do you know I'm not married? Or taken?"

"Your eyes gave me that answer the first time they locked with mine." I nodded toward her apron. "All the information you need to find me is in there. Now, I just need to know whether you're coming or not."

Her grin finally showed her teeth, but it only lasted a few seconds before she began to walk out of the first-class section, stopping just long enough to say over her shoulder, "For how confident you are, Mr. Spade, I'm surprised you need an answer."

Chapter Four

LILY

One day and one night—the amount of time Brady wanted to spend with me. A decision I'd contemplated while I finished my closing duties on the plane, still thinking about it when we were shuttled to our hotel, where the crew would be picked up the next afternoon for our return flight to Atlanta.

What I'd learned about him during our trip to Edinburgh was that he had clout. Only people with power were given their room numbers before they physically checked in to their hotels. I knew that because I spent seven days a week in hotels all over the world. And he spoke with authority—I could hear it in his words; I could feel it in his presence.

But he was more than just a guy who had extreme influence.

He was the type I could barely pull my eyes away from. The kind you just wanted to stare at because everything about him was so fascinating—from how he worked on his laptop to the intensity with which he watched TV, even the peacefulness on his face when he had taken that short thirty-minute nap.

Simple tasks that he made look strikingly sexy.

But beyond his provocative looks, I got the sense he was someone who had a stylist deliver his clothes, and the watch he wore—the same brand my ex had—was one of many that he kept in a locked drawer in his walk-in closet. He dabbled between first class and private jets; he preferred his scotch aged and worth hundreds, living a life that most could only dream about.

The reason I knew was because I'd dated someone just like him.

David was the reason why I was…emotionally unavailable.

Six months had passed since we'd broken up. Six of the longest months of my entire life, in addition to the year and a half we were together, equaling two years of hell.

Math that even I could calculate.

Since I'd called things off with him, I'd spent every moment I possibly could in the sky. What I hadn't done, during my little downtime, was do anything for myself.

Instead, I buried. I kept busy so I wouldn't have to think. I wouldn't have to face the ramifications of our past relationship head-on; I wouldn't have to process the damage it had left behind.

I saw the results.

I felt them.

Turmoil that still very much lived inside me.

So, I had to wonder why I'd gotten into a taxi and why I was opening the door to the backseat as the cab came to a stop in front of Brady's hotel.

If anything, my past made this decision even more confusing.

But as I'd stripped off my uniform about an hour ago, and gotten into the shower, and changed into jeans and a sweater—the only other clothes I'd brought with me—I'd told myself I was finally going to do something for me.

Tonight, I was going to attempt to forget David.

I was going to get out of my head, even if it was for a short period of time, and enjoy some unattached sex with a stranger who had promised to please me in ways I'd probably never experienced before.

As I walked into the lobby of the hotel, the tingle I'd felt on the plane returned. Still, I couldn't help but glance behind me, inventorying the people standing by the front desk and sitting on the chairs and couches in the center of the lobby and those alone, occupied by their phones or tablets. The throb between my legs completely consumed me as I went into the elevator, waiting for the doors to close before I hit the button for the top floor. My breath fully hitched as I found his door, my hand hovering above it.

Who am I right now?

I was someone who needed to relax and put her body first.

Someone who needed to think about how many orgasms she was going to have rather than her past.

Once I knocked, several seconds passed, and there still wasn't a response, nor did I hear any noise coming from inside his room.

Maybe he'd gone to sleep, and I missed my window.

Maybe he had gotten tired of waiting for me and went out.

Maybe—

The door opened, his face appearing in the crack. A smile immediately met my line of sight, and as the door became more ajar, I saw his chest.

His chiseled abs.

The trail of hair that led to the towel wrapped around his waist.

"You timed that perfectly."

His voice caused my stare to rise, but it didn't settle on his face for long.

It couldn't.

There was far too much of his body to look at.

The cords of muscle within his arms and pecs and abdomen. The veins that pulsed. The way each section was so defined, so clearly outlined, that I felt weightless, standing in front of him. The dusting of hair on each part only added to his masculinity.

A man who didn't just spoil himself with his power and money, but also took care of himself in ways that produced this.

This…perfection.

"Take your time. We have all day and night."

I cleared my throat, my gaze lifting once again, embarrassed that he'd caught me not once, but now twice. "I'm sorry."

"For what? You can take me in all you want. That's precisely what I was doing on the plane every time my eyes landed on you."

I swallowed, attempting to find my voice. "Except you're naked."

"I'm in a towel." Which then dropped to the floor, the hand that was holding it falling to his side. "Now, I'm naked."

I sucked in as much air as my lungs could hold and felt my eyes bulge. I was positive I looked like one of those cartoons, my neck craned back, my eyes so wide that they were protruding.

I couldn't stop the look; I couldn't even attempt to fade it away.

I was too focused on his hard-on, too shocked that he was standing in the doorway of his hotel room without a stitch of clothing on, unfazed if anyone walked by.

Was that cocky?

Or confident?

I couldn't remember what he'd said about the difference.

Not when I was obsessively staring at his dick. The tip, glistening with a bead of pre-cum, widened at the crown; the center girthier than any I'd ever seen; a length that would positively fill me; and there were more veins, like the ones in his arms; and short hairs that surrounded it, similar to his beard.

"This is what you do to me, Lily." He circled his hand around his shaft and pumped.

Once.

Twice.

He paused to say, "Do you want it?"

My eyes lifted unhurriedly. "When I called you cocky on the

plane, I had no idea you were *this* cocky."

He released a huff of air. "Come in so I can get you naked."

The second I crossed the threshold, I was in his arms. Our gazes locked even though his was several inches higher, the top of my head meeting the arch of his chest. He held my waist as he guided me toward the wall, and once my back was against it, his palms went to my face.

"I've been thinking about these lips since JFK."

That felt like years ago.

"Since I saw you in the airport, I haven't been able to get you out of my head." His forehead was pressed to mine, his thumb tracing my bottom lip. "You blew me the fuck away, so you can guess how happy I was when I saw you were working my flight."

I pushed my head back just enough that my mouth was pointed up at his. "I didn't see you."

"You wouldn't have. I was behind you."

"Except I always look behind me…and I would have noticed you."

"You did once you brought me the scotch, didn't you?"

His face moved to my neck, his lips gently grazing the skin between the collar of my sweater and my earlobe. Just enough movement and friction that my hips shifted forward, my back bending backward.

"You couldn't take your fucking eyes off me. Was this what you were thinking about?" A hand lowered to my side, gradually going down. "What it would feel like if my body was pressed to yours?" His hand stopped at my waist. "What it would feel like if my dick was grinding against your clit?" His fingers moved to the front of me, cupping the zipper of my jeans, his strength so firm that it felt like there wasn't any clothing separating us. "What it would feel like if I was inside of you, hitting that sweet spot, making you come so fucking hard?"

I shuddered. "*Mmm.*"

"I thought so."

He was barely doing anything, hardly touching me, yet it already felt so good.

"My plan was to pour us some drinks and get you to relax a little. I had a feeling you would need it. But now that I'm touching your pussy, I can hear it purring, telling me it's more than ready." His lips moved to my cheek. "You don't need booze. What you need is my goddamn tongue."

Clothes were suddenly stripped from my body. It happened so fast; I didn't even have time to take a breath before I was lifting my feet for him to pull off my shoes. My jeans were gone, my sweater removed. When all that was left were my bra and panties, he took a step back.

Like an artist who was standing too close to his canvas, he needed space to see the entire picture.

That was the way he made me feel. As though I were art.

And with his lips widening into a grin, his hand fisting his cock and stroking, a deep, guttural approval came from his throat, which told me he really liked what he saw.

"Jesus fucking Christ, Lily."

At least I'd managed to pack a matching set—the black lace panties sitting low on my hips, the bra hugging the bottom of my breasts, the push-up giving me more cleavage than I actually had.

I swore at least half of a minute had passed, and he wasn't moving or coming any closer; he was frozen in that spot the same way I'd been when he dropped the towel.

But he wasn't looking at my face, he was solely focused on my body, each second confirming a little more that he couldn't get enough of me.

Had a man ever made me feel this way before? That I was more than enough for him?

No.

I was sure of that.

"Do you want to know something?" He released his dick to wipe the corners of his lips. "I thought I knew what perfection was." His eyes fixed on mine. "I was wrong. Because never in my whole fucking life have I ever seen a body like yours."

I'd come here willingly.

I'd let him take off my clothes.

He didn't need to bullshit me. I was a done deal. Therefore, he didn't need to say anything at all.

But what he had said caused an explosion through my stomach, the embers lifting to my chest.

How could this complete stranger make me feel this way?

How could his words be more meaningful than any of the others I'd heard before?

"You've made me speechless," I admitted.

"You don't need to say anything at all. You just need to know"— he finally moved forward, his hands going to the wall above my head, his face leaning down toward mine—"that I cannot fucking wait to taste you." His lips hovered in front of mine. "Not just your mouth. I want to know the taste of your cunt. And the taste of your cum. And I want to know the flavor of your tongue when I'm making you scream louder than you ever have before."

His mouth slammed against mine, ravishing me with dominance and control.

I wouldn't have it any other way, not when it came to sex, despite that power being something I'd never experienced.

Because the two of us together were dripping with lust.

Passion.

And this was a man who wanted to please my body in ways I'd never felt.

As his mouth molded against mine, his tongue slowly dipping in, my bra was unhooked, my breasts freed, my nipples instantly pinched, using the power of his fingers. I didn't know how it was possible for him to do everything at once, but my panties were also lowered and now hugged my ankles.

Once I stepped out of the leg holes, his fingers dived between my legs, one on my clit, another probing my entrance until it was inside of me.

"So fucking wet," he moaned. "Just like I thought you'd be."

I pulled back from his mouth, needing the separation so I could exhale, "Ah." The feeling so overwhelming, I added, "Fuck!"

My fingers were all I'd experienced for the last six months. I knew what I liked, what I wanted, what would quickly do the job.

This was nothing like that.

He slid inside me with urgency, with a level of knowledge that led him straight to my G-spot.

That had me shouting, "Yes," within the first couple of plunges.

"Don't make it so easy on me, Lily. I want your first orgasm to be from my tongue."

I wasn't sure I could wait that long.

Not if he kept this up.

And certainly not if this pace continued.

"You'd better start licking now, then," I warned him.

"Is that what you want? For me to lick your pussy?" He stared at me with such hunger.

An appetite I wanted to feel between my legs.

"Yes."

"You're going to come on my tongue just like I want you to?"

I nodded.

"And you're going to let me taste it?"

"*Yesss.*"

He gave me another kiss. "Just to make it clear, Lily, doing this is just as much for me as it is for you." He instantly got on his knees, his finger no longer inside me, and in its place was his face.

I gripped his hair, locking our eyes, while he pressed his nose against the top of me, like he was trying to inhale me.

"I knew you'd smell amazing, but I didn't anticipate something as good as this." He stayed right there, closing his eyes, taking another breath. "The perfect body and the perfect fucking scent."

When his eyelids opened, he looked at me as if I were that piece of art. But not one he'd ever seen before. He stared like I was a painting that couldn't be valued.

That I was a piece desired by every collector in the world.

My head banged against the wall, trying to pull me from this moment, and I did it once more as I felt the first flick of his tongue.

It wasn't quick.

He dragged it down the whole length of my clit, from top to bottom, and just as I attempted to take in some air, he added a finger, plunging it into me.

"Brady!"

As soon as his name came out of my mouth, he focused on the peak, swiping across it with a heavy pressure. He would switch to massage mode, grinding his tongue against me before sucking my clit into his mouth. From there, he would hold the end and flick more.

This was a mix I'd never had, an erotic attack that had me screaming.

And every time I released more air, I could see the desire on his face.

He wanted me to come.

His eyes told me that.

His tongue proved that.

His finger solidified that.

So, I gave him one.

Because I literally couldn't hold it in a second longer.

"Yes!" I shouted just as the tingles from my stomach shot through the rest of my body, and what came with it, what it brought on, were shudders. They moved through me like waves, rough seas, a riptide that wasn't safe for swimming. "Brady!"

His hair wasn't strong enough to hold on to, so my palms slapped against the hardness behind me, pushing the sensations from my body into the drywall. It also helped keep me upright since the spasms were intense enough to take me down.

Not that Brady would let that happen. He had a grip on me that told me I wasn't going anywhere.

Once I stilled, the bursts quieting to a murmur, I expected him to stop.

But he didn't.

His licking was relentless, and even though he'd gotten what he wanted, it obviously wasn't enough.

"One down. One to go," he groaned as our eyes met.

He wasn't going to let up. He was going to follow through with everything he'd promised.

But I couldn't get off again. Not this soon. I was too sensitive. "I can't—"

"Don't say that word to me. You can. You will. And I'll prove it to you."

His tongue slid up and down, from side to side, switching between the pad of his tip and the sweep of the whole width, each change giving me a new flutter.

It confirmed one thing.

His mouth owned me.

"Why do you taste so good, Lily?" His lids were now closed, as though he was savoring something he'd been dying to have. "Why can't I stop? Why do I need more of you?" He moved faster. "And more."

Words I found so sexy.

But from a man who, after today, I would never see again. That admission caused an ache from somewhere deep inside. At the same time, I was comfortable with that decision. It went both ways. My routine didn't have room for him—or anyone.

There was just something about him being so different, about setting a precedent, that had me so turned on.

And it seemed he had the same reaction because his tempo increased, and so did his insistence—I sensed it each time his tongue neared the bottom and lifted. A pattern that repeated, but before I could get too used to it, there was a switch, and suddenly, everything became unexpected.

This man.

An experience I'd remember for the rest of my life.

And one I didn't have to focus on—there was no concentration needed. His actions kept me present. They overwhelmed me. Because when you combined the movement of his tongue and the turning of his finger inside me, I was consumed.

He was ruling my body. Taking it just where he wanted it to go.

And that was toward an orgasm.

"Brady!" This time, the build was more extreme. And even though I knew his style and the result, that didn't prepare me for what took hold of me. Because as it catapulted through my body, the force was even stronger than before. "Oh my God!"

The shudders hit harder, engrossing me to the point where I couldn't even draw in any air.

"Yes," he moaned, "that's what I want." He licked faster. "Give me your cum. Let me fucking taste it."

Hearing him beg for my orgasm was the hottest thing ever.

Something I'd probably never recover from.

Something I'd probably never hear again.

"Come on my fucking face."

The ripples were endless, like I'd lit a match, and they were igniting through every muscle, vein, even the blood in my body.

"*Ahhh*!" I swallowed, inhaled, and followed that up with, "Fuck!"

I was a mess of trembles and screams, and he licked past each one, waiting until the shimmying calmed. He lifted me, tossing me over his shoulder as if I were only a couple of pounds, and placed me on his bed. He left me to go into the closet, returning with a metal foil. He tore off the corner with his teeth and rolled the condom over his hard-on.

"Do you always travel with those?"

He climbed onto the bed, lying next to me. "I don't go anywhere without one."

I laughed, his truth unsurprising. For a man who looked like him, he probably got laid everywhere he went.

"If this is the way you treat all flight attendants, I imagine they come in handy."

"My company has its own jet. You're the first commercial-airline flight attendant I've met in years."

He climbed on top of me and kissed me, his lips still wet from me. His tongue covered in me. And his smile, when he pulled away, told me he knew that I was all over him, and that was one of the reasons he'd put his mouth on me.

He'd wanted me to taste myself, and he'd succeeded.

But instead of addressing it, I said, "I would have returned the favor had you not put the condom on."

"When I said I was licking your pussy for me, I wasn't kidding. That was no favor, Lily."

I touched his mouth, the thick whiskers that surrounded it, the softness of his lips. "You do that for everyone?"

"No." He chuckled. "But for some reason, I had to do it for you."

"You made it memorable."

He bit my lower lip, holding it in his mouth until he released it to reply, "I ate you like I couldn't get enough of you. I still can't." He rose from the spot next to me, and while he balanced on his knees, he positioned himself between my legs, lifting my ass just high enough that I was in line with his dick. "And I'm about to get more."

"Insatiable."

"With you," he said, "fuck yes." His tip was aimed at my entrance. "I need you to touch yourself."

"Now?"

His eyes narrowed in the most feral way. "Yes." He waited until my hand went to my clit. "I need you to rub it hard, like I just did with my tongue."

There was only one reason he would want me to do that.

"Because you're about to break me..."

He grinned. "Because you're about to experience what a fucking man feels like, and I need to make sure you don't get too far inside your head." My brows lifted as he added, "I get the feeling you would, and I'm not going to let that happen."

I'd only circled my clit a few times when his crown broke through, sliding into my wetness.

"Fuck," he moaned, his head falling back. "You're even tighter than I thought you'd be."

"And now, I know why you wanted me to touch myself," I panted.

If I really put my mind there, I could get lost in the pain. Sex with Brady was like being a virgin again. He wanted it to stay all about pleasure.

But what he didn't know was that I didn't have to touch myself to get lost. I could do that by just looking at him. The way his abs constricted when he drove into me. The way his lips parted, turning almost animalistic. The way his hands gripped me as if I were tinier than a stick.

God, he was beautiful.

The dominance, rhythm, the way he turned his hips, hitting spots within me that had never been touched before—it wasn't going to be long until I was screaming again.

"Why do you feel so different, Lily?"

"You feel"—I gasped—"so good."

"But this fucking pussy." He moved my hand away, replacing

it with his, thrumming my clit, pressing his palm against the top. "Where the hell did it come from…and how are you making me want to come already?"

I didn't have time to answer or respond before I was in the air, straddling his waist as he sat along the side of the bed, his large hands cupping my ass.

"Take it," he ordered. "Show me what you can do with my dick."

I had to find my breath, the movement so sudden that I needed my bearings. My hands balanced on his shoulders, my knees on either side of him, and I gently lowered myself onto his shaft, the sensation unlike when I'd been on my back.

This angle made everything more heightened.

It wasn't that I now had the control, nor was it the size of him or the depth in which he could reach.

It was how he looked at me with eyes that raged with emotion.

How he gripped my cheeks, like there was no way he would ever let go.

"Goddamn it," he hissed. "Yes! That's it."

I reached the bottom, using my hips to give him a quick buck. That was all it took, and the tingles returned. I gave him another thrust, shifting forward and back, and those feelings began to climb.

"I'm going to come again."

"I can feel it." His hand moved to the front of me, a finger rotating over my clit.

"Brady!"

"I didn't think you could possibly get any tighter, but, fuck me, you just did."

"Shit!" The crests shot through me, and so did his dick, slamming me with a speed I could take, and a persistence that was driving me right over the edge. "Ah!"

"You feel so fucking good."

I was no longer moving; I was frozen above him, unable to do anything except scream. He now held all the power, churning his hips, giving my body all the pressure it needed.

I couldn't breathe.

I couldn't even moan anymore.

I was out of everything.

Even when he lifted me and carried me to the wall, holding me against it. "My turn."

I tightened my legs around his waist and hugged his chest to mine.

"And when I'm done, we're going to do this all over again."

"Because you can't get enough…" I exhaled, using his famous statement.

"And because you'll still be here, which means I can have more." He gave me a quick kiss. "Since I have you until the morning, I'm going to spend every one of those hours inside your pussy, making you come." His lips pressed onto mine. "Again and again."

There was no part of me that doubted him. If today had proven anything, it was that Brady was a man of his word, that he knew his way around a woman's body, and that the pleasure he could give was record-breaking.

"I want you to come," I begged. "I want you to make me feel it."

"Say it again." His voice turned gritty, his strokes sharp and commanding. "But say my name this time. I want to hear it come out of your mouth." He leaned me more into the wall, freeing up a hand, which became wedged between the two of us, finding its place on my clit. "And I want you to do it while you're coming."

I thought it was impossible.

I thought that my body was done—at least for the time being.

Because there was absolutely no way I could get off again.

I was too sensitive, too spent.

But as he worked his way in and out of my wetness, grazing my clit, that familiar tug began to trickle through me.

"I cannot believe it," I moaned.

"And you doubted me."

Had I said that? Out loud?

I couldn't even remember.

All I could think about was that he'd brought me back to that place, and it was possessing every inch of me.

"I can feel it, Lily. I know how close you are."

"Then, fuck me harder." I shortened my grip around him. "Now!"

He gave me several pulses, shooting me higher, and I screamed, "Brady! Come!"

"Yes," he growled. "Just what I wanted to hear."

I didn't think he could pound me any harder, and, shit, was I wrong.

"I'm going to fucking fill you," he roared.

The two of us were tremoring in sync, our skin slick, our hands clutching whatever we could hold on to, our breaths mingling as our lips locked.

He knew just when to slow and exactly when to stop.

With both of us now still, our lips parted, but our faces stayed close.

"I'm giving you a small break," he offered.

"And then onto round two?"

He chuckled. "If that's what you want to call it." He kissed my cheek. "But I think we could use a shower first."

"Separate?"

He pulled me off the wall, and when he passed the bed, I knew he was carrying me into the bathroom. "And let you out of my arms? Fuck that."

I was wrong; his confidence trumped his cockiness.

• • •

I didn't want the awkwardness of a goodbye. I didn't want to be tempted to give him my number or ask for his—something that couldn't happen. I didn't want there to be a conversation that would haunt me.

I couldn't handle it.

Not now.

So, I waited until Brady was asleep, and I carefully slipped out of his bed and tiptoed over to the doorway, where he'd stripped off my clothes. His room was a suite with plenty of space between the bedroom and entryway; therefore, I was positive he wouldn't hear me. But I still moved silently, getting myself dressed, and just before I turned the handle to exit, I went over to the table, where there was a pad of paper and a pen.

A note seemed silly. So did thanking him.

I decided to draw a heart and put my name beneath it.

Did it matter if he saw it?

Did I even want him to?

I didn't know. I just felt like it was the right thing to do after the time we'd spent together.

I set the pen beside the pad and peeked into the bedroom, where he was soundlessly sleeping in the middle of the bed. His arm was gripping a pillow, and his leg was bent and extended toward the side I'd been on.

Both had, at one point, been wrapped around me.

And, oh God, had they felt good.

"Goodbye," I whispered.

I quietly went to the door and shut it behind me. I looked both ways down the hallway before I headed to the elevator.

When I was safely inside a taxi, a realization hit me.

It came on like the waves of my orgasm, but these were far more turbulent, causing a feeling in my stomach like seasickness.

I would never see Brady again.

But that was only half of it.

There was another side. A side that was just as agonizing.

A side that shook me so hard I had to roll down the window.

Will David find out?

Chapter Five

Brady

"What time does the game start?" Macon inquired while we were getting into the stretched SUV that had been hired to take us to Van Nuys Airport, where the Daltons' private jet was waiting.

"Are you really asking that question?" I shot back, taking a seat toward the center.

Macon sat across from me, his polo bright, his hair spiked in the front. The only thing he was missing was a goddamn lei.

"Yeah. Why?" he countered.

I looked at my middle brother, Cooper, who had just sat next to me, watching his thumbs quickly tap his phone. I knew who he was texting; I didn't even have to ask. This was the first time he'd be away overnight since his daughter, Rayner, had been born. I was sure his girl, Rowan, was holding shit down at home, but I could tell by his expression that the distance was going to challenge him. That just meant I needed to get him extra fucked up tonight.

"Because every man who follows hockey knows what time the

games start," I said to Macon. "What time dinner is—now, that's a different story. What time a concert starts—same deal. But sports? Come on, Macon. You're better than that. It's ingrained in our heads."

Macon flicked the air like I was a fly. "Will you just answer the question already?"

"Seven," I told him. "Like most NHL games on the East Coast."

As the rest of the guys climbed in, Macon looked at his watch. "And how long is the flight to Tampa?"

"Jesus Christ," I groaned. "What am I, your fucking travel agent?"

Macon smiled. "Such a dick."

Dominick had taken a seat along the back, and he replied, "Four and a half hours, give or take." He grabbed the bottle of whiskey that was on the floor in front of his brother Jenner, unscrewed the top, and took a swig. "I'm assuming your next question is going to be, *How much time do we have between landing and the game?* Am I right?" He chuckled while he handed the bottle to Jenner.

Macon pointed at Dominick and then at me. "No wonder the two of you are best friends."

Dominick flipped him off. "The answer is, a couple of hours. Don't worry, Macon, you'll have plenty of time to be fed a bottle and lie down for your nap before the game starts."

"I'm an expert at bottles," Ford, the youngest Dalton, said as he moved toward the front. "I'm pretty good at burping, too, if you need help there." He winked at Macon.

"That makes two of us now," Cooper added.

I put my hand over my mouth, laughing my ass off, while I took the liquor from Jenner.

Magic happened when the Spades and Daltons hung out. It wasn't just because we were practically family now—lots of families didn't hit it off. It was because there was an understanding between us, a mutual respect, the ability to throw all the shit we wanted and it was never taken as shade.

And one of our favorite things to do together was travel as a group. This trip had been planned during one of the nights I was out, having drinks with Dominick and the Weston family—a group of five siblings we did business with who owned high-end steak and seafood restaurants all over the world. Beck Weston, one of the brothers, played in the NHL for the LA Whales. All three families had box seats at the arena in LA and went to many of his games, but it was that night we'd decided to hit the road and attend one of his away games. After checking out the schedule, we'd chosen Tampa.

But for this trip, the whole crew hadn't been able to make it. Camden, the youngest Dalton, along with his twin sister's boyfriend, Declan, were in Boston, litigating a case, and had to pass. And there were also the Coles—Ridge and Rhett, Rowan's two brothers—who had been given a pity invite even though we knew they wouldn't come.

The three of them were now equal partners in our business—a merger I wasn't fucking happy about. The thought still pissed me off, but there was nothing I could do about it.

I wasn't surprised the Cole brothers hadn't made it. Their dad wasn't doing well, and one of them was always with him, but the real reason was that things weren't warm between us. They weren't cold, like they had once been, but I didn't see them vacationing with us anytime soon. Considering we had to work together and get along, at least things were headed in the right direction.

I took a long drink of the whiskey and handed it back to Jenner just as the SUV pulled out of the parking lot.

"Three weeks until Edinburgh closes," Jenner said to me.

My blood pressure spiked. "You never take a vacation from shop talk, do you, Dalton?"

He laughed. "You're telling me you do?"

He had a good point. Not a single motherfucker in this vehicle could separate himself from work. If we weren't chatting about law, their specialty, we were talking about hotels. I preferred the latter.

"Do you think it'll get pushed back?" I asked. "Or is three weeks a hard deadline?"

After several trips to Scotland, viewing all the available properties and land for sale, I'd decided on a rehab rather than a full build-out, and we were in escrow for a high-rise in the Old Town area of the city. Although my siblings had moved to the locations where they'd built hotels—Macon had gone to Hawaii; Cooper and Rowan and the baby would soon be headed to Lake Louise and Banff—that wasn't my plan. I would spend four days a week in Edinburgh and the other three back in LA.

A lot of fucking flying, but it was the way I wanted it.

"I'm about ninety percent sure it'll close on time," Jenner replied. "Dealing with laws outside our country is always a bit tricky, that's why I left the ten percent buffer in case Scotland decides to pull out some red tape." He shifted in his seat, turning more toward me. "How long will the rehab take?"

"I'm hoping no more than six months."

"Which means about a year," Jenner said.

If there wasn't gel in my hair, I would have dragged my hand through it. "I sure as fuck hope not." I set my phone on my leg, tired of holding it. "Since I'll be commuting back and forth, it's going to be a nightmare to share the plane with the other six partners. Shit, we're already struggling, and I haven't even started my weekly hauls to the UK."

"Before Walter and Ray signed the paperwork for the merger, I told them you guys needed a second jet. They didn't want to hear it. They wanted it to become your problem."

"Sounds about right," I groaned.

My uncle and Ray—who was Rowan, Ridge, and Rhett's dad—had wanted the two companies to become one, and when that was done, they let their heirs handle every internal fire. There were fucking hundreds that had ignited—from accounting to IT to HR. We were still dealing with kinks that were challenging our processes and testing our strength as a business. The mention of a second jet was something I'd brought up months ago, but with everything that was going on, it wasn't a priority to the executive team.

"And it's become a big problem."

"I didn't tell you to do this," Jenner started, "but, buddy, just go buy one."

Jenner was our corporate attorney. Aside from our accountant, there wasn't anyone who could give me better advice.

"You know I will," I told him.

He squeezed my shoulder, shaking it in his grip, and I glanced down at my lap, where my phone was vibrating.

I lifted it, reading the text on the screen. "Fuck."

"Don't even tell me it's a work crisis," Cooper said from beside me.

"Worse. It's a chick."

"The women never stop blowing you up, do they?"

"I don't know how they get my number. I don't give it out." I looked at my brother. "What the fuck? Are they detectives?"

"Your digits are probably written on every restroom stall in LA."

I glared at him. "Listen, man, going in, they know they only get me for one night. It should be no surprise to them when I leave."

"I'm sure they're hoping they can change you."

I held the phone toward him so he could see the text. "Like this one?"

Unknown: *Hi! Dinner last weekend was amazing. Wanna do it again? My place this time?*

"Brother, I'm shocked you even bothered with dinner and didn't just take her straight to your place."

"My place?" I huffed. "I don't take anyone there. The last thing I need is for my address to get out like my phone number and have women showing up at my goddamn front door."

"You don't think they can find where you live?"

The thought alone had me unbuttoning my shirt another hole, the collar now two buttons wide. "They can, I'm sure, but I bought it under the name of my trust, making it a little more difficult to find. Besides, I have cameras everywhere, and it would be impossible for them to get through my gate."

"Unless they climbed it."

"Dude"—I reached for the bottle and guzzled down several gulps—"stop."

He laughed. "What was her name?"

"Whose name?"

He nodded toward my pocket. "The one who texted you."

"I have no fucking idea."

He took the bottle from me. "You don't remember last weekend?"

"Listen, when it comes to that side of my life, things don't just go down on the weekends. I meet up with women during the week too. And between Wednesday and Saturday, there were three brunettes. So, at the moment, I can't differentiate one from the other, nor can I recall their names."

"You fucking dog."

I smirked. "Before Rowan, you weren't any better."

"That's the truth."

I took my phone back out. "One way to ensure they'll never see me again is to become clingy." I deleted the text and returned the phone to my pocket.

"You mean you'd be into one if she actually played hard to get?"

Would I be into one?

I thought about his question, really diving into the words.

I'd never come across a woman who captivated me to the point of wanting more. Who teased me enough to desire a second taste. Who enticed my brain to even ponder a future.

Except for one.

The flight attendant.

She hadn't given in during the trip to Edinburgh even though I propositioned her several times before we landed. I wasn't even sure she was going to show up to my suite. But when she did, we spent the entire day and most of the night together. When I woke early the next morning, she was gone. The only things she'd left behind were a note on the table—if I could even call it that, all she'd written was a heart and her name—and the memories I now had of her.

Memories I recalled often.

What is it about Lily that I just can't get enough of?

That was the thought that had run through my head the whole time she was in my hotel room.

When my hands were on her body, I wanted more of her skin to touch. When my lips were on hers, I wanted a longer taste. When my dick was inside her, I was already thinking about the next time I was going to have her.

But why?

Was it that she hadn't immediately given in to me on the plane? That she was the most beautiful woman I'd ever seen? That she didn't push for what was going to happen next or ask for my number or leave hers? Or that she disappeared without even saying goodbye?

Fuck if I knew.

But around six months had passed since I'd gotten even a whiff of her scent.

I wished I could say I didn't think about her, but I did. I wished I could say I didn't want to do that full day and night all over again, but I did.

I wished I could say my assistant hadn't reached out to the airline to see if she could find out Lily's last name, but she had. She'd also had no luck getting any information on her.

So, that was all Lily would ever be—a memory.

"Would I be into a woman if she played hard to get?" I repeated since I still hadn't answered Cooper's question. "I don't know. I suppose anything is possible, but the chances, at this point, aren't likely." I noticed we were pulling onto the tarmac, and Cooper was gripping his phone even tighter than before. It was time to shift the conversation off me. "You know, you can still back out if you're not feeling this trip."

His head slowly turned toward me. "Letting me off gently? Who are you?"

I laughed. "I'm still the asshole you know and love." I nodded toward his hand. "I can't help but see the way you're holding your cell. I couldn't pry that thing out of your hand for all the money in the world, which tells me something is up."

He drew in a long breath. "Rayner is running a little fever."

"Dude, go be with your daughter," I told him. The SUV came to a stop next to the jet, and Dominick was the first to get out. "Have the driver take you home or order a car service, but don't feel like you have to get on that plane."

"It's not the first fever she's ever had. But each time, I worry. Rowan assures me she's fine. The pediatrician has already come over and checked her out, and he says she's okay too." His head dropped. "One day, it'll get easier. Today is just not that day."

"You're a good dad."

He gazed up, his eyes full of emotion. "Besides her mother, she's the most important part of my life. Every sniffle makes my fucking heart stop."

There wasn't enough alcohol in Florida to get him through this trip.

"Cooper—"

"If I get to Tampa and I'm not feeling it, I'll fly back. But I want to at least try to go."

I put my hand over his shoulder, giving it a hard squeeze. "I support whatever you decide."

I slipped out of the backseat, and one by one, we crossed the red carpet and climbed the steps into the jet. I wasn't more than a few paces inside when a scent hit my nose. It was subtle. Like cologne the morning after, where it took a trained nose to catch those spicy hints that were barely strong enough to make their way off my neck.

But the second I breathed in that familiar piña colada smell, I was hit with a thought.

A memory came next.

My dick instantly hardened from it; my hands immediately clutched.

And suddenly, my entire fucking head was filled with images from the past, my eyes scanning the interior of the jet to locate the source.

That was all it had taken. One small whiff.

But as I looked, I saw no one.

It had to be a splash of tropical drink mix that had somehow found its way into the air or the aroma from the fruit platter that was placed by the first couch.

A coincidence.

And a goddamn tease that was cruel as hell.

I got deeper into the aircraft, finding a seat next to Dominick, and just as I began to turn around to sit, the flight attendant rushed out of the back of the plane toward our group.

She was blonde.

With eyes so deep and blue that a crayon could be named after her.

I blinked to make sure my fucking eyes weren't playing tricks on me.

And when my eyelids opened, nothing had changed.

She was still there.

With plump, full lips.

Fair skin.

A smile that showed the most beautiful white teeth.

My stare didn't have to dip down her body to know. I didn't even have to go as low as her neck.

Because not a single thing on her gorgeous face had changed in the time that had passed.

What are you doing here? Why are you in a Dalton uniform?

How long have you worked for my best friend?

Those were just a few of the questions that were filling my mind as she got closer, my nose confirming what I'd smelled earlier as her scent got stronger.

The erection in my jeans became relentless.

My fingers balled into a fist to stop them from reaching.

Because once we locked eyes, that was all I wanted to do.

"Brady…" She stopped at the back of Cooper's seat, one row behind Dominick's. Her eyes were wide, her lips hanging open for several seconds without anything coming out of them. "What a… surprise."

Chapter Six

Lily

When Aubrey, the full-time flight attendant for the Daltons, had trained me for this position, prepping for her maternity leave, she had told me that the Daltons ran things differently than most owners of private jets. They provided a list of what they wanted, including specific brands of alcohol, and instead of the attendant greeting the family at the bottom of the boarding stairs, like the pilots did, they preferred to be served drinks the second they boarded.

So, that was what I was preparing in the rear galley when I heard the chatter in the front of the plane. The sound was far too loud and animated for it to be coming from the pilots; therefore, I knew the passengers had entered the aircraft. I quickly finished pouring the several fingers' worth of scotch into the tray of glasses I'd set out, and just as I was walking down the main aisle, I saw him.

Brady Spade.

Tingles immediately swished through my body, and while I held the tray with one hand, I gripped the back of the seat with the other, a row behind where he stood, and I forced myself to breathe.

Because I couldn't.

Because everything, including my lungs, was frozen.

How was he here? How was he only a couple of feet in front of me?

How was this my luck?

He wasn't just a man I'd slept with. My first and only one-night stand. That title wasn't nearly strong enough; it didn't hold the same level of importance for the pedestal I'd put him on.

He was the man I'd been thinking about nonstop for the last six months.

But it didn't go beyond thinking since I'd refused to look him up online, even though I knew his full name, in fear that I'd be tempted to reach out.

Communication, a second night together—those just weren't possible.

"Brady…" I searched for something to say, doing everything I could to calm the jittering in my body. When the tray threatened to fall—something I couldn't let happen; I would never recover from the embarrassment—I released the seat and gripped the tray with both hands. "What a…surprise."

Surprise?

I could laugh at the little weight that word held.

Shock wasn't much better, but it was definitely a lot of that too.

Those eyes, that smile, his hands, the most incredible body I'd ever seen—I caught each one in my line of sight and shivered.

Brady was dangerous.

Not in a way that I was scared of him. In a way that I couldn't resist him.

"I didn't expect to see you again." His eyelids narrowed as they took me in, every inch causing more goose bumps to rise over my skin. "Certainly not on my best friend's private plane."

His best friend? Is a Dalton?

I knew the world was small. But this small was far too tiny.

I didn't know what to say, so I lifted a scotch off the tray and handed it to him. "Same." And then I realized that didn't exactly make sense, so I clarified, "Not on my best friend's jet. In general, I mean, I didn't expect to see you..." My voice trailed off as I came to my senses, knowing how ridiculous I sounded. "I'll bring you another scotch before takeoff."

I wanted to run, but I couldn't. I was the only flight attendant on board. I couldn't call in a backup. Aubrey had a newborn at home and hadn't returned to work yet, which was why I was here. Somehow, I had to make it through this flight, along with the two nights we were staying in Tampa, and then the return flight to LA.

All while having Brady within reach.

And whenever I came into contact with him, I had to hide the fact that there wasn't anyone in this world I was more attracted to than him. That no man had ever done to my body what he had.

Because I remembered.

Everything.

Even down to the minuscule details.

He lifted the glass to his mouth, watching me while his lips surrounded the edge, his Adam's apple bobbing as he swallowed.

That stare was unforgettable. It penetrated every inch of my skin. My goose bumps now doubling.

"I'll grab you a water too," I said softly.

A statement that had come out of nowhere. I'd just felt the need to break the silence because standing here, saying nothing, felt so strange.

He smiled, and it made everything inside me hurt. He even released some air, sounding like a semi-laugh, and that made me ache harder.

"You can bring me whatever you'd like, Lily." He licked the wetness off his lips, his gaze dropping down my body before he turned around and sat next to Dominick.

With his back facing me, I had a break from his eyes. I finally felt like I could breathe. But at the same time, now that they were gone, I missed them.

I wanted them back.

Because I never felt more beautiful or more wanted than when Brady was looking at me.

I couldn't stay in this position any longer. I still had a full tray of scotch I needed to hand out. With every ounce of willpower I had, I greeted some of my other guests, setting a glass beside each of them, asking the gentlemen what else I could bring them for the flight.

Memorizing their answers, I reached Brady's row. I said hello to Dominick and repeated the same question to him.

"I'll take the breakfast I ordered," Dominick replied.

"And for you?" I said to Brady.

He shook his head, his eyes not moving from mine. "Lily, you know exactly what I want."

Me.

That was what screamed inside me.

But in addition to his response, there was something about the way he had said my name that made me want to press my legs together, giving myself the pressure I needed. The grittiness of his voice was equally as stimulating, as it was the same tone he'd used when he moaned my name.

"Right," I whispered.

Another strange answer, but it was the only thing I could muster.

I asked the remaining passengers the same question and hurried to the back of the plane, gathering glasses of water that, once I returned to the main cabin again, I set next to their scotch. When I went back to the galley this time, the phone rang, and it was the pilot telling me we were cleared for takeoff. I hung up and finished my safety checks, letting my guests know we were minutes from taking off and requesting them to buckle their seat belts before I strapped myself into my seat.

I thought that once I removed myself from the main cabin, I would feel better. I'd be able to inhale air that wasn't filled with Brady's cologne, that I could exhale without the intensity of his eyes focused on some part of me. But from the angle in which I sat, I could see the left profile of Brady's face, his arm as it balanced over the armrest, the side of his leg, his foot tapping the carpet.

If anything, the anxiety in my chest heightened.

I had one month left of my contract before Aubrey returned as the Daltons' full-time flight attendant. I had worked with her back in Atlanta, and we stayed in touch. When she'd told me this temporary position was available, I'd jumped on it.

What I didn't understand was why this crew couldn't have flown to Tampa next month, after I finished out my contract and was no longer working for the Daltons, so I could have avoided this situation altogether.

Why did I have to be in Brady's presence again, which stirred up feelings that didn't make any sense?

Feelings that needed to stay buried.

Although a year had passed since my breakup with David, my life was no different than it had been when I met Brady.

I was still emotionally unavailable.

With shackles around my wrists, ankles, even my brain.

In fact, depending on how I looked at it, things had gotten even worse.

I made myself glance away from him, and I took the phone out of my pocket. I'd resisted for this long. So, why did I find myself typing his name into the search bar and watching the screen fill?

Articles, websites, social media accounts, his Wikipedia page—they were suddenly overwhelming me.

Brady wasn't just some guy.

Nor was he just a well-off guy—what I'd suspected when I

originally met him after taking inventory of his watch and clothes and hotel suite.

Brady's wealth was in a category of its own.

During all the times I'd said his name out loud and to myself, it had never registered.

But it should have.

Because he was one of the owners of Cole and Spade Hotels. The hotel we were staying in tonight. Resorts that were located all over the world. And the reason he'd gone to Edinburgh, according to the page I was reading, was because he was opening another one there.

He had a net worth that was well over a billion.

But to me, he was the man I'd given my body to post-David.

The man who had owned my mind since it had happened.

The man who wouldn't allow the goose bumps to disappear from my skin.

As the jet began to lift off the tarmac, heading for the clouds, I slowly glanced up from my phone.

Brady was looking over his shoulder.

At me.

As our eyes locked, even more emotion began to pour through my chest. It made my body throb. It made my legs squeeze together, but for an entirely different reason than before.

What have I done?

Chapter Seven

BRADY

As the wheels of the plane lifted into the air, I leaned closer to Dominick and said, "You want to hear something wild as fuck?"

"Always." He took a drink of his scotch.

"Do you remember, a while back, when I was flying to Edinburgh for the first time to look at property? I was on the plane, and you called right before takeoff, and I was telling you there was a flight attendant on board who I was going to taste before we landed?"

"The one who showed up at your hotel room, right?" He didn't wait for a reply before he added, "Sounded like you were impressed with her. Which is the only reason I remember her—because impressing you, my man, is no easy feat."

When I'd returned to LA and had drinks with Dominick, he had asked about her. That was the only reason I'd told him a few of the details. Otherwise, no one else knew.

I wasn't exactly the kind of guy who held it all in. But for some reason, I'd shared very little about Lily.

"That's the one," I told him. "And she happens to be your flight attendant, which shocked the hell out of me when I got on your plane."

He smiled, his head shaking. "I wondered how you knew her."

"How the fuck did she get this job?"

He cuffed the bottom sleeve of his button-down, moving to the other side to do the same. "We have three planes—you know that— and each plane has a full-time crew. Aubrey, the lead flight attendant for this one, was going on maternity leave. She came to us and said she had the perfect replacement while she was off, someone with years of experience. Aubrey trained her, and she's been flying with us for a few months."

"A few months," I repeated.

All this fucking time, Lily had been this close, and I'd had no idea.

Although we'd only had small bits of conversation in my hotel room, I knew LA wasn't her home base; it was Atlanta. Which meant she must have relocated to the West Coast.

But why?

"What else do you know about her?" I asked.

Dominick craned his head back to look at me, a grin slowly crossing his lips. "Why are you asking?"

"Just curious."

"Bullshit," he shot back. "You're never curious about the chicks you hook up with. You're asking because she was the one woman in your life who you didn't leave—she left you. And that's one of the reasons you're intrigued by her."

"Nah." I shook my head for emphasis. "You've got it all wrong."

His brows rose. "I do? Tell me how."

"You're looking too deep into it. It's not that complicated. I just asked a question. You're acting like I fucking want to marry the woman."

He laughed, banging my arm with his elbow. "Here's what I got for you: I know nothing aside from her name and that Aubrey vouched for her. But to be employed by our firm, she has to have a file with HR."

"I don't need to see it."

He smiled again. "I wasn't offering to show it to you."

"Jesus," I groaned.

"Question: now that you know where she works, what are you going to do about it?" He crossed his legs, holding his glass near his chest.

"I'm not going to do anything about it."

He chuckled even harder. "You mean to tell me you've thought about this woman for the last however many months, and you're not even going to talk to her?"

What the hell?

Was he inside my head?

"Maybe I'll talk to her," I said. "But if you think I'm going to ask her out or do anything beyond a simple conversation, you're wrong."

"For the second time, I'm calling bullshit."

"You can call it whatever you want. You know how I am about women. I'm not looking for a happily ever after. In my world, that doesn't exist, nor do I want it."

He nodded toward my glass as though he wanted me to take a drink. "You don't think you're being a little hardheaded?"

I turned in my seat, preparing to end this conversation.

It didn't matter what Dominick thought. I wasn't going there with him. Because nothing was going to happen with Lily.

But, goddamn it, she looked so fucking gorgeous—even if there was a Dalton logo above her tit.

Regardless, she'd made her decision. She'd walked out of my hotel room.

And whatever could have happened didn't.

"Unlike the rest of you motherfuckers, I don't want to get married, so there's zero chance I'm ever going to settle down. You're fighting for something that's never going to happen. Besides, she's the one who left. Maybe she realized she didn't want someone like me or she couldn't handle me. But if she wanted something, she would have left her number."

If she had, would I have reached out?

The answer to that scared the shit out of me, so I pushed that thought far from my mind.

"All right, my man. I'll play along and pretend you're right about everything you're saying. That you weren't drooling the second you saw Lily on the plane, and had she reached for you, you wouldn't have been putty in her hands." He mashed his lips together. "Only one of us in this row has his senses—and it's not you."

I tossed back the rest of my scotch. "I need a fucking refill."

He pointed toward the galley. "There're no rules on this plane. Why don't you go get one?"

"I think I will…"

"Don't take too long, or I might think you're talking to her."

Even though we hadn't reached cruising altitude and there was a bit of turbulence as we made our way through the clouds, I got up from my seat, flipped him off, and headed toward the back.

I could have waited until Lily came into the main cabin to bring us refills. But there was something about my conversation with Dominick that had me walking toward the back of the plane.

Was he right?

Should I have a conversation with her about why she had taken off without leaving me a way to get in touch with her?

Or was that topic a waste of our time?

She was sitting in the back, along the side, the position giving her a view of the whole main cabin, holding her phone not far from her face. She was so focused on the screen that she didn't see or hear me approach, but the moment my hand hit the counter, her eyes lifted. As soon as she caught sight of me, her chest rose much faster than a normal breath.

"What can I get you?" She went to stand and realized she was still strapped in.

"I can pour my own drink."

Since the Daltons had the same type of jet as us, I assumed they kept their booze in a similar location, and I opened the cabinets above the counter until I found the right one.

"But that's what I'm here for."

She was next to me, our arms aligned as we reached into the top cupboard at the same time. The outside of my triceps rubbed against hers. I didn't know why, but the contact, the closeness, the fucking scent that was coming off her body—that tropical oasis I just wanted to bury myself in—it was all giving me a goddamn hard-on.

"I'm happy to give you whatever you want."

"Whatever I want?" My arm dropped, and I took a step to the side, allowing her to grab the bottle. "Don't make that offer, Lily, when you don't mean it."

As she was unscrewing the top, she looked at me, the recognition of my reply slowly moving across her face. "I…" As her voice faded out, she glanced around the galley, as though my eyes had become too much for her, before her gaze eventually made its way back to mine. "I had no idea you were friends with the Daltons."

"Why does that matter?"

"I just wanted you to know that I didn't take this job to mysteriously put myself in your path or anything like that. I'm not that kind of woman."

"And if you had known we were friends"—I crossed my arms—"would that have made a difference?"

"Maybe."

My head shook as I processed her question. "You mean to tell me you'd have given up a job on the off chance you might see me? Or the opposite?"

She continued to hold the top of the bottle, which should have been opened by now, telling me she was no longer unscrewing it. "I just meant that if I had known, maybe I would have asked them for your number. You know, so I could have told you myself."

"No. I don't know." I leaned against the back wall. "You left my hotel room without giving me your number. You moved to LA, where you knew I lived. Knowing my relationship to the Daltons is insignificant." I wanted her to hurry so I could slam that scotch into my throat. "What would you have told me, Lily? Because I can't see how an explanation of your employment would have even mattered."

"I just..." Her voice got quieter. Smaller even. "I don't know..."

"If you'd wanted to reach out, you could have. You knew my first and last name, and there's this thing called Google. With all the information that's been written about me, it would have taken no more than a few seconds before you had my email, office line, and all my social media accounts."

She flinched, the hurt registering in her eyes before she said, "You're upset with me."

Upset was an emotion for the weak.

I was fucking angry.

"Pissed off is a better way to put it." Shit, I wanted to tell her I didn't care, but that would be a lie. "And mad—mad as hell that you didn't want me."

She set the bottle down. "Brady, you need to understand that I didn't look you up on purpose."

I did everything in my power to force my feet to start moving and walk back to my seat, but instead, I found myself not able to. And to make matters even worse, I replied, "Because?"

There was now a war happening in her eyes. A level of emotion I hadn't seen from her before.

"Because I'm not in a position to talk to anyone in that way." She focused on my right eye, gradually moving to my left.

"You told me you were single."

She nodded. "I am. And I was."

"Then, what the fuck are you talking about?"

She turned completely around, so we were facing each other. "I'm not in a place where I can get involved. Emotionally. Physically. And I was afraid that if I reached out, you would think—"

"That I wanted more?" I laughed. "No. That's not me. You've got the wrong guy."

She searched my eyes, but this time was different from before. This time, she was looking for an answer. "If that's the case, why did you want me to Google you?"

"I didn't say I wanted you to. I said you could have."

Her hands fell to her sides. "I don't want to argue." She tightened her fingers and then lifted her arms to wrap them around her stomach. "I'm sorry."

If she called this arguing, her past confrontations must have been weak. Neither of us was even raising our voices.

"Why are you apologizing, Lily?"

"Because that's what I know how to do."

I noted her response and assured her, "But you don't need to. We're not fighting."

"Things were left a little unsettled. I mean, I darted out without even saying goodbye. We both obviously have feelings about that, or we wouldn't be talking about it now." Her arms looked like they were tightening around her. "I just want you to know it's not you. You were...perfect." She drew in some air, holding it for several seconds before she said, "More perfect than I've ever experienced in my life."

What had happened to this woman? Where was the pain in her eyes coming from?

If she was single, why was she in a place where she couldn't get emotionally or physically involved?

And why did I feel the need to get the answer to that question?

Why the hell was it eating at me?

"I've never met anyone like you, Brady," she continued. "No one has ever made me feel the way you did."

Her admission hit me.

Not just a tap.

It fucking slammed into me harder than I had been ready for.

"Lily—"

My voice cut off as the plane dipped down several feet. A couple of heavy bumps of turbulence followed, and while she grabbed the counter to steady herself, I reached for her waist.

God, she felt so fucking good in my arms. She molded right to me, like her body had been carved from my outline, and while I held her against me, I let nothing separate us.

Not even air.

Her eyes immediately widened as my dick pressed into her, and as our stares locked, she licked across her lips. Not in a way that was sexual—although it was impossible for Lily not to look seductive while she was doing anything—but in a way that told me she was buying herself some time to come up with what she wanted to say.

Her hands moved to my chest, flattening over my pecs.

Holding them, not pushing them.

"Brady..."

I lowered my hands, stopping right above her ass, an area of her body I shouldn't be touching. Fuck, I shouldn't be touching her at all. I'd told her I didn't care, and my actions were showing her the opposite.

I needed to let her go.

But I couldn't.

"Yes," I replied.

The war was back in her eyes, but this time, the emotion was replaced by something else.

Something that looked all too familiar.

It stayed there, deepening, until there was a vibration in her pocket, the nearness causing the pulse to beat through me.

A notification from her phone—it had to be that.

But as soon as it happened—that simple alert that could have been spam mail—everything changed.

Her eyes.

Her face.

Her posture.

She pulled her hands away and clamped them around the edge of the counter. "I'll get you that drink, and I'll bring it to your seat." Even her voice turned a little sharp.

What the fuck?

The woman standing before me wasn't the same woman from a few seconds ago. The two of them told very different stories.

The previous one had had a look in her eyes that told me she wanted me to take her into the bedroom that was one door away and fuck her.

And the one looking at me now was regretting that expression had ever come across her eyes.

My palms slipped to her sides, and I watched her intake the longest, deepest breath. Her lips parted, her neck became covered in tiny goose bumps, her back arched as my fingers spread.

She fucking wanted me.

But something or someone was stopping her.

My hands dropped, and before I walked back to my seat, I said, "Make it a double."

Chapter Eight

LILY

I can't breathe.

That was what Brady did to me. He made it impossible for me to draw in any air. Or if there was some already in my lungs, I couldn't release it.

My body froze.

My mind became this giant game of dodgeball, where I was constantly ducking every thought and emotion thrown my way.

I didn't understand it.

I just knew that when his arms were around me, it felt as though nothing could ever get through. That cave between his hands and chest was the safest place ever.

Just him and me.

But the reality was, that was far from the truth.

Maybe with other women, that was possible.

Not with me.

That admittance was what took hold of me as I left my room and went down to the hotel lobby. The resort was beautiful, directly on the water, backed up to a marina. The front-desk clerk, when I'd checked in to the hotel with the pilots, told us we were in the Channelside section of Tampa. A quick search on my phone showed the list of bars and restaurants in the area. Every cuisine I could ever crave was nearby, along with outdoor and indoor bars, live music, and lots of walking paths and parks.

I had the next couple of days off, and for tonight, I planned on finding a spot outside, in an area that was well suited for people-watching, where I could order a drink and take in the scenery. But first, I wanted to wander. I wanted to cruise the boardwalk by the marina and check out the boats and smell the salty air. I wanted to meander under the bridges and experience a water taxi and have some ice cream and admire the windows of the shops.

As I reached the revolving door that separated the lobby from the street, there was a vibration in my purse.

A rattle that was as startling as a fire alarm.

I reached inside the small bag and pulled out my cell. As I read the words on the screen, my feet halted.

My free hand clenched into a fist.

My teeth ground together, my jaw locking, an instant headache splitting my skull.

Why?

Why?!

A word I found myself internally screaming so many times per day.

I looked at the sidewalk through the glass, craving the city I'd been excited to explore—the humid air, the scents, all goading me.

But I wasn't stepping out.

I was going back to my room.

I turned around and stopped at the store inside the lobby, robotically going over to the shelves that housed the alcohol to grab a bottle of vodka that I brought up to the register.

"There are mixers over there"—the woman behind the counter

pointed to the opposite side of the store—"if you're looking for some cranberry or orange juice or even tonic."

"No need." I kept my eyes on the clear liquid inside the glass. "I want it straight up."

"I like the way you drink."

I handed her enough cash that would cover the transaction and walked to the elevator, glancing behind me before I stepped inside. I leaned on the side wall prior to hitting the button for my floor. And I stared at the top of the bottle as the door opened, checking the space outside, and then I quickly made my way to my room.

When is this going to end?

A sentence I repeated every day as well.

Not just daily though.

Several times a fucking day.

And I never had an answer.

I tossed my bag on the desk and kicked my shoes off, closing the curtains and turning off the lamps. When the room was dark, I grabbed one of the glasses off the counter and carried it with the bottle into bed, pouring enough into the cup that I wouldn't have to constantly refill it.

I exhaled the air I'd been holding in and pressed my back against the headboard. My feet dived into the mattress, heels pushing as hard as they could kick. With my eyes closed, I tapped the back of my head against the fabric-covered headboard, the cushion preventing the banging from hurting.

By accident, my eyes opened toward the large rectangular windows.

I immediately regretted it.

Because I knew the view outside. I'd been admiring it for the last few hours. Now, it was blocked by the thick, heavy shade, where a small rim of light seeped out from the perimeter along each side. It wasn't sunlight; it was long past sunset. It was light from the adjacent buildings and the liveliness of Tampa.

It was a tease.

...

The sound of my phone caused my eyes to flick open, and I reached for my cell on the pillow next to me, checking the caller ID. I blinked a few times to make sure I was seeing the name correctly and connected the call.

"Hello?"

"Did I wake you?" Aubrey asked.

"It's okay." I rubbed my eyes. "Don't worry about it."

"What time is it there?" She paused. "A little past eleven, and you're already asleep? On your night off? You're worse than me, and I have a newborn."

"I went out earlier." I pushed myself toward the headboard, dragging the blanket up to my chest. The lie made me feel less pathetic even though I hated giving her one. "I had too many proseccos and tucked myself in." I glanced toward the bottle of vodka that was two glasses lower than when I'd bought it. "How are you? How's the baby?" I cleared my throat, trying to sound more awake.

"Colicky. I'm honestly wondering at this point if there's a way I can push him back inside of me. At least when he was cooking in my oven, I could sleep for increments longer than twenty minutes, and no one aside from me was screaming all day long." She sighed. "How's Tampa? How're the Daltons? How's life without a baby crying twenty-four/seven?"

"Everything and everyone are great." It occurred to me just then that if Brady frequently traveled with Dominick or one of the other Daltons, Aubrey could know him. "There was an interesting guy on board today. Brady Spade. Do you know him?"

"Do I know him?" She laughed. "I know him and his two brothers, Macon and Cooper, they've been friends with the Daltons for as long as I've worked for them."

My thumb instinctively went into my mouth, where I chewed the skin off the corner. "What can you tell me about him?"

She laughed again. "Do I sense a crush?"

"No."

"A visual crush?"

I filled my lungs, surprised that I could breathe, given the topic of our conversation. "He's undeniably handsome."

"That he is and very, very single as well. He's the only Spade brother who hasn't yet settled down. I've met Macon's girlfriend and Cooper's girlfriend—both are lovely."

"But you've never met anyone Brady has dated or someone he's brought on a trip?"

"You must not keep up with the LA gossip sites. The Spades and Daltons and Westons—another set of their friends—are constantly discussed, and Brady's love life is a hot topic."

"The only people I know in LA, aside from the pilots, are you and the Daltons." I crossed my legs under the blanket. "It wouldn't make sense for me to keep up with the gossip—I wouldn't know anyone they're talking about."

Now that I knew Brady was a conversation piece, maybe I needed to check out those sites.

But why?

Did it even matter what they said about him?

If anything, that was even more of a reason why I needed to keep my thoughts far away from him.

"Well then, let me fill you in. Miraculously, the baby is down, which means I have approximately ten minutes before all you hear is screams." Her voice was low, almost a whisper. "Brady Spade is quite the ladies' man. But he's never photographed with one on his arm, and he always attends events alone because he's not even willing to commit for a couple of hours, long enough to take one to a gala or an opening—can you even imagine?"

I couldn't imagine anything at the moment, and it wasn't the vodka's fault.

"Anyway," she continued, "he's seen around town with women— at concerts, restaurants, sporting events, just nothing major where there will be photographers. As for personality, he and his brothers are nothing alike. Macon is the bubbly, kindhearted one. Cooper is much more to the point and charming. Brady has the attitude of a lion. He's not rude; he's just extremely domineering and impatient and fearless. Fearless in a way where he knows what he wants and he's unafraid to go after it."

Nothing she'd said surprised me. That was precisely the way I'd suspected him to be.

"He's not going to give you the warm fuzzies," she went on. "Unless your idea of warm fuzzies is getting ravaged against a wall, after which it'll probably take a few days before you're walking straight again." She giggled. "If that's your thing, then that's your man."

"He's not my man."

He couldn't be.

But I certainly knew that what she'd described was his thing.

And after experiencing him, I knew that was my thing too.

"You know what I mean." She giggled. "They're honestly a wonderful family. I can't say a bad word about them. Respectful, mature, and it seems they really must have a good head on their shoulders because they're running an empire."

"Spade Hotels. That is an empire."

"Cole and Spade Hotels now since the merger, making their company even larger than it already was. I wouldn't hate waking up with that much money in my bank account. How about you?"

Money had never been my motivation as a kid or an adult. I just wanted to do what would make me happy. Even when my parents died and I inherited their house and savings, I didn't spend any of it.

I earned my own money and didn't need theirs.

And what I'd earned and what I'd inherited hadn't brought me happiness.

Because even though I was financially comfortable, happiness was an emotion I hardly ever felt.

But I'd felt it with Brady.

Aubrey didn't know that side of me.

No one did.

"Hey, Aubrey, do you know—"

My voice cut off at the sound of a knock on my door. Knuckles hitting three consecutive times in a row from a hand that had strength and power.

The pilots would have texted me if they needed something. Plus, they didn't know what room I was in.

That only left one other person it could be.

Oh God.

Every hair on my body was now standing straight.

My heart pounded so hard I swore it was going to come through my skin. My flesh went from cold to hot to cold again.

My mouth turned dry.

"Aubrey, I've got to call you back."

"If I don't answer, it's because the baby—"

A second set of knocks rapped against my door, and I pulled the phone away from my face and disconnected the call.

Chapter Nine

BRADY

"That was one hell of a win," I said to Beck, standing along the side of the locker room, in front of the bench where he was taking off his jersey and shoulder pads. "And that last goal? Shit, you were on fire."

The accommodations in Tampa were much different than his locker room in LA. The owner of the Whales spared no expense when it came to the luxury and comfort of his players. I couldn't speak about the room they provided for their visitors. For all I knew, it could look exactly like this one, but whenever we visited Beck after a game, it was as five-star as one of our hotels.

"Things weren't looking good at the end of the first period," he admitted, wiping his brow, the sweat still pouring from the top of his head.

"But you turned it around quite fast," Dominick replied. "The momentum completely shifted when you scored the goal at the beginning of the second."

"I thought you were going for a hat trick," Jenner said to Beck.

"I was." Beck smiled.

Jenner pounded Beck's fist. "You owe me a grand for not getting one."

"You took a live bet?" Beck asked him.

"After your second goal, I sure as shit did," Jenner responded.

Beck shook his head. "You should have heard the shit Bartosz was talking to me before the game," he said, referring to Tampa's goalie. He grabbed a towel and wiped his arms and hands. "I wanted nothing more than to make him pay for those words, so, yeah, I was going for three. I just couldn't make it happen. Their defense played better tonight than I'd thought they would."

"Still, two had to feel good," Macon offered.

"It'll feel even better when they come to LA in a few weeks and we crush them again." Beck dropped the towel onto the bench behind him.

"What's the deal with Bartosz?" Cooper asked. "Just some game-day sparring, or does it go deeper than that?"

Beck shrugged with a sly grin on his face.

"Maybe you should fuck his girlfriend and really stir shit up," Dominick said.

"Maybe I already have," Beck countered.

"My man," I said, grabbing Beck's shoulder.

"We're heading out for some drinks," Dominick told him. "Hopefully, you've got a little time, so you can join us. When do you guys fly out?"

"As soon as the team hits the showers, we're headed to the airport to fly to the east coast of Florida. We have a game there tomorrow night. Then, Nashville, Chicago, and home." He ran his hand over his wet hair. "Wish I could join you fellas. Tampa is a sick city to party in."

I squeezed his shoulder before I released him. "We'll see you when you get back to LA, and we'll do plenty of partying there. Glad we could catch this game."

"Happy you guys made it." He shook my hand.

As soon as he released me, he went around the group, shaking everyone else's hand, and then we made our way out of the locker room and through the exit on the side of the arena.

We were only a few steps past the door when Dominick, who was leading us, turned around and faced us. "My assistant made us reservations at a whiskey bar. It's within walking distance. We'll go there first and then head to the rooftop bar that's across the street from our hotel. We have a table there. If things stay hot, we'll stay until closing. If things die out, she reserved us a table at another bar down the street."

"Fuck yeah," Macon voiced. "Let's go."

The plans Dominick had arranged sounded fun, and I was on board for all of it. I wanted nothing more than to hang with these guys and get shit-faced.

But since we'd left the hotel and walked to the game, a thought had been nagging at me.

Non-fucking-stop.

And it was something I needed to do first before I even considered going to a bar and drinking more.

I shifted my stance, eyeing the Cole and Spade Hotel that stood taller than the others around it, with its mirrored facade and unique architecture. A property I hadn't spent much time at, but one I enjoyed far more than I'd expected.

"Aren't you coming?" Cooper asked.

I looked back at the group, realizing he was speaking to me and that everyone had joined Dominick, where they were all now standing several steps away from me.

Damn it.

I could already hear the words that were about to be shouted in my direction.

But that wasn't the only reason I was cursing in my head.

The other reason was because something had gotten into me.

Thoughts that shouldn't be in my goddamn head.

Thoughts that were mentally set in stone, especially as I said to them, "Text me the name of the whiskey bar." I slowly looked at Dominick. "I'm going to meet you there."

I could strangle myself for this. Because what I was about to do wasn't going to lead to anything good. I had several drinks already in me, and I'd had a hard-on for hours.

But as I gave the hotel another glance, I knew there wasn't anywhere else I wanted to be right now.

"Where are you going?" Macon asked.

I gazed back at the guys, the anger building in my chest.

It hadn't come out of nowhere.

I was mad at myself for doing this, mad about the entire situation.

Mad that I knew better and I couldn't fucking resist.

"You don't need to worry about that," I told Macon.

"You're really leaving us now?" Ford persisted.

"Brady, things are just getting started," Cooper said.

Enough with the fucking questions and guilt trip.

"I'll see you guys later," I told them.

Dominick nodded, knowing exactly what I was going to do, and said, "I'll text you the address."

As I turned around and walked toward the street, I heard, "Pussy."

I held my middle finger high in the air and went to the hotel's front entrance. After moving through the lobby, I stopped at the bank of elevators. Before I'd gone to the game, I'd called the hotel manager to get the room number I needed. Although it was against hotel policy to give out information on any guest, he couldn't deny an owner. So, when I stepped into the elevator, I knew just what button to press.

I waited for the lift to climb, and when it finally opened on the sixth floor, I went down the hallway, halting when I reached room 632. I stood in front of the door, my hand flat against it, as though I was waiting for the sense to be knocked back into me. My forehead was positioned the same way as my palm, landing just above it, my fingers now balled into a fist.

Why couldn't I resist her?

Why was she eating away at my mind?

Why had I thought of her scent and the feel of her pussy and the softness of her lips the entire time I was at the game?

Why was knowing she was behind this door, assuming she hadn't gone out, driving me to a level that was far beyond fucking wild?

My hand lifted from the hardness and returned; the sound it left was a heavy, deep knock, and in case she didn't hear the first one, I followed up with two more.

While I waited, I pulled my face away and gripped the frame on either side of the door. As the seconds passed, the little patience I had began to thin out.

And when I couldn't stand another second, my fist pounded a series of three more knocks.

She had the next couple of days off. I didn't know why my gut told me she was in her room since there was no reason for her to be. But I stayed right here, listening to every sound, and within a few seconds, there was the faintest scratch on the back side of the door right before I heard the twist of the knob.

Her face appeared through the crack, scanning the entire doorway even though I filled it. She kept it ajar and whispered, "Brady…"

"I need to know something."

I tried not to let her scent affect me.

I tried not to get hard from the quietness of her voice.

She clung to the edge of the wood, but didn't open it any further. "This isn't a good time."

"Why?" My teeth clenched. "Because you're not alone?"

Something else I hadn't considered. For all I knew, one of the pilots could be in her bed.

That thought had my goddamn fingers driving into the doorframe.

"Because I was about to go to sleep…and I'm hardly wearing any clothes," she replied.

An answer that made my grip loosen. But one that also made me do everything in my fucking power not to reach through the crack, open the door wider, and pull her into my arms.

Who was this woman? And what the hell was she doing to me?

Because wanting a chick twice had never happened before.

Yet this one had passed me up for six months; she hadn't wanted me enough to reach out—a fact that fucking ate at me—and I still found her irresistible.

Something I couldn't explain.

I just knew I couldn't leave this doorway without her lips touching mine.

"Lily, are you forgetting I've devoured every fucking inch of your body?"

Her lips parted as she inhaled. "I could never forget."

That reply, along with a few others she'd said on the plane, hit me hard.

"You were…perfect."

"More perfect than I've ever experienced in my life."

"I've never met anyone like you, Brady. No one has ever made me feel the way you did."

"Then, you know you don't have to hide your body from me," I ordered.

"But I do. And there are two reasons for that."

I leaned in a little further to get more of her scent. The tropical notes of the pineapple made me lick across my lips, wishing it were her wetness I was tasting. "What's the first?"

"I told you, I'm not in a position for this." Her head dropped. "My life is messy. Complicated." She finally glanced up, the hurt in her eyes evident. "You shouldn't want someone like me."

Someone like…*her*?

From where I was standing, she was everything I fucking wanted.

That face.

That body.

The sweetness that went beyond her scent.

"Let me be the judge of that."

"No—"

"Lily, let me be the judge of that," I repeated, the sternness thick in each word.

"You have no idea what you're saying."

The innocence was pouring off her.

But so was the honesty.

"I'm not the kind of man who says something and doesn't mean it. Words don't scare me." My palms ran down the doorframe. "Nothing scares me."

She stared at me. Silently.

"Nothing..." she said in the softest voice.

It wasn't a question; it was clearly a statement.

But I wasn't in a place to have that conversation—not now, not when I was this worked up.

"Let's not make this heavier than it needs to be," I said. "It's clear why I'm here and what I want. I'm not asking for anything more than that."

"But, see, that's the second reason I'm hiding my body from you."

My eyes narrowed. "Explain."

"You're looking at me like the moment you get through the door, you're going to strip off the little I have on, and I'm suddenly going to find myself in the air, against a wall, with you inside of me."

My teeth rimmed the lip I'd just licked, my erection painfully stiff as I took a step forward. "And you're telling me you don't want that?"

A second passed.

Two.

And then three.

"Answer me, Lily."

Chapter Ten

LILY

O nly a minute ago, I had been on the phone with Aubrey, every hair on my body standing straight from the sound of the knock. A noise and visit I hadn't expected.

Both terrified me.

I silently tiptoed to the door. When I reached the tiny peephole, I forced myself to suck in all the air I could hold and aimed my eye to the round opening.

Relief flooded me as I took in Brady's face.

But had it?

Although he wasn't who I'd expected, his presence came with a whole other set of problems.

After our conversation in the galley, I'd had a feeling he was going to approach me at some point during this trip. And as he was an owner of the hotel, I wasn't shocked he had access to my room number. What shocked me was that he'd waited almost no time at all to come here.

But maybe that wasn't shocking for a man, like him, who went after what he wanted.

Who wasn't afraid of anything or anyone.

But was this what I wanted?

What I...semi-feared?

It would take every ounce of willpower, while staring at this breathtakingly gorgeous man, to stay strong. To stay hidden in the doorway. To say whatever statement I could conjure up that would make him walk away.

Not because I didn't want him to touch me.

Because I knew it would be the worst thing for the both of us.

"Lily..."

The look on his face was hungry, feral, like he was about to pounce at any second.

It did things to my body.

Throbbing things.

Goose bump–like things.

Since the text had come through in the lobby, I'd been deep inside my head. Anxiety had been eating at me, to the point where the vodka didn't help. Neither had the nap or the conversation with Aubrey.

Brady was the only thing—the only person—who had halted my thoughts in the past and calmed my nerves.

I'd lost myself in him.

"Lily..."

And why should I deny myself of that?

Edinburgh was one.

Tampa would be two.

And then there would never be a three.

Once my contract was up with the Daltons, when Aubrey returned from maternity leave, I would find a different job, somewhere else, that would keep me in the sky for as many hours as possible.

"Answer me..."

But if I could just have this night, the mental freedom that it would bring, that would carry me over.

The same way Scotland had.

"Lily—"

"Yes." I opened the door an inch. Then another inch. "Before you say anything else"—I swallowed as the bursts of electricity he was causing to flicker through me set my stomach on fire—"that yes was my answer."

His hand lifted from the frame and slipped through the small opening. Half of it landed on my face. The other half was on my neck.

His grip was tight.

And then it tightened more.

"You're giving yourself to me..."

Why are those words so incredibly sexy?

Why do they make me even wetter?

And why do they confirm that I made the right decision even if I could possibly regret it later?

"For the night, I am."

The second that statement left my mouth, the door opened more, just wide enough for him to enter, and once he stepped through, his other hand was on me, and I was suddenly against the wall.

In the air.

Within his arms.

"Is this what you want?" His tone was as rough as his tongue had been when it was on my clit.

That memory. I could still recall it as though it had happened seconds ago.

"Yes."

Once my lips closed, his mouth moved to my neck, the spot right below my chin, and he stayed there, against my throat. "Say it again, Lily. I want to feel your fucking answer."

My eyes closed as my body turned to pudding—my muscles jiggly, my limbs barely holding steady.

Most of all, my mind was focused solely on one thing.

Brady Spade.

A man who made me feel so incredibly confident, powerful, and in control of what I wanted.

Most of all, he made me feel safe.

"I want you," I whispered.

A low, deep grumble came from his chest. "I should fuck you against this wall." He pulled me off the plaster and carried me toward the bed. "But I'm not going to. I need to touch you. I need to see every goddamn inch of your body. And do you know what I'm going to do then?"

"What?" The syllable came out as a moan.

"I'm going to punish you." He set me on the bed. "Six fucking months—I say that earns you quite the spanking."

"Brady—"

"You had full access to me, every means to reach out. You didn't." His stare dropped down my body toward my bare legs. "My tongue is going to remember that, Lily. When it's on your pussy, licking you, and you're fucking begging me to come—that's when I'm going to recall every one of those months of no contact. And that's when you're going to get punished."

Chapter Eleven

BRADY

"Brady!"

Lily's voice came out as a scream.

But she'd been screaming for the last thirty or so minutes. That was how long my face had been between her legs.

Punishing her with my tongue.

A threat I'd given to her when I first set her on the bed, where I then stripped off the little she'd been wearing and positioned her on the very edge of the mattress.

I spread her legs.

I got on my fucking knees.

And my face went to my favorite spot in the entire world.

What she didn't know about me was that if I made a threat, I followed through. I was a man of my word.

And this beautiful woman had gotten a lashing with the tip of my tongue, reminding her of every reason why she should have reached out to me.

It came in the form of denial.

I wouldn't let her come, licking her to the point where her body began to shake, the pitch of her voice turning its highest, her legs caving inward, her back arching, her hand pulling at the strands of my hair. Just as she was nearing the peak, I'd pull away.

Over and fucking over.

I even got up at one point. I walked my ass over to the minibar and slowly savored a small bottle of vodka, staring at her spread across the bed. Listening to her begging, seeing the slickness on her cunt, recalling the many trips I'd taken her toward an orgasm. And there, feet away from her pussy, I asked myself why I was doing this.

I wasn't going to settle down with her.

Date her.

I sure as hell wasn't going to marry her.

So, why the fuck did it matter that she hadn't reached out?

Because it pissed me off that she hadn't wanted more.

Because one time had been enough for her.

Because she hadn't thought about me, craved me to the point of needing to have me again.

Because she was the one woman who wasn't completely obsessed with me.

That was why.

I finished the rest of the vodka. I got on my knees, wrapping my arms around the inside of her legs, and I returned to the pussy that gave me more satisfaction than any of the others I'd had in the last six months.

I pressed my nose against her clit—a spot that had to be so worked up that only a little more pressure would set her off. "You can say my name all you want, Lily. You're not going to come."

"Please!" She tore at my hair. "I can't take it." She rocked her hips forward. "Not for another second."

I fucking loved hearing this.

Her begging.

Needing.

The scent of her every time I inhaled.

The feel of her wetness against my face.

"You think you deserve to come?"

"Yes!"

I chuckled at the sound of her desperation and pulled my nose away, aiming a finger at her pussy. So far, I hadn't fingered her. That would get her there even faster, and I wanted to draw this out as long as possible.

But the truth was, I needed her to come.

For me.

Because my cock wanted to be inside her so badly, and my stamina was starting to wear very thin.

"You'd better make me fucking feel it," I growled against her.

My finger dived through her tightness until I reached the back of my knuckle, and I turned my wrist, pointing upward toward her stomach, heading for the section of her body that would drive her fucking mad.

Her G-spot.

And that was when I began to lick again.

But I wasn't calm.

I wasn't slow.

I gave her hard, fast flicks with the front half of my tongue, pressing my finger in and out of her, and within a second, she was screaming.

"Brady! *Ahhh*!"

It wasn't just the noise that made my hard-on ache.

It was the sight of her body shuddering.

The way her cunt narrowed against my skin.

How her wetness thickened and I got to taste her orgasm and lick it off her.

"Oh my God!" She released my hair, her palm flattening on my head. "Don't stop!"

She didn't have to worry; I wasn't stopping until she stilled.

But I kept my eyes open, staring up her body to watch the entire thing, taking in every jitter and vibration. It was one hell of a view.

Beautiful and sexy.

Enticing as fuck.

And when her body calmed, the shouting finally quieted, her breath now coming out in pants, I carefully pulled my hand away, rubbing my nose against her clit before I completely separated us.

"That was"—she gasped again—"pure fucking evil." She looked down, her eyes wild like a goddamn animal, hair a mess, cheeks red, lips wet and apart. "I don't know whether I want to kill you or if I'm completely in love with you." Her hand went to her mouth, her eyes wide. "I didn't mean to say that—like that."

But she'd said it, and the word took hold of me.

Rocked me.

It was just a statement from someone who was still in that postorgasmic heat, but still…fuck me.

"Let's go with kill." I'd already taken off my shirt, but I was still wearing my jeans, so I reached into my pocket to get my wallet, grabbing the condom from inside. I put the wallet away, loosened my belt, button, and zipper, and I let my pants fall while I stepped out of my shoes. The only thing left was my boxer briefs. Since she was still on the end of the bed, I moved within a distance that she could reach. "Why don't you show me what you can do with your mouth?"

A smile came over her lips. "Should I punish you?"

My boxer briefs were suddenly around my ankles, my dick pointed at her mouth.

"You can. But you'd regret it."

"So, this is one-sided?" She wrapped her hand around the bottom of my shaft and began to stroke.

"I made it clear why you were getting punished. Me? I've done nothing wrong."

"That's what you call the last however many minutes?" She licked across my tip.

I hissed from how good it felt.

"Because not letting me come for that long makes you guilty as hell." She gave my crown a quick suck. "I think I should put you through the same thing you just did to me."

My eyes narrowed as I clamped her cheeks with both hands. "Try it. I dare you."

"You're threatening me, Mr. Spade."

I gave her nipple a pinch. "It's not a threat. It's a warning."

"What would that punishment get me? I need to know what the stakes are before I do anything…"

Never in my life had I negotiated while my cock was near a woman's mouth.

Yet every word she spoke was so fucking seductive; all it did was make me want her more.

"What you just experienced, that would happen all over again. But this time, I'd use a mix of my dick, my finger, and my tongue. You know, just to make it more interesting."

Her eyes grew wide. "You're a masochist."

"I've been called worse things."

She looked at my cock, like it was kinder than I was. A thought that made me want to fucking laugh.

There was nothing kind about my dick.

Not in the way I fucked.

Not in the way I drove orgasms through a woman's body.

"Would you ever let me win?" she pleaded.

A question that inconspicuously mentioned a future. Whether that was later tonight, tomorrow, or a week from now.

That was something I wanted.

And something I didn't.

Goddamn it.

"You just got my mouth. I'd say you already won tonight."

Her teeth nipped her bottom lip. "You know what I mean."

"Let's see how good you suck. If you're a rock star, that'll earn you a hell of a lot." As I nodded toward her mouth, I chuckled.

"Such an asshole."

"You love that about me."

She surrounded my head, taking several inches of my shaft into her mouth.

My eyes closed, and my neck fell back. My mouth opened, and I moaned, "Fuck, yes."

She used her hand at the same time, circling my base, her tongue rotating as she drew back, giving my tip some extra pressure before she bobbed. But as she lowered, she used her tongue again, dragging it across the sides, using her lips to protect my skin from her teeth.

I fisted her hair. "That's it."

For as long as I'd had a hard-on, it wouldn't take much more for me to fill her mouth, requiring her two swallows just to get it all down.

And if I had my way, that would happen at some point tonight— after a shower and a quick rest. But it wasn't going to happen now.

"Lily..."

I tightened my grip, urging her to slow down. But doing so only made her go faster. She was trying to earn herself that win, and she was quickly getting herself there.

"You'd better be careful." I glanced down, catching her eyes.

Although she couldn't grin, her stare told me she knew just what she was doing.

And she was enjoying it.

This fucking woman.

Before she could get any more pleasure out of this, I popped my dick out of her mouth and picked up the condom that had fallen to the floor. I tore off the corner of the metal foil, and I rolled the latex over me.

"What? You couldn't take it?"

I looked at her. "What did you just say to me?"

"I asked if you couldn't take it..." She was really smiling now.

"I could take it."

"But you were going to come. And you were shocked at just how good I sucked your dick and how fast I was getting you there." The pride beamed from her fucking face.

I was putting an end to that.

Now.

"Get over here." I reached under her arms, lifting her against me, and I took her place on the bed, setting her on top of me. "How about you ride me and make us both come?"

"You like this position. You made me do it the last time we were together." She wiggled her ass until her pussy was hovering above my tip. "Honestly, I'm surprised you give up the control."

"Ah," I exhaled as she sank me into her. "It's not about control. It's about having access to your entire body and watching you fall apart on top of me."

"Then, watch, Brady, because it's about to happen again."

There was zero inhibition in the way she fucked me.

Nor was there any hesitation, even with how large I was.

She took my cock like she fucking owned it, bouncing over my shaft, tilting her hips upward and back, grinding over the base so the top of me rubbed against her clit.

It was like she'd dreamed about this.

Maybe we both had.

And while she did everything in her power to milk the cum out of me, I focused on her body, surrounding her nipple with my mouth, dragging my teeth over the end. That little bud, the way it hardened and puckered, was so hot.

"Damn it, you feel good," I groaned.

I knew just how she was feeling.

I could hear it in her moans.

I could feel it in the way she was getting wetter with each dip.

I slid my hands across her hips, holding that deliciously meaty, perfectly curvy part of her body.

"Don't try to get me to slow down," she warned. "This is the speed that I want. Don't you dare tell me what you want."

Don't you dare.

She was using my words against me.

And I loved it.

"You're fucking me like you want to get me off."

She set her arms on my shoulders, pulling our chests closer together. "What if I do?"

She didn't pause. If anything, her speed was increasing.

"I'd lift you into the air and pound my orgasm through you."

Her hands lifted to my face. "No. No, no." She let out a long, deep moan. "You're not moving. You're staying right here. And you're going to take what I give you."

"Lily—"

"No argument. You lost that ability when you shifted the power to me." She nuzzled my lips. "So, take it, Brady, and enjoy it."

It was like her cunt was a fucking vacuum, her speed on sprint level.

"Oh fuck!" she screamed.

Just the sound I wanted to hear.

I cupped her ass—another one of my favorite parts of her body—and I held on.

That was all I could do.

What I'd been ordered to do.

And as much as I hated that, nothing made me happier in this moment.

Especially as her pussy practically fastened around me, as she began to buck over me, as the wave of wetness told me just what was happening in her body.

I couldn't hold it off.

Not with how incredible she felt.

Not with a view this stunning.

"Lily!" Within a few pumps, I was filling the condom. "Fuck me!"

"Yes!" she shouted. "Come with me!"

I gripped her harder, driving my fingers into the cheeks of her ass. "Damn it!"

Words were lost in my mind. I couldn't remember a time when something had felt like this. When an orgasm had projected through my body with an intensity this debilitating.

My muscles turned weak.

My breath became labored.

All I could do was grasp her, clutch her with both hands while she sucked everything out of me. And as she finished, when we both reached the end of our peaks, she lagged her thrusts until she was completely still.

It was then that my arms wrapped around her, making sure she didn't move.

I didn't even want her lifting off my shaft.

I was that sensitive.

"Don't you dare," I snarled, repeating that famous line as she slightly lifted. "You're staying right here."

She locked our eyes. "What's going on, Mr. Spade? Did I surprise you?" She smiled. "Did I give you exactly what you never knew you wanted?"

I chuckled.

This woman was full of surprises.

"You did all right."

Her brows rose. "Just all right? Because if you're telling me I can't move, then that's more than all right."

I wasn't going to give her a head that was as big as mine.

"I have an idea."

Her smile grew. "Yeah?"

"Why don't you stop asking questions and fucking kiss me?"

• • •

The second my eyes opened from the deepest sleep, piña colada was all I could smell. The scent was on the pillow my head rested on; it was in the air of the hotel room. Fuck, it was even all over me.

But it wasn't the aroma that made my brain go from zero to a goddamn million.

It was the fact that the sun was coming through the blinds and I was still here.

In her bed.

And I'd spent the night.

Something I'd hardly ever done with another woman.

But after a shower and a second round of sex, where I'd fucked her against the wall and on top of the desk before finally ending on the bed, I'd only intended to lie down and take a quick rest.

I certainly hadn't planned on staying until morning.

Because I never stuck around this long.

But something had made me so relaxed that I didn't get up. It hadn't been the drinks I had at the game or what went down in this room before I climbed under the covers.

What the fuck was it—

"Good morning."

Lily's sleepy, raspy voice pulled me away from my thoughts. A tone that was even sexier than she usually sounded.

She'd been dozing along my side, and with my arm stretched across the top of the bed, she was balled up under my armpit. She only had to glance up for our eyes to lock.

"Morning," I replied, sitting up a little more to rest my head on the headboard.

She looked past me to the nightstand, where there was an alarm clock. "It's eight thirty? My God!" She turned away from me and rolled onto her back, pulling the blanket up to her neck. "I haven't slept in like this in ages."

"That's what happens when you run into me on a private jet and answer a late-night knock at your door."

She giggled. "No kidding." An exhale followed her laugh. "Funny, the one time I sleep that hard and that soundlessly is with you."

"What's funny about that?"

She was quiet for a moment. "Girl things you wouldn't understand."

"Try me."

"Ah, but it's complicated."

"You've said that to me before."

"I wish I didn't have to say it again…but I do." She tucked her long blonde hair behind her ears. "Complicated should be my middle name, sadly." She focused on everything but my eyes.

"Why is it complicated?"

"Why…" she whispered. She finally looked at me after taking a break that was far too long. "What do you guys have planned today?"

A subject change.

Noted.

"Brunch," I responded. "That starts in about an hour."

She wrapped an arm around the top of the blanket, holding it in place, and reached toward her nightstand, grabbing her cell. She scrolled the screen, presumably looking at her notifications. Even though the comforter covered her chest, I could see the way it was moving, how it was rising much faster than normal. As she set her phone down, her cheeks turned red, her throat bobbed as she swallowed, her posture became incredibly stiff.

"I don't want to keep you from brunch. You probably have to get going anyway, so you can shower." She stopped looking at me. Even her profile was standoffish.

What the fuck had just happened?

Was she kicking me out?

"I don't need an hour. I'm quick."

"But I do."

When her eyes finally met mine, they were pleading with me. But why? Was she regretting last night? That I had woken up in her bed? That she'd even taken the job with the Daltons because that now made it much easier for her to run into me?

"I'm meeting up with a friend. At this rate, I'm going to be very late."

Was she telling me the truth?

Or was she looking for a reason to get me the hell out?

I was questioning every-fucking-thing when it came to this woman.

Because I'd become that guy, the one I no longer recognized.

Why? How?

Shit if I knew.

But what I did know was that Lily's body language, her tone, the emotion I could see in her profile had all changed since she'd looked at her phone.

And each one was telling me I needed to leave.

"Looks like I'd better get going."

She nodded, and then she slid out from the covers and hurried into the bathroom. I watched her the entire way, her ass looking so perfect as her hips swung with each step, her back a gorgeous arch, and thighs with just the right amount of muscle.

I was fucking hard again.

She returned seconds later, wrapped in a robe, the Cole and Spade new emblem on the breast pocket. I thought she'd come back to bed, but she picked up my clothes off the floor instead, each piece and layer, and brought them over to me, placing them on the blanket.

I couldn't help but chuckle. "I got the message. I'm going, Lily."

She'd acted this way on the plane when she read whatever had come across her screen.

What was it about her phone that felt so off?

. . .

"Dude, what the fuck happened to you last night?" Cooper asked as I joined the guys at their table.

There was only one chair available, between Ford and Macon, which had clearly been saved for me. If Dominick hadn't texted me the name of the restaurant, I probably would have bailed on brunch.

"I was busy." I set my napkin on my lap and took a long drink from the glass of water in front of me.

I knew my absence from the post-game partying was going to spark a shit ton of questions and accusations—none that I had any patience for.

I wasn't going to talk about Lily.

What had happened between us.

Where my head was at.

Because, fuck, I had no idea what I was thinking or doing.

"Busy doing who?" Macon asked.

I glanced around the circle, my best buds all staring back at me, grinning like fucking assholes. "Listen, there are plenty of other things we can talk about right now. Like what we're doing after this."

"Oh, we know what we're doing after this," Jenner said. "That was a conversation we had prior to you arriving. What's far more interesting is what you were doing before you got here."

"Give it up," I groaned, squeezing the wet glass, looking around the restaurant for a server I could track down so I could order a goddamn drink.

"If you just come clean, we'll stop bothering you," Ford said.

I glared at Dominick. "Dude, get your brothers under control.

Right fucking now."

My best friend laughed, seeing straight through my bullshit. "You realize what you're asking, don't you?" He leaned his elbows on the table. "There isn't a single motherfucker at this table who's going to lay off until you come clean. We both know that. The sooner you cave, the easier you're going to make this process on us."

Dominick wouldn't spill. We had that kind of relationship. But that didn't mean he wouldn't goad me into telling the rest of them.

"You all suck." I ran my hand over the top of my hair, strands that were still wet from the shower.

The one where I'd jerked myself off until I came into the stream of water. After seeing Lily's ass this morning, that was the only thing that would get rid of my raging hard-on.

A guy walked by that was wearing a polo with the restaurant logo, and I waved him over.

"Bring me a scotch," I told him.

"I'll let your waitress know," he replied.

"While you're at it, tell her to bring me two." When I looked back at the guys, I ground my teeth. Maybe if I gave them a bite, it would be enough. "I was with a woman. I'm not telling you anything you don't already know."

Cooper crossed his arms over his chest. "But to give up a night out with the guys for pussy? That's not you. You're the guy who gets pussy after the night is over, not when it's just beginning."

"I second that," Macon added.

"An opportunity presented itself. I acted on it." I shrugged. "Sue me."

"We're all family here, brother," Jenner said, nodding at each one of them as though he needed their backing. "There's no reason for you to keep anything from us."

My neck fell backward as I laughed.

Who the fuck was he kidding? There was every reason to keep

my mouth shut. Because the moment I opened it, I'd never hear the end of it.

I was the sibling and friend who had never wanted any of these guys to settle down. The one who had given them endless shit whenever they told me they were dating someone.

They knew I didn't hit it more than once. So, if I admitted Lily was twice...

Fuck me.

I might as well dig my own grave.

"You want to know the truth?" I leaned back in my chair, crossing my legs and wiping my hands over the top of my shorts. "When I went to the restroom at the game, I met a woman in the hallway. She was sitting in the suite next to ours. We exchanged numbers, and she texted me as soon as the game was over. I had a small window of opportunity." I took another drink of water, wishing it were scotch, which still hadn't been delivered. "That's where I was."

"And it lasted so long that you couldn't join us once you were done?" Ford asked. "Because it was after three in the morning when we returned to the hotel, and we were blowing your ass up with texts the whole time. That's quite a few hours. I'm sure you're a fucking superhero in the bedroom, but come on, man."

"Whose side are you on?" I shot back.

"The truth's side," he answered.

I shook my head. "I fell asleep. Stop making this into something it's not."

"In whose bed?" Macon asked. "Yours or hers?"

"Mine."

My attention was drawn to Jenner, whose hands were clapping, making a sound that captured all our focus. "That was quite the performance."

My eyes narrowed. "What do you mean?"

"I sat next to you at the game," Jenner said. "You didn't leave the suite once to use the bathroom. But if that's the story you want to go with, I'll give an A for creativity. As for truth, you failed. Hard."

The table turned silent.

And suddenly, out of nowhere, the waitress appeared, setting two glasses of scotch in front of me.

I picked one up and downed every drop.

As soon as I set the tumbler back on the table, Jenner said, "Fellas, I think we have our answer."

Chapter Twelve

LILY

Why?

That was what I'd been asking myself since the Daltons and Spades had boarded the plane over three hours ago. I wanted nothing more than to dissolve into the expensive carpet beneath my feet. It wasn't that the guys were giving me looks as though they knew I'd spent the night with Brady and the embarrassment was eating at me. There was none of that. It was having Brady so close for the entire leg of this trip.

All I could smell was his scent.

All I could feel was the touch of his hands.

All I could see was his stare.

And all of it…was way too much.

There was a little comfort in the fact that once he'd left my room, he never came back. He didn't surprise me the next evening with a knock at my door, and I never ran into him at the hotel. Based on what he'd said to me—that he'd gotten my message when I delivered his clothes to the bed—I hadn't expected to see him until now.

That didn't mean, deep down, I wasn't secretly disappointed.

That I wasn't asking myself why things couldn't be different.

Why I couldn't be different.

Why my life couldn't have taken a different direction.

Maybe then, every time I passed Brady in the aisle, our eyes locking, I wouldn't immediately look away. I wouldn't worry that if he showed up again, that could result in a second knock on my door.

A knock that would put us both in jeopardy.

As I gazed at him from the back of the plane, sitting inside the galley, where I could see hints of his profile, all I could think about was the two evenings we'd spent together. How after this plane landed, I would never get to experience Brady Spade ever again.

That thought, that dread, sent waves of emotion through my throat. I had to push it away as the phone against the wall began to ring.

I grabbed the receiver and said, "Hi, pilot. What can I do for you?"

"We're approximately twenty-five minutes from the airport. Please get everything prepared for landing."

"Right away," I told him and hung up.

I sucked in as much air as I could hold, and I made a final walk down the aisle, asking each of the guys if they needed anything. I got a few requests for water, one for a refill of scotch. When I reached Brady's seat, he took his time looking up at me.

But once those beautiful, piercing light-blue eyes connected with mine, a wave of tingles passed through me.

That was power.

That was emotion.

Because any of these men could give me the same look and nothing would happen inside my body.

Yet Brady only gave me a glance, and all the air I'd been holding was gone.

I was empty.

And there was no chance of me breathing anytime soon.

"What do you think I want?" His voice was low so only I could hear. Gritty. Controlling to the point where there was no possibility I could look away.

"Scotch?"

"Your phone number."

My phone number?

But I wasn't sure if my phone was safe. Part of me thought it was being tracked, that the calls were listened to, the texts were read. I'd been stupid enough to have a conversation with Aubrey about Brady the other night and immediately regretted it once we hung up, especially since we'd been interrupted by the banging on my door.

Talks like that needed to happen in person.

It didn't even matter if I got a new phone; I'd done that multiple times already, and the new number was always found. So, it definitely wasn't safe to give Brady those digits.

Besides, what would be the point?

After this flight, I only had four more weeks until I vanished from this job.

From LA.

From Brady's stomping grounds, where there was a chance our paths could cross again.

"Brady—"

"I'll get it from you when we land," he said, and his focus then returned to his laptop as though he was done with our conversation.

What the hell am I going to do?

I rushed toward the galley, gathering the water and refills, and delivered them to the appropriate guys. When I went to the back, I completed all the necessary tasks for the pilot. After I strapped myself into my seat, I took my phone out of my apron.

What do I do?

What do I do?

What do I—

An idea came to me. But first, I needed to confirm things with Aubrey, so I pulled up the last text I'd sent her and began to type.

Me: *So, question. I'm planning things out in my head, and I want to just confirm that you're definitely coming back to work in a month? And you won't be extending your maternity leave?*

Aubrey: *Girl, are you kidding? I'm starving for some adult interaction. I'd do anything to have a conversation with someone who actually talked back rather than just spit up all over me. Yes, I'm coming back. I'm counting down the days.*

Me: *Ha! That's what I thought—the return, I mean.*

Aubrey: *Are you back from LA?*

Me: *Landing soon.*

Aubrey: *Do you want to come over tonight for wine? We can gossip about all things Daltons and Spades. ;)*

Even though I trusted Aubrey—knowing whatever I told her, she would never speak about it to anyone—I didn't know if I would open up about Brady. There was really nothing to say about him. The two of us could never lead to anything. So, what would be the point in discussing a past that would only reinforce all the *why*?

Still, the only thing I had to return to in LA was a hotel room. On the eighth floor. With an AC that kept the space so cold, despite what temperature I set it to, that all I did was shiver all night. Conversation and company were things I welcomed when it was dark, late, and extremely lonely in there.

Me: *I'll see you at 7.*

Aubrey: *Stocking up on red and white—don't bring a thing. I CANNOT wait.*

Me: *Same!*

I placed my phone back in my apron and watched Brady as he spoke to Dominick, the two in their own world. A conversation that continued as the plane landed.

I unstrapped my belt and made my way down the aisle, feeling Brady's eyes on my back as I passed his seat. I checked in with the pilots, making sure everything was all right up front, and waited until it was time to open the cabin door. Airport personnel was waiting for us on the tarmac, placing the steps on the ground, and I rushed down them to position the red carpet. Two SUVs were parked nearby, the gentlemen's transportation, and the drivers were standing outside the doors to the backseat.

Just a few more minutes, and this would be over.

When I entered the plane, the passengers were getting up from their seats, gathering their personal items, and I thanked each one before they made their way down the steps. I wasn't surprised that Brady was the last in line. I'd expected him to lag. But what that did was give me a chance to get my thoughts straight, to prepare the words I needed to say.

So, when he approached, I was ready.

Except I wasn't.

Because as we stood face-to-face, we were alone on the plane—the pilots at the bottom of the stairs, waiting for Brady to disembark—and the privacy made the moment even more intimate.

All I could smell was him.

All I could see was him.

All I could feel...was him.

And what that was doing to my insides was making every part of me tremble.

How could a man I barely knew make me feel this way?

How could he have this much power?

As if on cue, there was a vibration in my apron, notifying me a message had come through my phone.

I didn't have to look.

I knew who it was from.

And every feeling, every desire I had for the man in front of me, was dissolved, as though acid had been poured over it.

"I want to see you again."

I swallowed the bitterness down my throat as the *whys* began to fill my head.

These were different from the ones from earlier.

Why does he want more from me?

Why does he think I can give him that?

His hand landed on my waist, his thumb flicking just above my belt, over my polo, so through the thin material, I could feel the heat from his skin.

It didn't feel like a touch.

It felt like an explosion.

One that would leave a permanent mark.

"Give me your number, Lily, so I can make that happen."

I hated myself for the thoughts in my head.

For the war.

For the whys.

I didn't trust my voice or what could possibly come out of my throat, so I rattled off the digits, watching him plug the number into his phone, saying not a word more, and when he read it back to me, I smiled.

A grin that hurt.

One that felt so ungenuine.

"I'll be in touch." His fingers squeezed me, and then he was gone.

Chapter Thirteen

BRADY

My phone was haunting me. The sight of the screen was like a goddamn flashing neon sign that reminded me of two things.

The first, that I'd sent Lily a text two days ago, and she still hadn't responded. For someone who flew for a living, with loads of downtime while she sat in the back of the plane and days off in a hotel room, I couldn't accept a busy excuse.

The second, that I was even bothered that she hadn't replied.

It had been a mistake to ask for her number.

To text her.

To tell her in the message that I wanted to see her, something I'd also mentioned to her on the jet. Had I just let things roll out the way I normally did, I wouldn't be haunted by a fucking thing.

Yet I was sitting at my desk with piles of paperwork surrounding me that needed my attention and an inbox with hundreds of unread messages, and instead of tackling any of it, I was staring at my phone, wishing for it to light up with a text from her.

I needed to stop.

I needed to set my head straight.

I tossed my phone into the top drawer, slid it shut with a slam, and put my hands on the keyboard, waking up my monitor. There was no way I could process anything of importance at the moment, so I focused on my email. I could knock out some responses, delete the unimportant shit.

I wasn't even through my first reply when I heard, "You got a second?"

Couldn't I just have a minute alone?

My jaw clenched, and I took an angry inhale as I glanced up.

Fucking Jenner.

"What are you doing here?" I asked, my memory immediately bringing me back to Tampa. "If it's to give me more shit about ditching you guys after the hockey game, don't bother coming in."

He laughed from my doorway and took a seat in front of my desk. "I had to meet with Cooper about Banff, and since I have news on Edinburgh, I came to talk to you."

I leaned back in my chair and crossed my legs. "I'm listening."

"The sale is coming along nicely." He adjusted his tie. "However, the governing officials of Scotland would like to discuss how you're going to change the facade of the hotel, along with the sidewalk and front entrance."

"Everything has been outlined in the proposal we sent them."

He nodded. "Yes, well, they'd like more than just a piece of paper. They'd like to talk about it all in person."

My eyes briefly closed. "You're telling me I need to go to Edinburgh?"

"As soon as possible."

This was a perfect example of why there was an endless pulsing of frustration that lived in my chest.

"That's all you have for me?" I snapped.

He smiled and set his arms on the armrests. "Unless you want to talk about Lily."

How the hell did he know her name?

"Are you fucking kidding me?" I thundered.

"You were last off the plane. Then, there was the expression on your face when you departed. And every time I looked at you, you were staring at her. I'm an observant person, no doubt, but this one wasn't hard to put together." His arms dropped, and his hands went to the end of my desk. "You think I'm going to give you shit. You're wrong. I'm proud of you, my man."

"For what?"

"Brady...come on. We're not going to sit here and play this game. I know your armor is thicker than your brothers', but at some point, you're going to want to talk about her."

I was so fucking tempted to reach into my desk drawer and pull out my phone, showing him the one-sided message, but the torture needed to end, so I spit, "There's nothing to talk about."

His head shook back and forth. "You just won't quit..."

My fingers clenched, and my fist pounded the top of my desk.

Maybe he'd caught me at a weak moment.

Maybe I was just fucking tired.

Or maybe I was just vulnerable enough to admit the truth.

"It's not that," I told him.

He was quiet for a moment, his brows slowly rising. "What is it, then?"

"Until I hear back from her, there's nothing to talk about."

"Ah. Got it." A smile crept over his face. "But I've got to say, you making the effort with her, it's good to see."

"I'm already regretting it."

His head dropped, like I'd worn him thin. "Take it from a man who wasn't looking to settle down either. When she comes into your life, whatever was holding you back, whether that be some outside circumstance or waiting for the right timing or a mental block, it all dissolves." He finally glanced up. Raw honesty stared back at me.

"And she's all that will matter."

Is that what's happening?

Am I already here?

Lily was all I'd thought about since I'd left her room in Tampa. But if I was being real, the thoughts had started long before then.

They'd started the night in Edinburgh.

Fuck.

My teeth ground together before I said, "I didn't know you were a lawyer and a shrink."

He chuckled. "You're something else." He got up from his chair and walked to the door. "Can I give you a piece of advice even if you don't want to hear it?"

"You're going to tell me anyway. I'm not sure why you're asking for permission."

He smiled. "You want her, you go after her. Don't let something like a reply stop you."

As his advice passed through me, I nodded, and I watched him walk into the hallway and disappear.

But even though he was gone, I couldn't get his words out of my head. They ate at me as my hands returned to the keyboard, attempting to pick up where I'd left off.

Shit, I couldn't.

Because Lily was all I could think about.

I just wanted a few more seconds to caress her body and place another kiss on her lips and one more graze across her soft, tropical-smelling skin.

I reached into my desk drawer and took out my phone, pulling up her Contact. Texting wasn't getting me anywhere, so I hit Call, taking the deepest damn breath as I held the phone to my ear.

After the second ring, I heard, "Hello?"

The voice was startling.

Because it was a man who answered.

"Is Lily there?"

"You have the wrong number."

My neck jutted back. "What do you mean, I have the wrong number? That's not possible—"

"Buddy, this is my cell phone, and my name isn't Lily. I don't even know who that is." He laughed and hung up.

There had to be a mistake.

Could phone lines get crossed? Was that even a thing?

Had she left her phone out and one of the Daltons disguised their voice just to piss me off?

I pressed the Call button again.

"You're not going to keep calling, are you?" the guy asked as he answered. "I told you, there is no Lily here, and this isn't her number. Please don't keep calling me." He hung up.

A bolt of anger shot through my chest, my hands shaking as I held my cell, staring at the home screen.

It couldn't be the wrong number. I'd typed it in correctly. I'd even repeated it to Lily to confirm.

That meant she'd either given me the wrong number or, somehow, this was one big mistake.

Regardless, I didn't fucking like it.

I picked up my office line, connecting to our assistant, and said, "Kathleen, I need you to book the jet for a trip to Edinburgh, leaving as soon as possible."

"Oh boy."

My eyes squinted shut, my jaw tensing. "What?"

"How quickly does as soon as possible mean?"

"Yesterday."

"Then, that's going to be a problem. It's currently scheduled about four weeks out."

Four fucking weeks?

This was getting out of control. We needed another plane.

I slammed the phone into the receiver and squeezed my cell so tightly that I wouldn't be surprised if the screen shattered.

No jet.

No phone number.

Fuck that.

I pulled up my Contacts again, searching for the number I needed, and held the phone to my face.

"What can I do for you—"

"Dominick, I need to borrow your jet. I need it within the next two days. And I need the one Lily works on."

Chapter Fourteen

LILY

Three weeks. That was how much time I had left with the Daltons. So, I spent my downtime planning on what I was going to do after this contract ended. I enjoyed all the years I'd worked for commercial airlines; at that stage of my life, the schedule had been perfect.

But that was no longer the case.

I needed to be in the air as much as possible, and the commercial airlines placed restrictions on how often you could work and fly.

At least if I continued in the private sector, working for businesses or families, my off time wouldn't necessarily be at my home base. It could be on overnight trips, like the one I'd done in Tampa and the many others I'd completed prior.

But no matter what, regardless of who I worked for or where I flew to, I'd be chained to a hotel room. At least they would be different rooms, in different parts of the world, looking at different sights through the window.

I didn't know why, but that sounded better than any alternative.

The best part about my present job was that the family was constantly flying. There were times when we landed in LA and immediately flew out less than an hour later.

That was the situation for today.

We had just returned from a trip to Boston, where Camden Dalton and Declan Shaw were representing Hooked, the famous hook-up app. It had been impossible not to overhear them discussing the case during both flights, but my NDA prevented me from ever breathing a word about it. We were only going to be parked in LA for about thirty minutes, just long enough for the pilots to swap out, fuel up, for me to clean down the interior of the plane, restock the food and drinks, and our new passengers would be on board.

Out of all places, we were headed to Edinburgh.

Not that the location surprised me since I'd already flown internationally multiple times with the family.

It was just a place that triggered many memories.

The thoughts in my head were so loud. The images so vivid—of when I'd knocked on his door, and when he'd placed me against the wall, and the number of times he'd made me come.

The magic in his fingers, his tongue, his dick.

My entire body was tingling by the time I finished wiping down the seats, my last task before I could focus on the paperwork that needed to be processed prior to taking off. I placed the microfiber towels into the laundry bin and lifted the pile of papers into my hand. I reviewed the details that were outlined and signed off, carrying the stack to the cockpit to give to the pilots for their signatures.

As I was passing the boarding door, an SUV was pulling up on the tarmac, which I knew had the passengers inside. The stairs had already been lowered; the red carpet was positioned at the bottom. For them, everything outside was ready to go.

I quickly set the papers in between the pilots so they could give the information a thorough read and said, "Looks like our passengers have arrived."

One of the pilots turned around to look at me. "Would you mind welcoming them at the bottom of the stairs? We still have some preflight checks we need to finish."

"I'm happy to," I replied.

From the doorway, I gave the interior a quick scan, making sure everything was in place, that I hadn't forgotten a bottle of cleaner on one of the seats or left a dirty glass on a table. Satisfied with what I saw, I ran my fingers through the sides of my hair and swiped around my lips and the corners of my eyes since I didn't have time to check my appearance in the restroom, and I descended the stairs.

The SUV came to a stop only feet from the carpet. The driver got out first, moving to the backseat to open the door. The way the vehicle was positioned, I wasn't able to see inside, especially with its dark-tinted windows. But I was curious as to who would be flying with us today.

I hadn't worked for the Daltons nearly as long as Aubrey, but considering how much time I spent with them, I knew them well enough to have favorites and preferences due to who was nicer and less demanding. For a location as far as Edinburgh, I hoped the group who was coming was on the less-demanding end.

As I waited, my fingers intertwined, my back straightened, my feet rocked over the short heels.

Beneath the door, a shoe hit the ground. Shiny black. A second one followed before a head towered over the top of the door, eyes immediately connecting with mine.

Eyes that were light blue.

A head that was covered in black hair.

A face with tanned skin.

Lips that I knew fondly.

My stomach flipped.

My chest tightened like it was a rubber balloon on the verge of exceeding its air capacity.

Brady.

Out of all people…

Brady?

What was he doing here?

Why was he on this flight?

How was I going to survive this trip when I'd barely made it through Tampa?

Oh God.

While the driver brought his luggage toward the back of the plane, Brady walked toward the steps.

His eyes didn't leave mine. They stayed fixed, sucking every bit of breath out of my body.

But his presence didn't just mess with my breathing.

Or my stomach.

Or my chest.

It tugged at my emotions in a way where they were skyrocketing out of control.

He halted at the bottom of the stairs, silence building between us.

Something told me I needed to say something, that I needed to be the first to break the quietness because he was too stubborn to do it.

My lips slowly parted, and, "Hi," came out in a voice so soft that I didn't even feel it leave my mouth.

He was so close that the word could have hit his face. If he swung his arm in the right direction, it would have grazed mine.

But there was no movement from him, not even his eyes—they just stared at me.

He didn't even blink.

And as time passed, his gaze grew, reaching beneath the surface of my eyes and skin and hitting the deepest, farthest part of me.

Once it penetrated, it stirred.

It stormed.

What felt like hours went by, and then, finally, he said, "Did you intentionally give me the wrong number, or is there a reason an asshole answered my call and hung up on me? Twice."

Shit.

He was calling me out.

A situation I hadn't anticipated happening because I didn't think I'd ever see him again.

I'd hoped that once he called the number I'd randomly made up, he would realize I didn't want to be found, and by the time he rode the Daltons' plane again, I'd be long gone.

I should have known that Brady didn't give up that easily.

It actually seemed as though he didn't give up at all.

I mashed my lips together, searching for a reason.

An excuse.

Something that would alleviate this situation.

But what could I say?

Another lie?

The truth? A truth I couldn't give him.

"I—"

"You don't have to answer me now." His stare intensified, which I hadn't thought was even possible. "We have a very long journey ahead of us. Hours that we'll be spending together. And since I'm your only passenger for this trip, you'll have plenty of time to explain yourself." He began to walk up the steps. "I'll see you inside, Lily."

Chapter Fifteen

BRADY

L ily left the galley with a tumbler in her hand and a look on her face that was slightly timid and a whole lot of shy. I tried to give her privacy and not watch her walk the entire way over to me, but with my head down, I could still see her, even if it was only in my mind.

I could feel her.

I could smell her.

She set my second scotch on the table beside me, and as she went to take her hand back, I captured it.

Partly for me. I needed to touch her, to get a sense of her skin and its temperature, and to remind myself why I'd arranged to take Dominick's plane to Scotland just to have a conversation with her.

Had I fucking lost it?

I searched for that answer as I held her.

Her flesh was warm, on the verge of hot, despite the plane being cold.

I waited to feel a tug, a clench, a stiffening.

None of that happened, nor did she pull away from me.

It almost felt as if her fingers collapsed, like she was giving me the weight of her hand.

She wanted to stay in my grasp.

No, I hadn't fucking lost it.

The phone number was one thing, but the way she responded to my presence was something entirely different.

I released her and said, "Why don't you pour yourself a drink?"

The monitor that hung on the wall showed a digital map of the flight's progress. We were somewhere over Arizona. I'd given her plenty of time to do the shit she needed to around the plane, for her to settle her thoughts since she'd looked like a deer in fucking headlights when I got out of the car. Maybe now, assuming she was calmer, we could really talk.

"I can't." She paused. "I'm working."

I glanced around the cabin. "Who's going to tell on you?"

Her fingers cinched her waist. "What would happen if there was an emergency landing? I can't be half in the bag while being responsible for—"

"One scotch isn't going to knock you on your ass, Lily."

What I hoped it would do was take the edge off.

There was a hell of a lot that I didn't know about her, but what I did know was that she was unlike most women. And what I couldn't figure out was her mysterious side, why a glance at her phone caused her entire mood to change.

Why she would become a completely different person.

I was going to get to the bottom of it.

I placed my scotch on her palm. "Drink this. I'll go get myself another one."

"No, I'm supposed to serve you—"

"Don't move."

I went into the galley and found a tumbler in the cabinet, along with the bottle of scotch, and filled the glass with several fingers' worth. When I returned to the cabin, she was sitting on the couch across from my seat, the glass still in her hand.

I nodded toward it. "Take a sip."

"For the record, I'm not caving because you told me to or because of peer pressure." She surrounded the rim with her lips and swallowed. "I'm drinking this because I need it." She took another gulp. "But you never saw this happen—got it? The trouble I would get in"—she shook her head—"would be endless."

She set the glass on her lap and looked at me. Multiple seconds seemed to pass before she spoke again. "I know you want an answer about the phone number."

"What I don't want is bullshit."

She nodded. "I get that." She crossed her legs, her body almost caving inward into the seat. "I hate that I have to tell you this. It honestly makes me feel sick to my stomach." She took another drink. "But, yes, I gave you the wrong number."

The anger that was always there came to a rippling boil.

I'd fucking tracked this woman down, only to find out she didn't want me to.

That didn't stop me from barking, "Explain."

"Explain to you that I'm a mess?" She sighed. "That my life is—"

"Complicated. I know." I crossed my arms over my chest. "Tell me something I don't know."

Her head shook, like she was in a field and didn't know what direction to take to go home. "I was hoping I could disappear before this conversation ever took place. I don't know what to say now that you know the truth."

"Let me get this straight." I was trying to keep my voice down, but the tone was as sharp as a blade. "You never wanted to see me again?"

"It's not that I didn't want to see you again. It's that I shouldn't. The difference between those two statements is huge."

Not a goddamn thing made sense to me, and that wasn't the

scotch's fault.

"What am I supposed to do with that, Lily?"

"You can't do anything." She seemed to sink even lower into her seat. "That's why I wanted to run. So we wouldn't have to face each other and I'd never have to look you in the eye and tell you that regardless of how I feel and what I truly want"—she paused to take a breath and then another—"you and I can never happen."

Each word was like a fucking slap against my face.

I was here, making more of an effort than I ever had in my entire life.

And this—this goddamn rejection—was what it had earned me.

No.

Fuck that.

I went to reach for the scotch, and my hand balled instead. "You gave me a fake number in hopes that"—my clenched hand circled the air—"this conversation, this meetup, would never happen."

She'd already spoken that answer.

But I needed to hear it again.

I needed it to sink so far into my head that it would burn the memories of her.

"Yes."

It was that easy for her, to just disappear, the two times we'd been together completely meaningless.

Yet this woman had lived in my mind since the first time I had seen her.

She'd dominated my thoughts.

And in return, she didn't want me.

So, I was going to make her feel as little and as shitty as I did.

"You know something, Lily? You read this situation all wrong." I finally lifted my drink and shot back at least a finger's worth. "You thought I asked for your number because I wanted to date you. That's not it at all. I don't date. I asked for it because I just wanted to fuck you again."

She pushed herself to the end of the seat. "Brady—"

"There's nothing left for us to discuss."

She held up her hand. "I didn't—"

"You can go back to the galley now." I nodded toward that section of the plane. "And I don't need you to check on me for the rest of the flight."

Chapter Sixteen

LILY

It was easier to make Brady hate me than to tell him he shouldn't want anything to do with me. Easier to feel the anger radiate from his body than feel the disappointment if I'd told him I couldn't cave on my decision.

What I'd said to him was the truth.

But I hadn't told him why.

Why I was running. Why I couldn't want him.

Why I was this emotionally unavailable, complicated disaster.

Since he'd dismissed me to the back of the plane, acting as though he was tired of even looking in my direction, it didn't even matter at this point.

What he didn't know was that I was sensitive. That the conversation we'd had, even though it was short and semi-cryptic because I hadn't explained myself, hurt. It was painful to admit what I'd done.

That even though I wanted to wake up in his bed tomorrow, that I wanted to go out on dates with him, that I wanted to explore what was happening between us, I couldn't.

And I didn't even have a chance to apologize.

Nor did I attempt to through the remainder of the flight or when we disembarked or got into the same vehicle to ride to the hotel.

The silence was so thick that I couldn't fill my lungs until I was alone in my room, my back pressed against the locked door, the view through the large window taunting me.

The *whys.*

They weren't just thrumming their regular beat; they were throbbing like techno through my entire body.

Of course, being back in Edinburgh only made everything feel worse. So did knowing he was staying somewhere in this hotel and that we had a return flight together tomorrow afternoon, where we'd be in close quarters for far too many hours.

But here, in Scotland, we had only one full day, and all of it was going to be spent alone in my room.

Except for the few minutes when I rushed down to the lobby to pick up the food I'd ordered. On my way back to the elevator, as I was passing the bar that was just to the side of the lobby, I couldn't help but notice Brady. He was sitting in the center, both arms resting on the bar top, with a small glass of what I assumed to be scotch in front of him.

Even if I wasn't so adamant on scanning every location I entered, I would have felt him anyway. I would have smelled him in the air. I would have somehow sensed his presence.

That was the kind of connection I had to him.

I stood midway between the bar and elevators and found myself frozen in this spot.

My feet wanted to walk to him, my hands wanted to place the food before him, my lips wanted to ask him if he wanted to share this meal.

But I couldn't.

I needed to keep my distance, return to my room, and pretend that I'd never seen him.

So, I urged myself toward the elevators, and just as I was about to take my first step, his eyes connected with mine, immediately halting my plan and the chance of walking away unseen.

To make matters even worse, I couldn't move. His stare was making my limbs lock in place, causing me to stay right here, vulnerable in more ways than one, while showing him how much his presence affected me.

I could only imagine what that looked like on my face when his light-blue eyes met my deep-blue ones.

A wave fluttered through my entire body. As it reached my chest, it took my breath away, like the plane and car ride, but this was worse. It was tighter. And as the seconds passed, my breath didn't return.

Only when Brady nodded at the spot next to him did I find myself walking, and it wasn't toward an escape—the elevators, a stairwell, even the lobby door. I was headed directly for him.

"Brady," I said as I approached, my brain a mess of thoughts, but there was something I absolutely needed to tell him. "I want to apologize—"

"I need to say something to you."

My heart was beating so fast that I placed my hand on top of it. "Okay," I whispered, cuddling the to-go food against me like it was a blanket.

He pointed at the chair next to his. "Sit."

I took a few seconds to inventory the room, looking at each of the faces that surrounded the bar, and when I was positive I didn't recognize any, I took a seat.

"I want to tell you something about myself." He held up his glass. "If I hadn't had four of these and a day of meetings that sucked the fucking life out of me, I don't know that I would be saying any of this to you."

His shirt was unbuttoned, showing a small hint of the dusting of hair on his chest. The gel he'd added to his locks had worn thin, allowing the strands to fall naturally. He looked like a man who had spent almost half of a day flying and most of the other half in meetings.

And he looked devastatingly sexy.

What I loved most about his appearance and the sound of his voice was that the edge was gone. This was the Brady I'd woken up to in Tampa. The one whose arms had wrapped around me in the middle of the night, as though lying next to me wasn't close enough. The one who had gazed at me in the morning like I was more beautiful in my half-asleep state than the sun coming in through the blinds.

The man I'd seen hours ago on the plane was his thick, crispy outer edge.

The man sitting next to me was the warm, gooey middle.

"I can't wait to hear it," I admitted.

His exhale came fast, through his nose, and when it hit my face, I smelled the scotch on his breath. A scent that, when mixed with his cologne, was more delicious than any of the food I was holding.

"I don't say I'm sorry. Not ever. I don't even know what that fucking word means." He turned in the chair, his body fully facing me. "But what I said to you on the plane was wrong. It was a lie. I didn't want your number just so I could fuck you." When he paused, I saw the passion flicker across his stare. "I do want to fuck you—I'm not saying that. What I'm saying is that there was more behind that statement, and I aimed those words at you because I was pissed. I shouldn't have pulled out a verbal weapon when all you were doing was being honest with me. You didn't deserve it, and for that, I'm sorry."

My fingers were on his arm. I couldn't recall when I'd put them there, but I was now squeezing him. It took everything in me to leave them there even though every warning sign was telling me to pull them back. "I owe you an apology too. I wanted to give you one on the plane. I just didn't have the chance."

"Because I took that chance away from you."

I nodded. "You were only focusing on half of what I'd said." I moved to the end of the chair as though the inch would allow me to lower my voice even more. "I wasn't telling you I don't want you. I was telling you I can't have you."

The corner of his lips lifted. "I don't like that response either."

"But it's better." I offered a small smile.

"Not really."

My fingers finally released him, and I reached for his scotch and took a sip. The burn in the back of my throat was appreciated. So much so that I took another drink.

"God, that's fucking hot."

I paused midair, the cup halfway between my mouth and the bar. "What I said is hot?"

"No, that you just took a drink from my glass."

"I hope you don't mind. I didn't even think to ask—"

"Lily, you can put your mouth on anything of mine."

My face flushed as I set the tumbler back on the bar top.

"I'm going to continue to be honest with you," he added, "and say this situation isn't something I've ever navigated before."

He moved a piece of hair off the side of my face. Just that small, intimate gesture, the ends of his fingers grazing my skin, was enough to ignite these tiny fires inside me. And the base of those fires was building a heat between my legs.

"I've never asked for a woman's number before."

"You haven't?"

He chuckled, not because he seemed to find it funny, but to emphasize his point. "I've never even been close to asking...until you."

"Seriously?" I held up my hand. "I'm sorry. I just find that really surprising, given how many women I'm guessing you've been with."

"My entire life, I've only ever wanted one thing from them. Once I get it, I'm out. It's a routine, you could say. I don't know what the fuck you did to me—maybe you played things just right, maybe it's that you don't want anything from me, maybe it's knowing that I can't have you—but I can't stop thinking about you." He pierced his bottom lip with his teeth, releasing it to say, "You not wanting us to hook up again or to go out on a date or for me to even have your number, well, given my past, I'd say that's just fucking ironic."

That admission made my eyes burn. It made my chest ache.

For reasons I couldn't explain.

For reasons he would never understand.

Why?

"Why is that, Lily?"

The question hit hard, but it wasn't unexpected.

He deserved an answer.

Maybe not the whole story, but certainly more than I was complicated, although that description was accurate. I couldn't break it all down—there was too much—and given that knowledge was power, I refused to let Brady hold any when it came to this situation.

This was my mess. No one else's.

But I could at least offer some type of explanation that would show him this had nothing to do with my feelings for him. Because those existed even if I couldn't do anything about them.

I unhooked my fingers, balancing them on my knees, and I swiveled the chair until my body was aimed at him.

I didn't know how I was going to get through this.

But I had to try.

Even if it was a topic I never discussed. Not with Aubrey. Not with anyone.

"It's been a year since I dated, and to tell you the truth, it's been that long since I even considered dating anyone. The thought of being with a man and getting involved again"—my head shook; my body recoiled—"that isn't something I've wanted. In fact, I've avoided men completely so I wouldn't send the wrong message or create an opportunity like the one that occurred between us."

My hand left my knee, and I shocked myself when it landed on his thigh.

"I've literally been hiding my heart and covering my eyes so something like this couldn't transpire. And then you came along, and to put it bluntly, you charmed the pants off me, and everything I'd been attempting to avert all went to hell."

My fingers began to tingle, and I pulled them back, squeezing them into a fist.

"Here's the thing, Brady. You're the first man to ever make me feel anything. And in the year since I dated, you're the first man to make me want to give my body to someone. You broke through a barrier that I never intended to lower."

How could I describe this? How could I make him comprehend the gravity of what I was saying without opening a wound and exposing him to the current I'd been drowning in?

"That probably sounds a little off the wall, doesn't it? Here's a woman who's been uninterested in men for an unreasonable amount of time, and I'm still in a place where I can't handle anything and—"

"You're making sense." His stare was softening. "Keep going."

I looked toward the lobby, viewing the faces that had recently walked in, the ones heading for the elevators, the new additions to the bar.

Even though the anxiousness was building in my stomach, I continued, "When I look at you, I see someone—*ah*!" My hand went to my shoulder as the pain shot through my muscle, my chest tightening into a ball as the wind was practically knocked out of me.

What just happened?

Brady immediately stood and reached behind me. "Are you fucking kidding me? Don't you see her sitting here?" he snapped to whoever he was gripping. "Are you okay?" he asked me.

I nodded.

"Lily, are you sure?"

"Yes," I replied.

My brain slowly started to piece together the last few seconds—the ache, the movement, Brady's reaction—and I figured out that someone had slid in between my chair and the one behind mine. There wasn't enough room, which had earned me an arm—or a sharp, pointed elbow—to the shoulder to give them more space.

But before I could take a breath, I peeked behind me to see who the culprit was. When I saw it was a man I didn't recognize, I gasped in some air.

"Dude," the guy huffed, "I've been waiting forever for a drink and—"

"I don't care how long you've been waiting. That doesn't make it all right to squeeze into a spot where there's no room and hurt someone in the process," Brady barked at him. "Apologize to the lady."

"I'm sorry."

"You're not even looking at her." Brady's eyes were rabid. "Say it to her face."

The space in the back of me was suddenly vacant, the body that had been wedged in there was gone, and he came to my front. Brady's hand was still clamped on the man's arm, his expression telling me he was being forced to do something he didn't want.

"I'm sorry," he groaned.

I was still rubbing my shoulder. "It's okay."

"It's not okay," Brady said. "But get the hell out of here."

The guy walked away, but Brady remained standing, his eyes glued on the man until he must have been pleased with his distance, and that was when he finally sat.

He massaged the back of my hand. "Are you sure you're all right?"

That was a loaded question.

Because physically, yes, I was fine.

But mentally, I was processing the intricate layers of Brady Spade.

A man who hardly knew anything about me.

A man who wanted more despite the little I'd given him.

A man who had defended my honor as though we'd been dating for years.

Never, in the twenty-eight years of my life, had anyone ever stood up for me the way he just had.

But it went even deeper.

What this situation just proved was that, as long as he could help it, he wouldn't let anything happen to me.

He was protection.

Security.

A guardianship that took away every one of my worries.

That was something I'd always wanted and never had.

"Thank you," I whispered.

"For what? I didn't do anything."

You did everything.

Instead of explaining, I said, "I thought you were going to strangle him."

His hand slowly slid up to my cheek. "I was going to do far worse than that."

Why was that response so incredibly perfect?

Why did it satisfy so many spots in my body, places that had been starving to hear words like those?

My eyes closed, and I nuzzled into his hand, a warmth swishing through me.

One that brought a calmness.

Reassurance.

But it only lasted a few seconds before the *whys* kicked in.

What am I doing?

"Brady..." My eyes opened, and I clasped his wrist, carefully pulling his hand off my face.

"It's been a year."

It took a moment, but I understood what he was saying. That twelve months should be an adequate amount of time to heal or move on from…whatever was stopping me.

He was right.

Except my situation was anything but normal.

"I know that seems like an eternity. And it is." I took in his eyes. His lips. The way it felt when they were on me. "But things aren't settled at all. They're—"

There was a vibration in my back pocket.

A notification, a sensation that made my spine straighten, like a string was attached to my head and someone was pulling it upward. My butt wavered over the seat of the chair, my balance still off, even after I stilled.

Like clockwork, my throat narrowed, every hair on my body rose, my heart pounded as though I wasn't just running, but screaming at the same time.

I hated this.

Oh God, I despised this.

Even more so when I had to say, "I have to go."

"Why? Because that motherfucker knocked into you? Are you hurting—"

"No."

His hand was on my waist as I stood. "Tell me why, Lily. Tell me what just changed that's making you leave me."

I shook my head, a war happening within those walls that couldn't be defined in a few sentences. "I can't."

"I'll go with you—"

"No." I squinted, the emotion burning my eyelids.

I wished I didn't have to give him that answer. I wished I weren't on my feet right now. I wished there wasn't something in my life that was causing this fear.

"I'll see you on the plane tomorrow," I said as loudly as I could even though it was so soft I wasn't sure he'd heard me, and I rushed toward the elevators.

Chapter Seventeen

BRADY

What the fuck just happened?

That was the question filling my head as I watched Lily run for the elevators, like a goddamn intruder was chasing her.

It couldn't have been something I'd said—I'd said nothing inappropriate.

Could it have been the way I was touching her?

But she had leaned into my hand, her eyes closed, a contentment coming through her expression, as if she were on the verge of falling asleep.

And then, out of nowhere, everything changed.

It happened as quickly as the flip of a switch. Even the way she looked at me was different.

The more time I spent with her, the more questions I had, and the more confusing things got. She had just started to open up, I was finally getting some truth out of her, and once that asshole had knocked into her, nothing was the same after.

Fuck.

As I reached for my scotch, needing a full glass, which I knew

I didn't have, I saw her bag resting right next to my tumbler. There were several containers of food inside. When she'd darted away, she'd forgotten it.

I couldn't toss it. She was probably starving and too stubborn to come back and get it.

Damn it.

I waved the bartender over. "I need my bill."

"Sure thing." He tapped the computer screen in front of him several times and handed me a paper slip.

I quickly filled out each line and dropped the pen, carrying the bag to the front desk, waiting until it was my turn.

"I need the room number for Lily—" My voice cut off as I was speaking to the clerk when I realized I didn't know Lily's last name.

I still hadn't asked her for it.

What the hell was wrong with me?

Why wasn't that one of the first inquiries I'd made during our flight today? I needed to think of a way around this. How could I get the room number for a woman whose full name I didn't know?

"The corporate account of Cole and Spade Hotels reserved four rooms for tonight," I said. "Mine, two others under male names, and the fourth is under Lily. I need the number to her room."

"I'm sorry, sir." She shook her head. "That's information I can't disclose to you."

"But my company is the one who reserved the rooms. Why can't I have access to room numbers that *I'm* paying for?"

I knew the answer. Because any employee at Cole and Spade Hotels would say the identical thing the lady was voicing to me now.

I just didn't want to hear it.

I took out my wallet, removed the thousand pounds I had inside, and slapped the money on the counter. "How about you reconsider?"

She glanced at the money, her stare slowly rising to me.

When she didn't move or say a word, I continued, "Mr.

MacGregor—your boss, the owner of this hotel—is selling the hotel to me in about two months. Once the sale goes through, Cole and Spade Hotels is who you're going to be working for, and I'm going to be your boss." My patience was dying with each word. "I understand why you can't give me that info. I'm asking you to look past those rules." I glanced at my watch. "Don't make me call Mr. MacGregor and ask him to get it for me since you won't."

I watched the information pass across her face. It didn't take more than a few moments before her hands were on the keyboard.

"You're Brady Spade?"

"Yes," I all but fucking growled.

The keyboard clicked again several more times.

"I see the four rooms." She paused. "Yours, the two that are under the other gentlemen." She glanced at me. "And the one under Lily's name."

"And her room number is?"

She sighed. "Three twenty-nine."

My hand lifted from the stack. "Spend it on something good."

"No, no, I can't accept that—"

"But you will."

I left the money on the counter and headed for the elevators, pressing the Up button until one of the doors opened. I hit the Three as soon as I got inside, slamming the button to close the doors so no one else would join me. Once the door slid open on the third floor, I was out, hurrying down the hallway toward her room, knocking the second I arrived.

It felt like twenty fucking minutes had gone by until I finally heard, "Brady, what are y-you doing here?"

"I have your food." I held it up so she could see the bag through the peephole.

"Just l-leave it outside. I'll get it-t in a little while."

Was she crying? Was that why her tone sounded so off? Why was there a shakiness to her words?

"Open the door, Lily."

"I c-can't. I'll see you t-tomorrow—"

"Like hell you can't." I held the doorframe and leaned closer to the wood. "I'm not going anywhere until you show me your face. I'll stay here all night if I have to."

"My f-face?"

"I need to put my eyes on you. Once that happens, I'll leave. You have my word."

"Why are you d-doing this?"

"Because I fucking care about you. That's why." My forehead pressed against the door, my fingers gripping the unforgiving lip of the molding.

What was she thinking? What was she going through? Why was she keeping it from me?

"Whatever you're hiding from, whatever you're running from, whatever the case is, you don't have to feel that way with me."

There was silence.

"Let me in."

More quietness ticked from the other side of the door until, finally, there was the sound of the chain moving and the lock turning, the door gradually opening just enough that her face appeared through the narrow crack.

"Baby," was what left my mouth before I could stop it.

But, goddamn it, I had zero regrets as it did.

Especially because I was taking in her flushed cheeks and puffy, red-rimmed eyes. Whatever makeup was left was smudged, the tears bringing the black flecks down her face.

I opened the arm that wasn't holding her food. "Come here."

A hand went over her mouth, her eyes filling even faster. "If I do that, I'll lose it."

"I think it's too late for that."

I reached through the doorway, my fingers wrapping around her waist. I wanted nothing more than to take the fucking door off the hinges and pull her against me. But her emotion was preventing me from doing anything that aggressive. I certainly didn't want to upset her more than she already was.

"I want to come in, Lily." When she didn't move, I added, "I just want to hold you."

As her hand left her mouth, her lips quivered, and she backed away, releasing the door so it began to shut. As if that was my cue, I grabbed the edge, pushing it open enough that I could step in. I set the food on the floor and wrapped my arms around her. As I pulled her against me, she felt weightless, as though she were the size of a doll and I was a giant, and I squeezed my body around her.

My lips went to the top of her head, and I breathed her in. "I've got you."

The clothes she had been wearing earlier were off. The only thing covering her now was a towel, but even if she was cold, I didn't believe that was the reason she was shaking.

"I'm not going to let you go," I whispered into her skull.

She became more emotional, her body quivering even harder.

So, I held the side of her head, pressing her other cheek onto my chest, and placed my thumb under her eye. I didn't want her to have tears, I certainly didn't want them to fall, but if they did, I wanted to be there to catch them.

Fuck, what would cause her to cry this hard?

I didn't want to ask. I didn't want to break this moment and make her talk about something that was obviously tearing her up.

But, shit, I wanted her to open up to me. I wanted to do more than just hold her.

I wanted to take whatever was eating at her and make it stop.

She gripped my shirt, clenching it into her fist, and when I thought she was going to use the tension to push me away, she did the opposite.

She held on tighter.

"Baby..." I exhaled again, but this time, she could feel the word as it came out of me.

I didn't let go.

I didn't move my mouth from her head.

I didn't stop circling her back and rubbing her neck and whispering, "I've got you," so she could hear it repeated over and over and know I wasn't going anywhere.

I didn't know how long we stood there or how long my fucking heart was tortured by the sound and wetness of her crying, but eventually, she lifted her head and looked up at me.

"Brady..."

"Tell me how to fix this."

A statement I'd never spoken to another woman. But I hoped she would trust me enough to take me up on it.

While she wiped her cheeks and the sides of her mouth, it appeared like she was attempting to catch her breath. "I'm going to go to the bathroom and clean myself up a little bit. I need a minute...okay?"

"Okay."

She was gone, locked behind the door of the bathroom, the faucet loud enough that I could hear it from the other side.

Jesus Christ...what was all that crying about?

I leaned against the wall behind me and dragged both hands across the top of my hair, recounting the last few minutes.

I needed answers.

I needed to know what the fuck was hurting her because that pain was deep. An ache so buried within her that I could feel the trembles inside my own body.

Even though there was a door between us, it didn't feel right to stand here. She deserved more privacy than that. So, I grabbed the food off the floor and carried it into the room, setting the bag on the dresser. Right beside it was her phone, the screen lighting up and vibrating as a call was coming through.

A call from someone named David.

As it continued to ring, I was unable to look away, not even when the call went to voice mail.

Once that screen cleared, the notifications showed.

And what it revealed was that this wasn't her first missed call.

It was her fourth.

All from David.

Who the fuck was David? A sibling? A friend? Her ex?

Someone she was currently talking to?

But she'd told me there hadn't been anyone else in the last year.

There had only been me.

The bathroom door clicked, and I turned around just as she was walking into the bedroom. Her cheeks were still red, and so were her eyes, but the emotion had died off, and the makeup was gone, and so was the towel. She'd changed into a pair of cotton shorts and an oversize University of Georgia T-shirt—an outfit that was adorable.

But she looked exhausted, like she was carrying the weight of the world on her shoulders.

"Are you all right?"

She took a seat on the bed, near the pillows, resting her back against the headboard as she tucked her legs up to her chest and circled her arms around them. "I'm sorry you saw that."

I held the edge of the dresser with both hands. "Don't be."

"But I shouldn't have broken down like that. Not in front of you anyway."

"Why? Is there a rule that you can't cry in front of me?"

"Brady"—her head dropped as she placed her forehead against her knees—"when I told you I was a mess, I wasn't kidding. I hope you believe me now."

"I never doubted you. I just didn't care. Because being a mess doesn't scare me."

I wasn't sure why. If a woman had ever said that to me in the past, I would have run for the fucking hills.

But Lily wasn't just any woman.

The way her pain was eating at her, the need to have her was doing the same thing to me.

There was no one in this world I would beg for.

That I would get on my fucking knees for.

But her.

When she lifted her head, her long blonde hair was in her face, and she pushed it away. "You're telling me that nothing you just witnessed—not me leaving you at the bar without any explanation or crying in your arms—bothers you? That you're not even the slightest bit alarmed that I'm a living, hardly breathing disaster?"

"No." I nodded toward her. "Stop looking for reasons that don't exist in my head."

She folded in even smaller and rocked back and forth. "What I'm doing is showing you the real me."

"And I'm still here." I walked to the bed and sat on her side, crossing my arm over her bare feet. "And now, I'm even closer."

Her eyes began to plead with mine. "But you shouldn't be in here."

My brows lifted. "Is there a rule about that too?" I moved her hair behind her ear when it fell back into her face and kept my hand on her cheek once I was done.

"You have no idea what you're getting involved in." Her voice had an eerie quietness to it.

"Lily"—I chuckled—"I've told you I'm not afraid of anything. Or anyone. I don't need a warning. I can handle myself and whatever or whoever is thrown at me."

She looked at me as if she was trying to see through me. "Make me understand. Help me make sense of all this because none of it is clicking in my head. I can't reconcile any of it, Brady. I've given you nothing. I've—"

"You've given me your body."

"But that's it." Her legs dropped, stretching out over the bed, her arms wrapping around her stomach. "I've given you nothing else besides every verbal alert I can think of and words of caution to run as far as you can. Yet you still want me. Why?"

That was a good fucking question.

I set my arm on her thighs, giving her some of my body weight as I said the first and only thing that came to me. "The moment I no longer felt like myself, I knew it was because of you. When you walked down the aisle toward my pod, you changed me without even trying. Without even knowing. And when I woke in Edinburgh and you were no longer in my bed, it was reconfirmed. Something was off, and it was you—you were gone. And I had no way to find you." I pulled my arm back to place my hand on her shin. "My assistant can find anything online, so I put her in charge of locating you. She did everything she could, but according to her, you don't exist."

"She's right. I don't." Her voice was still so small.

Most women her age had some kind of online presence even if that account was private. A place to post pictures, a ticker for random thoughts.

I wondered why she'd chosen to be invisible.

I didn't want to get off track, so I said, "I thought you were gone, that I'd never see you again. A memory I'd hold on to even though the thought of that ate me the fuck up. And then I walked onto the Daltons' plane, and it felt like my world shifted back into place. Everything that had been off for the six previous months was right again."

She dragged a finger across my thick, scruffy cheek. "All that for someone whose last name you didn't even know."

"And still don't. I was reminded of that tonight when I paid a thousand pounds to get your room number."

Her eyes widened. "What? You didn't really do that...did you?"

"I'd pay a million more to ensure you didn't cry alone in this room tonight."

Her gaze deepened. "But the truth is, Brady, what happened tonight is only a tiny piece of something that's so much larger and so much heavier than what you witnessed. There's history and muddiness and drama and…" She glanced up at the ceiling, her chest rising and falling so fast. "Why would you step into a sinkhole if you knew you were going to die?"

She was doing everything she could to push me away.

But I didn't get up from the bed.

I rubbed her leg with one hand and pointed at my chest with the other. "You've seen this fucking body. Sand, mud, whatever it is, I'm stronger." My hand stilled on her thigh as I smirked. "Nothing is going to drown me, Lily."

Her fingers intertwined with mine. "The second my contract ends with the Daltons, I'm going to get another job, and there's a very good chance it won't be in LA."

"I'll worry about that when it happens."

Because it wasn't going to happen.

Lily wasn't going anywhere.

"What else do you have for me?" I gave her a half smile.

As the seconds ticked by, the emotion grew over her face, but this round didn't fill her eyes. It just made them narrow. It changed her breathing; it thinned out what I wished were a grin.

"You need to hear me when I say this…it's not safe for you to be here."

"In your room? With you?"

She nodded. "Yes."

"I like it when things are extra dangerous."

"Brady, you're not taking me seriously."

I squeezed her hand. "You're saying someone is going to whip my ass for being here with you. Once again, it doesn't scare me." I leaned in so our faces were only inches apart. "No one is going to touch me.

Not with a whip or a fucking fist or even a gun."

Was she talking about David?

I wasn't going to ask; I didn't want her to think I had been snooping around her phone. When she was ready to talk about him— or whomever she was inferring to—she would.

But it didn't matter who it was or what they meant to Lily or what their past looked like; no one was going to jeopardize or threaten her safety or mine.

"You don't even realize what you're saying."

As she breathed out through her nose, the air exhaling hard and fast, it hit my face.

The scent made my stomach growl.

"Listen to me." I surrounded her hand with both of my palms. "I don't think you realize who you're talking to. You're forgetting—or maybe you don't know—that I'm a man with every resource at my disposal. Money is no object. I've dealt with assholes my entire life."

The Cole brothers were who immediately came to mind, a duo who were slowly integrating into our family, but that wasn't the way things had started off.

"Danger doesn't turn me off, it turns me the fuck on. So, yes, I realize what I'm saying, and at some point, when you're ready, I hope you'll be comfortable enough to tell me what's going on." I kissed her without any hesitation. "But until then, that doesn't change how much I want you, Lily. The only person who's going to stop me from having you is you."

She was quiet while she stared at me. "What that entails and what you're signing up for—it isn't light by any means."

She didn't kick me out. She didn't tell me she didn't want me.

She gave me a solid reply instead, one that had me moving even closer to her body.

"I'm still here." I smiled.

"And if it gets worse?"

I kissed the back of the hand I was holding. "You're worth it."

Chapter Eighteen

Lily

"*You're worth it.*"

Was this a dream?

It couldn't be because as he looked me in the eyes, I felt the truth in every word he'd voiced.

"You want to know something else?" He got up from where he had been sitting on the bed and walked around to the other side, climbing onto the mattress, positioned in a similar way that I was, lying with his back against the headboard and his legs extended out. "I'm staying right here tonight and tomorrow I'm going to walk out of this hotel with you, and ride with you to the airport, and fly back to LA, where I'm then going to take you home. To my home."

Was this another dream?

The man I'd grown to care about was willing to put up with all the emotional baggage I came with.

The flip side of that was, despite my warnings, he didn't really know what he was facing, and in no way was any of this going to be easy.

Yet not a single thing I'd admitted had fazed him.

And that was where another fear came in. Would things become too much for him to handle? Would he end up running, like he probably should?

Because if I grabbed my phone from the other side of the room, the screen would show several messages waiting for me to read and listen to. Texts and voice mails, where words would be screamed and threats would be made.

The darkness...

To the light who was lying beside me.

I looked at Brady, whose eyes wouldn't leave me. His stare alone could make me feel like the most regal, desired, cared-for queen.

"You really think we're going to figure this all out?" I asked.

"Trust me."

I wanted to.

But the last person I'd given my trust to had turned me into this.

"You're fearless—you know that?"

"And relentless when it comes to something I want." His arm slid around my shoulders. "I won't give up, Lily."

So far, he'd proven that.

"About tonight"—I glanced down my body, at my braless chest and cropped shorts; what I couldn't see was the ache in my chest, but I was consumed by it—"I need you to be easy on me."

He caressed my cheek. "I'm not even going to touch you. Not because I don't want to, but because I'd rather hold you instead."

Another dream.

This one I didn't want to wake up from.

My mouth opened, my bottom lip caving inward until my teeth were holding it, releasing it to say, "I need that."

"I know." He tapped his chest. "Come here."

I moved in closer, resting my face just below his neck, circling the small buttons on his shirt. I tried to find relief in the quietness, to ease the ache in my heart, to mute the questions, ones that were coming in so fast and hard that they were making it difficult to breathe.

"I can't shut my brain off. It's a straight-up war in there right now."

"How do you normally get your mind off things?"

I let out a small huff. "I don't. It keeps me up all night, so most of the time, I'm a walking zombie." I glanced up at him. "I sound like a good time, don't I?"

He fanned his hand across my face. "Tell me about the Bulldogs. I'm assuming you're one?"

He was talking about my T-shirt.

"I see what you just did." I attempted a smile.

"Answer the question, Lily."

"Yes, I am one." I closed my eyes, remembering the lighter days. "I was a marketing major. I'm not sure why. I had no real interest in working in that field. I really didn't know what I wanted to do at that age."

"Is Georgia where you grew up?"

"Buckhead. A really pretty part of Atlanta. School was about a two-hour drive, so I moved on campus as a freshman and then got an apartment my junior year, moving back to Atlanta once I graduated." My hand ran lower to the next button on his shirt.

"My parents passed a couple of years later. I could have moved into their house since I was already flying at that point. I just needed a crash pad during the little time I was home, but it didn't feel right to return to a house that no longer felt like home."

"Hold on a second." He sat up a little higher. "They're gone?"

"A car accident."

"And it killed them both?" When he saw my reaction, he continued, "Jesus, Lily. What happened? Unless you don't want to talk about it—don't feel pressure to."

My parents were easier to talk about than David, which made absolutely no sense. Maybe it was because I'd spent years working through the grief, where things with David were still so present and raw.

"It's okay. I don't mind talking about it." My hand flattened on the middle of his torso. "Have you seen the movie *Beetlejuice*?"

His eyes widened. "Don't even fucking tell me..."

"Instead of a dog, it was a guy who had lost control of his motorbike. They were on a two-lane bridge, and the motorist was weaving along the middle, where he shouldn't have been, and my parents swerved so they wouldn't hit him."

He held my cheek with such tenderness. "Fuck me."

"I found out when I landed in Rome. It had happened shortly after takeoff, and the police had been trying to get ahold of me for all those hours." My arm dropped, and I scrunched a pillow under my head, rolling onto my stomach. "It was a lot to handle at that age. I'd never dealt with any kind of death before. I didn't know what to do, how to tackle their finances, how to sell the house. I worked as much as I could just so I wouldn't be home."

He swiped my lips with his thumb. "I can't even imagine."

"They were all I had." A knot moved into my throat. I wasn't sure I had any tears left, not after all the ones I'd shed tonight. "And then, suddenly, I had no one, aside from my roommate and Aubrey—the Daltons' flight attendant who's on maternity leave."

When his lips parted, I put a finger over them, as I sensed what he was about to say. "Don't tell me you're sorry. I know it's horrible. I know you feel awful for me." I took several deep breaths. "I wish I could say that was where the darkness ended, but it didn't."

I was on the other side of it now—at least when it came to my parents. I thought of them every day. I missed them terribly. I wondered what my life would look like if they were still alive. If their support would have protected me in ways that I wasn't able to protect myself.

He kissed the back of my finger. "Tell me about flying. How did you start?"

"A much happier topic."

"Which is why I changed the subject." He ran his hand over the top of my hair. "How does one decide they want a career in the sky?"

I tucked the pillow under my chest, wrapping my arms around the sides of it. "A couple of weeks after graduation, I was sitting in a coffee shop, using their free Wi-Fi to apply to jobs. There were two flight attendants sitting next to me, and I couldn't help but overhear their conversation. I ended up talking to them, found out the airline they worked for, and applied. I was sent to training a week later."

"And you love it."

"Yes"—I nodded—"but I love it for different reasons than when I first started. Then, I wanted to see the world. After Mom and Dad died, I didn't want to be home. Now, I only want to be in the air."

"To run."

"And to hide."

"From the source of the darkness."

My head fell forward, my chin resting on the pillow. As I swallowed, the spit burned all the way down my throat. "I can't seem to escape it."

I'd thought a year would be enough time.

I'd thought my life would slowly return to normal.

I'd thought I would find happiness again.

Even with Brady in my room, who gave off more light than I'd felt in the last twelve months, I couldn't help but wonder if there would be a knock at the door tonight. Or if the front desk would stop by at some point to deliver a present that had been sent.

If not only text and voice mails would appear on my phone, but pictures too.

I know where you are.

I know what you're doing.

I know who you're with.

"What is the darkness, Lily?"

But what I'd learned was that I had no idea what he was capable of.

Because, like Brady, he was fearless.

Relentless.

And when he wanted something, he went after it.

I slowly glanced up at him. "Not what. Who."

Chapter Nineteen

Brady

If the darkness came in the form of a person, which she'd just confirmed, then my gut told me it was David. I could see the fear written across her face; I could hear it in her voice.

Whoever that motherfucker was, I wanted to wrap my hands around his neck and strangle the shit out of him.

What I didn't want to do was push her to talk about every hardship in her life. We'd already covered the shocking revelation of her parents, a period I couldn't even fathom, and then we transitioned straight into the asshole who was haunting her. She'd had a rough day as it was; I wouldn't continue pulling her down the rabbit hole of hell.

But, shit, between her expression and the way she'd broken down tonight, sobbing in my arms, it was no wonder she'd given me those warnings.

She was dealing with some heavy things.

But not heavy enough to make me get up from this bed and walk out.

Fuck that.

I wanted her.

And hearing that she wasn't perfect, that she had a tragic and difficult past, confirmed that this woman knew how to fight. She knew how to survive. That she hadn't let either of these scenarios break her.

That was what I wanted in my life.

That was what made me want her even more.

If David—or whoever this person was—became a problem, I would deal with him.

Because deep down, I was a fighter too.

Until then, there was no reason to even talk about him.

I traced down the side of her face, stopping when I reached the corner of her mouth, which hadn't grinned in far too fucking long. "How about I bore you with the history of Brady Spade?" I tugged at the section where her lips split. "Would that earn me a smile?"

She sighed. "Honestly, I would love nothing more."

I leaned forward to kiss her, inhaling the piña colada scent off her skin, slowly, carefully holding our mouths together. I'd promised her that my cock was staying in my pants. But any more of this, even the swipe of her tongue against mine, would jeopardize that.

Guaranteed.

I just couldn't get enough.

Once we were separated, I adjusted my back against the headboard. "The quick rundown is this: I'm LA born and bred. I went to college at UNLV. I wasn't there for the academics. I was there to party my ass off on the Strip. My dad and uncle started Spade Hotels—now called Cole and Spade Hotels, which is another story. My brothers—Cooper and Macon, whom you met on the Daltons' plane—and I worked for them through high school, and as soon as we graduated college, we joined the company full-time. That's where I've been ever since. Working, traveling, having a hell of a lot of fun."

"We need to back up for a second. Vegas? For four years? Whoa. The most I've ever done was a two-night stopover, and it kicked my ass. I wasn't sure I was even going to make my flight."

I laughed. "But it was a good time, wasn't it?"

While she filled her lungs, her lips began to tug wide. "A memorable time, I'll say that."

"My father's requirement was a degree. He didn't care where we went or what we studied. Now, my brothers took things a little more seriously. Double majors, minors. Academic honors." I placed my forearm under my head, using it as a pillow. "That's not me. I fulfilled what was asked of me, but I was really there to party. I wanted to get as wild as possible before my life became all business—maybe not all, but most."

"I'm going to ask you the same question you asked me. Do you love your job?"

I let out a mouthful of air. "The day-to-day? No. It's all bullshit busy work. Meetings, decisions, corporate policies—none of that interests me. I like being hands-on. Designing a new property or renovating an existing structure. I like overseeing the process from the ground up and watching the guests' reactions when they walk into one of my creations and they take it all in."

She rolled onto her side, folding the pillow to prop her up a little. "Sounds like you travel a lot for work?"

My hand went to her neck, cupping that sweet spot between her throat and collarbone. "Yes, and no. Once a property is up and running, my job is done. But to get that hotel where it needs to be requires an immense amount of travel. Once we close on the property here in Edinburgh, I'll be going back and forth once a week."

Her eyes widened. "Weekly?"

"I don't plan on moving here. My brothers typically do, they prefer staying in the location until the project is finished. In the past, I've done it both ways." I stroked her cheek while I studied her eyes. "For now, the weekly trips just feel right."

She glanced at the ceiling, the window, across the room toward the door. "This is the hotel you're buying, isn't it?" She glanced at me again. "I overheard you talking to Dominick on the flight to Tampa."

"It's going to look nothing like this once I'm done with it."

Her lips were pulling even wider. "Everything you do is fascinating."

"You haven't seen me in action. If you think I'm an asshole now, work mode is even worse."

She giggled. "I haven't seen you in action?" Her cheeks stayed red when she added, "By the way…I Googled you."

"And?"

"Your accolades are quite impressive, Mr. Spade. You have the largest five-star hospitality brand in the world—six of those properties being your designs, Scotland will be the seventh. Out of those six existing structures, two of them won architectural awards." With each point, she held out a finger. "You personally worked with an IT company to create proprietary software that streamlined the check-in process for your guests and a backend system for your whole network of hotels. And the rumor is, you're already setting your sights on Bangkok as your next location, which you think will be one of your most successful hotels."

"Bangkok," I sighed. "That was mentioned on fucking Google?"

Her hand shot out to my chest. "It wasn't online. I heard you talk about it during the flight to Tampa. And don't worry, I signed a fifteen-page NDA before the Daltons would let me step foot on their plane. I would never speak a word about anything any of you discuss. I'm a vault."

The anger lowered to a dull irritation. "I was about to have someone's goddamn head." I took a breath. "But, yes, that's where I'd like to build next. Jenner is starting to look at properties for me."

"And you'd live there, I assume?"

"It would be about a year and a half from now, and with the distance, I'd really have no choice." Hair seemed to constantly fall in her face, and I brushed some back. "Have you been?"

She nodded. "Twice. Both times for stopovers. So much to see and do. And the food? I die."

"Agreed. I just have to convince the team."

"The team is Macon and Cooper?"

I moved my arm out from under my head and rubbed my hand over my hair. "I fucking wish. That would make my life much, much simpler." I hissed out a mouthful of air. "My uncle recently retired, finally handing over the business to us boys and my cousin, but with that came a merger with Cole International. A transition that hasn't been easy on any of us. So, instead of there being four partners, there are seven."

She sat up. "I read about this too."

"You probably did. It made international headlines for quite a few weeks."

She wiggled over the mattress until she found a position she liked. "Let me get this all straight. There're three Spade brothers and a cousin?"

"Jo Dalton. She's married to Jenner."

"Oh, yes, I've met her. She's so lovely." She tucked her legs underneath her. "And then there're two Cole brothers and a sister, right?"

"Ridge and Rhett are the brothers. Rowan is their sister. Rowan is dating Cooper, my middle brother." I chuckled. "It's a lot to take in, I know."

"Good Lord." She rested her hands in her lap. "I'm pretty sure I've read about their romance. It hit the tabloids."

I clasped my hand around her shoulder. "Do me a favor—mention that when you see him. Nothing would please me more than the look on his face when you tell him there was a fucking article written about his love life."

She winced. "I'm pretty positive it was a magazine."

"Even better."

"I'm going to take a wild guess and say you're unhappy with having three more partners." She paused. "Am I right?"

It blew my mind how smooth it was to talk to her. How uncomplicated it felt. She wasn't drilling me or interviewing me, like many of the women I'd hooked up with in the past. She was truly trying to just understand it all.

And opening up—something I rarely did outside of family and close friends, and even then, I was usually tight-lipped about the personal stuff—wasn't hard to do.

"You're right." I rubbed the outside of her thigh, needing at least some part of me touching her. "Rowan's cool. My issue isn't with her. Although when she first started dating Cooper—given that she was one of our partners—that rubbed me the wrong way. Her brothers, on the other hand, have gotten under my skin since day one."

"I get the sense that's easy to do."

"You really think you know me, don't you?" I winked.

"Just a little hunch I have."

"Again, you're not wrong." My thumb stilled by her inner thigh. "But those fuckers came in with nothing but attitude. Granted, we're three cocky men who hate advice and compromising. I wouldn't want to deal with us, and I don't know how Jo does. But those dudes came at us all wrong." I flattened the top of my hair. "Ridge has a little girl, Daisy. She's a cute one, and he's the softer of the two, but Rhett"—I ruffled up my hair—"that bastard is something else."

She smiled. "Sounds like executive meetings are a blast."

My head shook back and forth. "They're getting better. They're nothing like when the merger first happened. Honestly, Rhett is lucky to be alive with how many times I've wanted to choke his ass out." My voice quieted a little as I added, "Macon wants us to give him a little slack. Their dad, Ray, is dying. He doesn't have much time left. It's tough."

"Are they close to their dad?"

"Very."

"Take it from someone who's been through it. He's going to need a lot of slack. I wouldn't wish that pain on anyone—not even someone I hate."

I moved my hand under her leg and squeezed. "For you, I'll think about it."

A sound went off on the other side of the room.

A vibration.

I didn't have to look to know what it was.

As Lily heard it, her posture changed. Her lips mashed together. Her chest was moving like she was panting and she couldn't stop fidgeting.

A conversation that had been going so well, and then this.

"Hey…" My fingers went to her cheek. "It's just us in here. No one else. Whatever is happening over there, ignore it."

At least I had confirmation that the sound of her phone was what changed her demeanor. That every time the fucker vibrated, it set something off inside her.

A trigger that went deep as hell.

I didn't think I could rewind her past and erase the damage that had been done, but I could certainly try to rub every spot that had been wounded and kiss those fucking scars in hopes that they'd never reopen again.

"It's so ingrained in my head. It's like…I'm always waiting for it." Her voice was barely above a whisper. "And when I don't answer or respond, the messages come in faster."

"I'll solve that right now." I got up from the bed and grabbed her phone off the dresser. Not only were there missed calls from David, but several texts had also come through. I hit the buttons that would turn her phone off, and when the screen went black, I returned it to the dresser and rejoined her on the mattress. "Now, you can't be reached, and you can't react to the messages if you don't know they're coming through."

Her eyes were getting emotional. Not teary. It was like I could see the fear within her irises. "That was probably a very bad idea."

"Listen to me." I grabbed both of her shoulders and moved my face close to hers. "I'm not going to let anyone hurt you or fuck with you in any way. I think you know me well enough at this point to know how serious I am when I say that."

"This is different." Her voice stayed flat.

"You're saying I should destroy your phone, then?"

She tucked her legs up to her chest, staying quiet for far too many seconds. "It wouldn't matter, Brady. He'd still find me."

Chapter Twenty

LILY

"I told you in Edinburgh that when we got off this plane, I was going to take you to my place, and I meant that," Brady said. "But as much as I want to tell you to come home with me, I want this to be your decision." He ran a finger under my cheek. "Bringing you to my place will change things, Lily. I want to be sure that's what you want."

As I sat next to him on the couch in the main cabin, expecting the pilot to call at any moment to instruct me to get the plane ready for landing, I was repeating his words in my head. Words that, before our last night together in Scotland, I never anticipated hearing.

Because I never thought it could ever be an option.

How could I bring someone into my mess?

How could I put them at risk?

How could I even think of dating when I wanted to spend every waking second in the air?

What I knew, what I felt, what I was absolutely sure of was that if I wasn't in the air, I wanted to be with him.

Still, it felt almost selfish of me to say, "It's what I want."

I didn't know if I was being fair. If I was making the right decision for Brady. If I was truly only thinking about a happiness that I'd wanted for far too long and I knew he could give it to me.

"That's what I was hoping you would say." He cupped my cheeks. "You know something? I've never brought a woman to my house before. You'll be the first one."

My brows rose. "Ever?"

"Ever."

I wasn't the only one who had changed.

Both of us before were so drastically different from who we'd become since we found each other.

Did that make us perfect for one another?

Or stupid to think this could last?

"And you chose me?" I exhaled.

"It wasn't really a choice. More like a need that would never go away."

I wrapped my arms around his neck, giving him a soft, sweet peck. The tingles immediately burst through my body, reminding me of the hold he had on me. Not that I needed the reminder. Everything he did just made me fall harder. But there was a giant elephant wedged between us, and it seemed wrong not to at least be honest about it.

"I have no idea if this can work."

"But you want it to."

"I do."

"Then, that's all I need to hear."

He slammed our mouths together, his kiss rougher, needier than the one I'd given him. His hands left my cheeks and dived into my hair, pulling me closer to align our bodies. The hardness of his muscles was like iron beneath me. The heat from his skin was making me scorch. The scotch on his breath and the spiciness of his cologne—a combination I simply couldn't get enough of.

I was being tugged between two directions. The desire to strip

off this uniform and straddle his lap and ride us toward the release
we both needed. Or to go to the galley and finish my duties, being the
respectable, responsible Dalton employee that I was.

Before I was faced with even making that decision, the phone in
the galley rang.

"*Mmm*," I groaned as I pulled away from his mouth. "I have to
answer that call."

"You're fucking kidding me."

I laughed. "I wish I were."

I wiggled out of his arms and rushed for the phone, listening to
the pilot make his request. I assured him the plane would be ready to
land and hung up, peeking my head into the cabin.

"Ten minutes until we're on the ground."

He looked feral as he said, "Get over here."

"I can't." I smiled. "Not yet at least."

"Hurry."

I went to the counter, making sure everything was locked up and
secured, and gathered my personal belongings from the drawer. My
phone was on top. I hadn't turned it back on since Brady had shut it
off in my hotel room.

That was so many hours ago.

I was terrified to see the messages that were waiting for me.

Since I was going to his house after this, I probably wouldn't
have a lot of alone time. This was my only opportunity to face those
messages head-on.

I didn't want to look.

I didn't want to torture myself.

But I also knew that if I didn't respond, things had the potential
of getting worse, and that wasn't what I needed right now.

I held my breath as the home screen loaded, filling with all the
notifications that had come in since last night in Edinburgh.

Five voice mails.

Twenty-eight texts.

All from David.

My spit felt like acid as it slowly dripped down my throat.

My hands shook.

The hair on my body was standing straight again.

I knew it was a mistake, doing this now, but I also knew I had no other choice.

I pulled up his text box and began to read.

David: *Why aren't you fucking responding to me?!*

David: *Are you fucking stupid? Haven't I told you countless times what happens when you ignore me?*

David: *Cunt.*

David: *Answer your goddamn phone, Lily.*

David: *You're nothing but a slut—you know that?*

David: *A little whore who had it perfect and fucked it all up.*

David: *That's what you do—you fuck everything up.*

David: *Bitch.*

David: *You're going to get it…*

David: *Now, my calls are going straight to voice mail? What the hell is wrong with you?*

David: *Is your fucking phone off?*

David: *You're going to be sorry you turned off your phone.*

David: *LILY, WHY THE FUCK AREN'T YOU ANSWERING ME?!*

I stopped reading and scrolled to the bottom, my hands trembling, trying to keep the phone steady as I typed out a reply, my heart pounding so hard that I couldn't inhale.

Me: *David, stop. I don't deserve to be treated this way. I've been in the air, and the Wi-Fi wasn't working. Stop throwing accusations at me that aren't true.*

I was just about to set my phone down and check the back exit when another text came in.

David: *Liar. The Wi-Fi doesn't die on private jets owned by billionaires. Do you think I'm an idiot who would believe you? You were probably fucking one of them on the plane. Weren't you?*

David: *Slut.*

Me: *You have no idea what you're talking about.*

David: *Yeah? Who's Brady?*

Every ounce of air left my body, and I leaned against the back wall, just to the side of my seat, giving it all my weight to make sure I didn't fall.

How does he know?

Was it because he'd listened in on my conversation with Aubrey?

Had he been in Edinburgh?

Had my hotel room somehow been bugged?

Me: *Excuse me?*

David: *You thought I didn't know? That I wouldn't find out?*

David: *Not just a slut, but a dumb slut.*

Me: *Again, you have no idea what you're talking about. You have it all wrong. Please, I beg you, stop accusing me of things that aren't true.*

David: *It's not an accusation.*

Me: *You know nothing. You're just reaching for things to use to punish me. I don't deserve it, David.*

David: *What about Preston?*

I felt all the blood drain from my face.

Me: *What about him?*

David: *Do you remember what I did to him?*

Me: *I remember what you accused me of, and you were wrong about him too.*

David: *I wasn't wrong. You were fucking him.*

David: *Slut.*

David: *And I made sure you never fucked him again. Is that what I have to do with Brady?*

Me: *No!*

David: *I don't think you're telling me the truth.*

David: *You reek of lies. Lying about the Wi-Fi, lying about—*

I stopped reading when I heard, "You're letting him win."

Brady.

Shit.

I slowly glanced up from my phone, and he was standing in the doorway of the galley, eyeing me up as though he were reading the texts over my shoulder.

"Do you want to tell me what he's doing to you?" He leaned his shoulder against the entrance. "Or do you want me to tell you what I think? How I can't stand seeing you like this, Lily. Watching the way he's affecting you. It's all over your face—the fear, the frustration, the anger." He held out his hand. "Give it to me."

"He's n-never going to st-stop."

The tears had already started.

So had the shaking.

I wanted to scream.

Why?

He shook his hand in the air. "Give it to me, Lily." When I didn't move, he nodded toward my fingers. "Give me your phone."

"What are you going to do with it?"

"I'm going to destroy it."

It wouldn't make a difference, but the idea of these messages vanishing into cyberspace was somewhat of a relief. At least I'd never have to read them again.

Until new ones came in.

I powered off the phone and placed it on his palm. "This isn't the first time I've gotten a new phone. Each time, he finds my number."

"But it'll be the first time you'll have a phone that's owned by me." He slid my cell into his pocket. "My assistant will bring it to you tonight at my place."

Tonight.

Oh God.

My head dropped. "About that…"

"Fuck no." He closed the distance between us, wrapping his arms around my waist, taking my weight off the wall to hold me against his body. "Whatever he said has freaked you out enough that you don't want to come over. Am I right?"

I nodded. And when that didn't feel like enough, I put my hand on his chest. "I can't get you involved in this. It's not right. It's—"

"Let me decide what I want to be involved in." He scanned my eyes. "You've warned me. It's clear how unhinged this dude is. My concern is keeping you safe. I'm not in the least bit worried about me."

"You should be."

His hand lifted to my cheek, his thumb rubbing my lip back and forth. "You keep forgetting who I am. The power I have. The resources that are at *my* disposal. Don't worry about me, Lily. Worry about him because if that motherfucker touches you, he will die."

Emotion was moving into my eyes.

It was falling over the rims of my eyelids.

"Brady…"

"Don't let him do this to us." He flattened his fingers over my cheek and moved his mouth closer. "I know what you want. I can feel it every time we're together."

He slid my hand to the left side of his chest. "Do you feel that? My heart is beating so fucking fast that it's ready to come through my skin." He pressed his forehead against mine. "That's what you do to me. What no woman has ever done to me before. I'm not going to lose that because some asshole is spewing threats—or whatever bullshit he's trying to fill you with. My bite is far deeper than his could ever be." He pulled back and held my face up to his. "I'm not going to let him ruin anything between us."

When the first tear dripped, he caught it.

"Brady…" I leaned my face into his hand, my body onto his, and I held on tighter than I ever had. Even though my brain was at war, the guilt was gnawing at me, the fear was flooding through me, I couldn't ignore my feelings. "I care about you. So much."

"I know."

When our eyes finally locked again, I felt that beat that he'd described. I felt more tingles. I felt the plane start to descend, and even at that speed, I didn't question if we'd be safe without being buckled into a seat. Because I knew—I felt that Brady wouldn't let anything happen to us.

I wanted that.

I wanted him.

"I promise," I whispered. "I won't let him ruin anything."

Chapter Twenty-One

BRADY

"You live in a palace," Lily said.

She sat on the couch in my living room, a glass of wine in her hand, her feet tucked underneath her. We'd only been back at my place for about twenty minutes. She'd gotten a quick tour, which she'd asked for, and we ended up relaxing on the large sectional in the living room.

I wanted her in a spot where she didn't have to think about anything or anyone. I hoped my house would give her that reprieve since she'd been a bit on edge during the plane's landing and the ride here. I couldn't blame her. That asshole wouldn't leave her the fuck alone.

Something I was immediately putting a stop to.

"I don't know if I'd call it that." I took a sip of my scotch. "But I think I did a pretty good job building it."

"You built this house?"

God, she was so fucking sexy. Even in her Dalton uniform with their logo sitting just above her tit—a shirt I couldn't wait to rip off her. I had all the love for Dominick, his family, and their company, but I didn't want his name anywhere on Lily's body.

I nodded. "I bought the land, knocked down the existing house, worked with the architect on the blueprints, and oversaw the contractor and interior designer. Not a single inch of this home was built without my eyes on it."

"A control freak or a perfectionist?" Her hand went to my arm as she smiled. "I'm kidding."

"But it's true. I'm very much a heavy mix of both."

She pushed deeper into the pillow behind her. "For the record, you're never coming over to my place."

"And why's that?"

She laughed. "I live in a hotel."

My brows rose.

"I knew things were just temporary in LA," she continued. "It seemed silly to sign a lease for such a short period of time. Plus, being there makes me feel like I'm not living alone."

I could hear what she wasn't saying. When dealing with a dude who bothered her as much as he did, being alone could trigger some terrifying thoughts. It could also give him more access to her. At least in a hotel, if she screamed or called for help, someone would be there instantly.

Fuck, I hated that either of us even had to think that way.

"What hotel?"

She covered her face with her hand. "It's not a Cole and Spade Hotel—don't kill me." Her hand dropped. "I checked, and your Beverly Hills location isn't in my budget. Or even close to my budget."

I pulled out my phone, clicked on my assistant's text box, and sent her a quick message. "You'll be checking in tomorrow. There will be a room waiting for you. And I assure you, it's in your budget." I put my phone away.

"Brady...stop. No. I can't—"

"Did you really think I was going to allow my girlfriend to live in a hotel that isn't part of the Spade brand? Come on. We both knew the second you came clean, I was going to change that."

If it were up to me, I'd have her move into my house, not the hotel. But I didn't want to pull a David. I didn't want her to think, in any regard, that I was making her a prisoner in my home. After he had taken everything from her, she needed her independence.

Still, I'd have my eyes on her the whole time she was there.

Her head fell back, exposing the sleek, smooth skin of her throat. "Your girlfriend…" It came out as a moan.

"I've been waiting to use it. The timing felt right."

Her cheeks were flushed, her lips in a smile as she glanced around the large space, at the high ceiling and open floor plan and the windows that had a direct view of the Hollywood Hills. "Your *girlfriend* is going to have a very hard time accepting your generosity."

"But you will."

"Reluctantly."

"But you will," I repeated.

"Yes, I will." She continued to smile. "Thank you."

By having her at my hotel, I could ensure her safety much easier than if she was staying elsewhere. I wasn't going to bring that up. She certainly didn't need to know that I was going to be watching to make sure there were no unwanted visitors to her room. And until that asshole was fully out of the picture, I was going to make sure he didn't even breathe in her direction.

"You know, if Edinburgh transforms into even a quarter of the beauty that you've built here in your house, that hotel is going to be absolutely amazing."

"It will. I'll accept nothing less."

She stared at me from the corner, pillows surrounding her side and back, wineglass not far from her lips. "Something I find so interesting about you…I'm far from perfect, and yet you look at me like I'm"—she gazed around the room again—"this."

"You're more beautiful than this, Lily. This doesn't even compare to you. Nothing does."

Her head shook. "When you say things like that, I feel it. The words literally sink straight into my soul."

"It's the truth." I untucked her legs and spread them out across my lap. "I didn't wait this long to be with a woman because I was looking for perfection. I waited because no one I'd met, been around, or seen even tempted me enough to want to be in a relationship. Until you, Lily. Until you changed every thought, want, desire, and every opinion I had on the subject." I curved my hand around the bottom of her bare foot. "None of us are perfect. We're all loaded with flaws, but when you find the person you want to be with, you ask yourself if you can tolerate those flaws."

"Have you had that conversation with yourself? About me?"

I huffed a bit of air out. "Several times. And you know what your flaws do to me?"

"Scare the shit out of you." Her voice shrank. "Make you want to run?"

I massaged her arch. "They turn me the fuck on."

"But—"

"No, no. We're not going to talk about buts tonight. I want you here. I want every part of you."

She raked her fingers through my scruff. "You make me feel like such a queen."

"Well, this is my palace, so that does make sense." I nodded toward my bedroom wing. "In my closet, on top of the island, are a few bags. They're for you. For tonight and for all the future nights that I can convince you to stay here instead of the hotel. In one of the bags should be a bathing suit. Why don't you go put it on?"

Her fingers froze. "Hold on a second. You got me…things? To stay here?"

"I didn't give you an opportunity to go back to your place and grab whatever you might need. So, I had my assistant do some shopping, and a bathing suit was on the list."

She looked at me in awe. "I can't believe what I'm hearing right now."

I began to rub her other foot. "We're going in my hot tub. If you'd rather go naked, I'm all for that. I'd actually prefer it." I shrugged.

She tightened her grip on my face. "Brady…that wasn't what I meant."

I laughed. "I knew what you meant."

"You're spoiling me." She dragged her teeth over her lip. "I hate you for that."

"You know what?" I growled. "That turns me on too."

She crawled out of the couch corner and straddled my lap, her arms resting on my shoulders, her pussy grinding over my hard-on. "How private is your hot tub?"

A few more pumps of her hips, and I'd be tearing off both our clothes.

"Private enough that I'm okay with you going naked." I grabbed her ass, squeezing those fucking cheeks, dreaming about my cock sliding between them. "Trust me, if I thought someone could see your body, I'd never allow it. No one is going to look at what's mine."

She lowered her lips to my mouth, pressing the softest kiss against me. "Take me there."

Chapter Twenty-Two

LILY

"My God," I moaned as my toes hit the water. Brady had carried me, naked, down the steps of his Jacuzzi, settling us into the center of the oversized tub, not near the inner row of seats or jets, just directly in the middle of it all. His hands surrounded my now-wet, slippery body.

"This feels incredible." My legs stayed circled around his waist, my arms on his neck, the water bubbling around us.

The moment he'd brought me out here, I realized he was right about the privacy. Despite the house being built on the edge of a cliff, his patio without a screen or fence around it, his home was situated in a way that unless someone was flying overhead, they wouldn't be able to see a thing.

Which alleviated my fear of David somehow peeking in.

Without that worry hanging over me, I could fully concentrate on the way Brady was touching me.

Kissing my neck.

Working me up to the point where I couldn't take much more teasing.

I needed him.

In every way.

"I missed this." He was touching the outside of my pussy, rubbing it with just a finger. After every few swipes, he would graze my clit and then focus on the top and sides. "I've fucking dreamed about this."

"It's yours."

Something I couldn't believe I could say—out loud, to his face— but it was true.

Since I'd met him on the commercial plane, Brady had mentally owned this body.

"Giving it to me, Lily, means I can do anything I want to it. You'd better think about that long and hard before you say those words to me again."

That statement ran from my head to my feet, and it brought chills and goose bumps with it.

I leaned into his neck, the steam making the ends of his hair wet, and they tickled my mouth as I whispered into his ear, "It's yours."

"Fuck me." His hands moved up my waist, over my navel, pinching my nipples on their way to my face. "I need you to be honest with me."

"I'd never lie to you."

He stilled my waist so I couldn't move. "Are you on anything?"

I nodded. "You have nothing to worry about. My IUD has been in for years."

"I've never gone without a condom. But the thought of putting one on right now, with you, I don't like it."

The stars and moon were above us, giving off just enough light that I could see the devilish look on his face.

"I'm turning you into the sinner…"

"I was one long before you, baby."

His grip lightened, and now that I could wiggle, his hard-on was positioned over my clit. I lifted myself up just enough that his tip was aimed at my entrance.

"Would the sinner like to feel how wet I am?"

"Lily..." His fingers dived into my damp strands, and he fisted a handful of my locks. "Do you know how good it's going to feel when your wetness is dripping over my dick?" He pulled my hair so my neck tilted back, exposing my throat, his lips landing just under my chin. "When I get to feel your pussy clenching and tightening around me." He kissed down to my collarbone. "When I get to fill you with my fucking cum."

I lowered a few inches, taking in his crown, stopping when I was less than halfway.

Without a condom on, he felt bigger, and I questioned whether I could even handle his size. But without the latex covering him, the feel of his skin was incredible. And with the slickness I was adding, I could bob freely, taking in more than I'd thought.

"Why don't you tell me how this feels?" I moaned so loud as I dipped again, halting when I reached his base.

"I could come right fucking now." His hands sank into my butt, ensuring I didn't move. "Goddamn, you're tight." He kissed up my neck. "And your cunt is so fucking hot." His lips hovered over mine. "And it's pulsing around me."

I also wasn't breathing, but he wouldn't know that.

The fullness had completely taken all the air out of me.

I didn't want it back.

I wanted to feel just like this forever.

"Give me those lips, Lily."

I held the back of his neck, bringing our faces closer, but there was still a small distance between us.

"I want you to give them to me because when I pull out and thrust back inside of you, I want to taste the pleasure on your mouth." He licked his bottom lip. "I want to feel your moan all the way in my body."

If there was a flaw in this man, I couldn't see it.

I couldn't feel it.

He was perfection.

And the moment I mashed our lips together, he reared his hips back and plunged into me.

"Brady!" A scream came first, followed by a moan. "Ah!"

"Fuck yes!" he hissed.

He didn't stop at one thrust. There was a pattern that went with the flick of his hips, sending me bouncing on top of the water. He then gyrated, hitting my walls and G-spot before he pulled back and did it all over again.

All I could do was hold on to him.

Because where he was in his dominant era, I was just taking it.

Swallowing it.

My body building around it.

The tingles instantly ignited, trickling their way into my stomach, where a heat was beginning to churn.

"You're going to come. I can feel it."

"I can't hold it off," I panted across his mouth.

"I don't want you to, but I want you to remember something…"

He wanted me to think?

Process?

Respond?

"You gave me this." He was squeezing my ass, but I was pretty sure he meant my entire body. "Which means I get to do whatever I want. You recall that, don't you?"

"Yes," I dragged out.

"Then, get ready to enjoy this…"

My orgasm was lifting, bringing a wave that I was fully unprepared for.

But something else was happening.

An invasion I didn't expect.

One that started with his finger, circling the rim of my ass.

An area of my body that had never been touched.

"Brady!"

"Is this a virgin ass?"

More than just a virgin—nothing, not even a finger, had ever been near it.

"Yes."

He growled, "Fuck." And then, "Don't worry, I'm going to be nice to it."

Even if he was nice, I didn't know what it was going to feel like. But right now, with what he was already doing to me and how he was making me feel, I was far too gone to even want him to stop.

"You have no idea how good you're about to feel." As his syllables hit my skin, they sent shivers through me.

I was taking in every second of this. Every bit of movement. My breath coming out in short gasps each time his finger shifted to a new spot.

I found myself arching toward him.

Almost...asking for it.

Not out of curiosity, but strangely out of need.

And after a few curves around, he slid in.

"Whoa," I exhaled, the feeling nothing at all what I had anticipated.

The little ache that initially came through was quickly dissolved.

And it became enticing.

Satisfying.

Fulfilling, like I'd needed this all along and I never knew I was craving it.

My upper body pressed against his, my arms suddenly holding on for dear life, my legs confined to his waist, locking me in place.

Because the last thing I wanted was for anything to change.

I wanted everything he was giving me, just the way he was giving it to me.

"Lily, you have one fucking tight little ass." When he shifted upward with his dick, so did his finger, both going in the same direction. "But you're taking that finger, and I can feel how much you're loving it."

"Don't"—I searched for my voice, unsure if I could even form a sound—"stop."

A deep, gritty chuckle hit my ears. "Never. Not when I know I'm making you feel this good."

It only took a few more beats of the duo, of the combined sensation, before I was screaming, "Brady," at the top of my lungs.

"You're tightening, damn it. Fuck!"

The peak slammed into me like two cars headed toward one another in the same lane. And when they collided—his finger and his dick—the impact was crushing.

That was what he did to me.

He imploded my orgasm.

"Jesus, you're so wet." He held our lips together, and I breathed him in. "That's it, Lily. Let me feel it."

Once my name left him, I connected our mouths.

That kiss just gave me one more thing to hold on to.

Because if there was an edge, he'd goaded me there, and I'd been teetering around it.

Except I no longer had a choice.

I had to let go.

And when I did, I didn't just tiptoe past it.

I fucking jumped.

"Give it to me," he barked, his speed increasing, the intensity doubling. "Fucking give it to me."

With that came shudders and more screams.

I didn't know if I was still kissing him.

If my eyes were closed.

If I was meeting him in the middle or moving at all because my brain was no longer connected to my body.

In this moment, all I could do was accept.

Feel.

Experience.

"Oh! My! God!"

The ride was nearing the end, the momentum slowing, the pressure fading. The fullness lightening until it was only half the friction since his hand was gone, leaving just his dick.

Even the breath that swished across my face, whispering, "Lily," was softening.

"I don't know what you just did to me." I sighed.

"But..."

I had to push the sexy aches away just to gather my thoughts. "But I want it again. And again."

He smiled only inches from my face.

It was the kind of smile that told me I'd seen nothing yet.

Which I couldn't fathom.

Because this was...this was more than anything I'd ever had.

"*Mmm.*" His lips moved to my neck, his hands on my breasts, pulling my nipples, rolling them between his fingers, veering me toward pain, but never taking it to that extreme. "It's time for you to come again."

Although he was still inside me, he wasn't moving. It was as if he knew I needed the sensitivity to go away first.

"Which means it's time for you to come," I told him.

His exhale was animalistic, rough, and raspy. "Right inside your pussy."

"I want that." I narrowed my grip around his neck. "I want that now."

He kissed me, delicately at first, like he was tasting, memorizing, learning me all over. That quickly switched to a tempo filled with need and desire. His hands caressed my back and sides, the top of my butt before he worked his way up, his thumbs soothing my nipples after he pulled them. The end of each of our breaths came out in a moan. And as he devoured my lips, he began to carefully move his hips, pulling back as far as his crown and sinking in.

"Oh, yes!" I gulped.

With each thrust, he went deeper.

He went harder.

He went faster.

And before I could even prepare my mind for what was happening inside my body, he flipped me around, gliding me across the water until I reached one of the corners of the tub.

"Hold on to the edge," he demanded.

As I found the roundness he'd referred to and clung to it, the waves from the movement splashing over my fingers, he positioned himself behind me, between my legs, extending them around him so I was straddling him backward. He then aimed me higher against the wall of the Jacuzzi so the jet was positioned right over—"Oh!"—my clit.

"You like that?"

"I—"

My voice cut off as he drove in, filling me.

Completely.

Holy fuck!

Aside from my ass, there wasn't a spot on my body that went untouched. The front of my pussy was stimulated by the power of the water, as though I were holding a vibrator against it; the inside was getting the friction it needed from his strokes.

"Brady…"

"Tell me. I want to hear it."

Nothing I could say could describe this.

It wasn't worthy of words.

I couldn't even begin to formulate how I was feeling, so I breathed,

"What is happening?" It was an honest question that I didn't know the answer to. Because I'd never had this. I'd never even come close to anything like this. "Brady, fuck!"

"Do you want more?"

How was that even an option?

"You can do more?"

"Ask me for it, Lily…"

"Give me more—"

Before I could get the whole sentence out, still curious what more would even look like, I quickly got my answer.

It came in the form of a pace. It was as if I'd wound him up and set him free, like he hadn't exerted any energy until now. As fast as the water was streaming in front of me, he was matching the intensity. But it didn't come just straight on, like the jet, he swiveled his hips.

He rocked.

He pumped.

And as my body began to reach that hard, overpowering crest, his moans told me he was as close as I was.

I looked over my shoulder. His gaze immediately found mine, and his eyelids narrowed, lips open and feral. The concentration and passion in his expression was the sexiest thing I'd ever seen.

"Make me come, Brady." I wrapped my fingers around the rough edge. "Make us come together."

"Is that what you want?"

I murmured, "Yes."

I didn't think asking for more was even a possibility.

But he proved me wrong.

Whatever he'd been reserving, he gave it to me. His strokes changed. They were sharper. Needier. They went from tip to base, entrance to G-spot before I could even take a breath.

But that wasn't all of it.

There was the jet that was massaging my pulsing clit.

"Oh fuck!" I shouted.

"Tell me you want me to come. I need to hear you say it."

"Please," I cried. "Come in me." I then begged, "Brady, I need it."

"Fuck!"

His voice, that grumble, tore through me at the same time my orgasm shuddered through my core. It was right at that moment, when I was hanging at the top, the sparks erupting, that I felt him lose it.

"Yes!" I screamed as he twisted even harder, as the wetness turned thicker, telling me he was adding to it.

Filling me.

Just like he'd wanted.

"Brady!"

"Your fucking cunt..." His movements still came in spikes, but not as fast. "I'm going to fucking fill you, Lily." He pounded me several times. "Hell yeah!"

My muscles were quaking as I started my descent, little screams leaving my mouth, my fingers squeezing whatever was within them.

I was coming down from one hell of a high, and with that came quietness and stillness.

When he reached the same level as me, he gently pulled out and turned me around, capturing me in his arms. He held me on his lap as he took a seat on the ledge and propped me up against him.

"You ravished me tonight." I was smiling, although I wasn't sure how; I had nothing left in me.

"I wasn't nice to her...was I?" He was rubbing the outside of my pussy, lightly tracing down to my entrance. "I can feel my cum dripping out of you." He whistled as the air left his mouth, his head shaking. "This is the first time I've ever felt that, and, shit, I've got to say, it's nothing like I expected."

"No?"

His lips nuzzled my ear. "Everything with you just keeps getting better."

Chapter Twenty-Three

BRADY

"Brady!" Lily screamed.

I glanced up from between her legs, where I'd been licking and sucking and fingering since I'd woken up a few minutes ago, and took in that gorgeous face. The way her mouth opened when she was getting close. How her head tilted back, lengthening her neck. How her legs clenched around me—whether it was my face or waist, she always tightened up.

Before we'd gone to bed last night, she'd told me she didn't think she could come again for a long time. Because things hadn't ended in the hot tub. I'd tasted her in the pool and again in the shower.

When my eyes had opened this morning, I'd decided to show her how wrong she was.

"Come on my face," I told her. "I want to fucking taste it on my tongue."

She was there—her clit was hardening, my finger was getting wetter as it dived in and out of her, her screams were heightening.

She just needed me to pop her past that edge.

I already knew her body like I'd spent the last ten years devouring it.

So, I knew that speed and pressure were exactly what she needed. I gave it to her.

"Shit!" She tugged at the roots of my hair. "Ah!"

That sound, the feel of her body when an orgasm was rushing through it, the taste, the look on her face—it was everything I'd been waiting for.

Everything I fucking craved.

Within a few more licks and arches of my finger, she was shuddering.

Ripples pummeled through her navel, and as each one passed, she yelled louder; she thrust against my face even harder, bucking, riding the orgasm out.

"Yes!" she cried. "Oh my God!"

As she was on her way down, I slowed my licks to laps, dragging my tongue across the whole length of her clit, transitioning things to a crawl until her breathing told me she was done.

I didn't hide my smirk. "I'm not going to say I told you so."

She let out a small laugh. "I'm terrified to tell you I truly don't think I can come again after this—so you didn't just hear me say it. Instead, you're hearing me say that I'm positive I can come a hundred more times."

I licked her off my mouth and gave her pussy a kiss.

A slow one.

A tender one.

A final one that soaked up the last of her wetness, holding it in my mouth, savoring it before I swallowed.

There was nothing in this world as sweet or addictive as Lily's pussy.

I moaned as the last of her went down my throat, and I worked my way up her body until I was hovered over her. "Want some coffee?"

She folded her arms behind her head. "I realize you just ate your breakfast, but I didn't."

I chuckled. "Eggs?"

"And bacon and yes to coffee and all the other things too."

"Let me see what I can cook up." I gave her a light kiss before I went into the bathroom, washing my face and brushing my teeth, and headed into my closet to put on some shorts.

Lily sat up as I walked back into the bedroom. "You know what's so funny? Ladies always talk about gray sweatpants and their obsession with men wearing them. But in my opinion, shorts are the new gray sweatpants."

"I'm lost."

She nodded toward my waist. "Mesh shorts are severely underrated."

I scratched my bare chest, trying to process what she was saying. "Still lost here, Lily."

"You know how a thong shows a woman's butt cheeks?"

I nodded.

"Gray sweatpants and mesh shorts, like the ones you have on, show your whole package."

"They what?" I glanced down to see what she was describing.

"I can see your crown and every delicious inch of your shaft."

I tried craning my neck forward to get a better frontal view. "You're fucking shitting me. I'm not even hard."

"You don't have to be. The material is lying right across your dick." When I gazed back at her, she added, "I might have just changed my mind about not being able to come again." She pointed at the door. "But breakfast first…before I die."

I didn't know what I was going to replace these shorts with and the thirty pairs I had just like them, but as soon as she left to check in to the hotel in Beverly Hills, they were all going in the trash.

"I'll see you in the kitchen," I told her.

I headed straight for the coffee maker, brewing two cups, and held the first mug, the contents black and bitter, up to my mouth to take a long sip. It was still early. I had plenty of time to fuck off for a little while before I needed to go to the office—something that had to happen at some point today so I could discuss the details of Edinburgh with the executive team. They were waiting for updates, and I'd been too preoccupied with Lily to fill them in.

"Mine?" she asked as she joined me in the kitchen, pointing at the mug still under the brewer.

She had on the button-down I'd worn yesterday and had clasped the middle three buttons, letting the top fall open, which gave off hints of her tits, and the bottom reached her mid-thighs, teasing me with her beautiful legs.

"God, you look sexy in my clothes." I took several dips down her body. "I didn't know how you took your coffee, or I would have gotten it ready for you."

She lifted the cup to her mouth and came over, leaning against the front of me. "I take it just like this." She closed her eyes as she sipped and swallowed. "What are you feeding me?"

I gave her ass a light slap and went over to the fridge, inventorying what Klark, my family's personal chef, had shopped and prepped. The meals that he'd prepared were in glass containers, the contents labeled and dated.

I looked at her over my shoulder. "I'm going to fry up some eggs and bacon, but tell me if any of these side dishes sound good to you—" My voice cut off when the tablet on the wall started ringing, notifying me that someone was at my gate. "One second. I need to get that."

I hit several buttons on the tablet to pull up the camera feed. Multiple angles were captured of the gate and call box, each showing a van, commercially wrapped with a logo and phone number and social media icons.

"Yes?" I said into the speaker.

"This is LA Flowers and Gifts," the driver replied, confirming the name on the van. "I have a delivery for Brady Spade."

I couldn't imagine who the hell would send me flowers or a gift from there. Maybe one of the guys was fucking around to be funny, knowing flowers would piss me off, or my assistant was being thoughtful since I was nearing the end of the Edinburgh closing.

I hit a button that opened the gate and said to Lily, "I'll be right back."

I went to the front door, waiting for the driver to pull up, and met him on the front steps, taking the long box out of his hand and locking the door behind me once I was back inside. I set the box on the counter and peeled the card off that had been taped.

"Flowers, huh?" She grinned from the other side of the counter.

"The guys are going to get a fucking earful from me—"

A bolt of rage erupted inside my chest as I read what was written on the card. My hands crumpled the edges as my grip tightened. My lips sank around my teeth as a goddamn snarl came out.

"What the hell?!" I released an unhinged breath. "That bastard is fucking with the wrong motherfucker."

"Brady?" She rushed to my side of the counter. "What's wrong? What happened?" She pulled at my arm, but it didn't move. "Who sent this?" When I didn't reply, she continued, "What does the card say?"

I didn't want to show her.

I didn't want to scare her; she was already terrified about the situation with him—a man who had now been confirmed as David— and this would only make things worse.

But I had to say something.

Something that couldn't be a fucking lie—that wasn't who I was, and it wasn't what she deserved.

"Lily…"

I held the card at my side, away from her line of sight because, shit, I didn't know how to tell her.

"Brady?" As she stared at me, taking in my face and the fury I couldn't hide in my expression, I could tell she was piecing it together.

Her entire demeanor changed with each second that passed.

Her shoulders rounded forward, her arms wrapped across her stomach, her body was sinking inward.

And on her face, the emotion, the fear, and the worry all returned.

"No." Her hand went over her mouth, her eyes widening as she said, "Don't tell me. Oh God, please don't tell me." Her head shook, her eyes beginning to well with tears. "It's from David, isn't it?"

Setting the card on the counter was the last thing I wanted. The thought of her seeing those goddamn words and getting instantly triggered made the rage in my chest come to a screaming boil.

That asshole had balls—I had to give him that.

But they were balls that I was going to fucking destroy.

This no longer involved just Lily and him. That had ended in Edinburgh the moment she became mine.

Now, this involved me.

"Please, Brady. Talk to me." She paused. "Tell me."

I lifted my hand from my side, glancing at the words again, my temper peaking.

MY BEAUTIFUL BLUE-EYED WIFE, YOU WILL ALWAYS BE MINE...

—DAVID

"Brady, please..."

It took everything in me to point the card in her direction.

As I watched her scan his message, her face crumpling, her body shrinking, my heart fucking shattered. The first tear dripped down her cheek, and instead of wiping it away, I dropped the card and pulled her into my arms. My mouth pressed against the top of her head, and I held her tighter than I ever had before.

"Wife?" she cried. "Is he fucking serious?"

"This will never happen again—I promise you that."

Her fingers dug into my bare back. "Why?" She sucked in more air. "*Whhhy?*"

I knew that wasn't a response to my statement.

She was questioning why David had done this.

"Brady, he won't stop. He's never going to stop." She pulled her face back to look at me. "He asked about you when he was texting me on the plane." She swallowed, her voice getting choked up from her tears. "Somehow—and I have no idea how—he found out about you. I lied. I told him there was nothing between us just to avoid this. And yet it happened. He did this because he knows, and…" Her voice trailed off, like she couldn't come to terms with what she was about to say.

I knew what those words were going to be and why she was shaking in fear.

She thought he was going to do something to me.

She was fucking wrong.

"He's finished—do you hear me?"

Her head shook, her crying now amplified. "It's not that easy."

I'd met very few people in my life who couldn't be touched.

I doubted he was one.

"I need you to tell me everything you know about this guy. The more information I have, the faster I'll be able to demolish him—"

"You can't." The loudness in her tone was gone. In its place was a voice so soft, just slightly above a whisper. "He's untouchable."

Now, I was really intrigued, and now, I needed some goddamn answers.

I gripped the back of her legs and lifted her onto the island, moving her thighs apart so I could stand between them. I kept my voice mellow and calm as I said, "Lily, I've given you time. I haven't pressured you. I've waited patiently for you to tell me about him. But that time has passed. My patience is long gone. You need to tell me everything."

Her hands covered her face, her neck dropping, the cries racking through her body.

Fuck me, I could barely take this.

I leaned into the side of her face, hugging my arms around her. "Nothing is going to happen to you, Lily. I've got you."

"It's not that." Her hands slowly slid down until her face was fully revealed. "This is the reason I didn't want us. Because of him. Because of what I knew he would do." Her eyes squinted shut, causing more wetness to drip down her cheeks. "Because of what he did to Preston and he's going to do it to you too."

I would address her concerns, but she'd just dropped a bomb that I couldn't ignore.

"Who's Preston?"

As her eyes opened, her hand went to her chest, as if she needed it to breathe. "A friend from work. One of the few I had." She paused to take a couple more breaths. "Preston didn't know the details of my relationship with David. I told no one. But he could tell I was torn up when we broke up, and to try to get my mind off things, he'd bring wine to my apartment or drag me out to a bar."

"And David found out."

She nodded. "He finds out everything. Always."

Another topic I'd circle back to, but first, what was Preston's role in her life?

She'd told me she hadn't dated anyone or been with anyone since David.

That I had been her first.

Was that not the truth?

"What did he do to Preston?" I asked.

"David went to his apartment." Her eyes turned into pools of tears, her lips quivering, even her fucking shoulders were shaking. "And he beat Preston to within an inch of his life."

The news didn't rattle me in a way where I was afraid David would do the same thing to me. David wouldn't touch me. But it rattled me for Preston, who was clearly someone Lily cared about.

"Brady, he spent almost a month in the hospital—that's how badly David had hurt him. I couldn't even go see him. I was scared that if I did, David would show up there and do something even worse."

She rubbed her hands over her thighs. "The thing is, Preston and I weren't even together. Our relationship wasn't anything like that or even close to that. We were friends—and Preston was in a relationship with another man. He was just a really good guy, Brady. I'd told David that a million times. He didn't believe me." She reached for my arm that was already around her. "I even showed David pictures of Preston's boyfriend and the two of them vacationing together, and David claimed that I'd Photoshopped the picture."

There was a bit of relief in hearing that Preston's preference wasn't Lily and that what she'd told me had held up.

But that David had almost killed a man?

That was some fucked-up shit.

The questions were multiplying in my head.

"How is David finding out these things about you? Is he following you? Tracking you?"

"I don't know." Her arms dropped to her sides. "Part of me thinks both since he seems to know where I am at all times—or at least some of the time." She gripped the edge of the counter. "He'll make random comments about my location or send photos of me walking into a hotel or getting off the plane, grabbing food, going to an appointment." She glanced down, no longer looking at me. "It's gotten to the point where I just stay in my hotel room. I've traveled to all these amazing places, and I don't explore them. I'm constantly nervous he's going to show up or come to my hotel room. I'm terrified of him, and I think he's so angry about our breakup that he'll hurt me. I don't know… I don't know what he'd do, but I don't trust him. I…" She slowly glanced up, the movement causing the tears to stream again. "I feel like a prisoner."

I fucking ached for her.

For what this despicable human had put her through.

For the anguish and uneasiness she had to live with on a daily basis.

"Two things. One, you're no longer living that way. When you travel with the Daltons, assuming you'll have time off, I want you out. I want you seeing every sight. I want you hitting up restaurants and boutiques. Whatever you would do if David wasn't a concern, that's what I want for you." I put my face closer to hers. "What I expect from you."

My hands went to the center of her thighs. "The second thing is, he will never step foot on any of my properties." I tried to keep my voice even, but the thought of him showing up at a Cole and Spade Hotel made my blood pressure skyrocket. "You have nothing to worry about. He will be stopped before he gets anywhere near your room."

She was quiet until she whispered, "But can you really stop him?"

I chuckled. "You have no idea what I'm capable of."

Stopping him would be one of the simpler pieces of this puzzle. But there were certain aspects I still didn't understand. That made no sense even though she was opening up more than she ever had.

"Why didn't David go to jail for what he did to Preston?"

"I told you, he's untouchable." She chewed the corner of her lip. "And when he does something, it's untraceable. That's who I got myself involved with. Out of all the guys I could have picked, I chose a man who's over-the-top obsessive. Irrational. Dangerous. Who creates scenarios in his head that aren't true. That's why I can't do this to you—"

"Lily—"

"Brady, it's only going to get worse." She was clutching me. Holding on like I was a rope. "This is just the beginning. Flowers are nothing compared to what he'll do."

"Not a fucking thing is going to happen to either of us."

I would repeat that over and over until it registered.

Until she believed it.

Until she could say the words and speak them with confidence.

"Rewind for me," I instructed. "Fill in some blanks by telling me how you two met and what he's like as a person. The more I know, the better it'll help me."

She was silent while she stared at me, her grip gradually lightening. "We met at a bar. I'd gone out with Aubrey one night, and he was there with some of his friends. He didn't come on super strong. That was what I needed—space and time to heal because, mentally, I wasn't in the best place. I was mourning my parents and emotionally wrecked and vulnerable."

"He picked up on that fast."

Which set off my anger again.

"Yep. He knew just what to say and how to get me to trust him, and at first, he was perfect," she continued. "But that didn't last." Her eyes turned haunted. "I should have run the second he began to change. My gut told me everything was wrong, and I didn't listen to it."

"He would have dragged you right back. I know the type."

The manipulators. They were all the same.

I'd done business with plenty of them. I could write a fucking handbook on their practices.

I ground my teeth together. "What did he do when he changed?"

"It started with control. Who I talked to. Where I went. Without me even realizing it, he was making decisions for me, like paying off the remainder of my lease so I could move in with him. But it didn't end there..."

She glanced at the ceiling. "I can't even believe I'm about to say this, but he told me to quit my job, and I listened to him." Several seconds passed before she locked eyes with me again. "He wanted me at his home. Accessible. That's what he said anyway, but I know it goes way deeper. He couldn't handle that I was gone, that I was with people who weren't him. That I was staying places overnight. He was constantly accusing me of cheating, of not being there for him, of being a terrible girlfriend."

The dude was a fucking psycho, and Lily hadn't been strong enough to fight him off, so he had taken full advantage of her.

But this was what manipulators did.

The way they acted, their timeline of events.

They didn't stop until they got everything they wanted.

"He treated you like property," I spit.

"And I stayed."

I cupped her cheeks. "But you found the courage to leave. That's what matters. And you must have found it because you're here."

She focused on my right eye and then my left. "I fled when I no longer recognized myself. That's when I knew it was time—when I couldn't stand another second of him."

The pain in her voice, the rawness—that was what I couldn't fucking handle.

Along with the thought of her running from him, knowing he would do everything in his power to make her life hell once she did.

My fingers tightened on her face. "Did he ever hurt you?"

"He physically never laid a hand on me. He threatened to many times, and after the whole Preston thing, I took those threats much more seriously. As far as if he verbally abused me"—she gasped—"yes, he beat me down."

My hands caught the tears that fell next.

"He made me believe I was worthless. That I was lucky he'd even given me a chance and that I didn't deserve him or anyone. The things he would call me, words he still uses—they're horrific."

"Baby…" I pressed my forehead against hers, stroking my thumbs over the corners of her mouth, thinking of how I was going to wrap her up and take her straight back to bed the moment this conversation was over. How I wasn't leaving her side until she was due to fly again with the Daltons.

The executive team could wait to hear the Edinburgh news. Lily needed me more.

I carefully pulled back, still keeping our faces close. "How did you get out?"

"I had to outsmart him, which was so difficult, given how much access he had to me." She put her hand on top of mine. "I had to move quickly, leaving when he was out on a job, renting the first apartment I found, getting my job back at the airline. I was in the air the next day."

"When he figured out you were gone, he blew the fuck up, didn't he?"

She sighed. "Within a week, he found out where I lived and would bang on my door for hours. I'd destroy my phone and get a new one, and like I told you, he'd somehow get the number. But that's not all…" Her exhale this time was labored. "He'd show up at the airport and at my favorite coffee shop. Wherever I was, he was there, too, trying to bully me into being with him, ridiculing me for the decision I'd made." She paused to catch her breath.

"When I couldn't take it anymore, I moved into a hotel. At least there, he couldn't knock for hours without getting kicked out. The knocking did stop when I relocated to the hotel, but he would still wait for me in the lobby and follow me to the elevator."

"When Aubrey told me she was going on maternity leave and that the Daltons were looking to hire a temporary flight attendant, I literally jumped at the opportunity."

With every description she gave, I hurt even more for her.

This wasn't a way to live.

And that was the whole thing—she hadn't been living. She'd been surviving because this motherfucker wouldn't stop punishing her.

"How long has this been going on?"

"A little over a year."

My brows shot up. "You're fucking kidding me…"

"Twelve-plus months, and he's still texting and calling, screaming when I don't answer, tossing every accusation my way."

"Verbally abusing you."

Fat tears immediately filled her eyes. "I hate that I have to admit that, that it even happened to me, that I allowed it."

The pieces were finally fitting together.

"Now, I know why my assistant couldn't find you online," I told her. "If you had a social media presence, who knows what he'd do?"

She nodded.

He had ruined her life for long enough.

As of today, that was coming to an end.

I wasn't a perfect man. Shit, I was so fucking far from that. But I could give her two things that she hadn't had in over a year.

Or possibly ever.

The first was love.

I didn't exactly know what that was, what it entailed, what it even meant, but the way I felt about her, the way I wanted to protect her, the things I wanted to give her, the amount of time I wanted to spend with her was different than I'd ever felt before.

That had to be love.

The second was freedom. She didn't have to worry about him showing up wherever she was, her phone filled with texts and voice mails of his abuse. She was going to live her life and experience the things she'd missed out on because of him.

That I would guarantee.

But there was one thing she hadn't yet told me.

One piece that didn't quite fit into the whole picture.

"Why didn't you ever call the police on him?" I pointed her face up at me. "You told me he's untouchable, but you never told me why."

She closed her legs around mine. "David comes from a family

who's involved in underground activity where he's high up in the chain of command. You'd think the police would be dying to get their hands on him and his family, but it's the opposite. He's in bed with the police—delivers an envelope of cash to the chief on the first of every month like clockwork." Her voice continuously softened with each sentence. "David and his family can do no wrong in Atlanta. So, you see, I couldn't go to anyone for help."

I'd suspected David was a bad dude, or Lily would have gone to the authorities. Therefore, I wasn't taken aback by the news. I just wondered how nefarious his family was, so I asked, "What type of illegal work are we talking about, Lily?"

"He supplies companies with illegal workers to keep their labor costs down. It's an empire, working off nothing but cash, that's completely off the books from both ends—theirs and the clients who hire them."

I almost wanted to laugh.

They could supply the entire East Coast with workers, and they still wouldn't bring in the revenue that the Spade and Cole families did.

If she'd said Mafia, organ trading, sex trafficking, drugs, or guns, his family's connections would run deep in a world that I wouldn't want to become the enemy of—but I would for her.

Sure, he had local connections that ran through Atlanta PD, possibly extending through surrounding states, but that didn't give him ties on a national level.

That also didn't downplay what he had done and continued to do to her; it just showed what I would be dealing with when I faced the bastard.

"Listen to me." I positioned my lips above hers. "I know what you're afraid of. I know you think I'm going to end up like Preston, that you were avoiding any type of commitment so you didn't get me involved. It's too late for that. I'm already involved, and I'm getting you out of this fucking mess."

"Brady…"

"And I'm doing it because I care about you. Because, at this point, I can't imagine my life without you. And because I won't allow him to destroy another second of your life."

She flattened her hands over mine. "If what happened to Preston happens to you, I'll never forgive myself, Brady. I won't survive it. I barely survived it then."

"Not something you even need to think about, never mind worry about."

She focused on my eyes, so much emotion still pouring from hers. "I can't imagine my life without you either." She ran her thumbs over my lips. "Or what I did to deserve you."

"I need you to do me a favor."

She didn't immediately huff out a laugh, but it happened after a bit of silence. "Okay."

"I need you to wrap your arms around me and kiss me."

Chapter Twenty-Four

LILY

I never understood or could relate to the saying, *You can't teach an old dog new tricks.*

Until now.

Because even though Brady had promised me that David wouldn't have access to me at the Beverly Hills location of the Cole and Spade Hotel, where I had just moved, I still scanned the lobby every time I walked in. And I inventoried all the faces around me after I stepped inside the elevator, prior to pressing the button to my floor, doing it again before I opened the door to my room.

The same was true this morning when I walked down the tarmac toward the Daltons' private plane, wondering if David would somehow pull up out of nowhere. Or when I climbed the steps and entered the cabin, I questioned if he would be sitting in one of the seats or couches. Or when I walked toward the galley, would he be there in the back, waiting for me?

When it came to David, I never knew what to expect.

So, I'd learned to anticipate him wherever I went.

Would that habit ever die? I couldn't imagine it would. Nor could

I fathom a day when I wouldn't fear his capabilities.

But the past two days, since the flowers had been delivered to Brady's house, my brain had taken a slight mental pause from David. Because, during those two days, I'd been completely wrapped up in Brady.

Spoiled.

Lavished.

And devoured.

That man was something special. Something perfect. Something I wanted and needed. And for as long as I'd fought this relationship, terrified that I was getting him involved in my mess, he'd assured me it was his choice.

And he chose me.

Before I left his house to move into his hotel, he promised I had nothing to worry about. That there was no reason to panic. The home I kept calling a palace had been built by him and he'd told me it was impenetrable. David had been able to reach the doorstep, where the flowers had been delivered, but he couldn't get through the walls. That also applied to his hotels and anytime I traveled with the Daltons or on my own.

According to Brady, I would be completely protected from here on out.

I didn't know how.

But I believed him, and I trusted him.

And as my guests boarded the jet and I greeted them in the cabin, Brady's promise began to make sense, and I understood just how he was going to make that happen from afar.

That insurance came in the form of Diesel, Dominick's passenger, the two going to Las Vegas, where we'd have a one-night layover and fly back to LA tomorrow. Although Dominick was tall and broad, like Brady, Diesel looked almost twice their size. He didn't have the body of a linebacker. More like a pro wrestler with muscles protruding from every part of him, a neck that was thicker than a tree trunk with tight, veiny skin, and hands like a catcher's mitt.

I hadn't worked for the Daltons for that long. I didn't know them as well as Aubrey. But my gut told me that Diesel wasn't a business associate of Dominick's, nor was he Dominick's bodyguard since neither he nor his family ever traveled with one.

I made sure the men had everything they needed and went to my seat in the galley, prepping for takeoff before I pulled out my phone to send Brady a text.

Me: *So...question. I'm not saying Dominick can't have a bodyguard, but given that one suddenly appeared, very randomly, seems more than just a coincidence. Which then makes me wonder, are you the reason why the largest man I've ever seen in my life is flying with me today?*

As I was strapping myself into the seat, the bubbles appeared under Brady's name, telling me he was typing.

Brady: *I might have had something to do with it.*

Me: *You got me a bodyguard?!*

Brady: *I told you, Lily, David isn't going to touch you or come anywhere near you. I can't guarantee that if I'm not there, but Diesel can. No one will fuck with that man—he'll eat them.*

Me: *HA! No, really, he's so large, I get the feeling he WOULD eat them.*

Me: *But also, I love the way you protect me.*

Me: *I really, really love it.*

Brady: *You'll be safe at the Cole and Spade Hotel in Vegas. I've got zero concerns about that. I just need to know that while you're out shopping and eating—things you'd better do, and do not fight me on that—that you're safe then as well.*

Brady: *If I hear you're only hanging out in your room...*

Me: *Your tongue will punish me? ;)*

Brady: *Don't send those words to me...not when you're that far* *away and not when all I can think about is eating your pussy.*

Me: *I die. <3*

Brady: *I also might have had something to do with the reservation you have for dinner tonight. It's at my favorite restaurant. I booked you a seat at the bar. I don't know how you feel about eating alone, but I thought the bar would be a good spot for that. Besides, Diesel is going to take you and be there with you, so you won't exactly be by yourself.*

Me: *You're so, so thoughtful. Thank you for taking care of me. I can't wait to try your fave restaurant.*

Me: *And thank you for Diesel. You're amazing. I hope you know that, and I hope you know how much I appreciate you.*

I peeked into the main cabin to check on my guests. Diesel was sitting on the couch, his frame far too wide to fit in one of the regular-sized seats. For the smallest of seconds, I envisioned David approaching us on the Strip in Vegas. Diesel wouldn't just palm him; he'd toss David straight through one of the metal grates on Las Vegas Boulevard.

There was no question I'd be safe with him.

Brady: *My family has known him for a long time, and all these years we've called him Diesel. I don't think I even know his real name. But I assure you, you're in good hands.*

Me: *When you told me nothing was going to happen to me, I believed you.*

Me: *But were you going to tell me, at any point, that you got me a bodyguard? Or were you just going to let me figure it out when this massive man started shadowing me?*

Brady: *It was a bomb I planned to drop before you landed. I figured I had a good hour or two before I sent that text.*

Me: *LOL.*

Brady: *I don't want to hide anything from you, so I want you to know that Dominick knows, which I'm sure you've figured out. I had* *to tell him to get Diesel on board. Your safety is also his number one concern.*

Me: *Is it strange that my boss knows I'm in danger-ish?*

Brady: *Your boss is the top entertainment lawyer in the country. He deals with celebrities and their protection for a living. Believe me, you're anything but strange to him.*

Brady: *He's also my best friend. A dude who has never seen me go wild for a woman until you. Even if David didn't exist, he'd want you protected. You're precious cargo, baby.*

The phone above my seat rang, and I quickly held it to my ear, listening to the pilot tell me we were about to take off. I hung up and checked the back exit, making sure it was locked, along with each of the cabinets and the restroom door. I made one final sweep of the cabin, asking Dominick and Diesel if they needed anything, and then I returned to my seat.

Me: *Don't growl when I say this, but you're quite possibly the sweetest man ever.*

Brady: *Sweet?*

Me: *Mmhmm. Extra sweet.*

Brady: *It's not a side I reveal often.*

Me: *Well, I'm obsessed with it. But I'm equally obsessed with your other side too. In fact, I'll take both—and lots of each.*

Brady: *Sounds like you're calling me perfect.*

Me: *What I'm calling you is my dream come true.*

Brady: *Fuck me, Lily. That is so hot.*

Me: *And I miss you. How's that for a topping?*

Brady: *Tell me how much.*

I stared at his words, thinking of how I'd felt this morning when I moved my things into his resort, a room that had at least twice the space of the previous hotel I'd been staying at. Something told me it wasn't a standard size either, that Brady had put me in an upgrade since it came with a walk-in closet, a seating area, a desk, and a full bar.

He was constantly taking care of me.

Thinking of me.

But it wasn't just that. It was the thought that tonight, when I got into bed, his arms wouldn't be around me. I wouldn't feel the warmth of his body. He wouldn't be the first thing I saw when I opened my eyes the next morning.

Things I'd grown to really love since sleeping at his house.

Things I was certainly going to miss during my trip to Vegas.

Me: *Knowing I'm not going to wake up to you makes me ache so hard.*

Me: *Honestly, the last two nights I spent at your house were everything I'd always wanted and never had. They were the best couple of days I'd had in years.*

Me: *Yes. Years.*

Brady: *Nothing makes me happier—aside from knowing you'll be back tomorrow.*

Me: *Does that mean I'll get to see you?*

Brady: *Fuck yes.*

Me: *Good. I can't wait.*

Chapter Twenty-Five

BRADY

"First order of business," I said while sitting at the conference room table in our corporate office, glancing around the large oval, where Macon, Cooper, Jo, Rowan, Rhett, and Ridge had joined me. "We need a second jet. And we need one immediately."

Rhett held up his hand. "Hold on a second—"

"What am I holding for?" I barked, cutting him off, not liking the way he had begun his reply. "We discussed a second jet months ago. It's apparent how badly we need one. That's why this isn't a discussion. This is me informing you that our company is buying one."

"You mean, *you* need a new jet now," Rhett responded.

There was no question; he was right.

But I didn't appreciate his tone, the sharpness of his words, or that he hadn't instantly agreed.

I leaned my arms on the table to get closer to the motherfucker as he glared from the spot directly across from me. "I'll be traveling back and forth to Edinburgh for the next six months or so. Our jet is booked out for weeks. It's not going to be available every time I need it. That's a fucking problem."

Rhett smirked. "That's a Brady problem. That's not a Cole and Spade Hotels problem."

This fucking asshole.

The one thing I had in my pocket was that my assistant had informed me there were several occasions when the Cole family had tried to book the jet and it was unavailable, causing them to take commercial flights. According to her, they had been just as unpleased as when it had happened to me. That told me Rhett wanted this jet. He was acting this way because I'd prompted the conversation and I was asking for it.

Which gave me an idea.

"The truth is," I started, "it would be beneficial if we actually purchased two jets. There are seven partners, plus our senior team, not even counting legal. Wouldn't it be nice to have Jenner only bill us for his hours rather than airtime and fuel, too, since he has to take his own jet whenever he travels for us? Which you know is billed at a marked-up Dalton rate, not at cost."

I looked at Jo for a rebuttal, knowing she'd surely have something to say about her husband.

She laughed and replied, "Do you really think my husband would charge us the full rate?"

"No fucking doubt about it," Cooper replied. "He knows we can afford it. He's giving us no breaks on his time, travel, or any expenses incurred."

Jo winked. "You're right."

Point proven.

Now, I needed to rub things in a little more, so I said, "Our hotel fleet has doubled since the merger. Edinburgh will be up and running in less than a year."

I nodded toward the bastard across from me. "You're looking at properties for us to purchase, and once one is bought, that'll take you away for an extended period."

I glanced at the other partners. "The rest of you travel nonstop. You're facing another wave of remodels and purchases, and that'll all take you away from LA, and you'll need a jet to get to wherever you're going."

I leaned back and crossed my arms. "The company can afford it, and we could certainly use the expense. Three isn't outlandish. It's more than reasonable for an organization as large as ours."

Ridge looked at Rhett. "It's not a bad idea."

Out of the two, Ridge had warmed to us first.

Not scalding—shit, not even toasty—just a hint of heat to take away the chill. That was where he stood with us.

"I think it's an excellent idea," Rowan chimed in. "I tried to book a flight to Banff last week, and the plane wasn't available."

"We flew fucking commercial," Cooper added, clearly annoyed. "Because Macon was in Hawaii with Brooklyn."

I rolled my eyes. "Don't get me going on Macon's Hawaii trips." I groaned. "He's the reason I've also had to fly commercial."

"Hey," Macon countered, "it's not my fault I'm more organized than you fools and I book my trips far in advance."

I tapped the screen of my phone as it sat on the table, pulling up my email, where I'd pre-written some information to the team, and I hit Send. "If you all check your inboxes, you'll see the planes that are available from the manufacturer I've selected. There are many builders. This one has impressed me the most. Their headquarters is in Dallas. I'll be going there soon to look at each of the jets on that list."

"And you're bringing us with you?" Rhett asked.

The asshole was suddenly interested?

I didn't play that way.

"That wasn't an invitation," I told him. "I'm going to Dallas alone. If I decide one of the jets is right for us, I'll make the purchase. You can then go look at the remaining planes to see if there's a third one you want to buy." I glanced at both families. "If anyone is opposed to this plan, speak now."

Not that I'd listen, but it was only right to give them a chance to voice their opinions.

Silence ticked through the room.

Until Ridge said, "I'd like to hear about what went down in Edinburgh."

Finally, a question that made fucking sense.

Before I answered, I peeked at my brothers, waiting for a smart-ass comment on why I hadn't been in the office for the last two days.

They knew I was home.

They also knew I wasn't alone.

But the two of them were tight-lipped.

Pleased that they'd refrained, I said, "The governing officials weren't happy about some of the changes I'd proposed to the facade of the property. They want the structure to be uniform with those around it. They're afraid I'm modernizing it too much."

Jo's brows shot up. "How did the conversation go? Or maybe I should ask, who bent first?"

"I told them to go fuck themselves," I replied, chuckling.

Cooper whistled. "Scotland doesn't realize who they've gotten in bed with. Poor bastards don't stand a chance."

"Trust me, they realize now," I said to my brother.

"You mean to tell me they're letting you change the exterior?" Rhett asked.

I licked my lips. "No. They told me to go fuck myself."

The room burst out in laughter.

"Sounds like you've met your match." Rowan snorted.

I held the edge of the table, hating that I had to admit, "I have to play nice, or they won't let the sale go through. They've made that clear. All I can do is clean up the exterior and give it the polish that it needs. As for the interior, they have zero say. That's a hundred percent me."

"So, things are moving along," Macon said. "When will you be closing?"

"Three weeks," I answered. "The plane will be purchased before, allowing my weekly commute to be seamless."

"Because your commute back and forth to Scotland is our top priority," Rhett said, his posture telling me he was ready to go to battle. "When, really, you should be moving there during the rehab, so you don't tie up the plane."

"I'm happy to buy the plane with my own money," I told him, leaning even further into my chair, my arms crossed over my chest. "I'll bill the company for the gas and the crew. Your choice."

"You just don't give a fuck, do you?" Rhett asked. "It's not about what's right for Cole and Spade—"

"There's where you're wrong." I slapped my hand on the table. "I do give a fuck. Edinburgh is going to be one of the largest rehabs we've ever done. I did my damn homework, and when that hotel is up and running, it's going to be one of our most profitable. But what you've neglected to ask me is why I'm not moving there." My eyes narrowed. "Ask the question, Rhett."

He continued to stare and said nothing.

"I'm revamping our payroll system. The same way I streamlined the check-in process for our guests and a backend system for our entire network of hotels. Had you read the email I sent yesterday while I was out, then I wouldn't have had to tell you. You would have already known this." I put up my finger when I could tell a response was about to howl out of him. "Now, you're going to ask who put me in charge of that task or what gives me the right to rewrite the system. That answer is me. As the chief technical officer, I have every right. And that's not something I'm comfortable doing from afar. I need to work with accounting to make sure every step of that process is done correctly." I rubbed my palms together. "Do you still call that not giving a fuck?"

He stood from his chair. "I've heard enough."

I nodded. "I don't blame you."

Ridge's head fell and shook. "You're certainly going to have your hands full, Brady." He pointed at the door. "I'm going to follow him out."

When they were gone and the door was shut, I looked at Rowan and said, "Your fucking brothers."

"What? That was the biggest improvement we've had," she replied. "Rhett wanted to choke you out and didn't. I would consider that massive progress." She smiled.

"Agreed," Macon, the goddamn golden retriever, said. "You can't convince me that wasn't one of our best meetings yet."

Rowan put her hand on Cooper's shoulder. "Congratulate your brother for not raising his voice at Rhett and ripping him a new asshole, please."

Cooper laughed at his girl. "Fuck shop talk." He looked at me. "I want to know why Diesel was on Dominick's flight to Vegas today."

"Jesus Christ," I growled.

"Diesel was on Dom's flight?" Macon said to Cooper.

"I can confirm that he was," Jo said, smiling.

"Oh, this is about to get spicy." Macon grinned at me.

"For the record, our brother hired Diesel to protect Lily, Dominick's flight attendant," Cooper replied. "So, when he tries to say he didn't and he attempts to avoid the topic altogether, you'll know the truth."

I pounded my fist down. "I'm in the fucking room, you know."

"She isn't just some flight attendant, is she, Brady?" Rowan asked. "She's your girlfriend."

"Who you haven't even admitted to us that you're dating," Cooper added.

I looked at Jo. "You're over there, fucking smiling, and I'm positive you have plenty to say. Do you want to come out with it or stay silent?"

"I'm enjoying every second of this without feeling the need to say a word." Jo winked.

I knew once this conversation was really had, I would get all the shit.

I deserved it for the things I'd said to them over the years.

But still, fuck that.

"Let me also say this," Cooper voiced, eyeing the hell out of me. "I know you're sitting over there, scheming your way out of this little chat we're about to have. But it's time you come clean, especially since we know you've been into her for a while."

"You don't know shit," I barked.

"No?" Cooper smirked. "The two of you hooked up when we were in Tampa. She's the reason you bailed on us that first night." His brows then furrowed. "Tell me I'm wrong."

Was it time to finally pull the plug?

Damn it.

"You're not wrong about the night in Tampa," I told them. "But you're wrong about when this all started."

"Now, I'm even more intrigued," Macon gloated.

I explained to them how I'd seen her in the airport when I flew commercially to Edinburgh and how she was—fortunately for me— my flight attendant in first class. I went on to admit how she'd taken off while I was asleep and the six-month gap that took place before I randomly bumped into her on the Daltons' jet.

I didn't give every detail. But I gave them enough.

The amount of pleasure on all their faces was fucking palpable.

"The one who left her mark before she got away," Jo said. "That's why you never stopped thinking about her. You didn't stop, did you?" She paused, knowing she wouldn't get an answer. "For once, you got a taste of your own medicine, and now, you're talking about her with dreamy eyes." She put her hand on my arm. "Whenever I fly with Jenner and happen to mention you, she has the same look on her face. Keep going. I need more."

Before I could say anything, Cooper practically sang, "Do you know what I am? I'm blown the fuck away. My big brother is finally ready to settle down. Shit, I never thought I'd see the day."

As wild as it was, I was here.

Ready.

But it was time to explain the elephant that stood between Lily and me.

"Guys, things are complicated, and I don't say that lightly." I ran my hand over the top of my head. "I've got it handled. That's why Diesel is on board and why he'll shadow her and make sure she's protected the entire time she's in Vegas and going forward."

"Going forward?" Macon mirrored. "Fuck. That doesn't sound good."

"She has a nasty ex-boyfriend." I ground my teeth together. "A motherfucker I'm ready to kill because he won't stop fucking with her. You know what that asshole did the other day? He sent flowers to my damn house with a card that called her his wife."

"And he still has a pulse?" Macon asked. "I'm shocked."

I was quiet for a moment. "He stalks her. Blows up her phone. Sends photos. Says things to her that makes my fucking blood boil." I flattened my hand on the hair I'd been rubbing. "I got her a new phone. She now has Diesel. I'm hoping, between the two, things with him will die down and he'll realize I don't fuck around and she's no longer his."

"She's yours," Rowan said.

I nodded. "I want her to be."

"Damn," Cooper said.

"Damn is right," Macon agreed.

Rowan looked at Jo. "I'm melting. Like legit, straight-up

swooning over here."

"Same, girl. Same," Jo replied.

"Never mind the girls," Cooper said, laughing. "What if her ex doesn't stop? What if this is just the beginning?"

My mind had been circling that question, thinking about it endlessly.

"I'll handle it," I told the group.

"How?" Macon asked.

"I'll make sure the dude doesn't have any fingers left to dial her fucking number or a tongue to talk to her with."

The room turned silent until Cooper said, "I've never seen you like this."

"Because Brady's in love," Jo replied. "Just like the rest of us."

"For the record, I'll take full credit for every bit of this," Macon said, grinning like a damn fool. "Because if I hadn't booked our jet to Hawaii, then you never would have flown commercial, and you wouldn't have met her."

While everyone laughed, I flipped him off. Even though the dickhead was right.

And for just that one instance, I was relieved he'd booked the jet before I'd had the chance.

"You know what hits me the hardest about you three?" Rowan said, looking at each of the guys. "When it comes to love, there isn't anything you boys wouldn't do for your girls."

• • •

Me: *You know what I hate?*

Lily: *What?*

Me: *When I take a breath and I don't smell you in the air.*

Lily: *Hands down one of the sweetest things anyone has ever said to me.*

Me: *That's the second time you've called me sweet in one day.*

Lily: *You've earned it, Mr. Spade. ;)*

Lily: *Do you want to know something I love?*

Me: *Tell me.*

Lily: *That I've thought about you all day. Not just because I've been with Diesel or that I have a dinner reservation coming up with food you recommended that I can't wait to devour. But because I've been walking the Strip and popping into stores—things I haven't done in a long time. Things I've missed. Things I'm doing because of YOU.*

Me: *Freedom sounds beautiful on you.*

She replied with a photograph, a selfie of her standing in front of the Bellagio fountains. The smile on her face was as wide as I'd ever seen it. But there was more. There was a happiness in her eyes that I'd only witnessed once before. It was the morning after the flowers had been delivered—when she woke in my arms, when I took her mind off everything, when it was just us in that bedroom, nothing and no one else.

That was the same grin staring back at me.

Me: *And freedom looks gorgeous on you.*

• • •

Lily: *That dinner…there are no words. I ate my weight in Wagyu, and I regret nothing. And the sides? I don't know what they put in that sweet potato casserole, but I will never recover from it. This next sentence is said with a screamy voice: I can't believe you paid for my dinner. Also screaming: You shouldn't have done that. Now with a loving voice: But it was so, so sweet of you. Thank you isn't enough, but it's all I have.*

Me: *More sweetness…*

Lily: *I can't help it. You're like the chocolate lava cake I'm still inhaling—mouthwateringly sweet.*

Me: *God, you're fucking cute.*

Lily: *Can I tell you what I hate?*

Me: *I suppose it's your turn. Go.*

Lily: *That when I'm in my room later, you won't be at the hotel to knock on my door.*

Me: *Don't tease me, Lily. You know I'll get on a plane right now and come to Vegas.*

Lily: *Would you really?*

Me: *For you, in a fucking second.*

Lily: *If I wasn't coming back to LA tomorrow, I might ask you to do that. But I'll get to see you once you leave work, and I'll get to spend the night with you, and I'll get to kiss you whenever I want. So, I think I can wait. It'll be difficult, LOL, but I'll make it.*

Me: *The places I want to kiss you…*

• • •

Lily: *Good night, B. Have the sweetest dreams.*

Me: *B…yes, I like that. Good night, baby.*

Lily: *xo*

Chapter Twenty-Six

LILY

I wasn't even all the way through the lobby, clinging to the small envelope that had just been placed in my hand, when one of the hotel employees noted my direction and rushed over to the exit to open it for me. I thanked him on my way out the door, where Brady was parked along the curb, another employee meeting me at the passenger side of Brady's Maserati, opening it enough to give me room to climb in.

It wasn't just the boss who made me feel like a queen; it was everyone who worked here too.

But today, they could try their hardest, and it still wouldn't take away the anxiety that was eating at my stomach.

"There's my gorgeous girl," Brady said before my butt even hit the seat.

He spoke like he hadn't seen me in months.

But that simply wasn't the case. The last several weeks had been full of encounters like this one. Pockets of time off, in between my flights with the Daltons, filled with nothing but him.

With a hand that wouldn't stop shaking, I secured the seat belt around me and attempted a smile as I finished. "Hello to you too."

He took in every inch of me before his gaze returned to my face. Still, the car stayed parked right where it was, showing he was in no hurry to leave.

"That's new, isn't it?" He nodded toward my dress.

I searched for air as I whispered, "It is."

Despite how I was feeling, I still couldn't believe he'd noticed.

Since we'd started dating, he'd seen almost my whole wardrobe. I'd lived in a uniform from the very beginning of my career, so I kept it casual during my downtime. An excessive amount of clothes had never been a priority. But once Diesel had become my bodyguard, I'd found myself doing much more exploring, and with that came shopping.

"Did you get that dress in Charleston?"

The last location I'd been with the Daltons, this time on a trip with Jenner that was for only one night before we returned to LA this afternoon.

"Yes, on King Street. Jo suggested I go there, she said it has the best shopping."

"Light pink. That's not like you at all." His hand was on my neck, just below my jaw, his fingers brushing my skin, as if he was trying to warm me.

I glanced down the front of me. The shade and color were very outside my box. I wasn't one for pastels. I liked boldness. I also wasn't one for pink. I preferred jewel tones. Poor Diesel had stood inside the store with me for far too long while I debated over several different dresses, eventually picking this one.

"I guess I wanted to try something different."

He nodded his head as he did another sweep. "And it worked. So fucking well." His stare was unhurried, like swinging in a hammock on a spring Sunday afternoon. "Kiss me."

"You know I have lipstick on."

He moved closer. "You know I don't care."

A trait I hadn't realized I was looking for until I met Brady. A man who was unafraid to get his lips stained in public—that was how much he wanted to kiss me.

I could only hope the sensation of his lips would force the anxiousness to die down. It would be short-lived. Once I gave him this envelope, the feeling was going to quickly return.

Our faces met in the center of the car, our lips aligning, a hunger coming from him. He didn't care that his employees were rushing past us in both directions, helping guests with their luggage and parking cars.

He just wanted this embrace.

Here and now.

And that was something I would never grow tired of, even if my head, at this very moment, wasn't in a good place.

"Do you want to know one of the sexiest sights?" he asked as he pulled away.

"Please."

Anything to occupy my mind.

"Watching you walk out of my hotel, knowing you were on that bed and that you showered in that bathroom and that your clothes are hanging in that closet." He let out a small but deep groan. "There's something so fucking hot about it."

"Why?"

"Because I know every minute you spend in there"—he briefly glanced toward the entrance—"you were reminded of me. Call me selfish, but I don't care, it's what turns me on." His eyes narrowed as he looked at me. "You're enjoying the hotel, aren't you?"

I nodded. "Yes."

I wished so badly it weren't temporary and that I didn't have my résumé in the hands of multiple private jet companies across the country, waiting to hear if they had any open positions. I could feel the sweat on my fingers as I gripped the paper package, a haunting realization that once I left LA, I wouldn't know what things would look like or what would happen to Brady and me. A thought that continued to nag at me even though I was trying hard to push it away.

I needed something lighter, something that hid the shakiness in my voice, so I added, "Now that I've done a bit of traveling with the Daltons, I've stayed at quite a few of your hotels, and they're all so incredible." But the more I attempted to fake how I was feeling, the weaker my smile got. "Vegas, Charleston, Manhattan, Seattle, Chicago, Miami, Beverly Hills—I can't choose a favorite."

"Edinburgh will be."

"Yes." I pushed a laugh through my lips. "For more reasons than one."

"It's good to have you back. Charleston was too far away." The narrowness of his eyes deepened. So did his gaze. "But something's off. Something's bothering you. What's going on, Lily?"

"Oh boy."

His brows furrowed. "What?"

I swallowed, the tightness attacking my throat. "When I was coming down to meet you, passing the front desk on my way out, one of the front-desk clerks stopped me and handed me this." I wiggled the envelope, my skin so slippery and my fingers jittery that I almost dropped it.

"What is it?"

"I took a quick peek before I came out here to meet you and…" My other hand went to my chest. "I had to stop. I couldn't look at it anymore." I put the padded mailer on his lap.

"Let me get this straight. I don't know what this is"—he lifted the envelope—"but you're telling me that one of my employees handed you this package without Diesel intercepting it?"

"Diesel came to the lobby with me. I got a call from the Daltons' assistant to schedule my next flight, so while I stalled to talk to her, he headed home. He's off tonight because I'm with you. And we're talking about a matter of seconds—that's literally how long I was alone."

"I'm not happy with anything you just said."

He lifted the top flap and pulled out the photographs, flipping through a stack that showed snapshots of me in different locations—walking the Strip in Vegas, shopping in Charleston, eating pizza in Manhattan, visiting Pike Place Market in Seattle, walking the Navy Pier in Chicago, sunbathing in a bikini on South Beach in Miami. But it wasn't just my travels that were included. There were also shots of me coming in and out of the Beverly Hills hotel, of me in Brady's car, of us pulling into his house.

With each picture he passed, his grimace grew.

Until there was nothing but rage in his eyes.

Before Brady, a look like that would have terrified me.

But not with him.

With him, there was no fear at all.

All it did was make me fall harder.

"Was there a note?"

I took the empty package off his lap and rubbed my finger over the name that had been written on the front. "That's David's handwriting. He didn't need to leave a note. Because now, I don't have to suspect if he's watching. I know he is." I set the envelope back down, disgusted to even touch it. "That's better than a note, and that was his intention."

He ground his jaw before he said, "This is the first time you've heard from him since the flower delivery, correct?"

"Yes."

"And there haven't been any texts or calls from him?"

"No, nothing."

I swore there was smoke coming out of his nose when he replied, "Stay right here. Don't move."

"Where are you going?"

"I'm going to fucking fire someone."

Before I could say another word, he was getting out of the car. He pulled one of the bellboys aside, their conversation brief, and while Brady disappeared inside the hotel, the bellboy positioned himself in front of Brady's vehicle. He looked in all directions, just like Diesel did whenever he was with me, which told me he was standing guard.

Oh God.

I felt awful.

My intention certainly hadn't been to get anyone fired. But when it came to David, I felt I needed to be fully transparent with Brady. I didn't want any surprises, and I knew he didn't either, so there was no way I could refrain from telling him about the photographs.

But really, they had come completely out of the blue. I hadn't heard a thing from David for the last few weeks. A break that was needed and appreciated.

In the time that had passed, my gut told me he wasn't gone.

A feeling that was similar to an invasion.

That somehow, some way, he was still here.

Watching.

Waiting.

Which I now knew was true.

What I didn't know was David's next move. That was the scary part. Because as loud as these pictures were, his silence was alarming.

When I couldn't look at the door for another second, waiting for Brady to return, I took out my phone to text Aubrey. Anything to get my mind off this.

Me: *How's the babe?*

Aubrey: *He's still the gold medal winner of crying. Dear Lord, I hope it stops soon. Aside from that, he's an adorable, very hungry, very poo-ey machine. And I'm a very tired and very in-love mama.*

Me: *Aw! I need to snuggle him soon.*

Aubrey: *I'm home for one more week. Come anytime—you know that.*

Me: *Your maternity leave flew by, girl.*

Aubrey: *For you. Not for me. LOL.*

Me: *Ha-ha, true.*

Aubrey: *How's the job search going?*

Me: *It's in full force. I'm confident I'll have something within the week. I've applied everywhere. I have to imagine someone is hiring.*

Aubrey: *With the résumé you have, your phone will soon be ringing off the hook. Anyone would be so lucky to have you.*

Me: *You're way too kind.*

Aubrey: *I'm honest. Knowing you took care of the Daltons while I was gone was the biggest relief. You're an awesome flight attendant, lady. I bet they're going to be very sorry they don't have another position for you.*

I quickly checked the doorway and saw Brady heading for the car.

Me: *Heart you.*

Me: *I'll keep you posted about the new job.*

Aubrey: *You'd better. xo*

He slid into the driver's seat, his hand going to my thigh while he gripped the steering wheel. "That will never happen again. They now know any package or mail has to go through Diesel or me—not you."

"I feel sick to my stomach that someone just got in trouble because of me."

He exhaled, the movement of air sending me a whiff of his cologne. "I didn't fire anyone. I just lectured the hell out of them. And I also met with the head of security to tell him to pull the camera feed of the front desk. I want to see if that motherfucker walked into my hotel and handed over that envelope or if he had someone else do it."

While he was breathing hard, I was holding in all my air. "What are you going to do with that info once you have it?"

"Do you mean, am I going to go to the police?" He shook his head. "No." His hand left my leg and landed on the gearshift, the engine revving as he shifted into first and pulled out of the hotel. "To be honest, I don't know what my plan is, but at least that will tell me if he's in LA or if he's having someone else do his dirty work."

"And what about Diesel? Did you call him and give him an earful too?"

"No. And not because you wouldn't want me to, which I know. But because you should have been safe in the fucking lobby of my hotel if my employees had just done their goddamn job."

I tried swallowing the lump in my throat. "Brady...it's him."

He looked at me when he reached the Stop sign. "How do you know that?"

"Because he would never have anyone else put their eyes on me. He wouldn't want them getting that intimate. He's too possessive. Every bit of this, down to the handwriting on the card he sent with the flowers, is all him."

"When you put it that way, I'm not surprised."

I put my hand on top of his. "I'm sorry. I'm so sorry."

He glanced at me even though we were in traffic. "This isn't your fault, Lily."

"But it is. All of this drama is because of me."

I could feel the emotion start to rise. I could feel it hammering in my chest.

Who starts a relationship this way?

Who comes with this kind of baggage?

When I'd texted Aubrey, it had given my brain a rest. But now, it was right back to the reality of the situation.

"Fuck, Brady, this is nuts. Every bit of this—"

"No, we're not going there. We're not letting him ruin another second—do you hear me?" He was at a red light, so his eyes were on me. "That dude isn't fucking special enough to warrant any more conversation about him. This is about us, not him. He doesn't have a place in this car, and he sure as hell doesn't have a place in this night I have planned."

I flattened my hand against my chest. "You're right." With my other hand, I squeezed the top of his fingers. "This is about us."

"I don't want you to be wrecked over this. I want us to have a good night—a night you deserve, baby."

The smile wasn't like the one I had given him earlier. It was smaller, weaker. Like a scab that was about to fall off. I wasn't going to continue to make David the topic. I was moving on from him completely, shifting my concentration, so I added, "What do you have planned?"

"I was going to take you down to Malibu and hit up Nobu and walk the beach after dinner but..." His voice drifted off as he analyzed my face. "You know what? I have a better idea."

"Yeah?"

He chuckled. "Tell me, Lily, are you afraid to get dirty in that dress?"

"Dirty?"

"And possibly messy."

I shrugged. "I have no idea what you mean...but as long as I'm with you, I'm not afraid of anything."

"The list of reasons I'm so fucking wild about you keeps adding up."

I giggled as he flew through the green light, weaving down several streets before he pulled into an In-N-Out Burger. I thought he was just turning around until he circled the lot and got in line at the drive-through.

That was when my laugh reached a much louder volume. "Burgers? That's your idea?"

"You hate it?"

"No." I moved my hand from his fingers to his arm. "I'll take casual over fancy any day."

He grinned at me and rolled down his window, saying into the speaker, "I'll take two Double Doubles with chilies and two Animal-Style fries."

"Anything else?" was said through the intercom.

"Two Cokes."

"You can pull up."

He paid at the window, collected the bag of food and parked behind the restaurant, handing me my wrapped burger and container of fries, positioning my Coke in the cupholder.

"I'm going to tell you two reasons we're here right now." He popped a saucy fry into his mouth. "The first is that even though Nobu is a restaurant I can't live without, I've been there before with other women. You deserve better, and I should have thought of that when I planned our night."

I unwrapped my burger, and the slippery bun, the chunky slice of tomato, and melted cheese proved just how messy this was going to get—and I loved it. "It doesn't offend me, Brady. I don't have jealousy issues like that. I know you've gone out with a lot of women. I would think there are very few restaurants in LA where you haven't taken someone." I winked. "But I'll also say this: I wore this dress because I knew you were going to take me somewhere nice. I'm just as happy— honestly, I'm even happier—in yoga pants and a T-shirt, wolfing down a Double Double and Animal-Style fries."

He wiped his fingers on a napkin and moved them to my face. "Something else that's so fucking hot about you." He finished chewing. "Reason two is that I've never brought another woman here before."

"That doesn't surprise me. Considering who you are and what you can afford, I'm sure they wanted the best."

"But when I tell you why I didn't bring them here, it will." He fanned his fingers over my cheek, keeping them there while I took a bite of my burger, attempting to lick the corners of my mouth, but knowing my face was the mess he'd warned me about earlier. "Going all the way back to high school, when I first got my license, this was where I came when shit got hard. When things spiraled out of control. When I needed a fucking break from everything and everyone around me. I'd order from the drive-through, and I'd sit in my car, just like this, and eat and give my brain a rest."

My eyes briefly closed, relating to that emotion. "I get that. On every level."

"College was no different. Post-college was the same." His hand moved to my chin. "When you showed me that package from David, I wanted to find that motherfucker. I wanted to wrap my hands around his throat. I wanted to do everything in my power to make sure that bastard never contacted you again." His voice rose, sharpened. But I felt the wave start to fall, the crest sinking into the top of the ocean as he said, "Sometimes, pouring myself a drink isn't enough. Neither is going to the gym, or out for a run, or hitting the bag as hard as I fucking can. I need something more."

"And that's when you come here, like you did tonight."

"With you." He wiped the corners of my mouth with his thumb and sucked off whatever was on his skin.

"You get turned on by me walking out of your hotel." I nodded toward his hand. "But whatever you just did, that's what does it for me."

He laughed. "That shit was good too."

I allowed a few moments of silence before I said, "I'm honored you took me to your place."

He took a bite of his burger, his mouth instantly cleaned with a napkin. "You know how fucking ridiculous that sounds? My place is a goddamn fast-food restaurant."

"Mine was a coffee shop in Atlanta. A little hole-in-the-wall that couldn't even make a latte and never had any paper towels in the restroom, so the floor was always wet from everyone's hands air-drying. I didn't care, I loved it." I took a drink of my Coke. "They had these cute little almond cookies that were bite-sized and chewy and kinda gooey—so yum—and I would order a bag of them and drink my black coffee. Nothing made me happier." I plowed several fries into my mouth. "What I'm saying is, who cares where the place is? What matters is that you have a place." I licked off the tiny onion that had been dangling on the burger for dear life. "And now, I know what yours is, and now, you know mine."

His stare intensified as his hands freed from the food and moved to my body. "You think the two of us are so different. But we're not."

"Can I tell you something?"

He nodded.

"The list of reasons I'm so fucking wild about you keeps adding up," I told him, using his own words.

His laughter filled the silence. "Kiss me."

"But I have In-N-Out sauce all over me."

He moved inches away from my face. "And you know I don't care."

Chapter Twenty-Seven

BRADY

My driver was about fifteen minutes early, so when I got to the plane, none of the crew was waiting for me at the bottom of the stairs. My unexpected arrival was even more apparent when I climbed the steps and walked into the cabin, looking toward the back, where Lily was bent over, taking bottles out of a box and arranging them in a cabinet. She hadn't bothered to bend her knees and crouch down. She was doing this all from a standing position, her ass high in the air, like I was behind her, pounding her in doggy style.

Fuck me, it was one hell of a view.

A view I'd seen a few hours ago, when she walked naked from my bed to the bathroom to shower and get ready for this flight—a quick one-day round trip that she didn't know I would be on or that I'd paid for.

I nodded at Diesel, sitting on the couch on the right side of the plane, and quietly made my way toward the galley. I didn't want to put my hands on her from behind and scare the shit out of her. Not when David was looming in these woods, which I was sure made her on edge.

So, I gave her a warning and said, "Now, that's one hell of an ass," and I halted in the doorway of the galley.

She froze, face pointed toward the ground, as though she was processing the statement and the voice that had spoken it, before she lifted and turned toward me. "Thank God it's you."

"Hi, baby." I wrapped my hands around her waist and pulled her closer.

The smile didn't take long to grow across her mouth. "What are you doing here?"

"I'm your passenger."

She gazed up at me with eyes so wide. "We're taking you to Dallas?"

"You shouldn't be shocked that I'd pay the Daltons to use their jet just so I could have you as my flight attendant."

She set her arms on my shoulders. "But I am. That's always the case when it comes to your decisions and the way they make me feel. Especially because you were with me last night and early this morning, and since this is only a day trip, you'll probably be with me tonight too." I went to reply, and she continued, "You're not sick of me yet?"

"Not even a little."

She nipped her lip. "I thought I was the only one who couldn't get enough. I'm glad I'm not alone."

I kissed her, making it last long enough that I not only took her breath away, but also reminded her that her lips were mine. "I'll let you finish up here. I've got some work to do."

"Do you want anything? A drink? Food?"

"Just some coffee, but don't rush. I've already had one. I don't need a second one anytime soon. Do your thing and come join me when you're done."

"Can I tell you a secret?"

I nodded.

She traced her hands down my chest, moving slowly before they fell to her sides. "Knowing you're the kind of man who would book a jet just to have me as your flight attendant makes me want you even more. And *more* is a word that, well, I didn't think was possible."

"I'll remember that tonight." I rubbed my thumb over her cheek, giving her a smirk, and I joined Diesel in the main cabin. "How are you doing, buddy?"

"All's good, my man."

Since our Vegas hotel was a casino, our IT department had developed software that scanned the faces of everyone who entered our gaming area, ensuring guests weren't wearing disguises to try to hide their identities. When a player was banned from our casino for reasons like cheating, card counting, or acting inappropriately, they were not allowed back. That didn't stop them from wearing fake facial hair, wigs, glasses, or hats in an attempt to throw us off.

When I'd spoken to the head of security of that hotel, I'd told him to use that software to comb through the video footage from Beverly Hills to check if David was the one to enter the hotel or if, at any point, he'd tried to hide who he was.

Knowledge, especially when it came to this motherfucker, was power.

The head of security had worked all night on this project. He raked through all the video feed—not just for the last forty-eight hours, but since the day Lily had moved in.

He'd emailed me his findings this morning while I was on my way to the airport.

Findings I didn't fucking like.

"We have a bigger problem on our hands than I originally thought," I told Diesel, keeping my voice low.

He didn't have a phone, a tablet, or even a newspaper in his hands—when this plane was grounded, his eyes were on the interior and exterior of the jet to protect Lily. So, when I spoke, it took less than a second before he looked at me.

"Tell me the details." He crossed his massive tree-trunk legs.

"As you know, Lily got a package of photographs delivered to the hotel."

Diesel hadn't just been told about the photos; he'd been sent copies since, in each of the locations they'd been taken, Diesel had been with Lily.

"I just found out that David was the one who delivered the package to the front desk."

"I was sure it was a gofer."

I turned on the couch to face him, moving my laptop bag off my shoulder and onto the seat beside me. "I was too." I glanced at the galley, hearing Lily working back there, but not seeing her. "Lily didn't agree; she knew it was him, but, fuck, I couldn't imagine this asshole coming all the way to the West Coast to hand-deliver some photos. Which then got me thinking. Was he the one taking them, or was he having someone else do the work?"

"Don't even fucking tell me," Diesel groaned. "It's been him all along, hasn't it?"

His voice was even large, carrying across the entire cabin, loud enough that Lily poked her head in and said, "Is everything all right?" She glanced from me to Diesel and then back to me. "You're talking about David, aren't you?" Instead of waiting for a response, she came closer and sat on the other side of my laptop. "What happened?"

I didn't want to hide anything from her.

At the same time, I didn't want to make her more anxious about the situation than she already was.

I kept my posture relaxed and my voice even-toned as I said, "It's been confirmed that it was David who delivered the package to the hotel. He attempted to go incognito, wearing a hat and a mustache, he doesn't have facial hair in any of the pictures we have of him, so we know he was trying to fool us."

"You have pictures of him?" Lily asked.

I hadn't asked her to provide any. I didn't want her to dig into a past she was desperate to forget. With the help of my assistant and the head of security, scouring online, we'd had enough documentation to make a comparison.

For someone who worked in an illegal, underground business, the asshole wasn't too careful about what he posted. There were far too many photographs of him on various social media sites.

That was his first mistake.

But what that told me was, there would be other mistakes. David wasn't careful. Which just meant I needed to find more of his mistakes to hit him where it hurt.

"My team has photos, yes," I told her. "What my head of security found was that he's been to the hotel multiple times. So far, he's only stayed in the lobby, but he's parked his ass there for hours on end, obviously waiting for you to come and go, so he can photograph you."

Her back straightened, and she wrapped her arms around herself, like a draft had blown in. "And to get close to me."

A thought that made my goddamn hands clench.

"Seems that way," I replied.

"So, we know it's him in LA." Diesel's leg dropped from the way it was crossed, and now that both of his feet were on the carpet, he leaned his arms on his thighs. "We know he's come to the hotel more than once. We know he's hiding his face, thinking he's outsmarting us." He paused. "What about the different locations? Was that him too? Or a PI?"

I moved the laptop bag and slid beside Lily, putting my arm around her. I fucking hated that she had to hear this. And I fucking hated that she'd been manipulated by this scumbag. "I think he's tracking this plane, following the flight paths. Maybe he's flying private, maybe commercial, but he has the means to get on a plane either way once he finds out where she's going." I let that statement settle. "What I don't like is that aside from taking pictures of her, he's not doing anything else. He's not threatening her or texting or calling."

"He's also not trying to get into her room at your hotel," Diesel said.

I shook my head. "He's never been on any of the elevators or entered the stairwells." I held her tighter, emphasizing those points.

"And in any of the locations he's followed us to, he's never attempted to get into her room or stop her on the street or approach her in any way," Diesel said. "He's just sitting quiet."

The way he looked at me told me he was thinking the same thing.

David was sitting quietly for now, but the pictures he'd delivered were a message.

Things were building.

And a build only led to one thing.

An explosion.

"That's not like him," Lily admitted. "He's not the quiet kind of guy. He's a talker—from the moment he wakes up to when he falls asleep. Words are his weapon, and he uses them nonstop." She gradually turned toward me. "Before getting my new phone, he was reaching out multiple times a day, throwing around all these accusations about you and about us."

"But I've stopped him from being able to reach you. I won that battle. He knows that. He fucking hates that. He also hates that we're together."

"Why the sudden change though?" she asked. "How do you go from screaming to silent when that's so out of character for him?"

Because the motherfucker was past mad. He was well beyond angry.

Screaming was no longer enough.

Things had progressed to a whole new, far deeper level.

That was the way I read the situation, and a fast glance at Diesel told me we were on the same page.

"I think he's shifting his focus," I told her. "I beat him once with the new phone. I beat him again by hiring Diesel. Now, he's scheming for a way to beat me."

She scanned my eyes. "What do I need to be doing differently?"

I lifted my hand to her neck, massaging the back of it. "You're doing everything just right."

"Brady…" Her shoulders rounded, her back hunched. She was caving inward, collapsing into her own body. "Why does it feel like something very wrong is about to happen?"

Chapter Twenty-Eight

LILY

"I'm dying to know where you're taking me," I said to Brady from the backseat of the SUV, the one that had picked us up directly after landing in Dallas.

The pilots and Diesel had stayed on the plane—something I found so odd—while only Brady and I took off. Things became even stranger when, so far, we hadn't left the grounds of the airport. Every time I thought we were going to turn off onto the main road, we just continued to circle.

"Let's say I'm tapping into your knowledge of aircrafts."

His eyes were an even lighter blue in the sun.

"My knowledge?" I laughed.

His fingers dived into the back of my hair. "With the number of years you have in your career, you know things from a perspective that I don't."

"Like?"

"What size cabin comfortably fits a certain amount of people. What type of storage is beneficial in the galley. What's the most practical layout for the main cabin. Shit like that."

"And why do you need that kind of information?"

The SUV came to a stop, and I peeked through the windshield. We were parked in front of a hangar where two men, professionally dressed, were waiting outside.

"Because I'm buying a plane."

The driver opened the backseat door.

And that was when Brady nodded toward the outside and said, "After you, my expert."

"You could certainly come up with a better title than that, couldn't you?" I winked at him.

"Are you sure you want me to? Because the title I come up with isn't going to be appropriate, and the last thing I want to do is to get you wet right now"—he tightened his grip on the back of my head— "and not be able to get you off for the next couple of hours."

A man who endlessly took care of me—not only mentally, but physically too.

Unicorns really did exist.

"That would be cruel." I smiled. "Let's go with expert, then. I kinda like the sound of that anyway."

I giggled as I climbed out, waiting for Brady to join me, and he walked me toward the men.

Introductions were quickly made, and I learned that one was the CEO of the aviation company while the other was the head of manufacturing. As we entered the large, oversized hangar, we were joined by the director of sales.

Although the majority of my experience was in commercial flying, I knew my way around an aircraft of any size and could easily answer the questions Brady asked as we toured the private jets in their fleet. There were seven for us to look at. Each one was a bit different in engine size, capacity, and layout. But it was almost as though the company knew exactly what plane would suit Brady's needs the most and saved that one for last.

As soon as we entered the final jet, there was no question in my mind that this was the plane he needed to purchase. Pure luxury, with details and finishes that had been selected by someone with an impeccable eye for design. An interior that would not only fit him, his family, his coworkers—whoever he needed to bring on board—but would also be a functional space to get work done, sleep, and even host a meeting.

The head of manufacturing finished the tour after pointing out all the important features, and Brady told the group he needed a moment alone with me to chat. The two men and woman departed the jet, leaving Brady and me in the center of the main cabin.

I took a seat next to him on one of the soft, buttery leather couches as he asked, "What do you think of their planes?"

"I can't comment on the engine or the cockpit—that's out of my realm of knowledge. But I can tell you that from the boarding door to the galley, these planes are gorgeous. And in comparison to the Daltons' jet, in my opinion, the ones we just toured are better."

"Wouldn't that bite Dominick's ass if he'd just overheard you?"

I laughed. "Let's keep that a secret between us, okay?"

He gave me a smile. "Do you have a favorite out of the seven?"

I nodded.

"Is it this one?" he asked.

"It is."

"Mine too. I can see myself spending a lot of time in here." He glanced around the cabin, giving me a view of his delicious scruff, his stare eventually returning to me. "Cole and Spade Hotels only has one plane presently that we share among all seven partners. It's a fucking shit show. We're constantly fighting for it, and the jet, on average, is booked out for weeks in advance. I can never get it when I need it."

"Will this be yours or the company's?"

He stretched his other arm out across the back of the couch.

"The company's, but mostly mine. I've told you I'm going back and forth to Edinburgh every week, this will be the plane I'll be taking. That doesn't leave much time, maybe two days a week, for my other partners to use it while I'm in LA."

"This will be the perfect jet for international trips." I pointed toward the rear, where a bedroom had been built, accommodating a queen-size bed. "You're going to be exhausted from that much travel, but having it equipped with a bedroom and a full shower is certainly going to help."

He reclined, putting his legs over the built-in ottoman, folding his arms behind his head. "You're right. It'll be a good fit." He was silent as he stared at me. "It's only missing one thing…"

I couldn't imagine what he was referring to. This plane had more upgrades and bells and whistles than any home I'd ever lived in. It wasn't higher end. It was the highest end.

"What would that be?"

A slow, beautiful smile came across his lips. "You."

"Me?"

"Cole and Spade Hotels would like to hire you to be the full-time flight attendant on this jet. The position would start in a week, after you've completed your contract with the Daltons. I have all the paperwork with me, so you can review the requirements and what it entails. Of course, it would come with full benefits, an extremely competitive salary, time off, a housing allowance—everything you need."

I felt my head shaking back and forth while I listened. While I processed. While I tried to decide if this was even real. "You're seriously offering me a job?"

His hand dropped from the back of his head and landed on my shoulder. "Yes, but I want to make something clear because I don't want the purpose of this to get misconstrued." He played with the ends of my hair. "I need someone who has your level of experience and can handle flying back and forth to the UK every week. That's why you're being offered this position, not because you're my girlfriend."

My thoughts were still all over the place.

A job?

With the Spades and Coles?

An opportunity that was exactly what I wanted, like the ones I'd been applying for.

"I appreciate your faith in me," I told him.

When he exhaled, the air hit my face. "You've told me you're applying to other jobs. Opportunities that could take you away from LA. Do I want you to go? Fuck no. I want you here. I want you with me. And I'd be lying if I said that didn't factor into it, but your skills and knowledge are the main reason you're being offered this." He paused, but his eyes intensified as they gazed at me. "I need you to know this, and I need you to believe me when I say this: If you don't take this position, that won't change the way I feel about you or what will happen between us. I don't want you to feel any pressure. It's either right for you or it isn't. But your decision won't affect us."

The excitement of the opportunity was building inside me, but it wasn't as simple as saying yes or no. There were other factors at play, like Brady having partners in the business. If Dominick knew about my situation, then I imagined Brady's brothers did as well. Brothers who would also be my boss.

What did they think about this?

Were they concerned that they were offering employment to someone with an ex like mine?

That I was entering their company with baggage no one, including myself, would want to deal with?

I turned toward him, positioning my elbow on the cushion, holding my face with the palm of my hand. "Let's say I take it. I'll be sleeping with the boss. Would your other partners be all right with that?"

"Macon is dating an employee. Cooper is dating one of our partners. My cousin, Jo, is married to Jenner—I've told you this. It's not an issue."

"But what about Ridge and Rhett? What would they think—"

"I don't give a fuck what either of them thinks. As far as I'm concerned, they're not allowed to have an opinion about this." As he studied my eyes, I could feel him hitting my soul. "Are you really worried about my partners' thoughts on us dating, or is it something else much deeper than that?"

I worried about everything.

Each layer.

Always.

That was the problem about me.

The other problem was that I used to keep those feelings in. I didn't share them with anyone. And instead of getting resolved, they would fester, making me feel even worse.

Until Brady had gotten me to talk and purge.

Like he was doing now.

"It goes deeper," I admitted.

"Talk to me."

I took a deep breath. "I don't want your partners to pity my situation and think I'm being offered this because it's your way of keeping me safe and protected."

"Lily…"

"I know it's not. I know you said you need a flight attendant with my level of experience. I believe all of that." A knot was forming in my throat. Still, after all this time, it was hard to admit that I'd gotten myself into this situation. "But my past is unique. It's challenging, it involves someone unstable and threatening, and I don't want them to think I'm some kind of—"

"I'm going to stop you right there." His hands surrounded my face. "No one enters a relationship without something. Shit, I came to you with the inability to commit because I never wanted to or cared about it." His voice was stern but soft at the same time, like he wanted to be heard, but he didn't want the words to hurt.

"You have an ex—so fucking what? Some people have a kid or five or, hell, twelve. Some people are in the midst of taking care of their ailing parents. Some are drowning in debt. Some don't have the ability to trust. Some are mourning."

He moved in closer. "What I'm saying is, my partners are far from perfect, and they don't expect you to be. But I promise, they'd never question my motive. They know I wouldn't bring someone into our company unless they were qualified."

He tucked a chunk of hair behind my ear. "I want you to think about it. You don't have to make a decision now. And if you want to talk about it more, we can. If you want to meet with my partners, we can do that too." He rubbed his thumb over my lips. "But if you say yes, this is going to be your new office, baby."

Chapter Twenty-Nine

Brady

"Where the hell do we start?" I said as Lily and I surrounded the island in my kitchen, where Klark had laid out a bunch of ingredients, leaving us to fend for ourselves.

It wasn't that my private chef had abandoned us. It was date night. So, instead of having him prepare something that I knew would be five-star, I'd asked him to leave everything he would use to make his world-famous spaghetti in hopes that I could re-create it. Sure, it would have been easier if I'd just had him leave a pot of it on the stove. But where was the fun in that? Even if I fucked it up royally, which I probably would, at least I got to attempt it with her.

And at least she got to see that I was trying.

"Cooking isn't my superpower." She smiled weakly. "Heating up, plating—I can do that all day. Knowing what flavors are missing or lacking or the sequence to make it all turn out magical, forget it. I'm a helpless cause."

I'd seen plenty of confidence over the years. Words intended to brag, impress, secure a second date that had no chance at all.

What I hadn't seen was this.

Vulnerability.

Admitting a weakness, and it was so fucking sexy.

"If it turns out like shit, we'll order in." I grazed her chin, a spot I was surprised I liked so much. It wasn't a beautiful feature compared to the others on her face, but it was what pulled everything together. A place that screamed to be held.

"I love that plan."

I ran my hand past her jaw until I was holding the back of her head, tilting it so her eyes were aimed up at me. "How are your knife skills?"

"I can spread cream cheese equally around the inside of a bagel." She giggled. "But I have a feeling that's not what you're asking."

God, she was so fucking cute.

"The onion, bell pepper, and mushrooms—can you handle that, or would you rather brown the meat?"

"Onions? Are you trying to ruin me?" She blinked several times as though the onions were already burning her eyes. "I'm kidding. I'll gladly take one for the team."

She wouldn't have to do that after dinner. Once we finished this meal, the night was going to be all about her pussy.

I kissed her softly. Slowly. Tasting what was mine before I pulled away to pick up the packages of meat that Klark had left. There were two kinds—ground beef and pork—and I combined them in a cast-iron pan on low heat and began to break up the chunks.

"Something fucking wild happened at work today," I said over my shoulder.

"How wild?"

"I went out to lunch with Ridge and Rhett." I continued to turn around to catch her expression, which showed she was as surprised as I'd thought she'd be. "There was alcohol involved, which was probably why the three of us survived the outing. But still, the three of us returned to the office alive." I left the meat and grabbed a pot from the cabinet, filled it with enough water, and set it on the stovetop to boil. "Honestly, that's a goddamn miracle."

"What prompted the lunch?"

I had to chuckle. "They wanted to pick my brain on how I was revamping the payroll department and how I'd done the same for our check-in and checkout process. They wouldn't say it, but I think they're impressed with my work." I gave the meat a quick stir. "Ridge is looking to spearhead a whole new app design for our company, so they wanted to hear my process."

"You're really letting him redo the app? That sounds like something you'd do, not him."

I sighed. "He's a single dad. He can't do a lot of traveling to open new hotels or remodel our current inventory. Although he's going to be doing an overhaul of our Malibu property and some updates to Beverly Hills, he's limited to only taking jobs around LA since he doesn't want to be away from his kid."

"Understandable." She sliced through the bell pepper. "Still, I'm a little blown away that they came to you. I'm happy they did. I'm just shocked."

"No one is more fucking shocked than me."

She brought over the cutting board with the chopped bell peppers and dumped them in with the meat. "Was I supposed to do that?" she asked after the last piece hit the pan.

I laughed. "I have no idea. Let's go with…yes."

She returned to the island and got to work on the mushrooms. "Do you think this is the start of a whole new relationship for you guys?"

I whistled out a mouthful of air. "I don't know, but it would be a hell of a lot easier if we had a relationship. There's so much tension. Not as much as when we merged, but enough. When I start Edinburgh, I don't need my time in LA to be fucking muddy because of them. It's going to be stressful as it is, balancing the payroll rollout with the Scotland remodel. If they add to that stress"—a short growl came from my throat—"they're going to like me even less."

"But lunch went well?"

I thought about the couple of hours we'd spent together. I knew Rhett had tagged along because Ridge had asked him to. A strength-in-numbers kind of thing. But there hadn't been any yelling. I hadn't even snapped.

"It was productive," I replied. "That's probably the biggest compliment I've ever been able to give to them."

She returned to the stovetop to add in the mushrooms. "And they say women bring the drama."

I stared at her profile as the mushrooms fell off the cutting board into the sizzling meat. "I know you're not calling me dramatic."

She winked when she looked at me. "I'm calling them dramatic." She returned to the island again. "One day, I bet the three of you are going to be friends. You're going to walk around the office with Ridge's daughter on your shoulders, and you're going to take Rhett to a hockey game with you."

"Did you hit a joint without me knowing?"

She laughed. "Mark my words. It's going to happen." She was peeling the onion, holding her face as far away from it as she could. "You didn't think you were ever going to settle down, and now, look at you. Cooking spaghetti and talking to me about work like any normal boyfriend would."

I dumped the noodles into the boiling water and faced her. "And I fucking love it."

"Me too."

"Your turn. Tell me about work."

A topic I'd avoided since we'd returned from Dallas a couple of days ago. I didn't want to push. I didn't want to rush her. When she made her decision, it would be on her time, and I'd be all right with whatever she chose.

But I thought about it all the time.

I even discussed it with my brothers and Jo. They knew what I wanted, and they were hoping it happened for me.

"Work," she said quietly as she cut the onion in half. "Well, you could say tomorrow is a bit of a monumental day for me."

"Why's that?"

"It's my last overnighter with the Daltons. A quick trip to Manhattan with Dominick before my contract ends at the end of the week." She finished up the onions and stirred them into the meaty mix.

I added in the two jars of sauce, along with the seasoning Klark had left on the counter. I didn't know how much of each; I just gave the bottles a heavy shake into the sauce.

"How do you feel about it coming to an end?" I asked.

"I thought I'd be sad. The end of that job signified so many changes ahead. I didn't know where I'd end up or what I'd do or where I'd be living. And then add in the whole David fiasco, and it's a lot to think about."

While she worked on combining everything in the cast iron, I assumed the noodles had to be done, and I drained the water and added the spaghetti to the meat. With the large spoon, she began to marry it together.

Within a few rotations, she said, "But I'm not sad at all—don't get me wrong; I'll miss those guys. The Daltons were so good to me, but my next opportunity is just as amazing." She gradually gazed up at me as I stood at her side. "Actually, it's even better." She leaned her body into mine. "I want to accept the job you offered, but…"

I didn't put a hand on her.

I didn't even kiss her.

I gave her the moment to get out whatever she needed to, making sure my mouth or fingers didn't influence what she was about to say.

"I don't want to sign a year contract. I want to go month to month, and I understand if that's a hard limit for your company and you'd rather go with someone else. I just feel more comfortable with a much shorter contract."

"No one will have an issue with that."

Her hand went to my chest. "You have to know, it's not that I think something bad is going to happen between us—I don't believe that at all. But if it did, I don't want either of us to feel like a contract was keeping me in a place that neither of us wanted me to be in." She moved her hand to cling to my fingers. "With that said, I would never leave you high and dry. I would stay until another flight attendant was found, and I'm happy to put that in writing."

My other hand went to her waist. "Done. Any other stipulations?"

"Nope."

"Come on, Lily. Don't make it so easy on me. You must have other demands that weren't met in the paperwork I gave you."

She shook her head. "You almost doubled the salary the Daltons are paying me. You're giving me more benefits than I had when I worked for a commercial airline. The housing allowance is enough that I can afford the Cole and Spade Hotel in Beverly Hills—yes, I plan to pay for it, you're not giving it to me for free. I can even ditch the car rental and purchase a vehicle now. And the best part"—she arched her back, fully pressing us together—"I get to be with you."

She was giving me everything I fucking wanted.

An eruption came from my throat. "And you're good with that?"

"Beyond good."

I felt the truth in her words. I saw it in her face.

But I just needed to double-check.

"You're absolutely sure?"

She dropped the spoon and put both hands on my shoulders. "Not just sure. I'm positive." She took in my eyes. "This is what I've wanted, a position just like the one you're offering. I didn't want to go back to commercial. I wanted to stay in the private sector. Why not do it here, with you...when all I want is to be with you?" Her lashes fluttered as she stared at me. "I weighed every angle. I slept on it for more than one night. And I couldn't come up with a single reason not to take the job."

I rubbed my nose over hers. "You've made me so fucking happy."

I didn't wait for her to respond before I slammed our lips together, the taste of her so much richer than the last time I'd done this. My tongue dipped in between her lips, circling her tongue, my hands lifting to her face, holding her cheeks, keeping us together.

"You know what I love?" I asked when I finally pulled back.

"Tell me."

"That I won't have to miss your lips while I'm in Edinburgh. That I'll be able to do this whenever I want."

There was a raging hard-on in my pants.

One that had sprouted the second she gave me her answer.

One that reminded me whenever I wanted her pussy in Scotland, in addition to her lips, I'd be able to have that too.

One that couldn't wait to sink into her.

"More sweetness. I can't even handle it." A smile covered all the skin that wasn't hidden by my hands.

If she heard the thoughts in my head, she wouldn't agree with her last statement.

"Let's inhale this dinner so I can show you a side that isn't as sweet."

"Hurry." She laughed. "Please."

I released her to grab two plates, dropping twirls of noodles and sauce on each one, and carried them to the table. On my next trip, I added napkins and silverware, along with the glasses of wine that I'd poured before we began to cook.

"I don't know why…but I'm nervous to try this," she joked as she dipped her fork into the pasta.

"It can't be that bad. It's cooked. It's mixed. It just might not be…" I took in a mouthful. "Shit, this is good."

Her eyes widened as she chewed. "I know…this is kinda excellent. Like way better than I expected."

The sauce was flavorful, and the meat was savory. The noodles were a little overdone, but it wasn't a deal-breaker.

"I don't hate it." I circled my fork through the heap and chomped up my second bite. "I think I actually like it."

"Same." She swallowed. "I really like it in fact."

But even though I continued to eat, chewing several more bunches of noodles, they weren't hitting the spot.

They weren't filling me.

They weren't giving me what I needed.

I set my fork down and got up, grabbing the bottle of wine from the counter, and knelt on the floor beside her. I slid her chair until she was facing me.

A smile immediately reached her lips. "You're already full?"

I chuckled. "Not even close."

I moved her legs around my waist, and I lifted her off the chair, pushing her plate and wine so I could place her on the table. I got straight to work on her jeans, yanking them down, past her bare feet. I didn't bother with her panties; I just ripped those fuckers off.

"But what I am is thirsty as hell, and the only glass I want to use is you."

My face nestled between her legs, and I held the bottle above her pussy, pouring the dark red cabernet down her clit. I kept my mouth beneath her, catching the slow stream, not letting a drop hit the floor.

"Oh my God."

I glanced up, catching eyes that were watching me.

That were fucking smoldering.

I splashed more down her body, lapping the drips as they ran over that perfect, gorgeous pussy.

"You are…"

I continued to gaze at her, waiting for her to finish her statement.

"I'm what, Lily?" I paused. "Hungry? For you? Yes, I'm plenty of that. And when I'm done drinking, I'm going to eat your fucking cunt."

Chapter Thirty

LILY

Brady had set me across the glass table we'd been eating dinner on, covered my pussy with the red wine we'd been drinking, and buried his face between my legs. He hadn't just used me as a glass. He licked me. He fingered me. And he was currently nearing me toward a second orgasm.

As my body climbed toward that riveting, steep point, my arms tried extending over my head, desperate to find something to hold on to, my fingers teasing the mound of spaghetti on his plate. I tried moving them sideways, and they hit my plate and glass of wine.

So, I held on to his hair and screamed, "Fuck," while I twirled his thick black locks, clenching them in my grip.

That tongue.

"There's nothing in this fucking world that tastes as good as you," he rasped.

And there was simply nothing in this world that felt as good as him.

The way he knew just where to flick. That he focused on the spot at the very top, using the flatness of his tongue to massage and the tip to sweep. The way his finger knew what speed and angle to slide into me.

How the combination of the two almost immediately brought me back to that place again with hardly any rest in between.

"Yes," I cried. "Don't stop."

"I want you to come on my fucking face."

He didn't even need to ask.

I was already there.

"Right now, Lily. Right fucking now."

"Oh, yes!"

A rush shot through my body, starting at my clit that throbbed with sensations each time the wetness from his mouth slipped across it. From there, the passion trickled across my stomach, rose to my chest, and tingled its way down my legs.

But those were just the tail of the orgasm.

The core lived within my pussy, exploding with these fiery prickles, each one pounding harder, like fingers on piano keys during a song that was rising in sound.

"Brady!" I couldn't get out more than one word. But that wasn't the only thing that came out of me; there were moans too. Ones so loud that they vibrated through my body. "Ah!" And as those moans cascaded from my lips, they hit the air as if they were bolts of thunder.

Waves of shivers collided in my stomach, causing shudders to rocket through me. "Yes! Brady, fuck!"

He didn't slow. What he did instead was lick until there was nothing left in me but breath, and when he was sure I had hit the sensitivity phase, my body completely still, he lifted my shirt to kiss across my stomach and my breasts. He shifted to my neck, throat, and chin, settling against my mouth.

"Kiss me," he pressed. "I want you to know just how good you taste."

His kisses were as ravenous as when he'd licked my pussy.

The sound of his belt buckle and zipper filled the silence. When those noises quieted, he pulled back to say, "I could have eaten your pussy all night."

"It almost feels like you did." I held his face. "For the record, I never wanted you to stop. I loved every second."

He nipped my lip. He wasn't soft. He wasn't gentle either.

"Fuck me, you're wet." His dick was probing my entrance, a door that he was lightly knocking against, as though he knew I needed a few seconds to catch my breath and find my bearings before he dived in. "Is she ready for me?"

"Yes." As I inhaled, I let out a small laugh. "I love that I'm still on the table and all I can smell is spaghetti and how it's not even a little distracting."

"All I can smell is your pussy. Which is distracting because I want to eat it again." He slowly sank into me. "Goddamn it, Lily. You feel fucking incredible."

His pace was unhurried, his body heating mine as it lay on top of me. A weight I found so incredibly sexy because it didn't crush me.

It held me.

And that was everything I needed from him, even as my breath hitched from taking in more, inch by inch, until he was fully buried.

That was when I really moaned. When the sound from my throat became so guttural that I was positive he could feel it within his shaft.

"Fuck yes," he hissed. "This is exactly what I wanted." He leaned up, pulling me to the table's edge, and while he stood in front of me, my legs wrapped around him, he took his first stroke. "Jesus, Lily. You get tighter every time I fuck you."

His thrusts were getting deeper.

If there was an end, he was now hitting it. But not like a hammer. He was circling that spot, the one that craved his presence, and all it did was add to my wetness.

And make me moan louder.

"Harder." I didn't know how my body could so easily and so quickly find that place again, but I was there, dangling, dominated, and desperate for that feeling I knew he could give me. My nails stabbed his hands as they roamed my chest, his landing on my breasts, pinching my nipples through my bra, mine resting on top of his, pushing him to do it even stronger. "Faster!"

"You want to come again?"

The way I exhaled gave him the response he didn't need since I was sure he could feel what was happening inside my body.

But I added, "Yes. Please." And then, "Now," in case it made him fuck me even rougher.

Not a roughness that was careless and reckless. A roughness that came from a man who knew what I could handle and just how I wanted it.

But even after my begging, he didn't give in. His speed stayed exactly the same, as though he was building me up first. What did change was his thumb. It pressed against that tender spot he'd licked earlier. He didn't just hold it there; he brushed the pad of that finger back and forth.

"Wetter. Just what I wanted," he exhaled.

He was working me.

Leading me.

"Holy! Shit!" I unraveled my legs from around him and set my feet on the lip of the table, keeping my thighs wide and open. "Yes!"

The new position took away all restrictions. He now had full access to do whatever he wanted.

And what he decided, was to send me so far over the cliff that my whole body was wriggling with spasms, my stomach shuddering, my lips screaming, "Brady!"

That was when he went faster.

When he finally caved and his movements became harsher.

When he twisted his hips, aiming for every angle, adding to the overwhelming ache inside me.

"You're getting tighter again. Fuck me."

Within a few more strokes, I was nearing the comedown—a place I never thought I'd reach at this rate.

He lowered his upper body, shortening the space between us so I could wrap my arms around his shoulders and bury my face in his neck.

I was spent, exhausted.

I just needed to breathe.

I needed to hold on.

I needed to give him my weight that I could no longer bear myself.

Rather than staying still, he lifted me into the air, circling my legs around his waist, bouncing me over his dick as he carried me. With each jump, he spread more of my wetness over him, but what he also did was release the lingering jitters that had been stranded in my stomach. Somehow, he even knew the lasting spasms were hiding within me, and he set them free.

After each bump, I clung to him.

I yelled for him.

I moved with him, meeting him in the middle, moaning from the friction as he slipped back.

He held on to my hips and said, "Jesus, you know how to fuck."

I expected him to walk us into his bedroom, a mattress to be beneath some part of me, the crackling of his fireplace as the background noise.

But when he reached the living room, he placed me on top of the couch, the hard edge no wider than a balance beam with cushions directly behind my ass. And as he set me there, he tore off my shirt and bra, leaving me naked while he removed the remaining clothes he had on.

Finally bare, he pressed our bodies together, sliding back in like he'd never left.

"And you're still so fucking wet," he groaned.

"Because I want more."

"Insatiable...like me."

I ran my fingers over his chest, across the deep grooves and solid, rock-hard muscle before dipping down his abs, feeling the way they outlined, becoming more defined as he thrust into me.

"But just with you," I clarified.

It wasn't only his body that I was obsessed with, watching the cords and etches as he fucked the breath out of me. It was also the way he looked at me while he did it that owned me like nothing I'd ever experienced.

That feral nature in his eyes.

The desire.

Need.

I couldn't get enough, and there was no way I ever would.

"Brady"—I pulled his mouth toward mine—"I want you to fill me with your cum."

"Don't say that to me. It'll make me go fucking wild."

The smile was already on my lips, but it grew for him. For the anticipation of what he was about to do to me. For what was going to happen when the wildness took over. For the realization that my fourth orgasm in less than an hour would feel as good as the first.

"But I want it," I told him. "I want to watch you come, and I want to feel it drip out of me."

"So fucking naughty." He kissed me. "And all mine." He reared his hips back and plunged in, twisting, rocking as though he wasn't afraid to send me flying into the cushions. "Are you sure this is what you want?"

"Yes," easily rolled off my lips because I was almost there again.

The build nagged at my insides, the satisfaction growing with every pump.

Just like the table, I bent my knees and rolled my bare feet over the tough corner and used my hands to balance, squeezing the section of the couch by my heels.

What this position allowed was one hell of a view.

Of his body and those delicious muscles.

Of his cock driving in and out of me, covered in a glistening slickness.

And of his face as the pleasure spread across it.

My God, he was handsome, especially when he was having an orgasm.

Like he was now.

"Lily..." He dragged my name out in multiple syllables, getting deeper as his growl turned louder. "You'd better fucking come."

He didn't have to order that demand.

I was there.

Shouting, "I am!"

The beat was climbing, summiting, a steady pulse that had me yelling his name over and over. I was paralyzed by the euphoria torturously running through me. Rapture so intense that I was lost.

I was locked.

I was over capacity.

"Brady!"

"Fuck yes," he crooned. "Make me feel it." His pounding transformed into quick, sharp thrusts. "Milk my fucking cock."

I didn't know what my body was doing to him internally. I only knew how I was feeling, how loud I was shouting, how I was quivering from every part of me. And as those tremors slipped through me, he was clinching me tighter, stroking me harder, emptying himself inside me.

I knew because I could feel it.

The way the wetness was increasing.

The way it was thickening.

And, *oh shit*, there was nothing hotter.

"Brady, yes!"

"You like that, don't you?" He held my face with so much strength. "You fucking love when I fill you with my cum."

My arms rotated around his neck, my legs doing the same to his waist while I moaned, "Give me more of it."

And he did.

Several more strokes' worth until we were both completely still.

Panting.

Sweaty.

And, dare I say, satiated for the moment.

"You are...something else." I laughed.

He cupped my chin. "I'm going to bring you into the shower and clean the wine and cum off your pussy, and then we're coming back out here and finishing that meal."

"Love that idea." I smiled. "But I'm surprised you're still hungry after all that eating."

He gave me a quick kiss and bent over to pick up the clothes he'd stripped off us. "Don't tempt me, Lily. I can easily go for another round after our shower."

By now, I knew the sound of Brady's notifications. The low ding that was assigned for texts had gone off several times in a row.

I nodded toward his pants. "I think your phone is about to explode."

He set his pants beside me, where he draped them over the back of the couch, and he reached into his pocket to grab his cell. "I just want to make sure it's not anything serious..." His voice faded before he shouted, "What the fuck?!"

Anger was immediately present in his expression, his teeth bared, as though he were about to attack.

I couldn't imagine what he was reading.

Was it about work? Edinburgh?

Shit...could it be about me?

I grabbed his hand. "What's wrong?"

"I'm going to fucking kill him."

Him?

Did that mean… David?

Or someone else?

I continued to grasp the back of his hand. "Brady? What happened?" I waited, and when I got no response, I added, "Talk to me."

His eyes slowly shifted from the screen to me. "Lily…" His head shook back and forth, the rage building in his eyes. "I don't want to show you this."

David.

It had to be.

And as that realization began to take hold, my heart pounded inside my chest.

A boulder wedged its way into my throat.

Every bit of pleasure I'd been feeling was instantly drained from my body.

"Please." I sounded breathless. "Just get it over with."

Gradually and reluctantly, he tilted the screen so we could look at it at the same time.

Unknown: *A few more to add to your collection, you motherfucker.*

There were four photographs attached to the text from Unknown. The first was of a bed that looked vaguely familiar, a pair of boy shorts and a T-shirt on top.

Boy shorts and a T-shirt that were mine.

A sickness was rising in my stomach as I flipped to the second picture. This one showed the interior of my suitcase, where my two packing pods had been unzipped; a pink lace bra and matching thong poked out of one, and my Dalton polo, which was part of my uniform, had been pulled out of the other.

My heart began to throb as the third photo showed my cosmetic case as it sat on the counter of the bathroom. My perfume had been taken out and was resting in the palm of a hand, fingers wrapped around it, nails that were rugged and chewed.

A hand I knew all too well.

"That was my hotel room in Charleston." My throat was so tight; I could barely speak. "I recognize the bed and the bathroom." I tried to swallow and couldn't. "He got in. Oh God." My hand went over my mouth. "He'd come into that room while I was out…and I didn't know."

The fourth photo made my eyes fill, tears streaming down my face as I continued to stare at it. It was a photo of the inside flap of a wallet—David's wallet—where a picture had been secured. The shot was of David and me, on his couch, during the beginning of our relationship. His arm was around my shoulders, his lips were on my cheek, and there was a huge smile on my face.

I'd taken the selfie, and during our relationship, it had become the home screen of his phone. I didn't know he'd printed it or that it lived in his wallet, but it was a picture that should have been tossed when I broke up with him.

After a full year, it was still there.

To me, a scar.

To him, a possession.

Something he'd never let go of.

Someone he'd never stop fighting for.

When I opened my mouth, I tasted the saltiness.

The fear.

The promise, which I voiced to Brady in the quietest whisper. "He won't ever stop."

Chapter Thirty-One

BRADY

What Lily didn't know was that once David had texted me the photos of her hotel room in Charleston, proving that he'd somehow broken in, that wasn't the last time I heard from him.

It was only the beginning.

The motherfucker was now messaging me daily.

Sure, I was goading him. Responding. Letting him know that I wasn't going to tolerate his goddamn nonsense. But what I was learning from our exchanges was that it didn't matter what I wrote back. He was going to do whatever he wanted, and that had started long before the Charleston incident.

But my question was, where would it go from here?

Me: *She's not yours. She's mine. How does that feel? That you lost her. That she'll never be with you again. Is that sinking in yet? Does it fucking kill you?*

Me: *For the record, going into her hotel room will be the last time you ever get that close to her. Do it again, and you're dead.*

David: *You're a funny man, Brady. You think you have me pinned down. You're not even close.*

Would he eventually get Lily's number? He hadn't, or I would know since she'd promised she would tell me.

My number was much easier to find. All it would take was a solid internet search, where the mobile number of every Cole and Spade executive was listed somewhere. One day, I would only use this phone for business matters, but I hadn't bothered getting a personal line yet.

Even though he hadn't gotten access to her cell, that didn't mean he wouldn't start showing up at my house. Or the restaurants we ate it. Or the locations we flew to.

When it came to him, was anything off-limits?

Because what I'd learned was that he'd walked right through the lobby of the Charleston Cole and Spade Hotel and not a single person who worked for me in that location stopped him. Although the entire staff had been tipped off that he could show up—something I did whenever Lily traveled overnight with the Daltons—and the security team at that hotel had been told to use our software that would detect disguises. But when David sauntered through the lobby, the security team was outside on the back patio, dealing with a drunk, disgruntled guest who had been making a scene and yelling at some of our other guests. Therefore, security wasn't viewing the feed, and that window became the perfect opportunity for David to slip in, unnoticed.

Had he set that up purposefully?

Fuck, I didn't know.

Nor did I know how he'd gotten a key and entered Lily's room. But the feed, once it was reviewed, showed a key in his hand and him waving it in front of the reader at her door. He'd been in her room for a total of ten minutes before he took the stairs to the lobby and walked out the same way he'd come in.

David: *How does it feel that you're trying to keep me out and I continue to find a hole to get in? Does it hurt that you can't protect her? Does it, Brady? You're a fucking joke.*

Me: *You haven't laid a finger on her, and I guarantee you won't.*

That's protection. That's the comfort I can provide.

David: *But I laid a finger on her panties, and she wore them the next day with my scent all over them. That's called satisfaction.*

Me: *You're a sick fuck.*

He'd backed me into a corner, and the asshole knew it. Because Lily was adamant about not going to the police, saying that it wouldn't fare well for us, given that David had the Atlanta law enforcement sitting in the palm of his hand. When I mentioned that this wasn't Georgia, that I'd be dealing with the troop in LA, her answer didn't change. She said it didn't matter what police department was contacted; David would continue to get away with what he was doing because he was an expert at disappearing.

My fucking hands were tied.

My frustration was building.

How the hell did I make him stop?

Until I had that answer, all I could do was step up the security that surrounded us.

Diesel had now traveled back and forth to Edinburgh the three times we'd gone so far. During those trips he took with us on the new plane, I parked him outside my room whenever we were gone. And while I was working during the day, he was with Lily, and just like when she had been employed by the Daltons, he wasn't to leave her side.

David: *You're one jealous dude. Jealous of how much power I still have over her. Jealous that she thinks of me.*

Me: *There's no jealousy. There doesn't need to be. If Lily wanted you, she wouldn't be with me. End of story.*

David: *But will she always think of me? Fuck yes. Is it my dick she fantasizes about when she touches herself, alone in her hotel room during the nights you work late? Fuck yes.*

Me: *I'm done engaging. You're one nasty motherfucker.*

These were messages she didn't need to see. That she didn't need to stress over. That she didn't need to know even existed. What I wanted was for her to continue living freely, like she had been since I'd hired Diesel as her bodyguard. She would not go back to spending her days inside our hotel room, feeling like she was locked in a prison. Edinburgh was a large city, and she needed to spend time exploring and enjoying everything it had to offer.

Because there was nothing better in this world than a happy, smiling Lily.

David: *Now that you just got home, how was your trip to Edinburgh?*

David: *Do you really think Lily enjoys following you back and forth to Scotland like a little puppy? You've taken away her identity and made her your shadow.*

Me: *I'm protecting her from you.*

David: *If I wanted to put my hands on her, do you really think Diesel could stop me? Do better, Brady. Do much fucking better.*

Me: *Stay away from her. I'm warning you, David. Don't take my words lightly, I'll fucking kill you myself.*

David: *You make me laugh.*

Just like the grin that was on her face now, as we were tucked in a corner table of a restaurant with an interior that was designed to look like a castle. We'd started with an appetizer of oysters and shellfish bisque, and while Lily was digging into her main course of lamb, I was nursing my grilled lemon sole.

I didn't want this meal to ever end—it was that fucking good.

This was our fourth trip to Scotland. One of the best parts about being in a new city with my girl was getting a break from the food in LA, establishments I'd gone to with other women, and getting to check out restaurants with her that I'd never eaten at before.

"Goddamn it, this is exceptional." I glanced up from my plate to see that gorgeous smile was still across her lips. "Is yours as good as mine?" I reached my fork over the length of the table and took a small chunk of her lamb, popping it into my mouth. "Fuck, that's delicious too."

"I've been moaning over every bite. You haven't heard me?"

Because of the tall ceiling, the sound spread, and it was slightly noisy in here. Not a bad thing at all, but it had prevented me from hearing those tiny little groans.

"If I had, my dick would be hard right now."

She laughed. "Tell me you're going to have a restaurant like this in your hotel so I can dream about eating this again and again." She moved some blonde locks off her cheek.

"I am—the meat part at least. You haven't met the Westons yet—a family of five who specialize in high-end steak houses. They're going to open their signature restaurant, Charred."

"We went to their LA location, didn't we?"

I nodded. "One of the brothers plays for the NHL—that's the game we were attending when we flew to Tampa."

"I'm connecting the dots." She wiped her mouth with her napkin. "Does that mean you'll be kicking out the three restaurants that are in the hotel now?"

Even though it was under construction, the hotel was still operating. We'd broken the rehab into sections, so many parts of the hotel were still functional. Floors would get renovated one at a time, giving plenty of rooms for us to rent out, and restaurants would close similarly—when one left, a new one would come in, allowing guests to have places to eat in the interim. We were trying to make the process as seamless and convenient for everyone while maintaining a steady stream of revenue.

"Yes," I replied. "The current restaurants don't provide the five-star quality of food I'm looking for, so they're gone. Aside from Charred, there will be two others that will focus on local cuisines, providing experiences that will blow their minds."

I lifted my glass of scotch, holding it while I stared at her. "I want to tell you something. Something I've been keeping from you."

"Change of subject, I see." Her brows shot up. "Something you've been keeping from me, huh?"

I took a drink and set down the tumbler. "Well, I didn't want to say anything until I was positive."

"Okay..." She placed her fork on the side of her plate.

I knew how her brain worked. She thought that whatever I was going to say was going to be about David.

It irritated me to no end how that asshole wedged himself into conversations and thoughts without anyone even mentioning his name.

I was ready for that to never happen again.

"I told you that Jenner was getting me a list of properties in Bangkok because that's where I want my next build-out to be."

She sat up straighter in her chair, and before I got a chance to continue, she said, "Actually, if we're being technical, I told you I heard a rumor that Bangkok was going to be your next location. That's when you told me he was gathering a list." As her face warmed, she winked.

"That's right." I chuckled. "Regardless, the purchase is going to happen. Over the last week, I reviewed all the available properties, and at the beginning of next month, on our way back from Scotland, I'm going to pick up the family in LA and head there to look at them." I paused, really taking in her eyes. "I'd like you to come with us."

Her face tilted to the side. "The whole family?"

"The whole family," I repeated. "Including Jenner and Jo. And we're going to stay for several days and vacation at one of the prospective hotels." I chuckled again. "So, we'll all be together."

"Throwing me straight into the wolf den, aren't you?" She put her hand up to stop me from replying. "I'm kidding. I've already met most of them anyway, and I can't wait to bond with the rest."

I liked that answer.

But I needed to break things down a bit further before she gave me her final response.

"Here's the thing." I leaned my elbows on either side of my plate.

"If you come, I want to get a temporary flight attendant for that trip. I don't want you working. This will be a vacation, and I want my family to get to know the personal side of you, not the professional side. And I don't want you to take offense to that because I know you, and I know you would tell me that it's no problem for you to be a part of the flight crew for that trip and that you'll be able to balance both." My eyes narrowed. "And for the record, I have no doubt that you could. But I want you to have the time off, to enjoy yourself, even though it's your plane. And for once, I want *you* to be waited on."

"Mr. Spade…"

"Hold on. I'm not done." I set my hands where my elbows had been resting and gripped the edge of the table. "I don't want to put any pressure on you, so I want you to know that you don't have to come. I want nothing more than to have you there. But if it feels like too much, too fast, I understand. You can sit this one out, and it won't change the way I feel, or change us, or change how much I want you." I ran my tongue over my lips.

"I appreciate that you're giving me a choice, but I want to be there." She reached across the table and put her hand on mine. "I want to hang with your family. I want to be the first woman who's ever been introduced to them as your girlfriend." Her smile was the biggest it had been tonight.

"I could semi-strangle you for bringing another flight attendant on board. I'm a bit territorial when it comes to your new plane, and it kills me to have someone else working on it." She gave her head a little shake. "But I understand why you want to do so, and I don't take offense to it." She squeezed my fingers. "Just know that I'm letting it slide this *one* time. But never again—do you hear me?"

"You know, you're so fucking adorable when you try to be stern with me." I rubbed my thumb over hers.

"In other words, it didn't work?"

"No." I huffed. "If you think I'm letting you work during any of our vacation trips, you've got another thing coming."

"You spoil me, Brady."

"I can afford to. And I want to."

She pulled her hand back and gazed at me, staying silent for several beats. "I never knew it could get better. That it could be like this. That as time went on, things became stronger, and feelings grew, and that I could actually experience a deeper level of happiness every day."

"I didn't either."

No truer words had been spoken, and I was positive we both knew that.

"I'm so, so everything for you."

I laughed at the cuteness. "That makes two of us."

"Is it ironic that we're learning this at the same time?"

I went to lift my fork, and there was a vibration in my pocket. It couldn't be a text or a social media notification—I'd silenced those. The only thing that could come through was a phone call.

As I was taking my phone out of my pocket, just to make sure the call wasn't an emergency, I replied to her, "Nah. I think it's perfect. I wouldn't have wanted to know what everything felt like before you. I only want to experience it with you."

I paused to look at the screen of my cell, the caller ID showing that it was my Edinburgh hotel. Something felt off about that, especially at this hour, knowing the contractor and his staff had already gone home.

I said to Lily, "Hang on a second. I need to take this," and I held the phone up to my ear. "This is Brady."

As the head of security spoke, everything in my body stopped.

My heart.

My breathing.

And what pulsed instead was an anger I'd never felt before.

My teeth bared, my chest heaved, and my fucking tongue vibrated as I roared, "What the fuck?!"

Chapter Thirty-Two

LILY

"No," I cried into the base of my hand so the word wouldn't hit the air. "No. No. No!"

My tears were like burning lava as they rolled over my eyelids and down my cheeks.

Everything quivered—my lips, my chin.

My body.

There was a weakness moving through me, where everything felt so light and uncontrollable, that I didn't know if I was sitting or standing or even breathing.

I just knew what I was seeing.

The truth that was lying in front of me, covered in blood, marred with cuts and bruises.

But how?

But why?

And how could this have happened again?

First Preston.

Now Diesel.

And as if his injuries weren't the biggest knife to my soul, watching Brady from the doorway of the hospital room only slid the blade in even deeper. Because as Brady looked at his friend, holding his hand with such tenderness, careful not to bother Diesel's IV, there was the sharpest ache in Brady's eyes and guilt in his expression.

His injuries shouldn't have occurred.

But Brady had assigned him to stand guard outside the door of our hotel room while we were at dinner. Since the Charleston incident, he didn't trust that David wouldn't try to break into our room.

This evening, David proved he didn't need to go into the room to hurt us.

He had done his damage directly in the hallway outside our door.

Oh God.

If it wasn't for me, Brady wouldn't have had to hire Diesel. He wouldn't have gotten that call while we were at the restaurant. We wouldn't have had to rush to the hospital.

And Diesel wouldn't be in that bed. His face…unrecognizable.

But that wasn't it.

There were other spots on his body that David had attacked.

Before we'd come into his room, the nurse had told us they were still assessing all his wounds, waiting for test results, warning us that many more tests would have to be run.

This wasn't even the beginning of a long recovery.

"Jesus, Diesel," Brady exhaled, still clutching his friend's hand. "What the fuck, my man? He did you wrong. So fucking wrong." He was hovering over Diesel's face, taking in his swollen eyes, the cut on his cheek that had been stitched shut, and what appeared to be a broken nose that caused deep purple marks across the bridge toward both sides of his cheeks. "I'm sorry. I'm so fucking sorry."

Not nearly as sorry as I was.

Brady had nothing to apologize for.

This was all my fault.

I held the doorway, squeezing it hard enough to keep me standing.

Without it, I didn't think I'd be on my feet.

My knees no longer wanted to hold me.

My thighs felt wobbly and powerless.

Even my feet were unsteady and hating me.

But somehow, I found the energy to push myself off the doorframe, dragging my body toward the bed, my breathing more labored the closer I got.

It was one thing to see the damage from afar.

It was a whole other thing to view it this close.

There were pads on his chest, an oxygen tube in his nose, and machines behind him that were monitoring his status.

The *beep, beep, beep* was all because of me.

The bruises were a midnight purple, not a violet, like I'd originally thought.

The cut on his cheek was much more rooted and jagged than it had looked from the doorway, the stitches so thick that I could see the exact spots where they had been weaved and sewn through his skin.

I could only imagine what was beneath the blanket. The color of those bruises. The cuts. The blood.

Oh God.

My knees buckled and slammed onto the floor beside his bed. "Diesel..." I sank to the ground, my forehead resting on his arm, a spot that was just as battered. I didn't want to hurt him more, but I needed to feel him at the same time. "I'm sorry. From the bottom of my heart, I'm so, so sorry."

That wasn't enough.

It wasn't nearly enough.

"I'm going to be okay." His voice—guttural, scratchy, and hoarse—cut straight through the air.

A reply that might as well have twisted the blade.

"I need you to be okay." I wrapped both of my hands around his, looking up across his broad chest. "I need you to make a full recovery.

I need you to be the same person you were before tonight."

In every scenario I'd ever seen him, he looked massive.

But not here.

Here, in this bed, he looked small.

Frail.

Fragile.

I tried not to squeeze his palm, but I couldn't help it. "I'm not going to leave you, Diesel. No matter how long you have to stay in Edinburgh, I'll be here. At your side."

I couldn't do that for Preston. I'd wanted to, but I couldn't. If Brady had to put a guard at the door of Diesel's hospital room, I didn't care; I wasn't leaving this man alone. Not when he'd risked his life for us.

I rubbed his hand over my cheek. "I promise you'll have me here until you walk out of this hospital."

He locked his thumb around my hand. "You've got a good one here, Brady."

How could he say that?

After everything that had happened tonight?

A night that still didn't make sense to me. All I knew was the phone call had come in from hotel security, telling Brady that they'd found Diesel on the floor in the hallway outside our room. That the ambulance brought him to the hospital. We'd immediately left dinner and caught a taxi and come here, where we were taken into the emergency department.

What my gut told me was that David hadn't been caught by the hotel security. That somehow, he'd slipped in and out without being detected.

Like a cockroach, scurrying toward a tiny hole, never getting slapped or stomped on.

That was David.

"Tell me how you're feeling, buddy."

It wasn't a chuckle that left his busted lips, but an attempt at one. "I've had better days. Doc is mostly worried about my lungs and spleen. Hoping it's nothing too—"

"We need to take you in for X-rays," a nurse said as she poked her head into the doorway. "We don't know if you'll be coming back to this unit or going onto a floor or straight into surgery. Best say your goodbyes now." She held up her finger. "I'll be back in one minute."

The moment she was gone, Brady said to Diesel, "Have the police been by yet?"

"Not yet," Diesel answered. "I was only in this room for a couple of minutes before you guys came in." His mouth was the only thing that moved when he talked. His face was too puffy to blink or wrinkle, to even raise his eyebrows.

"I'm sure they'll be here at some point to question you," Brady told him.

As if my stomach couldn't go any lower, it practically sank to the tiles beneath me, my mouth filling with a salty taste from the tears.

"You're all set with your story?" Brady inquired.

Diesel gave him a thumbs-up.

Brady then softly put his hand on Diesel's shoulder. "We'll be back to check on you. If you need anything in the meantime, you know how to reach me." He walked to my side of the bed and put his hands under my arms, helping me get up.

"I don't want to leave you," I said to Diesel.

"I'll be all right," he voiced to me.

Just all right?

That wasn't a good enough answer.

I needed certainty.

I needed a guarantee.

"I'll be back as soon as they let me see you," I whispered through a sob, and I let Brady take me out of the emergency department, the cool evening instantly slapping my wet face.

I couldn't take another step.

Not until I knew what they had been talking about.

So, I halted under the awning by the exit and waited for Brady to look at me. "What is he telling the police?"

"Nothing. He's paid to keep his mouth shut."

What did this mean?

Why couldn't I process anything?

"What about the footage from the cameras at the hotel?" I asked. "Won't there be proof—"

"There is no footage, Lily. With the renovation, the security feed is choppy at best. It hasn't been working correctly since the rehab started on the floors of the hotel."

That wasn't true.

I knew there was footage. I'd heard Brady ask about it at the restaurant.

"Are you telling me the truth?" I pressed.

"No." His voice stayed low. "But that's what the police will be told by every member of my security team." He rested his hands on my neck, his fingers fanning up to my face. "Georgia can't protect that motherfucker here. I could easily turn him into the authorities and have them deal with the bastard."

David would run.

He'd never let the police in Scotland find him.

He was probably already on his way back to the States.

"Brady—"

"But that would be too easy." He rubbed my cheeks as though he was trying to calm me. "Edinburgh won't give him the punishment he deserves, which he's going to get the second I put my fucking hands on him."

This was too much.

I couldn't handle any more.

I couldn't breathe.

I wiggled out of Brady's hold.

"Where are you going, Lily?"

"I need air," I said over my shoulder.

He moved in beside me, his hands somewhere on my body, but I was too numb to place their location; I could just feel the heat his fingers were giving off.

With each step, the weight of my feet was becoming too much.

So were my legs.

And my torso.

And my damn chest and head.

"This is my fault." The tears were coming much faster now. But instead of feeling like hot lava, they were more like acid. "Diesel is lying in that bed because of me. Every discoloration on his skin and cut and bit of swelling is because of me. And that's just on the surface. I don't know what's happening underneath." I tried to draw in some breath. "The same thing happened to Preston. Don't you understand, Brady? I'm the problem. I can't—"

"Don't start blaming yourself." He moved in front of me, blocking me so I couldn't continue to walk. "Diesel knew what the job entailed before he took it. He knew something like this—or even worse—could happen. And he's not the only person who would stand in the way of harm to protect you, Lily." His hands returned to my face, tilting my chin so my eyes were pointed at him. "I would do the same. I would take a fucking beating if that meant keeping you safe. I'd take whatever that asshole gave me as long as I knew you were okay and that he didn't lay a finger on you."

How?

Why?

I don't deserve this. I don't get to have someone like him.

"Brady..." I gasped in some air. "Why?" My head shook. "Why would you do this for me? Why—"

"Because I love you." He pulled me against him, holding me in his arms. A place I never wanted to leave. A place that felt more like home than anywhere I'd lived since my parents had passed. "Because I fucking love you—do you hear me?"

With our chests aligned, I could feel the beating beneath his skin.

And the strength in his hands as they held me.

And the warmth from his body, protecting me from everything, even the chilly breeze.

"I love you. Oh God, I love you."

When the words were said a third and fourth time, they weren't uttered in his voice.

They were spoken in mine.

Chapter Thirty-Three

BRADY

David: *You thought Diesel would stop me, you stupid motherfucker. Do I need to remind you to do better? Feels like I do.*

Me: *You're fucking dead. Wait until I get my hands on you.*

David: *Diesel has about 100 pounds on you. What, are you going to kick my ass? Spank me? First, you'll have to find me. I know you've been looking. Haven't you? You're just not good enough.*

• • •

David: *It's really fucking sad that Lily chose to be with a moron like you.*

Me: *Fuck you.*

David: *Fuck me? You're getting funnier by the day.*

Me: *I'm going to fucking kill you.*

David: *I think we know it's the exact opposite. I'm going to kill you.*

• • •

David: *You have two choices: stay with her, which won't end*

pretty, I promise, or give her back to me and all of this will stop.
Me: *It's not a choice.*
David: *Then, watch your back, Brady. I'm feeling…revengeful.*

• • •

"Welcome home," Dominick said as I stomped into his office, shut the door behind me, and collapsed in the chair across from his desk.

I'd been back in LA for less than three hours, and after dropping my shit off at home, this was the first place I came.

I didn't know where else to go or who else to turn to.

My brothers couldn't help with this situation.

Dom was my only shot.

David: *Already leaving Lily all alone? You think keeping her in your house with a security system and a guard by the door is going to stop me?*

David: *Fucking idiot.*

I shoved my phone into my pocket, dropped my elbows onto my knees, and dived my fingers into my hair. I was surprised there were any strands left by the way I'd been tearing at them lately. "I need advice."

"About…"

I glanced up. All the rage, all the resentment, all the furor was coming to a head. "I don't know what the hell to do about David."

"The ex?"

"From hell," I added.

He adjusted his cuff links before setting his hands down on his desk. "Before we get to him, how's Diesel?"

I hissed out the air I hadn't realized I'd been holding in and leaned back in the chair. "Two weeks…" I couldn't stop the growl from coming through my lips. "Two fucking weeks he spent in that hospital. Can you believe that shit? A concussion, broken collarbone, four broken ribs. A ruptured spleen. A bruised lung." I let my hands fall after using them to count each one of his injuries.

"David used a fucking crowbar on him, Dominick, and came at him from behind. It's no wonder Diesel didn't stand a chance." My chest began to pound. "The footage... I could barely watch it. Makes me fucking sick to my stomach."

"Damn, dude." Dominick crossed his arms over his chest. "Doesn't sound like David gives a fuck about anything, and he won't stop until he gets what he wants."

"That's the thing. Once he got Diesel down on the ground, he didn't stop. He probably wouldn't have, but two of our guests came off the elevator, heading in his direction to get to their room, and David obviously didn't want to be seen or caught, so he took off for the stairs."

Dominick knew the basics. We'd spoken multiple times while I was in Scotland the past few weeks. What he didn't know were the finer details, things I hadn't wanted to discuss over the phone.

I crossed one leg over the other, my foot swinging in the air. "He set up a distraction to get the security team away from the feed. Same thing he had done in Charleston, which we thought was a coincidence at the time, and now, we know it wasn't. This guy knows what he's doing."

"He's a calculated motherfucker."

I nodded. "No shit." I wiped my hands over my jeans, the sweat pouring out of my body—I was so worked up. "We'd been to Edinburgh three times before our last visit, and David didn't do anything. Diesel sat outside our room during every one of those trips. And then—boom—out of nowhere, he strikes."

"Sounds like there's no rhyme or reason for when he attacks. He just goes straight for it."

My eyes shut as I exhaled. "Except for his texts. They come in daily. Threats, bullshit. He won't stop." When my hands were done rubbing my jeans, I gripped the armrests of the chair. "I've looked for him. I've had my assistant, who's as good as a PI, try to find him. I even hired a PI to locate him. He's untraceable."

Dominick's brows rose. "What would you do if you found him?"

I stayed silent, staring at my best friend.

"All right," he voiced when he realized I was going to say the words he feared, "let me ask you this: what do you think it'll take for him to stop?"

I clenched my fingers into a fist. "He wants me to give her up."

"That's not an option."

I blew out some heavy wind from my chest. "No, it's not a fucking option."

"The police can't take care of this, correct?"

"Correct." I shook my head. "I've beefed up my security. Lily is never alone, no matter where she goes. I'm carrying a fucking gun on me at all times in case the asshole jumps me in public." I lifted the bottom of my polo, showing him where the gun was tucked into my pants. "That's why I'm coming to you. I don't know what the hell to do at this point."

He leaned onto his desk. "First off, you're not going to have blood on your hands. I won't let that happen. You have too much to lose—Lily, your freedom, your business."

It wasn't easy to wrap my head around any of this.

What it meant.

What I was willing to do.

How that blood would be on my hands for the rest of my fucking life.

But I saw no other way around it. If I couldn't go to the police, who else was going to make sure the bastard didn't hurt Lily?

"I don't have any other option," I admitted.

"But you do, my friend." He glanced toward his office door before he moved his chair in closer. "You know my buddy Brett Young?"

It took a moment to move the anger aside and focus on something besides David and what I planned to do to him.

"The entertainment agent. Of course I know him." I'd seen him at plenty of Dominick's parties. We were acquaintances, but we'd never hung out personally.

"Yes, him. Now, stay with me because this is going to get a little convoluted." He folded his hands together. "One of Brett's partners is a woman named Scarlett Davis. Scarlett's best friend is Pepper Michaels. Does Pepper's name ring a bell?"

My teeth ground against each other. "What does this have to do with me?"

"Trust me, Brady." He nodded toward me. "Have you heard of Pepper?"

"Fuck, you're making me think." My head dropped toward my legs as I silently repeated her name, waiting for it to hit me. When it did, I said, "She's the owner of the sex club, isn't she?"

I'd never been, but I knew several guys who had checked it out and spent some time there.

"Yes, that's her." He reached to the bottom of his desk, where I assumed was a keypad because I heard the beeps as he tapped the different buttons. When his hand returned, he was holding a small black card that he pushed across his desk toward me. On it was a phone number written in white ink. "Pepper's boyfriend, Bale, is who you need to talk to. That's his number."

"Who the fuck is Bale?"

He slowly licked his lips. "The man who's going to make this all go away."

"And you keep his number locked in your desk?" I took several deep breaths.

His smirk was the kind of reply I was looking for. "You never know when you might need it. It came in handy today, didn't it?" He tapped his desk, his eyes narrowing. "Do yourself a favor—don't call him unless you're absolutely ready." He leaned in even closer to me. "Because once you talk to him, there's no turning back."

I held the card, flipping it to check the other side, but there was nothing else written on it. "You're guaranteeing me that he'll get rid of David? You're positive about that?"

Dominick smiled. "I've never been surer about anything in my life."

The way he spoke those words was haunting.

I could feel them inside my body.

I could still hear them in my head.

Dominick was my closest bud, and we were always honest with each other. Something told me that if I asked him who else he'd given this card to, he wouldn't tell me, nor would he admit that he'd ever given it out before.

But what I knew was that he wouldn't bullshit me.

I'd come to him for help.

And he'd just given me everything I needed.

"So, I just dial his number and…" My voice trailed off to let him fill in the blank.

"And follow his instructions when he answers—and he will, regardless of what time you call. You'll pay a fee, he'll give you a time frame, and you'll be given proof that the job was done."

I stared at his digits again. "It's that easy."

"No."

His reply made me look at him again.

"Nothing about this is fucking easy," he continued, "and you'll think about it until the day you die. But it's necessary—we both know that."

Chapter Thirty-Four

LILY

Brady stared at me from the other side of the main cabin with the most devilish smile on his face. We were only three hours into our trip to Bangkok, and every few minutes, I would find myself glancing in his direction, and each time, his eyes would already be on me. It didn't matter if he was in deep conversation with his brothers and Jenner or that I was sitting on the opposite side of the plane, chatting with the ladies.

When it came to him, his gaze was never far.

That was one of the many things I loved about him.

And I wanted him to feel the love flowing through me, but Jo was dragging my attention back to our group of girls as she said, "I have to tell you that I've never seen Brady like this in my entire life." She tapped her hand over the side of my leg. "He has heart eyes over you, girl."

I didn't know if it was her lotion or perfume—or both—that was the most delicious scent of pumpkin.

Wedged between Jo and Macon's girlfriend, Brooklyn, with Rowan sitting across from us, all of us forming a small circle, I took my time looking at each of their faces as I replied, "I'm nuts about him." I grinned and then gave my man a quick glance, our gazes locking before I added, "Honestly, he's the best thing that's ever happened to me."

Within the first twenty minutes of the flight, it almost felt as though I had three new best friends. Brooklyn and Rowan were just as warm as Jo and immediately embraced me. It was shocking, given that I was employed by the Spades, that I hadn't met either of them yet, but so far, Brady was the only person I'd flown with.

"Is it just me, or does it look like Brady's about to take you into the back bedroom and do the extra naughty to you?" Brooklyn said.

"I was thinking the same thing," Rowan agreed. "He can't take those heart eyes off you."

Jo smiled and laughed. "He's my cousin, I can't go there, you guys."

"He won't go there either," I said, giggling to Jo. "And don't worry; he might look like he wants to take me into the bedroom, but he wouldn't dare with all of you on the plane."

"But when we're not on the plane..." Brooklyn sang.

I shrugged. "Admittedly, anything is possible."

Everyone laughed.

"It's funny, when I first met Brady, I wasn't a fan." Rowan kept her voice down as she spoke. "He wasn't super excited about my relationship with Cooper. One, because he was losing his drinking buddy and partner in crime, and he hated that. Two, because I had become an executive at the company, and he didn't think, in our position, we should be dating."

"Even though Macon did the same thing." Brooklyn rolled her eyes.

"No kidding," Rowan replied to her. "And three, he didn't want my family's business to merge with his, and that pissed him off to no end."

"It was quite the trifecta," Jo added.

Rowan said, "One I didn't think we'd survive, but fortunately, we did."

I'd heard Brady's side of the story. I'd never heard Rowan's.

So, I asked cautiously, "Was Brady...mean to you?"

"Not mean. He was just spicy." Rowan let out a laugh. "Which is something I understand well. My oldest brother, Rhett, is just like Brady, so I know the behavior. Good thing is, Brady came around pretty fast, and underneath that rough, growly exterior is someone absolutely amazing." Her grin grew. "But seeing you two together puts things in perspective. You could say, it gives me hope for Rhett."

"Brady's problem was that he was missing love." Brooklyn's icy-blue eyes held me while she talked. "Now that he has it, he's a whole different person. He's fulfilled, and his attitude—or lack thereof—really shows it."

Rowan put her mocha-colored hair into a low ponytail. "His smile gives that away." Her eyes shifted to me. "Your boy never smiled before."

"It's like an emoji has taken over his face," Jo said, laughing.

"The heart-eye emoji!" Brooklyn said a little too loud.

They were all trying to inconspicuously glance in Brady's direction.

But I didn't have to. I knew exactly what they were talking about.

Because it was the expression that almost always stared back at me nowadays, except when we were talking about David or Diesel.

What the girls didn't know was that beneath the hearts was a feeling of contentment.

Of knowing we were in the right place with the right person.

Something neither of us had known we wanted until we found it.

"I need to add one more thing," Jo said, looping her arm through mine. "Given that Brady is my cousin, I've spent more time with him than I can even count. And never, in all these years, has he ever brought someone home or on a vacation with us." She dragged her teeth over her bottom lip. "The man is thirty-one years old. Can we take in how big of a moment this is?"

Her expression let me know she wasn't done. "But what's equally important is that he didn't just bring any woman with him, he brought you." She squeezed tighter. "I know we've gotten to spend a bit more time together than you have with Brooklyn and Rowan, and in that time, I've grown to adore you. I'm so happy you're part of the family."

"I feel the same," Brooklyn added. "You remind me so much of my sister, Clementine, which means I automatically love you. Gorgeous, caring, with old-soul vibes—you're fabulous, Lily."

"Something tells me we're all going to be great friends," Rowan said.

"I hope so." I didn't think my smile could grow, but it did. "And I have to add, I'm looking forward to meeting your brothers at the end of this trip even though we'll only get to spend a little time with them," I said to Rowan.

"Yes"—Rowan laughed—"that." She shook her head. "Believe it or not, Brady invited them to join us for the entire trip, and part of me thinks they would have taken him up on the offer, but Daisy's mom was just returning from a work thing out of state, and there was coordinating to do, and Ridge couldn't make it happen. So, one night with them is all we get."

"Rhett doesn't have the same excuse," Jo said.

Rowan voiced, "You're right about that. I just don't think he was ready to make that kind of leap without his brother. And given my relationship with Cooper, I don't exactly make the best wingwoman for him."

"I have to admit, I get his stance," I said to the ladies. "We all know Brady on the outside isn't the warmest person in the world, so if Rhett is like him, which you said he is, I can see his hesitation. Guys like them can't just jump into the pack. They have to dip their toes in first and feel out the temperature of the water. The best news is, he's coming, even if it's for only a short time." I put my hand on Rowan's arm. "I know Brady had lunch with your brothers not too long ago, and he said things went well. Another huge step in the right direction."

"You're right," Rowan said after a few seconds of silence, but she wasn't looking at me; she was staring at Brooklyn and Jo. "She's perfect for him, and I love her."

. . .

"Get over here," Brady said as he swam over to where I was sitting on the edge of the pool, taking in the gorgeous scenery around us. He moved in between my legs, giving me a one-second warning before he pulled me into the water.

"Ah!" I giggled as he slid me into the coolness. My arms and legs circled him, our faces aligned. "Hi."

He dipped us as low as our necks. "I've missed you."

"You just went over to the other side of the pool to grab a fry from Rowan's lunch."

"And I missed you while I was gone."

I gave him a quick peck on the lips. "Please don't ever stop feeling that way about me. It fills me in ways you can't even imagine."

"A feeling that will never die, I promise."

Sun-kissed.

Rested.

Smiling.

That was how the two of us looked after four days in Bangkok.

Away from David, as far as I knew, and assured that Diesel was healing back at home, we could actually relax.

When we'd left LA, I hadn't been sure how a vacation with a group of people I didn't know that well—and some hardly at all—would go. But every moment had been perfect—from the walks I took with the girls in the morning to the meals we all ate together, the time we spent at the spa, and the sightseeing.

I understood why Brady enjoyed vacationing with this crew. There wasn't a second when we weren't laughing or having fun.

I nodded toward the far side of the pool, where Rhett and Ridge were hanging out with Cooper and Rowan. "We should go join them."

"We should?"

"Yes." I hugged him tighter. "They're Rowan's brothers. They're your partners, and technically, they're my bosses. We should spend as much time with them as possible."

"At the moment, I'd just like to focus on how you feel in this fucking bikini." His hands rubbed down my back, around my ass, and up my sides. "Fuck me, I wish there weren't anyone in this pool right now."

"I think this position is getting you a little too worked up." I tried to wiggle, but he wasn't letting me go anywhere.

"It's not the position, Lily. You could be wearing a goddamn snowsuit, and we could be in the center of a fucking snowbank, freezing to death, and I'd feel the same way."

That feeling.

How did he do it?

How did he consistently make me experience it?

They were just words, yet they were so much more with him.

I kissed him.

And then I kissed him again, but slower this time, tasting the sun and pool and French fry on his lips.

When I pulled away, his hard-on was pressing against me.

I had two options. I could either go up to the room with him— something I wanted more than anything—but that meant we wouldn't be seeing the group for at least an hour, and I really thought we needed to join Rhett and Ridge, or I could change the subject.

"You know," I started, "every morning, during our walk, the girls can't stop saying how blown away they are by you."

He chuckled. "And what does that mean?"

I ran my hands over his scruff. A thickness that I loved feeling with my fingers and when it scratched the sensitive skin between my legs. He wasn't allowed to ever shave it.

"Apparently, you're a whole new guy, and they love the version you've turned into."

"You mean, an emoji with heart eyes?" he growled. "You guys weren't exactly quiet on the plane."

I laughed. "They've been calling you that ever since."

"I know. Macon and Cooper found out about it and have been giving me endless shit." He aimed his tip against me. "Which I'm fine with because it's true." His hands returned to my ass, palming each cheek.

He was slowly moving us through the water. He wasn't bringing us over to Ridge and Rhett; he was just circling the section of pool that was surrounded by the suites our group was staying in.

Brady had booked the highest-rated hotel in Bangkok for us to stay in. After touring a few of the available properties, the six other partners agreed with the one Brady had picked to purchase, and Jenner was going to submit the offer. Once the Edinburgh remodel was finished, Bangkok would be his newest destination. And when that happened, his hotel would be the highest-rated resort in the city.

But with that decision came questions.

Many that had been filling my head over the last few days.

"How long do you think the rehab here is going to take?" I asked.

"Why?"

I arched my neck, soaking my hair in the water before I faced him. "I assume you're going to move here, it's too far to go back and forth weekly. That means the plane will be used by your other partners, and I'll be everywhere but here."

Not that I minded working for his other partners—that wasn't the issue. It was the thought of being away from Brady for any extended period of time. I didn't like the idea of that at all.

"You're saying you're going to miss me?" He dived into my neck, kissing up my ear and across my cheek until his lips were hovering over mine. "Is that what I'm hearing?"

"I think that goes without saying."

"Six to eight months is my guess." He traced his thumb over my bottom lip. "I can tell you one thing: there's no fucking way I'm going to let my wife be away from me for that long."

My eyes widened. "Your wife?"

"And if it were up to me, my wife would be moving to Bangkok with me." His other hand left my ass, and both palms were now holding my face. "I won't make that decision for you. But I don't want to be away from you, and I hope you don't want to be away from me."

"What…" As my voice trailed off, I couldn't stop staring into his eyes, waiting for the intensity in his expression to die down. It didn't. It just continued to see right through me, confirming the seriousness of what he'd just said. A statement that had taken my breath away. "That's a title I've never been called before."

"It's not just a title, Lily. It's going to be a reality very soon."

Chapter Thirty-Five

Brady

"Hey!" Cooper yelled to get my attention from the other side of the van, a vehicle large enough to hold our entire party. "You planned one hell of a trip, my brother." He put his arm around Rowan's shoulders. "We had a blast."

The old me would have smirked and taken the credit. Because I just didn't give a fuck.

But Lily was right; there was a change. I felt it in everything I did and the things I said.

And it was all because of her.

"You mean, our assistant planned one hell of a trip." I knew Bangkok well enough that I had a preference on where I wanted all of us to stay, but she had booked our spa visits and the sightseeing and every restaurant we had eaten at.

"Who gives a shit who planned it?" Macon said. "This was fun as hell."

Brooklyn put her hands up in the air. "I second that."

"You know we loved every second of it," Jo added.

"Fuck yeah," Jenner agreed.

I linked my fingers through Lily's and pulled her closer.

Goddamn it, she smelled good. The pineapple coming on strong since she'd just showered.

"I'm glad you guys came."

My stare landed on Rhett and Ridge. They'd joined us yesterday, staying just long enough to view the properties Jenner had found, get in a little relaxation, some dinner, before flying home with us this morning. What was wild was that I'd actually had a good time with them. Rhett had loosened up a bit, and Ridge was more talkative than he'd ever been.

"And I'm glad you guys came too. It was nice to see you both relax." I let out a chuckle to let them know I was giving them shit.

Ridge laughed. "I'm not going to lie…I wish I'd been able to come sooner and spend some more time here."

My brows rose. "Was that a compliment?"

"Probably the biggest one I could ever give you," he replied.

I pounded his fist. "I'll take it." I turned my focus to Rhett. "And you? Can I count you in for the next trip?"

"I came to this one, didn't I?"

That was Rhett's way of giving a compliment.

I knew his style.

Before Lily, I would have said the same thing.

I held out my balled-up fist to him. "Happy you did."

After he knocked his knuckles against mine, I turned to Lily.

There was so much conversation happening around us that no one could hear anything I was about to say.

Except she beat me to it and whispered, "Do you see me beaming?" Her smile certainly was. "I couldn't be prouder of you right now."

"Because of what I just said to Ridge and Rhett?"

She nodded.

"Lily, it wasn't more than a few words of conversation."

"But it was a start—and a big start."

I kissed her cheek, moving my mouth to her ear. "I'll give you that."

She cuddled up to my side as the van pulled into the entrance of the private airport. Once we cleared security, the driver continued onto the tarmac and parked a few feet from the plane, where one of the pilots was waiting at the bottom of the stairs.

Before the driver even had a chance to get out of his seat, the pilot was pulling at the handle of the van, sliding the door open. He peered inside with a peculiar look on his face, scanning everyone until he found me. "Brady, we have a problem."

Those were words I didn't want to fucking hear.

Words that instantly triggered my heart to start pounding.

The pilot's statement could have been referencing anything, but I still glanced at my newly hired bodyguard, who was sitting closest to the door, making sure he was on alert. When I saw that he was, I gave Lily's hand a squeeze and climbed out of the van, joining the pilot on the tarmac.

"What's going on?" I asked him.

The bodyguard got out and stood behind me.

"I've been calling and texting you," the pilot responded. "I was hoping to talk to you before you arrived so I could warn you."

I pulled out my phone. There were several missed calls and texts from him.

What the fuck?

I checked the settings, seeing the mode for Do Not Disturb was on, which was why I hadn't heard any of his attempts to reach me.

"Sorry about that. It won't happen again. Fill me in on what's going on."

He crossed his arms, like he didn't know what to do with them. "The crew arrived at the plane about an hour ago to do our usual preflight checklist and flight plan, and when we got on board..." His eyes dropped to the ground, a redness heating his cheeks.

What the hell?

What was he about to tell me?

"The plane," he began, "was a mess."

"A mess?"

His head shook as though he was afraid to say anything else. "It's been vandalized."

"It's been...*what*?" The pounding in my chest turned to a fire. A fire with flames that were about to lick straight out of my mouth. "Tell me you're fucking kidding me right now. Wasn't it locked?"

"Yes, of course it was."

"Then, how the hell—" I cut myself off because I knew how this had happened.

Instead of saying another word, I took the steps two at a time, and as soon as I turned into the main cabin, I saw the destruction.

My stomach instantly sank.

Motherfucker.

I gripped the headrest of each seat as I walked through the cabin, knowing my knuckles were turning white from the pressure, the anger in my body building with each step. David had written *MAKE YOUR CHOICE* on the back of every fucking seat, along with the walls and windows, with what looked like black marker. The base of the seats had been sliced with a knife, where there were multiple rips in the leather, running vertically and horizontally, so the stuffing was coming out. The carpet was in similar shape, torn and shredded in many areas.

This was more than a mess.

This was devastation.

I headed for the galley, where bottles had been shattered, liquor and condiments splattered all over the walls, where the same words had been written across the wallpaper and over each cabinet. The flight attendant was in the restroom, the door open, where she was trying to clean up all the glass from the mirror he had shattered above the sink, where he'd also ripped off the toilet seat and graffitied the walls inside.

I couldn't fucking believe what I was seeing.

David wasn't just trying to make things difficult for me.

He was defacing and demolishing everything that meant something to me.

He was kicking me where it hurt.

But what was next?

My life?

Cooper's? Macon's?

My parents'?

Lily had said it before…and she was right.

He wasn't going to stop.

My phone was still in my hand. My damn fingers shaking in rage as I turned the screen toward me, trying to flip through the notifications, finding the text I knew was waiting for me, but all I could see was fucking red.

David: *Keep taking what's mine, and I'll keep taking what's yours.*

David: *It's your choice.*

David: *NOW, MAKE A FUCKING DECISION.*

"What the fuck?!" Cooper yelled from behind me.

I turned around to see my brother's face full of shock and concern.

A few seconds later, Macon appeared beside him, shouting, "Who in the hell would do this?" as he scanned the interior.

Rhett and Ridge were behind them, the same look coming through their expression.

"What the hell happened here?" Ridge demanded.

"This is bullshit," Rhett added. "Who would do something this fucked up?"

"Oh God, no!" Jenner shouted as he joined us.

Aside from Ridge and Rhett, the guys knew there was only one man in this world who had balls big enough to do this.

Before I could reply to any of them, the pilot voiced, "We've been trying to clean things up. We don't have a product that will take off the marker. But when we get back to LA—"

"I'll have it taken care of," I told him. "It's not your responsibility to clean it. I appreciate you trying." A thought hit me, a worry that went so fucking deep that I had a hard time getting out the question. "Was there any damage to the cockpit? Can you fly the plane?"

"The cockpit wasn't touched," the pilot responded. "Neither were the twin engines or anything external from what we can tell. I'm having a flight engineer check things out to be sure. So far, the damage only appears to be in here."

Cosmetically, it could all be repaired. If he'd fucked with the guts of the plane, that would have made things much trickier.

"Brady…" Lily gasped as she stood in the mouth of the cabin, her voice small, weak. Her hand went over her lips as she took in what was before her.

She knew who had caused this wreckage, and her eyes told me she was blaming herself.

She was horrified.

Mortified.

Embarrassed.

I wanted to fucking murder that bastard for the both of us.

"Brady—"

As she started to say my name again, I cut her off with, "Cooper, Macon, Jenner"—I stopped to think for a second, questioning if I should include Rhett and Ridge since they knew nothing about the situation, but quickly realized they owned as much of this plane as I did and they needed to be included—"Rhett and Ridge, I need to talk to you outside." I pointed at the door and nodded, signaling for them to start moving.

I then walked over to Lily and put my hands on her cheeks. "I'm going to go talk to the guys about this. I'll be right back."

Her eyes were already filling with tears. "I'm sorry, Brady. I c-can't... I don't... I'm s-so, so—"

"Baby, this isn't your fault."

"How c-can you say th-that?"

"Because it's my fault. My fault that I haven't stopped this motherfucker yet." I pointed her eyes up at me, catching the first tear as it dripped. "Are you okay if I leave you for a few minutes?"

She took a breath instead of answering me.

"I need to know you're okay before I can go anywhere, Lily."

She nodded. "I'm okay."

I gave her a quick kiss.

Now that the women and bodyguard had boarded the plane, I called Jo over, waiting for her to wrap her arms around Lily before I took off for the steps and met the guys on the tarmac. I knew they were going to tell their women about the conversation we were about to have. I was fine with that. I just wanted to have it with the men first, and I didn't want to have to filter what I was about to say.

"Most of you know it was David who did this to our plane." I crossed my arms before I threw my phone across the fucking runway. "I don't know how he got it unlocked, but the motherfucker somehow made it happen, and he left this mess."

Knowing Ridge and Rhett were lost, I said to them, "David is Lily's ex-boyfriend. The dude isn't right in the head."

I gave them a quick rundown of his behavior, a fast-forwarded synopsis of what he'd done to Diesel to give them an idea of the type of person I was dealing with and why I couldn't go to the police. I even pulled out my phone and showed them his most recent text.

"Aside from telling him you're going to kill him, what else have you done?" Macon asked.

I explained how I'd researched David, how I'd had our assistant look into locating him so I could confront him myself, and how all attempts had been unsuccessful.

"He has a presence online. Loves to post on social media. I just can't nail him down."

"What would you do if you got your hands on him?" Jenner asked.

I hissed out a mouthful of air, my jaws locking, as I was holding them together so tightly. "I think the real question is, how long can I let this go on for?" I rubbed a palm over my other balled fist, envisioning what it would feel like if it connected to David's face. "The biggest thing I'm worried about is his next move. Who else is he going to hurt? One of you? Lily? Our parents?" I let the reality of that set in for the second time today, and all it did was work me up more. "Is he going to burn down our corporate headquarters? My house?" I looked at each of their faces as I clenched my teeth. "Is he going to kill me?"

I wanted to fucking scream, and I wanted to beat something. I wanted to hit it so hard, again and again, until there was blood on my skin.

This wasn't rage.

This went far beyond that.

"The asshole is getting through my personal security," I continued, my voice as rough as sandpaper. "He's getting through the security at our hotels. He's getting through locks." My arms dropped at my sides, both hands now squeezing into fists. "The dude's like a goddamn ghost. How the fuck do you stop someone who's as invisible as him?"

"There's only one way," Cooper said, his tone harrowing.

I ignored him and bellowed, "Because it won't end unless I give her up, and I'm telling you all right now, I'm not giving up a woman who's going to be my wife." I shifted my gaze around the entire circle to reinforce that point.

There was a vibration in my pocket, and I lifted my phone to my face.

David: *Are you asking yourself who or what is next?*

David: *You should.*

When I showed the new messages to the guys, Cooper roared, "End him. That's my answer. That's how all this stops. There's no alternative. I'm telling you right now if some asshole was pulling this shit with Rowan, I would do the same thing."

"He's right," Jenner said. "You have no other choice."

The group turned silent until Rhett broke the quietness with, "I think you all know I would have killed him already." He rubbed his hand over the side of his black beard, showing the lion tattoo on his thumb. "He's making your life hell. He's making Lily's life hell. This isn't a job for the police. This is a job for someone who will put a bullet through his fucking skull."

Ridge nodded. "I agree with Rhett."

Jenner added, "You don't want blood on your hands, brother. There are people out there you can hire who can do a much better job than any of us could."

I nodded. "I've got a name."

Macon was the softest of the group. That didn't make him feeble. He just had a heart bigger than the rest of us. As I looked at him, I saw nothing fragile in his stare.

"If he hurts you or Lily or any of us, which he will, then this isn't even a discussion. You need to protect your family, Brady, and Lily's part of our family."

Chapter Thirty-Six

LILY

B rady reached for me the second I climbed into his bed and pulled me toward him, immediately snuggling me against his chest. My head nestled in the spot just below his neck, my arm wrapped around his stomach, and our breathing matched as the quietness of the room took hold.

It was just us and the fireplace across from us, the gas spitting off a dull white noise.

But it felt like there was so much more happening inside this room. It felt like there were a thousand people in here, all screaming, *David*, at the same time.

We'd gotten home from Bangkok yesterday and not left his house since. We could probably use the excuse that we were getting reacclimated to the time zone, battling jet lag, and resting up before we had to leave for Edinburgh in a few days.

But I was positive that wasn't the case for either of us.

Especially because Brady had made it clear that he wasn't comfortable with me going to his Beverly Hills hotel to grab what I would need for our next trip. He said his assistant would go for me and bring anything I requested.

I'd become a prisoner again because of David.

But this time, Brady was too.

Not just in the physical sense, but mentally as well.

From the moment I'd stepped on the plane in Bangkok, David was all I'd thought about. My brain an endless maze of questions and worry.

Why was this man trying to destroy everything I cared about?

What would it take for him to stop?

Leaving Brady?

Having to make that impossibly painful decision just to save whoever he planned to victimize next?

Maybe that was what I needed to do.

Maybe this had to be on me, not Brady, even though he'd insisted he was taking care of things.

"How far are you inside your head right now?" he asked.

His voice was like a blade, cutting through the semi-silence, the point startling me enough that I jumped.

I was so far into my head that I hadn't realized I'd been rubbing his chest or that my breath was coming out in pants or that my entire body had tightened into a ball.

I tilted my neck back to glance up at his face. "Clearly, you're seeing straight through me."

"I've been doing just as much thinking." He brushed some hair off my forehead. "On the flight, since we've been home—he's the only thing I can focus on."

"Same." Lying down no longer felt like the right position, so I sat next to him, crossing my legs in front of me. "Everything aches, Brady. Everything is so..." My voice trailed off as I thought of a more accurate description. What I was experiencing was deeper than an ache. It was a heaviness that lived directly above my heart, a weight that wouldn't lift. That made it hard to breathe. That sent tears shooting into my eyes. "So fucked up," I finished. I wiggled my fingers, trying to move the numbness out of them. "Something has to give. Something has to be sacrificed. It's the only way he'll stop. And it has to be me—"

"That's what I want to talk to you about," he said, cutting me off, his hand going to my leg at the same time. "Normally, I'd just make the decision and do whatever the fuck I wanted. But having you in my life, I can't do that. Your opinion matters, certainly when it comes to this." He sat up a bit higher, reclining against the headboard behind him.

"What are you saying?"

He reached toward his nightstand and grabbed his phone, tapping the screen multiple times before he faced it toward me. "I haven't told you everything."

I took the cell from his hands, the screen showing a text box with David's name at the top. "You've been texting him?"

"For a while." He nodded toward the phone. "He reached out to me first, and it's been ongoing. Read what he's sent."

For...*a while*?

And he hadn't told me?

There was an instant narrowness in my chest as I scrolled to the very top, when the first message from David had been sent, and I read their exchanges. Words full of hate. Anger. Accusations. And there were multiple messages a day.

I reached the section where David spoke about hurting Diesel, and I couldn't believe what I was seeing.

How did I ever live with that man? How did I give my body and heart to him?

How did I trust him?

He had been a monster when I was with him, but this person—this level that he'd reached—was worse than when he'd beaten up Preston. This was a revengeful, immoral, despicable human.

It was like every day that had passed fueled him a bit more.

Until he became this. Someone willing to do anything and everything to get what he wanted regardless of what that meant and who and what he destroyed in the process.

His texts, the ones he'd sent over the last couple of days, made it clear that Brady had a choice.

He could either give me up and the pain and ruin would be over or David would continue this path of wreckage.

I knew how Brady felt about me. I knew how much he loved me.

I felt the same.

But I couldn't put this choice on him. It wasn't fair that he had to make this type of decision, putting his home and business and family at risk.

David was my problem, not his.

Therefore, I had to make the decision for him.

"Brady…" The phone dropped from my hands, as I no longer had the strength to hold it. "I—"

"There's only one way to end this," he said, once again trumping my thoughts with his. "Since I can't predict how he's going to strike, I need to prevent him from even trying."

I nodded. "I know." I unraveled my legs, bent my knees, and pulled them against my chest, holding them as I rocked. "Damn it, I know."

"I have a solution. That's what I want to talk to you about."

I couldn't believe we'd reached this place.

I'd thought Brady would be the man I would marry.

I'd thought he'd be the father of my children.

My happily ever after.

But David had ruined that.

He was taking that happiness away from me.

Because he couldn't have me.

And he was forcing me to make this decision.

"Before you say anything, I need to get this out." I kept the emotion in my chest, not letting it travel to my throat or as high as my eyes. I needed to stay as strong as possible or I'd never get through this.

"When I left David, when I realized what that meant and what that was going to look like, I knew my life would never be the same. Just like when I lost my parents, things would always be different for me, and it's something I've accepted." The rocking made my stomach feel worse, so I let each knee fall to the side, pressing my feet together and wrapping my fingers around them.

"I've learned to find happiness in the little moments. Things that most people wouldn't even recognize, and that's why I know we'll be okay—why both of us will be...okay."

My memory took me back to all the sunsets I'd watched from the windows of my hotel rooms, walking through lobbies to hear the laughter and chatter from other guests so I wouldn't feel so alone.

"I don't want to do this—oh God, I don't, Brady. I can't even imagine my life without you, but there's no other choice—"

"Don't say it. Don't even think it. It's not happening." He pushed himself forward, holding my face. "Do you hear me? It's not happening."

"Brady—"

"David isn't going to come between us. It's not what you want, and it's sure as fuck not what I want."

I could no longer stop the tears. My strength to keep them in my eyes was gone.

This was just too much.

Because this wasn't the first time we'd had a conversation like this, when he'd told me that David wasn't going to get in the middle of us.

Yet here we were.

Again.

And now, it was even worse.

"H-his texts," I cried, knowing what I was going to have to tell Brady and knowing how much it was going to hurt. And knowing this would be one of the last conversations we'd ever have. "He wants y-you to make a choice."

"And I have."

I searched his eyes for what he wasn't telling me.

But before I could really look deep, he was reaching into his nightstand again, this time returning with a black business card. On it, written in white ink, was what looked like a phone number.

"This is the man who's going to make David stop."

I glanced from the number to Brady and back, several times, waiting for the meaning behind those words to hit me. "What are you saying?"

He took the card from me and held my palms together, surrounding the backs of my hands while our gazes were fixed. "David gave me an ultimatum. But I'm not giving you up, and I'm not letting him hurt anyone or anything I care about. I'm taking back the control. I'm putting a fucking end to this."

What?

How?

And then it hit me.

Not like a slap. Not even like a punch to the nose.

This was ammunition that shot straight between my eyes.

"You're telling me that man, the one whose number is on the card, is going to…" I couldn't even say the words. They wouldn't come out of my mouth.

"Yes, Lily. That man is going to kill David."

I couldn't move.

My head wouldn't even nod or shake.

That was how frozen I was.

And when I blinked, nothing came out of my eyes. Not a single drip. Even those had halted.

The only thing that was happening within me was his statement repeating over and over in my head.

Like the record was skipping.

Like my finger was slamming on the rewind button.

"That's what I wanted to talk to you about tonight," he said. "That's why I told you I would normally just make the decision, but I can't do that to you. I need you to be a part of it."

I tried to pull in enough air to say, "Do you understand what just came out of your mouth? What you're saying?" I tried to swallow. I tried to stop the screaming inside my body. "You want me to just be able to say yes? We're talking about a person's life!"

"A person who's trying to destroy us, Lily. The person who's not going to give up until he gets what he wants. I'll say it a hundred more times if I have to—I'm not going to let that happen."

"So, you're just going to kill—" I put my hand on my throat. "I can't even voice it out loud. I think I'm going to be sick…"

"Listen to me." His hands moved to my knees as he knelt in front of me. "You don't have to make the decision. That's on me. I just need you to be aware of it. I need you to know why I'm doing it. I need you to be able to look me in the eyes and know I'm doing this for us. Because, so help me God, if that motherfucker ever lays a finger on you, I will never forgive myself." His voice was beginning to get deeper, rougher, louder.

How could he say this to me?

How could I even give him an answer?

How could I make a decision this large?

A decision that would affect someone's life.

Even if he'd hurt me. Even if he'd made things hell for me. Even if he was the worst person in the world.

I swallowed, the lump so large that my throat was on fire. "I can't…"

"You can't what?"

"I can't tell you to do it."

His light-blue eyes were pleading with mine.

"I can't have that on me."

"Baby…" He pulled me into his arms and held me, using an unforgiving strength. One that I needed. "This isn't on you. You don't have to say anything."

I was trying to piece this all together. What it would feel like to live without the constant fear of David. Where I wouldn't have to worry about him hurting Brady or anyone else. Where we wouldn't need security. Where I could live a life without having to be shadowed. Where I could walk into Brady's plane and not wonder if David was hiding somewhere inside. Where I wouldn't have to wonder what he was going to do next.

That was what I wanted and why I was going to end things with Brady.

But this…this wasn't my plan.

This was unfathomable.

"Listen to me." He pulled back so I could look into his eyes. "What I need to know is, if I call the person whose number is on that card, will you still love me?" His hands moved to the back of my neck, his thumbs pressed against the sides of my mouth, his eyes locked with mine.

He would do that for us.

For my protection.

For our safety.

So the two of us could start living in a way we deserved.

But, oh God, I knew what that meant.

I knew what that decision would ultimately do.

Could I live with that?

Could I stop it from eating at me?

Could I sleep at night, knowing I was a part of this?

But didn't I deserve peace?

Love?

Freedom?

"Brady…" My head would have dropped if he wasn't holding it. My stomach was rattling, churning, the emotion moving through me in steady bolts rather than sporadic waves.

"Will you be able to look at me as the man who protected you and not the man who had your ex-boyfriend killed?"

Brady was the first boyfriend I'd ever had who considered my feelings.

He was the first boyfriend who valued me, who cared what I thought of him, who showed that my feelings mattered.

I wasn't just a piece of arm candy to him. I wasn't someone he wanted to possess.

He was giving me a voice, and he was telling me to use it.

My eyes closed, and the wetness on my lids ran down my cheeks.

My heart throbbed.

My hands shook as they clung together, fingers knotted.

I knew… I knew David wouldn't stop. I knew his fearlessness would take things to a point where someone would eventually die. An innocent bystander David murdered just to get back at Brady.

I couldn't let that happen.

I wouldn't let that guilt be on me.

My eyes opened, my lips purging, "I love you."

"Lily, I need you to answer me."

I couldn't tell him to do it. I couldn't give that order and live with myself. So, I nodded and whispered, "Yes," before I collapsed in his arms.

Chapter Thirty-Seven

BRADY

One of my favorite parts about every evening was watching Lily sleep. The way her face was so relaxed and beautiful. Peaceful. Her breathing quiet and rhythmic. Her fingers usually clinging to me, like she needed to know I wasn't going anywhere, but tonight, there was a pillow under her hand. And she was breathing harder than normal, her expression a mix of emotion, the dream appearing as though it wasn't a good one.

I could understand.

It had been a hard evening.

But it hadn't ended when she gave me the answer I wanted to hear. What followed was a deep, thorough conversation, filled with details she needed to understand.

How it would work.

Who would be doing it.

How I'd gotten Bale's information.

Was there a chance I could get blamed? Could it be traced back to me? Would it stay confidential?

Did the family know?

Would anyone say anything?

The inquiries went on for quite some time, early into the morning. She was emotional, apprehensive, and with good reason.

This decision would be final.

It would change everything.

It shouldn't be taken lightly from any angle.

And it wasn't.

I'd been thinking about it since Dominick had placed Bale's number in my hand. But for Lily, this was all new. It was something she hadn't even considered. In fact, her plan had been to end our relationship so she wouldn't put anyone at risk.

God, that gorgeous woman was willing to sacrifice so much.

But I wouldn't let that happen. Because even if she left, that didn't mean David would stop. He wasn't exactly a man of his word; I couldn't trust anything he said.

The only thing I could trust was that he couldn't hurt anyone I loved when he was dead.

I waited until I was positive she was sound asleep, a slumber so deep that she wouldn't feel me leaving the bed or hear me quietly walking out of the bedroom. With Bale's card and my cell in my hand, I went into my office and shut the door, flipping on the light before making my way over to my desk.

I set the card on the wooden desktop, staring at the numbers before I unlocked my phone and pulled up the keypad and hit the appropriate digits.

I didn't immediately press the green Call button.

I focused on it for several minutes.

It wasn't that I was wavering on my decision.

I knew what needed to be done.

I just needed a fucking moment to get my head straight.

And as though David could hear my thoughts and wanted to confirm I was making the right decision, a text from him came across my goddamn screen.

David: *Too afraid to leave your house? Unsure where I'm going to hit next?*

David: *Jesus, you're a fucking baby.*

David: *A real man would come out and face me.*

Me: *I've given you every opportunity to face me. You'd rather do everything behind my back. Because you're afraid of what will happen if I get my hands on you.*

David: *I think we both know I'm not afraid of anything.*

He wouldn't say that when Bale confronted him.

Motherfucker.

I returned to the keypad and hit the green Call button.

Within two rings, my call was answered, and I heard, "Brady Spade."

Bale knew my name and must have had my number saved in his phone. I wasn't surprised. Someone in his line of work didn't get random calls and was tipped off before his number was handed out.

In this case, I was sure Dominick had let him know I would be phoning soon.

What was interesting was that Dominick had told me Bale would answer regardless of the time.

It was four in the morning.

Apparently, Bale nor David ever slept.

"Bale..." I replied.

"What can I do for you?"

I moved his card into the top drawer of my desk. "There's a man." My eyes closed as I envisioned David's face, which I'd only ever seen through pictures. "David."

"David..." Bale repeated. "Yes."

"How does this work?"

"I'm going to text you an address. We'll meet there and discuss things a little more in detail."

I rubbed my hand over the top of my head. "I have a tail."

"You'll lose it the moment you enter the guarded garage."

"Perfect."

"I'm going to ask you a question. It'll be the most important question you ever answer."

I pushed back my chair and crossed my legs. "All right."

"Is she worth it?"

My head hit the cushion of the chair, bouncing ever so slightly, a smile pulling at my fucking lips. "Hell yes."

"I'll see you in a couple of hours," he said, and the phone went dead.

• • •

David: *You fucking asshole, you leave her in that house like a prisoner. You've got some nerve.*

Me: *Go fuck yourself.*

• • •

Bale's description of the garage had been accurate, which I learned the moment I approached the gate. It was located on the first floor of the high-rise, where there was an armed guard at the entrance. I gave him my name and showed identification, and he instructed me to park in spot 107 on the east side of the lot. From there, Bale's instructions were to get out of my car, lock it, and come to spot 162 on the west side of the lot.

There were no windows in the garage, no access to the outside, except for the entrance I'd just come through. One of the reasons, I assumed, Bale had chosen this spot. Unless David killed the guard, there was no way he could get in here.

The only thing I'd brought with me from my house was my phone, and I had been told to leave that in my car. So, that was what I did as I climbed out, locked up, and walked to the opposite side of the large space, passing all the rows of vehicles.

The numbers hung from the ceiling, making it easy to find 162, where a black Suburban with tinted windows was parked. As I approached, I heard the locks. I took that as a signal that Bale was unlocking the passenger door. To check if I was right, that was the side I went to, wrapping my fingers around the wide handle, the door instantly becoming ajar.

He looked down at me from the driver's seat. "Brady…"

I took in his black hair, blue eyes, and thick beard; my first thought was that he didn't look like a killer.

But who does?

"Bale," I said as I climbed in, shaking his hand.

There was a timer glued to the dashboard. One that we would have used in high school when we were running sprints. He hit the side of it, and a countdown of four minutes was underway.

"That's how long you're giving me?" I asked.

"In my line of work, time is crucial. It must match up perfectly. Four minutes is two minutes longer than I gave my last client. If you have questions, you'd better start asking them."

I didn't know what to expect from this conversation. Dominick hadn't told me much about Bale or his personality or how the process worked.

The beginning sounded like the best place, so I said, "What's the first step?"

He reached into the pocket of his suit jacket, removing a small envelope, and he handed it to me. "In there is my fee and where I need you to take the cash."

I began to lift the corner flap.

He said, "Do you really want to waste time looking at that information? You have three minutes left. Given that money is the least of your concern, why don't you focus on more pressing matters?"

He had a point.

I didn't know if I liked that about him or hated it.

"How are you going to do it?"

He folded his hands in his lap. "With a bullet."

"Where?"

His brows rose, his forehead folding with deep lines. "Where am I going to put the bullet, or where am I going to take him to do it?"

"The latter," I said.

"I can't tell you that."

"Then, when are you going to do it?"

He tapped the side of his head, like he was scrolling through an invisible calendar there. "Within a week. David's case isn't overly messy, so I can work within a short time frame. But there're some loose ends I'll need to tie up in his home in Atlanta. I need to clean his phone. And I need to make sure his family—whose ties are thin, but they still have ties—doesn't connect any of this to you or Lily."

I hadn't mentioned Lily's name to him, but I wasn't shocked to hear that he knew it or where David lived or his family's affiliation.

There probably wasn't anything in this world that Bale wasn't privy to.

"I have a request," I told him.

"What is it?"

From the moment Dominick had given me this option, I'd thought about every detail of this. I'd analyzed all the layers. I'd considered every scenario.

I knew what I wanted.

Now, I needed Bale to give it to me.

"I want to be the one who pulls the trigger."

"Absolutely not." His voice wasn't a bark, but it came out with a serious, caustic bite.

"Why the hell not?"

He set his hands on the steering wheel. "Clients are liabilities. I don't work with them, I work for them, and I only work alone."

"Make an exception."

He shook his head. "My answer won't change."

"Fuck—"

"Brady, listen to me. You might think you're comfortable holding a gun in your hand and pulling the trigger and putting a bullet in a man's skull. But when it comes down to it, it's nothing like it sounds. Trust me, I've been doing this a long time." His voice echoed in my ears. "These jobs come with risks. Timing. I'm not willing to ruin a job over a client having an emotional crisis seconds before the mark is to be killed."

"Are you going to send me proof that he's dead?"

"Proof? Another liability." He let out a shallow laugh. "This job will be untraceable. No, I will not send you proof."

"Then, I don't know if I can do this, Bale. I need to be able to close my eyes at night and know this man isn't going to kill Lily, my family, or me. It's not that I won't take your word for it. But without being there, without seeing, I can't—"

"Fine…" He released a long, loud sigh, and I could feel his annoyance from the other side of the car. "I have an idea."

• • •

David: *How do you know I'm not going to blow up your house? You think you're keeping her safe, but you don't know me at all. You don't know what I'm fucking capable of.*

Me: *If you've ever questioned why I'm protecting her from you, it's because of that statement right there.*

David: *Of course I'm going to fucking say that. SHE'S MINE.*

Me: *She was never yours.*

David: *If I were you, I'd be nervous about getting back in your car.*

David: *I'd even be nervous about walking out of your office building right now.*

• • •

Me: *Yet I'm still alive. Why is that? Because there's one person more powerful here, and it's me.*

David: *Because I've shifted my focus to Macon. You have two brothers... I don't think you need both.*

Me: *You're pathetic.*

David: *You won't be saying that when he's dead.*

• • •

David: *Putting the whole family on lockdown now, huh? Someone took my threat seriously.*

Me: *What happened to you? What made you so fucking miserable that you've dedicated your life to hurting people? Did your parents not love you? Did they choose a favorite child, and it wasn't you? Were you fucking dropped as a kid? Forgotten?*

David: *You took what's mine. I've made that very clear.*

Me: *Let me make something clear to you—and I won't say it again. She's mine now. She's going to be my wife. She's going to be the mother of my children. She's going to be with me until she takes her last breath. I'm telling you this so you won't ever forget. I want those facts to stay in your head for the rest of your fucking life.*

David: *It's already forgotten.*

David: *Asshole.*

• • •

David: *Come out of your fucking house.*

Me: *I'm done having any conversation with you...and I'm done with you.*

• • •

David: *If Rowan was smart, she would drive faster to work, or I'm going to catch up to her.*

David: *Or maybe it's Brooklyn I'm tailing.*

David: *Or your mom while she drives to the nail salon...*

• • •

David: *Have you really gone silent on me?*

David: *You've got nothing to say?*

• • •

David: *Answer me, Brady.*

David: *FUCKING ANSWER ME.*

• • •

David
2 Missed Calls

• • •

David
4 Missed Calls

• • •

David: *Answer your goddamn phone.*

• • •

Me: *Goodbye, David.*

Chapter Thirty-Eight

Brady

I was already in my office when the FaceTime call came through, lighting up the black screen of my phone. Bale had given me a three-minute window just after two in the morning. Instead of setting an alarm, in fear that it would wake Lily, I stayed up and came in here with plenty of time to spare.

There was no fucking way I was going to miss this chat.

I connected the video, waiting for the background to come into focus. The darkness of the basement—or wherever Bale had taken him—made it a little difficult to initially see.

There was still no question what I was looking at.

David.

In the fucking flesh.

With hazy brown eyes and curly, messy hair and scruff that came in spotted.

He looked like a goddamn kid. But he was the same age as Lily. He just had a face and demeanor that had never matured.

He'd been placed in a chair with rope tied around his chest, wrists, and ankles. It appeared that a rag had been balled up and stuffed in his mouth with a piece of duct tape spread vertically over his lips, preventing him from opening them.

"Say what you want to say, Brady," Bale ordered.

I knew there was a smile on my face. There was something so fucking satisfying about seeing him shackled and restrained, the fear and vulnerability in his eyes now that he was the prisoner.

"You thought you'd won, didn't you?" I didn't take my eyes off him as I spoke. "You thought you were going to hurt me enough to let her go, wear me down so badly that I'd just hand her over to you." I chuckled. "Look where we are now, motherfucker."

My smile widened as I pointed behind me, unsure if he could see my finger or not. "Lily's asleep in my bed. She's moving in with me. In no time, we're going to be engaged, and she'll be my wife." I paused. "What about you, David? Where are you right now? What's your future going to look like?"

I exhaled a deep sigh. "I got the girl, and you're…going to die."

He made no reaction, nothing in his face, no movement in his body. He didn't even try to buck in the chair.

"Bale, do me a favor," I said. "Give him a nice punch in the face for Diesel. For what that bastard did to my friend, he deserves a broken nose before he enters hell."

The phone was sitting on a stand, Bale standing at a side angle. As soon as I gave him the request, he crossed into the full range of the camera, reared his arm back, and connected his fist to David's nose.

David began to groan, and once Bale took a few steps away, clearing my line of vision, I was able to see the blood dripping from David's nostrils.

"Last words, Brady," Bale voiced sharply. "Say them now."

"Fuck you, David. Fuck you for the torture you put Lily through. Fuck you for what you did to Diesel. Fuck you for what you did to my plane. And fuck you for making me resort to this."

There was a flash of black that came from Bale's hand, and a sound, a thunder, rang through the speaker of my phone as he pulled the trigger.

The bullet landed straight between David's eyes.

There was a look that came across his face. Almost a peacefulness as his life left his body, a paleness that rose through his skin right before his head slumped forward.

It was then, that exact moment, when his eyes were no longer visible, that it hit me. That it strung an intricate, complicated web within my chest. That it burst through my veins and muscles.

When I saw the result of what I'd done.

More blood pooled across the chest of his oversized button-down. I didn't know if it was coming from the wound in his skull or if it was still pouring from his nose or if it was a mix of both. His fingers loosened on the armrests of the chair. His posture, although forced by the rope, became relaxed.

As I continued to watch, I was positive of two things.

David was dead.

And I would never tell Lily about this video chat.

I would burn down the world for her, but I would never subject her to what I'd just witnessed. She didn't need to know that love had made me want to see him suffer. That love had made me want to watch him be killed.

That love had made me want to protect her at all costs.

Chapter Thirty-Nine

LILY

My eyes were only open for a few seconds, the morning sun not yet risen in the sky, when Brady told me it was done. That David would never bother me again. I didn't ask for proof—I didn't want to see it or know what was involved. All that mattered was if Brady told me David would never terrorize me again, he meant it.

I didn't feel this deep sadness that a life had been taken. I couldn't grieve a person who had tried to destroy me and the man I loved.

What I had to do now was learn to live without fear.

But in our minds, it was hard to believe that David wouldn't be waiting for us the moment we stepped outside. He wouldn't be watching. He wouldn't be reaching out, texting in detail about where we were going and what he was going to do to us.

Unlike all the other times before, Brady's phone stayed silent while we were gone.

It stayed silent when we came home.

It stayed silent the next morning and afternoon and evening.

The first week didn't seem real. Neither did the second week. By the third, there was still that cinching in my stomach whenever I walked down the hallway to our hotel room in Edinburgh, or when I was getting in an elevator, or when I moved my things out of the Beverly Hills location of his hotel and into Brady's house. In the back of my mind, I could hear David's opinion, his anger and rage that I was going to be living with Brady.

But that was all it was—thoughts.

The man I'd been fearing all this time, whose words had abused me, whose control had turned me into someone I despised, was no longer alive.

Each day, that resonated a bit more.

And each day brought an endless amount of relief.

Brady and I were still feeling it even a month later, sitting at the same restaurant in Edinburgh where Brady had gotten the call that Diesel was in the hospital. But now, we didn't need a bodyguard standing behind our table, which had become our norm, and there wasn't one waiting outside the door of our room at the hotel.

We were free.

We had come back here because the food was so good, but the memory of it all was horrible. Brady wanted a redo. Since the renovation had him working much longer hours than he'd anticipated, oftentimes, we ended up getting food delivered or devouring room service. He was just too tired to go out, and that was why it had taken so long to make our way back.

But tonight, he'd finished up early.

We'd just gotten our first round of drinks, and before we even had time for a toast, he was pulling out his phone and typing something onto the screen.

"I just sent Diesel a text," he said, smiling over the top of his cell. "I wanted him to know where we are and that we're toasting him." He held up his glass and clinked his scotch against my wine.

After we took our sips, he glanced back at his phone. "He's having a little scotch himself, apparently."

"Ask him how he's doing." I licked the wine off my lips. "And tell him we miss him and we have to do dinner when we get back in LA."

Brady laughed. "He said he's only saying yes to dinner because you're asking." He set his phone down. "And he said he's doing awesome."

My head shook back and forth. "Thank God for that. I mean, it's not like we haven't been checking on him nonstop, but still, I'm just so relieved he's doing okay."

He reached across the table, his thumb brushing the back of my hand. "You look fucking gorgeous tonight."

The heat instantly spread across my face.

It didn't matter how many times he complimented me or how often; it always felt like I'd never heard the words before. "Thank you."

"Is that dress new?"

I glanced down the front of me, where the spaghetti straps rested on my shoulders and the low-cut satin was hugging my breasts, the dress tightly fitting to the middle of my thighs.

Peach was the color I'd gone with.

Of course, Diesel hadn't been part of this shopping trip—for reasons I appreciated, but something I missed at the same time.

"I picked it up this morning during my walk. I wasn't sure about the color, but I tried to choose something far outside my comfort zone—"

"It looks incredible on you." His eyes dipped, taking their time to linger as low as the table would allow, slowly rising back to my face. "I've yet to see anything on you that I don't love."

"Even your clothes."

He chuckled. "Especially my clothes."

I twisted the stem of my wineglass. "Can I tell you a secret?"

He nodded.

"You told me once you would do anything in your power to

protect me."

"That's not a secret. I believe I've said that to you more than once." He swished his drink. "It was true then, it's true now, and it'll be true forever."

A man who always kept his word.

"The secret is…Brady Spade, I'm going to love you until the day I die."

He pointed at his lap. "Baby, get over here."

I wiggled in my seat. "If I do, I know what you'll do, and we're in a restaurant. Down boy." I took a sip. "Can I tell you something else?"

"Is it going to make me growl?"

I laughed. "When the construction is done, I'm really going to miss it here." I glanced up at the ceiling, the way the entire place felt like you were in the belly of a castle. Even the smell, the scents that went beyond the food, gave off the same feel.

But I wasn't just referring to the restaurant.

After all the time I'd spent in Edinburgh lately, it had really stolen a piece of my heart.

The landscape. The architecture. The residents.

All of it was a combination I loved.

"Then, I'll buy you a house here, and we can come whenever you want."

I smiled. "You can't help yourself. You just have to be that kind of extra, don't you?"

He pulled his hand back and took a drink. "When money is no object, it's hard not to be extra." He wiped his lips, his stare turning even more intense as he took me in. "You can think about it."

"Or we could just stay at your hotel whenever we want to visit."

"We could. It just doesn't give us the privacy I'm after."

I pushed my hair off my shoulders. "What kind of privacy do you mean?"

He leaned his arms on the table. "Like the nights I make you scream so fucking loud that I know the neighboring rooms are reporting us to the front desk." He lifted his glass. "I don't want my wife to have to muffle her screams or get looks from the hotel staff because they know you scream."

He took a drink. "I want you to be able to swim and go in the hot tub naked, and I don't want my employees looking at you in your bikini or that peach dress"—he nodded toward me—"and thinking how fucking hot you are and what they'd like to do to you. Because they're thinking that, I promise you. And those thoughts of theirs, they drive me fucking wild."

"They shouldn't because I'm a million percent yours."

His eyes closed and a warmth spread over his face. "Do you know how much I love the sound of that?"

Something in the distance was dragging my attention away from Brady's face.

It was a gaze that I could feel directly on me.

When I finally located it, a smile moved quickly across my lips. "You're not going to believe who's walking through this restaurant right now."

"Who?"

"Dominick, Jenner, and"—I craned my neck to the side to see who was hiding behind Jenner and squealed—"Aubrey!"

"What the fuck?" He looked over his shoulder just as the three of them were approaching our table, and he stood. "What the hell are you guys doing here?"

While he man-hugged Dominick and Jenner, I threw my arms around my girl. "I can't believe you're here—in Scotland, my gosh. It's so good to see you."

"Same, girl. Same. When the guys said we were stopping here, I thought about texting you, but I figured surprising you would be even better."

I pulled back just a little. "You look amazing."

"Stop." She waved me off. "I have fifteen pounds I still need to lose. They're the stubbornest pounds ever." She sighed.

I held the outside of her arms. "You honestly look fabulous. Please don't lose an ounce."

"And what about you? Can we talk about that dress and how I'm dying to have your boobs and not the milk jugs that I've been carrying around?"

I laughed. "Once you stop breastfeeding, they'll deflate to my size."

She rolled her eyes. "You're funny—you know that?"

I wrapped my arm around her and faced the small group of men. "So, what are you guys doing here anyway?"

"Jenner says he has some good news for us," Brady replied. "And for some reason, the motherfucker couldn't just pick up the phone and call me."

"Where's the fun in that?" Jenner said. "We were actually in Ireland, doing some business, and thought with you being so close by, why not come here and tell you in person?"

"Tell me what in person?" Brady said.

Jenner put his hand on Brady's shoulder. "The Bangkok deal is going through. Congratulations, my man. You just scored yourself another property."

"No shit?" Brady shot back.

"The contract is signed, sealed, and"—Jenner handed Brady the envelope he was holding—"delivered."

Brady looked at me, his eyes beaming. "We got Bangkok, baby."

"I'm screaming for you right now." I winked, and he knew exactly what I meant by that.

He shook hands with Jenner and then Dominick, Dominick voicing, "I'm so fucking proud of you, brother. You're crushing it."

Dominick was right. My man wasn't just rehabbing Edinburgh; he was working with HR at their corporate office to streamline their entire payroll process, and he was helping Rhett and Ridge with a new app.

But he wouldn't mention any of the backend stuff to the Daltons while they were boasting about his accolades. Because my grumpy alpha also had a bit of humility. That wasn't something I'd seen in him at the beginning of our relationship, but it was certainly there now.

It reflected in his smile, in the way he was accepting their praise.

"I appreciate it," Brady said. "Are you able to join us for dinner, or are you heading back to the plane?" he asked, looking at each of them.

Jenner replied, "We were planning on joining you whether you wanted us to or not."

We all laughed.

"I'll go let the waitress know so we can get a bigger table," I said.

"Already done," Aubrey responded, squeezing me. "We let the hostess know on our way in."

"Even better." I smiled at her.

Our waitress approached and led us to a new table on the other side of the dining room. Once everyone got seated, she took the drink orders of the newcomers and promised to bring Brady and me refills since our glasses were almost empty.

As she left, I looped my arm through Brady's and whispered, "Bangkok. I'm dying at the thought of that."

"We'll be moving there right after Edinburgh." His brows furrowed. "Won't *we*?"

I grinned. "Yes, we'll be moving there together." I chewed my lip. "Like I could ever be away from you for more than a couple of nights. Come on."

"Kiss me."

"Right now?"

He growled, "Right now."

I gave him a quick peck on the lips, and shortly after I pulled away, he took out his phone.

"I have to tell the guys," he said.

I stared at his screen while he typed.

Me: *Fuckers, guess what I got?*

Cooper: *If you tell us you got pegged, I'm leaving this fucking chat.*

Macon: *Jesus.*

Ridge: *Cooper, your mind is always in the sickest places.*

Rhett: *Well?*

Me: *I got Bangkok. It's a done deal. I have the paperwork in my hand right now.*

Rhett: *Dude, that property rocked.*

Cooper: *HELL YES.*

Ridge: *Best news I've heard all week.*

Macon: *Another one for team Cole and Spade. You're kicking ass, Brady.*

He put his phone away just as the drinks were getting delivered, and everyone held their glass up in the air.

"Does anyone mind if I give the toast?" I asked the group.

"I'd love nothing more," Dominick replied.

Jenner nodded in agreement.

I gave Aubrey a grin and turned toward Brady. "To the man who has given me everything I've ever wanted. It's your turn, baby. You deserve this more than anyone."

"I love you," he said as though it were only the two of us at this table.

I shook my head as I stared at his handsome face. Moments like this one, where I still couldn't believe he was mine. My protector, my everything. "I love you more. Cheers."

Epilogue

BRADY

"Harder!" Lily screamed from the top of her lungs. "Fuck yes, Brady! Don't stop!" She reached behind her head to dig her nails into my shoulders, her leg locking around me.

We were lying on our sides, where I was ravishing her from behind with a speed I usually reserved for the end. But my girl was asking for it, and she knew she could get anything she wanted from me.

Fuck me, I couldn't get enough of her body.

My hand glided across her stomach. Her hip. The outside of her thigh. Her tit as it sat in the base of my hand, grazing her nipple with just the pad of my thumb. With each swipe, she drew in more breath. She arched. She squeezed me from the inside.

"Brady, please."

And then there was the begging.

I couldn't handle the sound of it.

The neediness.

The desire.

The way, only minutes ago, she'd pleaded with me to give her an orgasm, followed by a second, and now, she was craving her third.

It wouldn't take much more for her to come. She was tightening around me, her pussy getting wetter with each thrust, her noises getting louder, her breathing becoming more labored.

As for me, I was doing everything I could not to get off. But a few more strokes as deep as the one I'd just taken, and her pussy would be sucking the load out of me.

Which was most definitely going to happen because, now, she was moving with me, pumping her ass forward and back, meeting me in the center. In the middle, where we collided, I gave her a quick twist, my shaft hitting every angle, spreading the friction through her body.

When I drove us apart and slammed back in, my balls slapped against her, and my finger rubbed her clit in circles, flicking the top with the flatness of my nail.

"Yes!" she yelled.

The wetness that had been keeping her slick was thickening.

She was past close.

She was there.

"Lily…" The intensity had reached my voice. I could hear the grittiness in my pitch.

She knew just what I wanted, what I needed, what I yearned for.

And her cunt was giving it to me.

A pussy that had been built for me, fitting around me so perfectly, keeping me in nice and snug.

"Oh shit," she gasped.

As soon as the words left her mouth, there were two changes.

She became extra taut, and there was a slipperiness that told me she was coming.

"Ride it, baby."

Her movements increased, but so did mine, and I rocked into her as hard and as fast as I could.

"Yes, just like that. Don't stop."

It only took one more plunge before the tingles burst through my balls, the wave coming on sharply, the orgasm lifting to my shaft. "Fuck!"

"Ah!" She sucked in some air. "I'm coming!"

As her shouting hit my ears, my first shot released, and once it exploded from my tip, I joined her with my version of a scream, which she knew was a growl. "Lily!"

"Yes!"

I reared back as the second stream began to build, my hips plummeting forward, working through her as more of my cum dripped out, filling her pussy with the rest of me.

I joined her moan with a, "Fuck yes," and exhaled into the side of her face, the bucking dying into a slow rhythm before we completely stilled.

Even after we were empty, we continued to cling to each other.

It didn't matter how much time we spent together, how I came inside her daily; it would never be enough.

"If I roll around to face you, you'll no longer be inside me," she said.

"And?"

"I'm not ready for that yet."

Could this woman be any fucking cuter?

I gently pulled out and moved her onto her back, hovering over her, pressing my lips to hers. "I'll never grow tired of hearing you say that." I kissed her again. "Good morning, gorgeous."

A smile was already there, her cheeks now warming. "Good morning to you."

"Instead of getting right into the shower, how about a dip in the pool?"

She nodded. "I would really love that."

I connected our lips once more. This time, slowly and tenderly, separating us only to say, "I'll meet you in there."

I shifted my weight, giving her enough room to slide out of the bed. She didn't grab a robe before she opened the sliding glass doors that led to our patio or put on a bathing suit. She didn't have to cover herself in any way. We had a private pool outside our rental in Bangkok, a small villa located down the street from the hotel I'd just started rehabbing, and the outside was surrounded by thick plants and trees, giving us full privacy.

While she walked down the steps and dunked under the water, I went into the other bedroom, grabbing the folder that I'd hidden at the top of the closet—a package I'd received yesterday from Jenner.

I'd planned to wait for the right moment to give it to her.

Now felt like a better time than ever.

On my way back through the living room, I caught sight of her from the second set of glass doors. She was in the center of the pool, facing me, her head reclined so her hair was floating. Her back was arched, putting her chest on full display. Tits that were the perfect teardrop shape, nipples that were hard and perky.

She wasn't just the most beautiful woman I'd ever seen. She was a vision so fucking breathtaking that while I stood here, staring, gawking, I had to ask myself... *Is she really mine?*

And, damn it, she was.

She'd stayed with me in Scotland.

She'd moved with me to Bangkok.

She'd loved me even after I had David murdered.

And even though I had so many plans for us in the works, an idea in my head of how I wanted to do this and what it should look like, I knew I couldn't wait any longer.

I needed her answer now.

I returned to the guest room and lifted the mattress, searching the top of the box spring. Once I found what I was looking for and it was secured in my hand, I made my way outside.

"Hey, handsome." She nodded toward the folder. "What's that?"

"A present."

She grinned. "Because you haven't given me enough already."

I closed the sliding doors. "Baby, you know I'll never stop giving you everything. Spoiling you is my hobby."

"But you've already given me the world."

I made my way down the steps of the pool and walked over to her, handing her the folder. "Here's something to add to your world."

"What is it?"

"Open it," I instructed.

She didn't want to drag her gaze away from mine. I could tell by her smile, the quirkiness across her lips. But she eventually moved to the side of the pool, where she set the folder on the edge. She then shook her hands in the air to dry them off and finally opened the lid.

"Brady...oh my God. You didn't..." she panted. "You did!"

I moved in behind her, resting my chin on her shoulder, her ass brushing my dick. I was doing everything in my fucking power not to get a hard-on again. That moment could come after, but not now.

"I think I'm in shock," she continued. "I'm most definitely in awe. And speechless—add speechless to that list." She gradually turned around to face me. "You are..." She scanned my eyes. "I don't even know. You're just everything."

"Everything you've ever wanted?" My hands lowered to her hips and went around to her lower back.

"That goes without saying."

"How about you're in love with our new home?"

Her head shook as she stared at me. "I'm more than in love with it." Her eyes continued to search mine. "I cannot believe you bought us a house in Edinburgh."

"I told you I was going to."

"No, you told me that when money is no object, it's hard not to be extra and that I could think about that purchase."

I chuckled. "You have me there." My hand lifted to her face. "One of the things I've tried hard not to do is make decisions for you. At one point in your life, you weren't allowed to make any. I'll always be the man who gives you choices, not the one who takes them away."

My other hand rose, but I kept it behind her, holding the back of her head. "I bought Scotland without asking you first, but let me explain that even though it's a gift to you, Lily, it's more of a gift for me."

I lifted her out of the pool and set her on the ledge next to the paperwork, separating her legs so I could move in between them. "We spent over seven months in Edinburgh, and every time we were there, when things in our life changed, when the evil was finally gone, I saw something in you. On your face. In your eyes. In the way your lips pulled wide every time you looked around the city."

I wrapped an arm across her back while I kept the other one behind me. "LA isn't your favorite town. You've never said that, but I know. Atlanta will never be your home again—I know that too. What I love about Edinburgh is the way it looks on you. How happy it makes you. How you feel comfortable in that space. How you've even made friends there. And in return, that makes me the most content man alive." I paused, watching the sun glow across her skin. "Seeing you that way, feeling you that way—that's all I want. So, yes, I gave you a home there. A place outside the hotel that you can make into our escape, our bit of paradise. But knowing you're filled with that much pleasure is really the biggest present I could ever have."

She whispered my name, running her hand over the top of my hair and around to my scruff. "I'm the luckiest woman alive."

"Woman…" I said. "I'd rather you call yourself my wife."

"You and that wife nonsense—" Her voice cut off, her eyes widened, her hand immediately covered her mouth as she saw the diamond ring I was holding in her lap.

I didn't fuck with the box; the pool would have made that too tricky. So, I just held the platinum band that was embedded with over a carat and a half of diamonds and a five-carat oval in the center and set it against her thigh.

A ring I'd designed myself.

I'd planned candlelight. Rose petals. A location on the Gulf of

Thailand that would have music and a photographer, scheduled to take place in a few weeks.

But it wasn't nearly as private as this.

I knew my girl. She would rather have this moment with just us. Naked. In our pool without a single spectator or a camera from the photographer flashing in her face.

"Lily Roy," I said softly as I looked into her eyes, "I want nothing more than to spend the rest of my life protecting you. Having children with you. Making memories like this with you. Loving you." The first drip was sliding down her cheek as I added, "There has never been a question in my mind. You are mine." I smiled. "But the choice is yours, baby. So, I'm going to ask you, will you become my wife and I will be yours forever?"

As her head nodded, more tears fell. "The answer was yes long before you asked me."

I slid the ring onto her petite finger, and I pulled her off the edge of the pool and straight into my arms. Her legs wrapped around my waist, and her arms circled my neck.

"Mine," I growled, a tone I'd already used this morning, but this one was different.

This one was territorial.

Permanent.

Guarding.

"I know you're going to tell me you love me," she said, "but you need to know that I love you more."

• • •

The Heartbreaker, book four in the Spade Hotel Series, features Ridge Cole. It is a sizzling single dad romance with all the spice and swoons.

Here's a sneak peek...

Chapter One

RIDGE

Out of all the places I expected to end up tonight, a strip club wasn't one. Shit, I wasn't complaining. Spending an evening looking at naked women wasn't exactly a bad time in my book. Especially when the ladies left the stage and pranced topless around the lounge where all the patrons, including myself, were sitting. That gave me an up-close, personal look at their bodies. Asses that were covered by only a thin, usually sparkly thong. Nipples so hard it was as though they'd been rubbed with ice. Eyes that taunted as they locked with mine and skin so heavily perfumed, their scenes lingered long after they passed me.

I wasn't a virgin when it came to strip clubs. I'd visited my fair share over the years, so I knew that inside these walls was nothing more than a fantasy. The strippers were saleswomen. The nods and smiles and words that were exchanged were all selling tactics.

The only real thing that came out of a place like this was a fucking hard-on.

That was why, earlier tonight, when the thirty or so of us were packed in a party bus, celebrating Brady Spade and Lily Roy's joint bachelor and bachelorette party, and Brady announced this was our next stop, I wasn't excited. Brady was one of the executives at Cole and Spade Hotels, our company, and the last of the Spades to settle down—something I never, in my lifetime, thought would happen with a reputation like his.

But he proved everyone wrong—and, by everyone, I meant all of California and probably half the West Coast.

Rhett looked about as amused as me, so I rested my arm across his shoulder and said, "I never thought I'd say this, but I'd rather be a club right now."

"That sounds as insufferable as this," he replied and stood. "I need another drink."

I wasn't positive if that was code for something else, like he was calling a ride share to get out of here, so I asked, "Are you going to take off?"

"If I do, don't come looking for me." He disappeared toward the bar.

I tried not to think about Rhett while I turned toward the crew. The couples all seemed to be having a blast, the women far more engaged with the strippers than their men. The only singles that were part of the gang, aside from Rhett and me, were the Weston's. A family of five siblings—four men and a woman—who owned high-end restaurants and clubs across the world, many of those located in our hotels. Although Eden couldn't attend, she was away on business, the four brothers were here. Since the merger, I'd gotten the opportunity to work with them, even hang out outside of normal business hours, and would consider them friends.

Which was why I knew things were about to get rowdy.

If there was one thing this group did well together—the Cole's, Spade's, Dalton's, and Weston's—it was having a good time.

And it seemed like everyone was.

That was all the more reason to shake Rhett out of my head and focus on the party. Especially considering this was my first time out in a while. Daisy's mother was back in town after a long stint on the road and she had Daisy for the next week. Knowing my daughter was safe and in good hands gave me a chance to let loose and unwind. I wanted nothing more than to laugh my ass off, catch a buzz, and go for a long run in the morning to sweat out all the excess booze.

But before this night was over, I needed to make sure I had enough material to rouse up the guys during our next executive meeting. I fucking loved digging the fellas on all the shenanigans that went down after a night of debauchery.

One way to ensure that was more alcohol.

There wasn't a waitress anywhere near our tables nor was there any walking around the VIP area. So, I turned around to scan the other side of the lounge, looking for someone capable of taking an order of shots, and that was when I saw her.

A woman so fucking beautiful, my eyes wouldn't leave her.

Even if there was a reason to drag my stare away, I wouldn't.

I couldn't.

She was that breathtaking.

That gorgeous.

That enticing.

I pushed myself to the end of my seat, knowing I was about to get up at any second because I needed to talk to hear her voice. I needed to talk to her. I needed to be closer to her than I was now.

That was how drawn I was to her.

And while I stayed here, somewhat frozen, I took in the details I'd missed when my eyes first landed on her. I certainly couldn't have ignored her red hair. That was what initially mesmerized me. But the more I looked at the long waves, strands that hung down her back and over her shoulders and hugged the sides of her face, I realized it wasn't just a deep auburn. The color reminded me of a burnt fall sunset.

Her face was a combination of soft features that even individually screamed a level of beauty I'd never seen before. Lips that were plump and glossy. A small button-like nose. Smooth, sun kissed skin. Eyes that I couldn't see the color of from here, but I could feel how alluring they were.

And then there was her body.

A chest that was the perfect size for her petite frame, hips and a waist that dipped in just right, and an ass with the amount of thickness I desired.

She didn't run in a straight line from head to toe.

She had curves.

Curves I wanted to fucking devour.

There had been a dullness in my chest when I'd walked into this strip club tonight.

Now, I was on fire.

And there was no way I could let another second pass without buying her a drink.

"Going to grab a cocktail?" Beck Weston asked as I stood, his chair directly next to mine. "Do you mind grabbing one for me too?" The NHL star was loving his off-season life, freeing up his time to attend things like this.

"I'm not headed to the bar."

He chuckled. "Where else would you be going? The restroom?"

I nodded toward the redhead, watching Beck's stare land on her. "Enough said." He pounded my fist. "Go get her, my man."

I took off before anyone else could distract me and delay me even more and I walked out of the VIP area and into the general lounge, stopping at the base of the stage where she was standing.

Now that I was nearer, I could fill in all the blanks, like the color of her eyes, which was the lightest brown. There was a dusting of freckles that ran down the middle of her nose. Skin that wasn't just smooth and pale, but silky and creamy. Thighs that had the faintest definition of muscle.

And, *goddamn it*, nipples that were the lightest pink.

I didn't care that she was standing on a stage with only a thong covering her. I sure as hell didn't care that she was a stripper. Nor did I care that every fucking man in this room had his eyes on her.

What I cared about was that as soon as she stepped onto the floor, I grasped every bit of her attention.

Despite this being an imaginary playhouse, I was about to find the authenticity in this room.

And I was going to show her that in me.

Luckily, I didn't have to wait long, the song was ending, and she was making her way to the steps, holding her bra and the cash she'd collected from the stage. A bouncer helped her down the short staircase where I waited for her.

As he moved away, helping the next stripper onto the stage, I said, "Hi," just loud enough that she could hear me over the music.

Her smile tugged from the side and lifted. "Hi."

"You were incredible up there."

She knew how to shake her body, how to use the pole, how to squat with her legs spread wide while her hair whipped across her face.

"Thank you."

I kept my eyes fixed on hers, not allowing them to dip even though I wanted them to. "Can I buy you a drink?"

She slipped her arms through her bra straps, wrapping the lace around her tits before she clasped the hook behind her back. "Why would you want to do that?"

"I was watching you from the VIP lounge and hauled my ass over here to talk to you."

"Aren't you charming." She batted what I assumed were fake lashes considering how long they were. "There's a stage in there too, was the dancer not entertaining enough?"

My hands were at my sides, but I wanted them on her waist, so I could feel just how velvety her skin was. And while I was there, I wanted to wrap her legs around me and carry her somewhere quiet. "She's not you."

She laughed, showing teeth that were white and beautifully straight. "I'm not sure what to say to that."

"Say you'll have a drink with me."

"You're cute, you know that?"

"Follow me," I instructed.

She stayed planted. "I think you're forgetting where we are."

"I know exactly where we are."

She combined all her hair and laid it over one shoulder. "Then you know I can't join you. It's not that I don't want to. I'm just not allowed. If I'm not up there"—she pointed behind her at the stage— "then my job is to roam the room until I book a private dance."

"What does that entail?"

"The private dances?" When I nodded, she continued, "You've never had one?"

I chuckled at the way she was looking at me. "Why does that surprise you? You know nothing about me…" I gave her a wink.

"I just assume most people who come here are knowledgeable on the services that are offered. If I'm being honest, I'm glad a guy as handsome as you isn't a regular here."

She thought I was handsome.

Finally, I felt like I was getting somewhere.

"Because?" I questioned.

"Regulars can be a little creepy…if you know what I mean."

I crossed my arms over my chest. "Trust me, I'm not that."

She laughed again as she shifted her weight, the sky-high heels bringing the top of her head to my throat.

"I don't mean any disrespect when I say this, but I don't make it a habit to come here." I kept my voice gentle. "My friends and I are celebrating a bachelor and bachelorette party and ended up here."

Her brows rose. "Is it your bachelor party?"

An appropriate question.

I whistled out a mouthful of air. "Fuck no."

It seemed my answer registered through her before she nodded toward the VIP area. "Back there, there are private rooms. You can rent them for a dance, two dances, three dances—however many you want."

The more I spoke to her, the more I realized there was no way I could have left here without talking to her.

I would have regretted it for the rest of my life.

Because looking at her from where I'd been sitting with the group wasn't nearly enough.

Neither was this conversation.

Whoever she was, however her story unraveled—I wanted to know both.

"I'd like to rent a private room for the entire night."

Her eyes widened. "Really?"

"If that's the only way I'll get to spend time with you, then yes. Take me there."

The shock was evident on her face. "I think there are some logistical things we have to work out first."

I reached into my pocket, took out my wallet, and grabbed the wad of cash from inside. I didn't need to count it; I knew just how much was there and I placed it in her hand. "That should more than cover it."

She slowly glanced down at the stack. Her chest rising and falling several times. "You're giving all of this to me?"

"Pay the house or whatever you have to do to cover your bases. The rest is for you."

Her head shook, giving me the impression she didn't want to take it.

That gesture, that modesty made me want her even more.

"Are you sure?" she asked.

I almost laughed.

A greedy person would take the money and immediately lead me toward the private rooms. She wasn't greedy at all. And something told me the redhead was a lot different than most of the people in this establishment.

"I'm positive," I told her.

She nodded. "Okay. Come with me."

I followed her through the main lounge and past the VIP section where she stopped at a window. I kept my distance, giving her the privacy she needed while she spoke to the cashier. She counted out an amount I could vaguely see and palmed the rest. When she made eye contact with me, waving me forward, I moved in beside her, and we entered a small room.

With the walls, ceiling, and floor all black, it was difficult to see with just a dim, single spotlight above. But it gave off enough of a glow that her skin sparkled and the whites of her eyes and teeth really stood out.

"Why don't you sit here." She stood at the side of an armless chair.

There were two in the room, and they were identical, placed a few feet apart.

As I got comfortable in the seat, she made her way to the front of me and put her hands on my shoulders.

The stage, where I'd met her, had been too congested with scents, so I wasn't able to detect hers. But now that she was in this position, I knew why I hadn't been able to smell her. Her perfume was too light. But in here, the subtleness of her vanilla latte aroma was just right.

"Just so you know, there are cameras in here." The ends of her hair dangled in my face. "My manager can see everything we're doing."

A warning I didn't need.

"Are you saying that for your protection?"

She stilled. "I would say that to anyone I brought in here."

"I realize you really don't know me, but I didn't bring you in here to touch you or do something that would cause your manager to be alarmed."

"Why did you bring me in here, then?" She spoke so quietly.

"Let me clarify something first because I don't want to be misleading." I rubbed my hands together before I set them on my legs. "Touching a body like yours would be a fucking dream and I'd love nothing more, but that's not my motive. I want to get to know you. That's why I wanted to buy you a drink and that's why we're in here." She said nothing. "What's your name?" I was met with more silence. "I'm Ridge."

I could feel the hesitation before she voiced, "Addy."

"Addy"—I lifted her hand off my shoulder and escorted her to the other chair—"why don't you sit. That'll make it easier to talk."

"You're sure you don't want a dance?"

If we were anywhere else, this would have gone so differently.

I wouldn't know that her fucking nipples were the lightest shade of pink. I wouldn't know that she had a patch of freckles, like her nose, that ran up one of her ass cheeks. And I wouldn't have to move her to the chair next to mine since the chances of her straddling me right away would be slim.

"We're just talking, remember?" I waited until she sat. "I'm one of the good guys. I know you don't believe that, but you will before the night is through."

"How good?"

I chuckled. "Fuck, you must meet some real assholes in here if you have to ask that question."

She turned the chair to face me and moved it closer, her knees briefly rubbing against mine as she crossed her legs. "I don't know if I should admit this or not, but this is only my third shift and my very first time bringing a guest in here. So, to answer your question, I'm sure there are lots of assholes, but I'm not seasoned enough to know just how spicy they can get."

For some reason, I really liked hearing that she was new and unseasoned.

"Third day on the job and your first private booking. Is it safe to assume you weren't a stripper before you took the job here?"

She let out a burst of air that sounded like it came from her nose. "No."

"New profession, then."

Her head dropped. "New and very temporary." She wrapped her arms around her stomach.

"Can I ask you a personal question?"

Her eyes lifted. "You've already seen my boobs, Ridge. I think we're past personal, don't you?"

I laughed. "This question digs in a bit."

She shrugged. "Try me."

"What makes one decide to strip"—my hand went in the air— "I'm not knocking the profession, I want to make that clear. I'm just curious what made you choose this path."

"Ah. That." She sighed. "It's a very good question. I think everyone in here probably has a different reason." She glanced toward the door, which was closed, her arms appearing to tighten around her. "I'm not even going to lie, I almost chickened out before my first shift, wondering if I would survive and trying to come up with another option. But I figure I can do it for a couple of months—or however long it takes—and be done. It won't be the hardest thing I ever overcome in my life, that's for sure."

"If it's any consolation, you happen to be really good at it."

"Oh Ridge," she exhaled, "I don't know if I should laugh or cry from that statement."

"Laugh. Always laugh." I winked at her.

Her head shook. "I picked the wrong profession—my parents warned me when I declared a major and I didn't listen. I went with my heart instead of my bank account. Wrong move, I guess."

"And which profession is that?"

She smiled. "One that pays like shit."

She wasn't ready to open up. I could understand that.

The environment, I was sure, had something to do with it.

"Or maybe I should say, it's a profession that doesn't pay as well as this," she clarified.

"Listen, there's no shame in hustling. We all have to do it at some point or another and that hustle looks different for everyone." I was tempted to take out my phone and show her a picture of Daisy, but I kept it planted in my pocket. "I've got a little girl. I can tell you right now, there isn't anything I wouldn't do to provide for her. She's my priority. She's the reason I work as hard as I do."

"How old?"

"She's six, going on twenty-five. Smart as a whip. Hell of a lot smarter than me."

She nodded, grinning. "And her mom?"

My head tilted as I took in Addy's stunning face. "If her mom were in the picture, I wouldn't be in this room right now. Remember... I'm one of the good ones."

Her smile stayed wide.

"I want to go back for a second." Because it was a question she'd danced around. "I've told you my daughter is my reason and she's what motivates me. What's your reason?"

Whatever her answer was, was her breaking point. And I knew, without even hearing it, that it would teach me so much about who she was and what her life looked like.

One thing I knew for certain, this job wasn't for the weak. It took serious balls to walk in that door and accept a position that came with the requirements she faced.

So, whatever drove her, it made her one unique woman.

She leaned forward, resting her arms on her thighs. "You really want to know me, don't you?"

"You could say I'm interested."

"In what?"

"You." I cleared my throat. "All of you."

She released a small noise that didn't sound like a sigh or a moan. "Ridge..."

"You're not asking me why I'm interested. Or how I'm interested. Or when I became interested."

"I don't have to, because we're in a private room of a strip club and you saw my moves on the stage, courtesy of high school and college cheerleading, and thought to yourself, she'd be a good lay." She chewed her lip. "Am I right?"

"Addy, you're not giving yourself nearly enough credit." I paused. "Were your moves noticed? Sure, they were. Was your body appreciated? Fuck yes. But I would have appreciated your body if we'd been in a bar, and you were in jeans and a T-shirt, and my imagination was filling in the blanks. Being in here and what you're wearing"—I nodded toward her—"have nothing to do with my opinion. I would have reacted the same way regardless of where we'd met." I crossed my legs. "I could have paid you for a dance in the VIP room. I could have let you dance topless on top of me when we came in here. I told you, that's not what I want or what I'm looking for."

"Tell me, then, Ridge, why are you interested?"

Acknowledgments

Nina Grinstead, this wasn't our easiest, was it? Brady tested me in ways I hadn't expected, but you stayed with me—through the tears, through the rewrites, right up to the very last second. You never lose faith in me, you never give up, and you never stop fighting to help me find my best—because even when I don't see it or feel it, you do. That's more than having my back; that's being the best thing that's ever happened to me. Just like I said last time, to many more framed text messages on my wall. I love you. To the moon and back.

Jovana Shirley, how you put up with me, I'll never know. My emails at the eleventh hour, asking for all the things, ha-ha—and this book was certainly no exception. Thank you for always finding a way to make it all happen, for saying yes to all my shenanigans, and for your support, which truly means the world to me. At the end of every book, I always write, I can never do this without you, and I mean it more and more each time. Love you so, so hard.

Ratula Roy, there aren't many people in this world who will drop everything to keep my head above water and who will send me virtual tissues and who will tell me to pull my shit together (with love, of course), and who will answer my messages at any hour, day or night, but you do. We've been at this a long time together, and you know, every time, what I need and how to stop the world from spiraling. I hope you know I can't be me without you. I love you more than love—and I'll never stop saying that to you.

Hang Le, my unicorn, you are just incredible in every way.

Judy Zweifel, as always, thank you for being so wonderful to work with and for taking such good care of my words. <3

Vicki Valente, you've been the most wonderful addition to my team. Thank you for all your hard work. I appreciate you so much.

Nikki Terrill, my soul sister. Every tear, vent, virtual hug, life chaos, workout—you've been there through it all. I could never do this without you, and I would never want to. Love you hard.

Pang, I treasure you. In all the ways. And I'm so, so lucky to be able to work with you.

Sarah Symonds, I love you, friend, and I miss you terribly.

Brittney Sahin, another book that I survived because of you. I swear, you keep me going in ways you don't even understand. Love you, B, and I love us.

Kimmi Street, my sister from another mister. Thank you from the bottom of my heart. You saved me. You inspired me. You kept me standing in so many different ways. I love you more than love.

Extra-special love goes to Valentine PR, my ARC team, my Bookstagram team, Rachel Baldwin, Valentine Grinstead, Kelley Beckham, Sarah Norris, Kim Cermak, and Christine Miller.

Mom and Dad, thanks for your unwavering belief in me and your constant encouragement. It means more than you'll ever know.

Brian, my words could never dent the love I feel for you. Trust me when I say, I love you more.

My Midnighters, you are such a supportive, loving, motivating group. Thanks for being such an inspiration, for holding my hand when I need it, and for always begging for more words. I love you all.

To all the influencers who read, review, share, post, TikTok— Thank you, thank you, thank you will never be enough. You do so much for our writing community, and we're so appreciative.

To my readers—I cherish each and every one of you. I'm so grateful for all the love you show my books, for taking the time to reach out to me, and for your passion and enthusiasm when it comes to my stories. I love, love, love you.

About the Author

USA Today best-selling author Marni Mann knew she was going to be a writer since middle school. While other girls her age were daydreaming about teenage pop stars, Marni was fantasizing about penning her first novel. She crafts sexy, titillating stories that weave together her love of darkness, mystery, passion, and human emotions. A New Englander at heart, she now lives with her husband in Sarasota, Florida. When she's not nose deep in her laptop, working on her next novel, she's scouring for chocolate, sipping wine, traveling, boating, or devouring fabulous books.

Made in United States
North Haven, CT
16 July 2024

54863660R00212